THE KEEPE

"This book is like the finest pastry, layered with flavor and bursting with happiness! It's gloriously sweet and extraordinarily delightful!"
—Sarah Beth Durst, *New York Times* bestselling author of *The Spellshop*

"Another masterpiece from one of my favorite authors in cozy fantasy!"
—Rebecca Thorne, *USA Today* bestselling author of *Can't Spell Treason Without Tea*

"I deeply enjoyed every inch of this novel. In fact, I think I'm going to take my next vacation in Shpelling."
—Olivia Atwater, author of *Half a Soul*

"A refreshing fantasy adventure written for anyone with a heart. Full of delightful twists and turns, fights with sentient objects, and scheming mages."
—John Wiswell, Nebula Award–winning author of *Someone You Can Build a Nest In*

"With sweet humor, delightful characters, and a touch of romance, *The Keeper of Magical Things* is an enchanting tale full of whimsy and gentleness. I adored every minute of it!"
—Maiga Doocy, *Sunday Times* (UK) bestselling author of *Sorcery and Small Magics*

"*The Keeper of Magical Things* is a story about finding yourself and finding love in the most unexpected of places (a sleepy village called Shpelling). It has everything you can possibly want from a cozy fantasy: a fish-out-of-water main character, an icy love interest with a secret heart of gold, a tonne of outlandish magical objects, heaps of humor, and, obviously, a catdragon. A hilarious, cozy page-turner." —Genoveva Dimova, author of *Foul Days*

Praise for
THE TELLER OF SMALL FORTUNES

"If you're running a little low on serotonin, trust me: Brew yourself a hot drink, curl up with this treasure of a tale, and thank me later!"
—Sangu Mandanna, national bestselling author of
The Very Secret Society of Irregular Witches

"Warm, welcoming, and endlessly inventive . . . feels like being invited in for tea with a dear friend (and expert storyteller!)."
—Grace D. Li, *New York Times* bestselling author of
Portrait of a Thief

"Joyful, heartwarming, and utterly charming, Leong's cozy fantasy debut is a cup of hot (fortune-telling) tea straight to the soul."
—Amélie Wen Zhao, *New York Times* and international bestselling author of *Song of Silver, Flame Like Night*

"A warm and lovely book that will soothe your heart. Its gentleness and coziness are such a delightful gift."
—India Holton, international bestselling author of
The Geographer's Map to Romance

"An absolute delight from start to finish. Settle in for a cozy, heartwarming journey full of twists and turns, found family, and appreciating the little things alongside the big ones."
—Genevieve Gornichec, author of *The Witch's Heart*

NOVELS BY JULIE LEONG

The Teller of Small Fortunes
The Keeper of Magical Things

THE
KEEPER OF
MAGICAL
THINGS

JULIE LEONG

ACE
NEW YORK

ACE
Published by Berkley
An imprint of Penguin Random House LLC
1745 Broadway, New York, NY 10019
penguinrandomhouse.com

Copyright © 2025 by JL Writing, LLC
Readers Guide copyright © 2025 by JL Writing, LLC
Penguin Random House values and supports copyright. Copyright fuels creativity, encourages diverse voices, promotes free speech, and creates a vibrant culture. Thank you for buying an authorized edition of this book and for complying with copyright laws by not reproducing, scanning, or distributing any part of it in any form without permission. You are supporting writers and allowing Penguin Random House to continue to publish books for every reader. Please note that no part of this book may be used or reproduced in any manner for the purpose of training artificial intelligence technologies or systems.

ACE is a registered trademark and the A colophon is a trademark of
Penguin Random House LLC.

Book design by Alison Cnockaert

Library of Congress Cataloging-in-Publication Data
Names: Leong, Julie, author.
Title: The keeper of magical things / Julie Leong.
Description: First edition. | New York : Ace, 2025.
Identifiers: LCCN 2025010218 (print) | LCCN 2025010219 (ebook) |
ISBN 9780593815946 (trade paperback) | ISBN 9780593815939 (ebook)
Subjects: LCGFT: Fantasy fiction. | Novels.
Classification: LCC PS3612.E5788 K44 2025 (print) |
LCC PS3612.E5788 (ebook) | DDC 813/.6--dc23/eng/20250325
LC record available at https://lccn.loc.gov/2025010218
LC ebook record available at https://lccn.loc.gov/2025010219

Printed in the United States of America
1st Printing

The authorized representative in the EU for product safety and compliance is
Penguin Random House Ireland, Morrison Chambers, 32 Nassau Street,
Dublin D02 YH68, Ireland, https://eu-contact.penguin.ie.

To everyone who's spent too long chasing someone else's idea of greatness—your magic was never theirs to measure. Be kind. Kindness is great enough.

ONE

CERTAINTY BULRUSH WAS in the midst of arguing with a particularly intractable quilt.

Which, as far as morning chores went, was not really something to complain about. Not when other novices were stuck transcribing dusty old scrolls, or mucking out the stables by hand for reasons as dubious as "it builds character" and "the horses like to see you work." No; Certainty knew she was lucky to be warm and dry in the laundry rooms, with only a few dirty blankets between her and freedom.

But still. It'd be so much easier if the bedding could just be a little more *reasonable*.

"Don't you want to be nice and clean? That ink stain makes you look a mess; why don't we just get rid of it . . ."

"I am a quilt. I display patterns. My purpose is to be beautiful." The object-voice of the quilt was soft and muffled in Certainty's mind, but gave the strong impression of pouting nevertheless. The problem was simply that the quilt *liked* its splotchy new ink stains.

"Yes, but you're also meant to keep people warm in bed, and no mage wants to sleep under a dirty quilt," she cajoled.

"I'm not dirty," it insisted. *"I'm decorative."*

But she sensed a tremor of hesitation in its words. *Aha*—there was her angle of attack. What objects wanted, above all else, was to be used. To fulfill the purposes for which they had been made. To be *valued*.

Certainty knew this well because she was a physical mage. (Well, a mage-in-training.) However, unlike the Guild's more powerful physical mages—ones who could hurl boulders great distances (preferably in the direction of an enemy army), or ones who wove enchantments into precious metals—her abilities were slightly more . . . mundane.

By touching objects, she could speak with them to understand their purposes and convince them to do small things for her. She could sweet-talk a cup of tea into being less bitter; she could shame a shirt into unwrinkling—but, unfortunately, that was about the extent of her powers.

Hence her being here in the Guild laundry rooms. A sixth-year novice, magicking ink stains out of bedsheets while trying not to think about how her entire family had pinned their hopes on her magical career.

Certainty set her jaw and pressed on.

"Just the other day, I saw a steward get rid of some pillowcases. A novice spilled some potion ingredients all over them—wyvern blood, you know, impossible to clean—so the pillowcases had to be thrown out."

There was a pause as the quilt absorbed this information.

"Thrown out? You mean—discarded?"

"Left for rags," she confirmed. *"Latrine wipes, I think."*

The fringes of the quilt twitched in alarm. *"But I'm a good quilt! I'm very comfortable . . ."*

"I'm sure that's true." Certainty patted the quilt, trying to be both stern and reassuring. Then her fingers skimmed over its

dark splotches, and she frowned. Now that she was looking more closely, there was something funny about the way the ink had spilled... It almost looked like a floral pattern—were those roses? *"How did you get this stain, anyway?"*

"It's not a stain," said the quilt, still sulky. *"I made it with some of the extra magic floating around. I thought people would like it."*

Extra magic...? What could that mean? Sometimes objects spoke in riddles. Certainty supposed that they experienced the world rather differently, on account of being things and not people, and Mother and Sons knew that people were hard enough to understand as it was. She shrugged it off.

"I'm afraid not. And even if they did, you'd never match with the rest of the decor, see? Look, you're a lovely quilt already, we can all see that—quality stitching, padding still nice and thick—so let's just shake off all that messy ink so we can put you back where you belong, hm?"

The quilt wavered, rustling indecisively under her hand. *"... latrine wipes? Really?"*

"Really."

The quilt shivered once more, and then—thank the Mother—finally complied, with a reluctant sigh like the whisper of fabric against skin. The ink welled up from the fibers, tracing the quilt's edges before dripping in dark rivulets onto the floor. A puddle of ink gathered on the stones, and the quilt was soon crisp and clean once more.

Certainty beamed down at it. Hours of scrubbing saved, just like that.

"Well done, quilt. Thank you!"

A sullen silence was her only response. Certainty shrugged and withdrew her magic. Carefully, she refolded the quilt and balanced it atop the basket of clean bedding in the corner. The quilt was the dean's favorite, apparently; the laundry staff would be grateful that she'd managed to salvage it. The Guildtower servants always were whenever Certainty was able to help with a favor like this. It was just too bad the servants weren't the ones who decided which novices got to advance to magehood.

Certainty sighed and went to fetch the next basket of laundry—and that was when, as her da would say, everything went thoroughly pear-shaped.

First came the sudden deadening of noise—a heavy, disorienting silence that plugged her ears up as if she'd just jumped into a lake. Then there was a great shrinking sensation, as if the Guildtower itself were contracting with Certainty at its center. Her stomach swooped in a highly unpleasant fashion, and a little late, she wondered whether she ought to start panicking—then—

WHOMP.

The sound was so loud, yet of so low a register, that it vibrated right through the stone walls of the laundry room, rattling the contents of the shelves, the baskets, and Certainty's skull in the process. She wobbled and grabbed at the wall for balance, heart thudding and breath coming short and jumpy. Was the Guildtower under attack? Had the alchemists blown up their laboratories in the Paper Quarter again?

But no further *whomp*s or strange shrinking sensations followed, so Certainty edged toward the door, cursing the fact that she was alone. Blasted unlucky that the laundry staff were all taking their break and gossiping in the courtyard instead of here with her, where they might be able to protect her from . . . whatever this was. Certainty was *not* built for combat.

Still, a weapon couldn't hurt. She grabbed a wicker rug beater from its hook on the wall before poking her head through the doorway to see if anyone else knew what was going on.

"Hello?" she called out.

Nobody responded, but strange and muffled noises were coming from the kitchens down the hall . . .

Mustering her courage and brandishing the rug beater like a floppy sword, she followed the sounds down the stone corridor and approached the kitchen entryway with caution. Then she breathed a sigh of relief. Everything inside looked fine: There were partially sliced loaves of bread on the counter, glistening chickens and ducks roasting on their hooks above the fire, an enormous stewpot simmering merrily away in the corner, cabbages rolling around on the floor . . .

Wait. Cabbages?

Ordinarily, the kitchen was staffed with a dozen-odd people: cooks, bakers, off-duty pages loitering hopefully near the ovens, and so on. It had been bustling and noisy with the day's preparations when Certainty passed by earlier.

But now . . . the kitchen staff was nowhere to be seen.

And instead, there were a number of large, round cabbages, green and squeaking on the kitchen floor.

"Oh dear," Certainty breathed.

The Guildtower was, of course, a place of magic. Unusual things happened often in places of magic; Certainty had seen her fair share of them. But they generally happened in controlled environments under the supervision of a senior mage—and transforming the kitchen staff into leafy greens didn't seem likely to be on anyone's syllabus.

She crouched down to examine the cabbage closest to her. It was a marvelous specimen whose size alone would have made it a prize contender at any Spring Fair. It looked properly vegetal—as cabbage-like as a cabbage could get, really—yet somehow, it *also* bore an uncanny resemblance to Ger the head cook. Something about the bumps and veins on the outer leaves . . . tentatively, she reached one finger out to prod it.

"Squeak!" said the Ger-cabbage, wobbling indignantly.

Certainty nearly fell over. She sprang to her feet, making a vaguely reassuring gesture with her hands while trying to remember the protocol for magical emergencies. "Don't worry, I'll get help! Stay here—"

She wasn't sure if Ger could understand her, but supposed it didn't really matter, as he didn't look capable of going very far in his current state. *Notify the dean*—that was the first step. She dashed out of the kitchens, running so fast that she nearly knocked over the uniformed errand boy conveniently headed down the stairs.

"Oy! Watch where you're goi—"

"The dean," she said, grabbing at the boy's shoulders. "There's been an emergency in the kitchens! Fetch the dean, and any other senior mages, too—"

"What? What kind of emergency?"

"The kitchen staff have all been turned into cabbages—a transformation spell—look, *just go get them*, would you?"

The page's eyes went wide, and he sprinted back up the stairs much more quickly than Certainty could have managed. She flopped against the wall, trying to catch her breath. She hated how powerless she felt. Undoing transformation spells on any living thing—let alone a person—was far beyond her capabilities; she knew better than to even try. So all she could do was send for help and wait for the *real* mages to show up. Stupid mages with their stupid circles, and spells that actually worked when they cast them . . .

The distressed squeaking increased in volume behind her, and it occurred to Certainty that the Guildtower's kitchens were home to several cats and at least one dog, any one of which might pass by and decide that the cabbages rolling around on the floor looked like fun new chew toys. Sighing, Certainty headed back down the stairs to guard them while she waited. At least there was *something* useful she could do.

FORTUNATELY, NO CURIOUS animals appeared, and it was only a quarter-bell or so before a gaggle of senior mages clustered in the entrance to the kitchens. They looked as out of place in their elaborate robes as peacocks in a chicken coop. (It wasn't often that senior mages deigned to descend all the way down to the kitchens, but Certainty imagined that the sudden and unexpected transformation of Guildtower staff into cabbages ranked fairly high on the faculty agenda.)

It wasn't only senior mages, either. A woman whose dark hair was threaded with silver strode to the front of the group with a no-nonsense air, and Certainty swallowed. The High Mage herself had come.

High Mage Melea looked both older and sharper than Certainty remembered from the last novice assembly. Unlike the other mages, she wore plain blue robes adorned only by two golden pins: one bore the Guild circles, and just below, the other displayed the twin lions of the Eshteran Crown. It was this latter that marked her as elected leader of the Guild of Mages and Minister of Magic to the Crown, and therefore the most powerful mage in the kingdom—politically speaking, anyway.

Behind her spectacles, the High Mage's shrewd gray eyes took in the kitchen, the squeaking vegetables, and then Certainty in an instant.

"Novice . . . ?"

"Certainty, High Mage." She bobbed a nervous curtsy.

"Novice Certainty. Report, please." Her voice was crisp and authoritative.

There wasn't much to report beyond the obvious—*the*

kitchen staff seem to have turned into cabbages—but Certainty did her best, beginning with the strange sensations she'd felt immediately before finding them in their current state.

"Hmm," said the High Mage. She made a complicated gesture with her fingers that Certainty recognized as a spell of magic detection, and her eyebrows drew together. "No spell signature. It wasn't a mage who did this. Dean Leverin, would you kindly return our cooks to their original forms?"

The dean, a heavyset man with a neatly trimmed beard, nodded and rolled up his sleeves. He took on a look of great concentration—then muttered a spell that was followed by a gentle *pop*, and the cabbage by the stove abruptly turned into a woman wearing an apron and a bewildered expression. All watched (Certainty with a particular envy) as more *pop*s followed, and one by one, with gasps and cries of relief, the kitchen staff reappeared safe and whole in their human forms. Many touched their limbs and faces anxiously, as if to make sure they were still there. Certainty couldn't really blame them.

"Thank you, Leverin. Nicely done." The High Mage turned toward one of the other mages. "Mage Farid, your theories as to the cause of this?"

A mage wearing pointed shoes was running his hands along the kitchen walls with a look of concentration. "I cannot be certain yet, High Mage. I'll need samples to study. There are several possibilities—"

"Perhaps accidental ingestion of a transformation potion..." mused a female mage with a belt full of glass vials. "Something in the stew?"

But Certainty suddenly remembered what the quilt had said. "Extra magic!" she blurted.

The senior mages looked at her in faint surprise, as if they'd forgotten she was still there.

"What do you mean, Novice?" the High Mage asked.

"I mean—" Certainty felt their eyes on her and swallowed. "I think the transformations might have been caused by an excess of magic. I was doing laundry just next door before it happened, and there was a quilt I was speaking with—my ability, you see—and it said something about there being . . . extra magic."

A muttering arose from the mages at this, and the High Mage nodded thoughtfully. "Magical spillover . . . interesting. Farid—could this be possible?"

Mage Farid stroked his beard. "Well—yes, I suppose. My thaumic compass has had some erratic readings lately. I thought the thing was just old and needed replacing, but perhaps the girl's right, and we've surpassed the safe threshold for magical energies."

"But how?" blustered Dean Leverin. "We've always taken great precautions to prevent magic leakage in the Guildtower! Our spells cast only within containment fields, our magical artifacts stored only in warded vaults—"

A small noise interrupted him. It came from within the group of mages. It sounded like a cough that didn't especially want to be noticed.

"Mage Mortimer," said the High Mage, narrowing her eyes at its source.

An unkempt-looking mage sidled reluctantly to the front. He was an older man with gray hair that shot out in all directions from beneath a red felted cap and bloodshot eyes that blinked a little too often. He looked how Certainty had felt the one time she'd accidentally taken a sip of dragon reviver instead of berry cordial; she hadn't stopped vibrating for days.

"I sent you a memo last week, High Mage," he said. His voice was scratchy, like a quill dragged across parchment. "When those adventurers delivered us another haul of artifacts from the Dungeons of Drakmar, if you remember? Two wagonloads! Mostly junk, mind you, all low-grade enchantments, nothing valuable—but still, there was nowhere to put them, because our vaults are so blasted full. They've been full for months, High Mage; I put in an official request, all the proper paperwork and everything, but the bursar said something about budget cuts—*budget cuts*, I tell you—"

The High Mage cut him off with nothing but the tiniest narrowing of her eyes.

"And *where*," she said, her every word crisp with intention, "are these artifacts now?"

Mortimer blinked his jittery gaze away and mumbled something.

"What was that?"

"Thekitchenpantry," he said, still barely audible. He looked as if he wanted to transform himself into one of the flagstones beneath his feet, or possibly a very small root vegetable.

There was a loud groaning from the other senior mages, and the High Mage drew a deep, vexed breath and opened her mouth—but Certainty couldn't know what she would have said to the unfortunate Mage Mortimer because at that moment, there was another vast sucking noise, that same unpleasant swooping in her insides, and then—

WHOMP.

It began to rain figs.

A GREAT DEAL of organized chaos followed. As Certainty kept out of the way and watched, High Mage Melea took charge of the situation with frightening efficiency. The raining fruits were banished with a spell; the kitchens were to be closed until the pantry was adequately warded (one of the mages looked mournfully at the roasting chickens); the kitchen staff would be given several days off to recover from their brief spells as vegetables; and Mage Farid was to immediately take measurements of the thaumic levels in the vaults and all other parts of the Guildtower to detect any other leakages.

"And you," the High Mage said curtly to Mage Mortimer once they were no longer being pelted by fruit and the other mages had been sent away to their tasks. "Come to my office as soon as you have a proposal for remedying the artifact overflow situation."

Certainty fidgeted. Nobody had asked her to do anything; could she just leave? She was going to be late to her afternoon classes, but then again, maybe the dean would excuse her—*I'm quite shaken by seeing Ger like that, sir; not sure I'll be able to concentrate on Advanced Spell Components today*—

But then the High Mage's eyes snapped onto her, and her expression was calculating in a way that made Certainty nervous.

"Actually . . . Mortimer, I may have a potential solution for us. Novice Certainty, I'll need you to join us in my office."

"I—" She had nothing to do with any of this; she'd just been unlucky enough to be on laundry duty at the wrong time! But there was only one correct response to such a request. "Yes, High Mage."

So High Mage Melea turned to exit, followed by the miserable Mage Mortimer, and Certainty saw no alternative but to troop out of the kitchens and up the stairs toward whatever it was that fate had in store for her.

TWO

CERTAINTY, MAGE MORTIMER, and High Mage Melea strode out of the kitchen and through the corridor, then up the wide, spiral staircase that was the spine of the Guildtower.

As they passed each landing, Certainty caught glimpses of the four curving corridors branching out from the stairs to stretch north, east, south, and west, all looping back to the central column like the boundaries of a clover. The novices' quarters, the classrooms, the libraries—a kaleidoscope of rooms snaked throughout the tower, the varied fiefs of the Guild's vertical demesne. But they only continued to climb up and up, and Certainty tried not to wheeze too audibly; physical exercise was not traditionally a mage's strong suit. Finally, they turned off into a corridor lit brightly with magelamps, and halted before a set of ornately carved doors.

"I need a few moments to discuss matters with Mage Mortimer first," the High Mage said to her. "Wait here, please."

The High Mage and Mage Mortimer disappeared between the heavy doors. As soon as they closed, Certainty let her shoulders slump, and she looked glumly around at the ornate tapestries adorning the whitestone walls. On one of them, a mage appeared to be riding a gryphon while hurling fireballs at the battlefield below. *Charming.* Whether it was meant as an inspiration or a warning, Certainty wasn't sure.

It was Certainty's first time on this particular floor of the Guildtower. She'd never been called to the High Mage's office before—she wasn't nearly important enough for that. Well, neither important enough nor enough of a problem, she supposed. Sometimes a novice could get in enough trouble that the High Mage would expel them from the Guild personally, but as far as she knew, she hadn't broken any Guild rules.

Her conscience gave a guilty twinge.

All right, fine, she hadn't broken any rules *lately*. That incident last spring with the starfruit wine and invisibility potions didn't count, surely. It had all been Dav's idea, and everyone's heads had reappeared eventually.

But besides a few such minor infractions, Certainty was by and large a rule-abiding novice. She'd never do anything that put her in real risk of expulsion; why would she? She liked her life in the Guildtower. Granted, she was more than ready to move on from it—but only with a mage's circles pinned firmly to her robes.

It had to happen eventually; that was what she kept telling herself. (And her family.)

She shifted her weight to her other foot, watching the closed doors with growing anxiety. What could the High Mage possibly want with her? Surely she didn't blame her for the cabbages. Certainty tucked a loose curl back behind her ear but it sprang free again; her hair, like her, had a mild tendency toward rebellion. She accepted the futility of trying to make it behave and simply stood there trying to quell the nervousness that churned her stomach. *Blast.* She should've just signed up for door duty that morning instead of laundry. Better to have to wrangle eager applicants and fill out paperwork for the Guild testers than get caught up in . . . whatever this was.

Then the office doors finally opened again, and Mage Mortimer's bloodshot eyes peered out at her. "You can come in now," he muttered.

Steeling herself, she followed him in and found herself in an office that was grand without being ostentatious. Along the eastern wall, an immense window stretched from carpeted floor to inlaid ceiling. Through it was a magnificent view of the White Palace, gleaming in the midday sun and draped in a lush shawl of gardens. In the center of the room was a large desk crafted from dark wood that was presently covered in scrolls, parchments, and books whose disarray suggested they had very recently been rifled through. In front of the desk were two cushioned chairs, worn but expensive-looking, and seated behind the desk, wearing a thoughtful expression, was the High Mage.

Certainty ducked another quick, nervous curtsy. (It never hurt to be polite.) The High Mage gestured toward the chairs, so she sat in one while Mortimer merely stood to the side, twitching faintly and looking like he wished he were anywhere else.

The High Mage studied her for a moment. Then she pulled one of the parchments closer and peered down at it over her spectacles.

"Certainty Bulrush of Potshire. A novice for six years now. The longest-tenured of our current novices, in fact. Accepted for training at seventeen, with a highly specific aptitude in physical magic—the ability to communicate with objects via touch. Is that all correct?"

"Yes, High Mage."

A highly specific aptitude. It didn't sound so bad when you put it like that.

"And yet, your magic has failed to progress sufficiently during these six years to qualify you for full magehood. You've attempted the advancement trials twice, and have failed twice."

Certainty's stomach clenched. Had the Guild's patience with her finally run out? But if so, why was the High Mage delivering the news herself? Surely the dean could have handled something as minor as one novice's disappointing performance review.

Certainty tried to keep her voice level. "Yes, High Mage. But I've been training hard, practicing my spellcasting—I'm hoping that next time . . ."

Truth be told, she could barely even convince herself that she was improving. Sure, she could speak with objects all day long, but *true* mages didn't rely solely on their unique magical talents. They learned to cast spells from across the magical disciplines; augmented their natural specialization with at least a basic repertoire of utility charms and incantations. But Certainty . . . even the simplest of spells were still a struggle for her.

The High Mage's gaze flicked up at her and Certainty trailed off. Glumly, she wondered how much detail, exactly, was on that parchment. Depressing to think that her six-year Guild career could be summarized on a single page.

The High Mage went on.

"Your instructors report that you're a good novice. Diligent. Cheerful. A little impertinent, at times, but hardworking. Always willing to help."

"Um. Thank you?"

High Mage Melea put the parchment down and leaned back in her chair.

"But Novice, I'm sure you've read all of the texts on the subject of magical development by now. So you know as well as I do that if your magic hasn't gotten any stronger by now, it never will."

Her words stung all the more so because they were true. All mages eventually came up against a natural limit to their powers, and Certainty had found hers far too early. The innate magical spark that the Guild testers had seen in her at seventeen had simply never kindled into anything more.

It didn't matter how hard she trained, how many books she read—the spells she cast always sputtered out as her feeble pool of magic spent itself dry. Even though, Mother and Sons knew, she'd *tried*. For six years, she'd tried! Everything from meditation techniques to questionable back-alley tonics; anything at all that offered the possibility of expanding her magic beyond the marginal and the mundane. But all she'd ever gotten for her efforts were splitting headaches and heartburn.

Certainty pressed her lips together, willing down the unpleasant creep of shame.

"Please don't expel me from the Guild. Please. I'll try harder. I'll . . ." She wasn't too proud to beg—wasn't too proud to do anything at all that the Guild might ask of her.

But what *could* she do? More laundry? More chores?

She certainly couldn't slink back to Potshire, to her family, with nothing to show for her six years in Margrave. She didn't want to think of what her parents would say, let alone Asp. He'd looked at her like she was a heroine from the stories when they told him that she'd been accepted by the Guild. That his big sister was going to become a *mage*, fancy robes and all, and that she'd send home money to secure his apprenticeship—a future beyond the farm—as soon as she succeeded.

Gods, the day she'd left, he'd hugged her so tightly it'd hurt.

But across the desk from her, the High Mage looked surprised.

"Expel you? That's not why I asked you here."

Certainty let her eyes lift from the desk's swirling woodgrain. "It's not?"

"No. The Guild has a task for you, Certainty. It's unglamorous but essential. And, as your earlier insight demonstrated, one that may be uniquely suited to your particular ability."

Mage Mortimer made a skeptical-sounding noise—but Certainty's heart had leapt to her throat. *A task.* Novices were rarely given formal assignments of their own. That sounded promising. Like the sort of thing that would incline a Guild committee to look favorably upon her candidacy for magehood. She sat up straighter in the chair, attempting to look very serious and responsible and mage-like.

"What would you like me to do, High Mage?"

"You heard Mortimer speak of the Guild vaults when we were down in the kitchens, yes? I presume you know what they are."

"They're where all of the Guild's magical artifacts are kept."

The High Mage nodded. "Our treasury, of a sort. The vaults contain the enchanted items crafted by our greatest artificers, alongside relics recovered from the Mage Wars. And Mage Mortimer here . . ." She cast a sharp glance at him. "He is, at present, the Keeper of the vaults. An important responsibility, because these magical artifacts can be immensely dangerous—not only to their users, but to all around them. As we've seen."

"It was an oversight," muttered Mage Mortimer. His felted hat had slid askew and he looked even more unbalanced than before. Certainty couldn't help but wonder if constant exposure to powerful artifacts had affected his mind. She'd heard stories: cursed rings of power, demonically possessed lamps, that sort of thing. Or perhaps Mortimer only suffered from the particular brand of madness brought on by decades of bureaucracy and administrative work. "One mistake in years. *I submitted the memo!* The bursar—"

The High Mage only lifted one well-practiced eyebrow, and

Mortimer subsided into sullen silence. He had not missed the "at present," Certainty surmised.

"Mage Mortimer has brought to my attention that our vaults are over capacity. The hired heroes of Eshtera have been doing too good a job hunting magical treasures, it seems, and the Guildtower now has a dangerous surplus of artifacts. As a result, many are stored improperly, posing an immediate risk of further . . . *incidents*. We can contain the thaumic leakage temporarily, but there is an urgent need to move some artifacts out of the Guildtower as soon as possible."

Certainty was beginning to put together the pieces. "You want me," she said, speaking slowly, "to transport magical artifacts out of the Guildtower?"

"Precisely."

"But . . ." Some of those artifacts must be centuries old! Objects of indescribable power—they could level cities, part oceans—and they wanted to trust *Certainty* with them? "But surely—"

Her alarm must have been written all over her face. The High Mage shook her head, looking amused.

"Obviously we wouldn't send the important ones with you. Just the recent delivery currently cluttering the kitchen pantries, and perhaps some other minor items. Mage Mortimer assures me—*and will verify*, won't you, Mortimer—that only lesser artifacts with enchantments of the third degree or lower will be sent."

"Lesser artifacts," repeated Certainty. "So . . . junk." At least that sounded far less likely to result in her bringing magical destruction upon the kingdom.

"Yes," said Mage Mortimer. He still sounded disgruntled, though Certainty thought it very possible that that was just his default state of being. "Even a novice physical mage should be able to handle them. It'll buy us some time to expand the vaults properly. Safely."

Even you, Certainty heard. But the High Mage had said something else.

"And my ability is uniquely suited to this because . . . ?"

"Because all artifacts must be identified and recorded before being stored." He harrumphed. "You can talk to objects, the High Mage says. That should make identifying their enchantments nice and easy for you. Cheaper than using up hundreds of identification scrolls, anyway."

"I see." Just like doing the laundry. "And where will I be transporting them?"

The High Mage pulled a scroll out from underneath a tottering pile and unrolled it to reveal a map of Eshtera. On it Certainty saw Margrave, with the royal lion crest alongside, as well as markings for the other major cities and the mighty Saltpeaks. But the High Mage's finger hovered over the parchment, searching, until it stopped somewhere in the blank space of the southeastern farmlands above a tiny black speck.

Certainty leaned forward to squint at it. The dot could easily have been mistaken for a stray dust mote. Someone—not the original mapmaker—had scribbled in beside it something that started with an *S*.

"Shpelling," said the High Mage.

"Pardon?"

Beside her, Mortimer snorted, but the High Mage ignored him. "The village of Shpelling," she clarified. "That will be your destination."

"Oh. Why . . ." Certainty tried to say the village's name without spraying the map. "Why Shpelling?"

"Mage Mortimer and I examined the records. For decades, the Guild hasn't accepted a single novice from Shpelling, or in fact from a many-league radius around Shpelling. It seems that this magical drought may have been caused by something that happened there during the Wars. A powerful earth mage overextended himself."

"Burned himself out," added Mortimer. "Sucked the place dry of every drop of natural magic it had."

"We therefore have good reason to believe that this village is now the least magical place in all of Eshtera. No preexisting thaumic energies, which means . . ."

"Less risk of the artifacts' magic interacting and spilling over," finished Certainty.

"Correct."

Low-grade artifacts, non-magical village. So far, it all sounded reasonable enough. "Well, of course, I'd be honored to do what I can to help," she said, trying to sound honored instead of apprehensive.

The High Mage gave her an approving nod. "I'm glad to hear it. Because I've also decided that Mage Mortimer would benefit from the assistance of a Deputy Keeper, and your completion of this assignment would provide a very strong case for placing you in that role. And given that such a position is required to be held by a mage . . ."

Certainty's breath caught sharply.

". . . it would obviously require your advancement to magehood."

Advancement to magehood.

No longer Novice Certainty, but Mage Certainty. The golden circles pinned on her chest—her own room on the upper floors of the Guildtower—and a mage's stipend! Enough silver to pay Asp's apprenticeship fees, to rebuild the old barn, to buy her ma a new spinning wheel . . . Everything she'd ever hoped for since her family sent her off on the mail coach to Margrave carrying a cheese sandwich, a pouch of pennies, and the weight of their family's future. *Finally.*

"Yes, High Mage," she squeaked, and tried not to wince at how high her voice sounded. *Gravitas, Cert. Mages have gravitas.* She cleared her throat. "Thank you, High Mage! When do I leave?"

"Tomorrow morning." The High Mage rang a small silver bell on her desk, summoning a page from outside the door. She said something in his ear; the boy nodded and rushed off again. "But you won't be going alone. You're not a mage yet, Certainty, which means that technically you can't take sole possession of Guild artifacts, even lesser ones such as these. And you'll need a partner with more—well—*reliable* spellcasting abilities."

Certainty's excitement dimmed, but only a little. A group project, then; that was fine. "Mage Mortimer?" If she was going to work for him in the vaults, it made sense to start now.

But he shook his head. "I'm needed here at the Guildtower. Got to oversee the vault expansion."

The High Mage steepled her fingers together. "Novice, I've decided that Mage Aurelia Mirellan will accompany you."

Ah. Certainty knew there had to be a catch.

Mage Aurelia, the ice witch. Or at least, that was the epithet assigned to her throughout the novices' quarters. So named for her silver-blond hair, her frosty disposition, or both—Certainty wasn't entirely sure, as she'd never spoken with the mage herself. Well, unless you counted the time in the library when she'd giggled too loudly at Novice Francesca's story of a run-in with a former fling, and Mage Aurelia had emerged from a study booth like an avenging angel to glare at them. She doubted Aurelia remembered, though. The woman probably terrified multiple novices into silence on a daily basis.

But novices gossiped like it was their job, and the topic of which mages' stars were rising or falling was always a popular one. Aurelia was said to be a brilliant scholar. Even though she'd come to the Guild late at twenty-one, she'd excelled in her classes and trials and been raised to full magehood in near-record speed. Not only was she a strong spellcaster, but she also had a powerful magical talent: farspeaking, the rare and coveted ability to open channels of communication over great distances.

And yet, puzzlingly, despite Aurelia having advanced to magehood two years ago, she still hadn't been sent out on her first official assignment. Instead, Certainty had heard that she spent all her time at the Guildtower in Margrave doing magical research. It was the sort of desk work usually given to older mages who, after decades of service among far-flung postings, were allowed to trade in their seniority for the comfort of tenured office—unusual, however, for a promising young mage.

Naturally, rumors swirled as to why Mage Aurelia remained tower-bound: The High Mage was punishing her for some grave transgression; she was having a torrid affair with a Palace Minister; no, she was having an affair with a Minister's *wife*—

But now, it appeared that Mage Aurelia was finally to be sent on her first assignment. With Certainty, the Guild's least-promising novice—to a village called *Shpelling*, or the geopolitical equivalent of a sneeze.

"Will that be a problem, Novice?" The High Mage was watching her closely.

"No, High Mage. Not at all," Certainty said hastily. "I'd be happy to work with her." And that wasn't even a lie; she'd partner with a basilisk if that's what it took to finally earn her circles. She could handle one sniffy and supercilious mage, no problem, sign her up.

But she couldn't help wondering how Mage Aurelia would take the news...

Then the door to the High Mage's office opened, and a tall, attractive woman not much older than Certainty strode in. A pale braid fell over her shoulder, not a single shining hair out of place. The golden interlocked circles of the Guild were polished to a gleam on her immaculately pressed robes, and her chin was lifted high.

"High Mage," said the woman. Mage Aurelia, Certainty recognized. Her voice was clear and clipped, with a crisp Margravian accent. "You sent for me?"

"Yes. Mage Aurelia, are you acquainted with Novice Certainty?"

The blond mage looked over at Mage Mortimer, noting his presence, then at Certainty. Aurelia's eyes were a startling green, and they lingered for a moment on Certainty's face. Certainty felt uncomfortably like a research specimen being examined and found wanting.

"No, High Mage."

Clearly, the library incident hadn't merited any space in Aurelia's memory.

"It's nice to meet you," Certainty ventured. Aurelia gave her the barest of nods in return.

"Novice Certainty's physical magic enables her to speak with objects," said High Mage Melea. "As such, I've tasked her with transporting lesser artifacts from the Guildtower to a safer location—the farming village of Shpelling—as well as completing a thorough inventory of the artifacts once there. And you, Mage Aurelia, will accompany her on this assignment."

Aurelia's expression was unreadable as she digested this, but Certainty thought she saw a muscle in her jaw twitch.

"Inventorying minor artifacts," the mage said, her tone flat. "In a farming village."

The High Mage frowned. "It may not seem like a particularly

glorious assignment"—and that was definitely an admonitory note in her voice—"but it's vital to the safety of the Guildtower. It should be straightforward—I imagine it will take no longer than a month and a half, two at the most. You'll need to work together to see it done: Certainty leading the cataloging, and you, Aurelia, warding the storage site and performing any other spellwork that may be required."

There was an uncomfortable moment of silence.

"I look forward to working with you, Mage Aurelia," Certainty said, offering her a polite smile. "I've heard a lot about you."

The look Aurelia gave her in return was scathing. Certainty's smile dropped, realizing the mage must have misunderstood. "I didn't mean . . . I just—"

"High Mage, is this assignment compulsory?" Aurelia interrupted, turning away from her.

The High Mage sighed. "Aurelia, it's well past time you complete an assignment outside of the tower . . ."

"But why this one? It's a novice's task! A quartermaster's, even—or anyone with a rudimentary grasp of spellwork—"

Certainty felt her cheeks warm.

"You know very well why," said the High Mage sharply. "We are none of us so mighty that we will not do what needs to be done. Yes, Aurelia, this assignment is compulsory. And besides, time away from the Guildtower may be beneficial to your *studies*."

She placed a strange weight on the last word that Certainty didn't quite understand. She opened her mouth to ask what the High Mage meant, but Mage Aurelia shot her a furious look, so she promptly closed it again. *Right. Not my business.* Certainty could almost feel the chill emanating from her partner-to-be.

"The artifacts are being loaded as we speak." The High Mage's voice brooked no argument. "Mage Aurelia, Novice

Certainty—take the rest of today to see to your affairs. Be ready to leave in the morning. I expect an initial progress report sent to me in two weeks' time. Am I understood?"

Aurelia was glowering at her polished boots. If looks were spells, they might have burst into flame. "Yes, High Mage."

"Then both of you will see Mage Mortimer and Fanya in the stables immediately after breakfast tomorrow; you'll be provided with everything you'll need then. Novice, Mage Mortimer, you're dismissed—but Aurelia, kindly remain for a moment so that we can discuss further."

Aurelia's jaw ticked, and she didn't turn her head as Certainty and Mage Mortimer exited the High Mage's office. As Certainty passed by Aurelia, she caught the faint whiff of parchment—the scent of the library, of hours spent with books and scrolls—but underneath it, too, was something soft and floral. A strange but not unpleasant combination.

Gods. What was she doing, sniffing her colleague? In the middle of the High Mage's office, no less. *Stop being weird, Cert!* Luckily, it didn't seem anyone had noticed. She hurried her steps as she followed Mage Mortimer out.

But as the office doors closed behind her, she couldn't help sneaking one more look over her shoulder at Aurelia. That hadn't been the most promising introduction.

It's fine if she doesn't like me, she told herself, making her way back down the whitestone stairs and ignoring the knot twisting her stomach. *She doesn't need to. We just need to get through this assignment, and then I'll be made a mage, and we can go right back to ignoring each other's existence. Simple as that.*

Too bad nothing magical ever turned out to be quite as simple as one thought.

THREE

"WAIT, TELL ME again. You're being sent where, to do what, exactly? With who?" Saralie's nose wrinkled as she processed Certainty's news.

"*Whom*," said Davish, walking beside her with an armful of books. "And don't be snobbish. Novices never get sent out on Guild assignments! I don't care where it is, *I'm* jealous of Cert."

Certainty grinned at him. "Shove off, Dav; you've never been jealous of anyone in your life. Least of all me."

He shrugged an easy shoulder and probably would have responded with something witty and charming, but then around the curving corridor strode a mage with loose curls and a jawline like carved whitestone.

Brannon. Certainty felt a pang. They'd been friends several years ago—and flirtatious enough to possibly become more—but as with so many of her Guildtower friendships, they'd grown apart once he'd earned his circles and moved to the higher floors of the mage quarters. Moved up and on, while Certainty stayed behind.

She tried to catch his eye, but Brannon swished past without even a glance. Magehood had changed him—but then again, perhaps it'd change her, too, if she ever got there. Certainty supposed that, from a mage's point of view, novices were just scurrying notetakers who bumbled about causing accidents and asking for letters of recommendation until they eventually became mages themselves, and therefore competition.

"Yum," said Saralie emphatically as they watched Brannon disappear down the corridor. His silver robes fluttered dramatically from broad and well-muscled shoulders.

"I don't see all the fuss about Mage Brannon. He's not even that handsome." Davish sounded disgruntled. Neither of them knew that Brannon had been Certainty's friend, once upon a time. "Just because he's not old yet, and a fancy fire mage, and washes his hair regularly . . ."

Saralie raised a pointed eyebrow, and Dav's words disintegrated into grumbles. Certainty smiled to hide any lingering sadness she felt at seeing Brannon again.

At least she had Dav and Saralie, though she still couldn't help feeling like a hanger-on to them sometimes. They were inseparable. Certainty would bet all her (admittedly meager) coin on the two of them eventually marrying each other—or at least spending a good deal of time in each other's beds—and whenever that happened, she'd become a dot outside their line, instead of a corner of their triangle. But for now, somehow her two otherwise intelligent friends still hadn't discerned their feelings for each other and instead spent all their time bickering in a poor substitute for proper courtship.

Certainty had thought about saying something but decided that it wasn't her place to intervene. Besides, it was more fun this way.

The three of them were on their way to the dining hall for a late supper (made possible, despite the closed kitchens, by a delegation of servants being sent to raid the city markets—and a good thing, too, for the senior mages would almost certainly have viewed a late mealtime as an even graver emergency than the Guildtower collapsing into a thaumic sinkhole).

Certainty had been excused from her lessons given her impending departure and had spent the last several hours wondering what it was, exactly, that she ought to be doing to prepare. *See to your affairs*, the High Mage had said, but Certainty didn't really have many affairs worth speaking of.

So she'd packed her bags, tucked in the corners of her bedsheets neatly, and wrote a letter to her family. In it, she shared the details of her assignment, but decided to not yet mention the magehood that had been dangled alongside it. (She figured that she ought to see how things in Shpelling went before giving them reason to hope; she'd learned from her first advancement trial, when they'd baked her an entire celebratory apple cake that had to become a consolation cake instead.) When she'd finished writing the letter, she'd given it to the Guildtower's messenger station with instructions to deliver it to her father.

But once that was done, she'd found herself itchy with anxious energy, so she'd tracked down Dav and Saralie in the library to tell them about her impending departure. They'd reacted predictably, peppering her with excited questions, before the librarian on duty had hissed at them with sufficient venom that Saralie had dragged both of them out of the stacks to go to supper instead.

Now they walked through the whitestone passages of the Guildtower's fifth level, joining the river of other white-clad novices on their way to the dining hall. Unlike the other rooms and wings of the Guildtower, the dining hall had no doors; instead, a stone archway yawned wide enough to not impede the flow of bodies during mealtime rush. Through the arch was a high-ceilinged room that looked far too large to exist as it did within the confines of the narrow Guildtower—but it was the Guild of Mages, after all. She assumed that the mages who had constructed the Guildtower had some magical means of making things bigger on the inside.

Certainty, Davish, and Saralie joined the queue for the steaming platters of roasted meats and boiled vegetables set out at the far end of the dining hall, exchanging nods and greetings with other novices they knew along the way. Most of the queue wore novice's whites, although a scattered handful of mages were just leaving the hall now.

They piled their plates high with food before claiming three empty seats at a long table. Certainty took a big forkful of the roast beef and gravied peas and leaned back, sighing contentedly. Six years in the Guildtower hadn't yet dulled the shine for her of having meat at every meal, in servings as large as she wanted—and without having to fend off her bottomless pit of a younger brother, too.

"Look," said Saralie. She was sitting across the table from Certainty, facing the entryway, and nodded toward it. "That's her, isn't it? The mage you'll have to work with?"

Certainty and Dav turned to look, and indeed, there was Mage Aurelia, shoulders back, striding into the dining hall while novices parted before her like blades of grass before a highly polished plough.

"That's her."

She wondered why Aurelia was only coming to supper now; as a mage, she had the right to eat one bell earlier and avoid the rush. Most mages took advantage of that privilege—but tonight, Aurelia clearly had chosen not to. Lost track of time while preparing for their assignment, perhaps? Or had she intentionally come later to avoid the company of her fellow mages?

If the latter, Certainty wasn't sure it had been a good trade;

dozens of curious eyes tracked the mage as she lined up for her food. She seemed to ignore them entirely. The three of them watched as Aurelia collected her plate and carried it to the farthest end of the emptiest table. Then she sat, alone and aloof, an island of silver robes and blond hair.

Aurelia looked up briefly, and her sharp green eyes snagged on Certainty's from across the room. If possible, her expression grew even stonier. The mage glared back down at her food and speared a boiled sprout with savage precision.

"Yeesh. I take it back, Cert; maybe I'm not jealous of your assignment after all." Davish craned his neck again to look. "She's pretty, though. Ow!"

Saralie had leaned across the table to whack him on the shoulder.

"Stop leering at mages who outrank you, Dav. As if she'd ever give a novice a second look."

He shrugged. "I'll have my circles next season, won't I? Mage Lemma told me she thinks I'll pass my trials—" He broke off awkwardly, looking at Certainty. "Sorry, Cert, I don't mean to bring it up . . ."

Certainty gave him a half-hearted smile. "It's fine." She was about to have the best chance she'd ever had of earning her own magehood, after all. And she could never be mad at Dav.

Like Saralie, he'd been at the Guildtower for two years now, and had quickly become one of Certainty's closest friends. He was quick to smile, with expressive eyebrows and a seemingly endless supply of suggestive jokes, and as the second son of Efreeti merchants who had emigrated from the southern borderlands, he had the easy, comfortable confidence of one born to a well-to-do and loving family. His parents regularly sent coin and parcels to the Guildtower for him—fashionable clothing, new books, the candied orange peels he liked—and Certainty found it hard not to envy the way he seemed to sail through life on ever-fair winds. Once he received his circles (and he *would*, as a reasonably powerful harvest mage; of that she had no doubt) Cert thought he'd hardly even notice the difference they made. Dav already carried himself as if he wore a mage's robes, and the mage's stipend that would mean so very much to the Bulrush family of Potshire would probably just disappear into his monthly drinking budget.

But Dav did chores like the rest of them without complaint, and whenever they went out to the taverns, he always bought everyone a round. He didn't seem to care much either way that Certainty was a farmer's daughter, or that Saralie's mother was a baroness. And she was sure that when Dav became Mage Davish, he wouldn't stop associating with Cert for fear that her novicehood would somehow tarnish his newfound status.

. . . well, mostly sure.

Certainty's glum thoughts must have been showing on her face. "I hope Mage Aurelia doesn't make things more difficult for you," Saralie said, looking worried. "On your assignment, I mean."

Certainty shrugged. "Surely she wants to succeed as much as I do? If anything goes wrong, it'll look bad for her, too."

"Desires can be conflicting," Dav said with equanimity. "And they aren't always rational."

Saralie rolled her eyes at him over her peas. "Typical man. Haven't even met the woman, and you're already spouting off about what she does or doesn't desire—"

"It's not about her being a *woman*; it's about my being older and wiser than you—"

"You're *three months* older, you lout—"

"—and at least three times smarter—"

Certainty let them bicker while she finished her food. She'd miss this while she was gone. The easy camaraderie, the sense of belonging in a place she knew intimately... The High Mage had said the assignment shouldn't take them longer than a month or so, but to Cert, that sounded like a very long time indeed. A long time to be without her friends, and with Mage Aurelia as her only connection to the Guildtower.

"Aurelia's a farspeaker, you know," Certainty mused. "Do you think she'd be willing to send messages back to the Guildtower for me? If I wanted to reach you two without waiting for the couriers?"

Dav snorted. "The ice witch? I doubt she'd—"

But then Saralie cut him off with a sudden choking sound, her eyes wide and urgent across the table.

"Mage!" she blurted out, looking somewhere over Certainty's shoulder. "Good evening—"

Suddenly, Certainty caught the scent of lavender and parchment. Her stomach plummeted. She looked behind her, dreading what she knew she'd find there. Sure enough, Mage Aurelia's green eyes met hers.

"Novice Certainty," Aurelia said. Her voice was quiet, and somehow it was infinitely worse than if she were shouting.

Certainty scrambled to stand. *Shit, shit, shit.* There was no way Aurelia hadn't been close enough to hear Dav call her *the ice witch.*

"Mage Aurelia," she said weakly. "I was—that is, we were just having dinner..."

"Yes. I see that." Aurelia's voice was as brittle as flint. She didn't look at either Davish or Saralie as she spoke. "I've been studying the maps. Shpelling is 17.4 leagues to the southeast of Margrave, and I wanted to inform you that we should be prepared for an outgoing journey of several days at a minimum, possibly up to a week."

"Yes. Um." Certainty's words tripped over themselves in their haste to escape. "Thank you, I'll be ready."

"Good."

They stood there for another moment looking at each other, Certainty's mind racing through possible things to say—*sorry my friend called you an ice witch; please don't wreck my chances of magehood; what potions do you use to keep your hair so shiny*—but none seemed exactly appropriate, and like a book slamming shut, the moment passed her by. Aurelia jerked her chin in acknowledgment, then turned abruptly and strode out of the dining hall.

Certainty's stomach sank as she watched her go. Had Aurelia come to dinner late specifically to speak with Certainty about their assignment? But then, why had she sat at a different table? And why did she have to come by at *precisely* the wrong moment?

Certainty blew out a breath, wishing she could simply cast a spell to undo the last few minutes. She wasn't entirely sure what it was that she was feeling, but whatever it was, it wasn't good.

Because for just a heartbeat, in the flash of their eyes meeting, Certainty thought she had seen a ghost of something in Aurelia's face that she hadn't expected, and hadn't been at all prepared for.

Something a lot like hurt.

FOUR

CERTAINTY HALF HOPED that Aurelia wouldn't show up at the stables the next morning, unlikely as that was—but of course, the blond mage was already there by the time Certainty arrived. She'd probably reported for duty at the first crowing of dawn. Aurelia stood stiffly beside the stable entrance, arms crossed, traveling pack by her feet.

Certainty's own bag was both larger and more sloppily packed; not having much idea of what she'd need in Shpelling, she'd thrown in all her possessions: her clothing, her books, her sewing kit, and sundry other supplies. The bag was now so stuffed that it threatened to explode and shower anyone in the vicinity with ladies' undergarments and quills.

"Good morning," Certainty said brightly to Aurelia as she set her pack down. It was a new day, a fresh start, surely they could both forget that awkward encounter in the dining hall last night...?

"Novice."

Perhaps not, then.

At least Fanya was glad to see Certainty. The wiry, gray-bearded dwarf who opened the stable doors to let them in was one of the Guild's quartermasters, and Certainty had previously done them some small favors, using her magic to fix some finicky equipment in less time than it would have taken to bring in an appropriate craftsman.

"Novice Certainty," said Fanya, drawing out her name in a way that made her smile. "So the High Mage is sending you off on a grand quest! In such a rush, too—it must be urgent indeed."

Beside them, a rumpled-looking Mage Mortimer let out a snort. He was wearing the same clothes he'd been wearing the previous day, and clearly hadn't slept much.

"It's just a minor assignment," Certainty said diffidently. She nodded at Aurelia. "And this is Aurelia. She'll be my partner for it."

"*Mage* Aurelia," Aurelia said curtly. Fanya's grin faded, and they shot Certainty a look of sympathy.

"I see. Well met, *Mage* Aurelia." They mimicked Aurelia's emphasis and the mage narrowed her eyes as if unsure whether to take offense. "Here's your cargo for the journey, all loaded up and ready to go."

They gestured to two large wooden traveling wagons painted the reddish-brown of Eshtera's flag. *Sanguine umber* they called it, but to Certainty's eye it mostly just looked like mud that had wine or blood spilled on it—which, when she thought about it, was a fairly good representation of Eshtera's history, so maybe that was all right. Besides their questionable paint job, the wagons looked perfectly ordinary—except for the Guild's prominent interlocked golden circles on the sides, the vaguely ominous magical auras surrounding them, and the notable lack of horses.

"Official Guild transports! I'm surprised we get to use them for this." Certainty ran one hand over the side of a wagon, feeling the strong currents of magic underneath. Curious, she let just a little of her magic slip into it.

"*—onwardsonwardsonwards, four leagues south, east at the crossroads, onwardsonwardsonwards, protect the cargo, left at the Moot, onwardsonwards, destination of Shpelling—*"

She jerked her magic back, reeling; the wagon's object-voice had barreled through her mind, tripping over itself like the spokes of a wheel. Powerfully enchanted, indeed.

"This lot might be low-grade stuff, but they're still magical artifacts," Mage Mortimer said irritably. "Would be irresponsible to send them off with you without some form of protection."

"Aye," said Fanya. The dwarf slapped the side of the wagon with the fond air of a proud parent. "Fully warded, and already enchanted to take you to your destination. The second one's spelled to follow the first, so you two can sit together in the front one, all cozy-like. They'll stop at inns along the way when you need to rest, too. Junk artifacts or not, the High Mage is a careful woman—with these beauties, there isn't a bandit in all of Eshtera who'd be fool enough to try to waylay you."

Certainty recalled learning about an incident years ago when an enterprising band of criminals had the bright idea to ambush a Guild transport. The ward's defensive spells had been *mostly* undone when the thieves were finally released from their pens, but it was said that their leader still had a tendency to shed feathers and honk in moments of stress.

"But you'll have to send them back promptly once you arrive. We haven't got enough of these to let them just sit rotting in some village. The journey out shouldn't take you more than a week, so I'll be expecting them back in twice that time, yes?"

"Understood," said Mage Aurelia. She opened the back door of one of the wagons, her nose wrinkling with displeasure as she examined its contents. Certainty joined her to look.

Inside were stacks and stacks of plain wooden boxes, as well as loose items of various shapes and sizes. A drinking horn. A rusted helmet. A cloudy, tarnished mirror. Some of these items had paper labels tied on with thread, but many others had no such identification and were simply strewn haphazardly across the boxes, dingy and dusty and forgotten to time.

It looked, largely, like a pile of junk. Broken, useless things that the Guild no longer had room for.

Just like you, whispered a voice in Certainty's mind. But she quashed the thought firmly. The High Mage had been clear. If she could complete this assignment—and she didn't see any reason why she wouldn't be able to, even if Aurelia's glowering presence put a bit of a damper on things—then she could finally prove her value to the Guild and earn her place. *Deputy Keeper Certainty.*

She didn't love the title, but maybe it'd grow on her.

"Can we get a move on?" Mage Mortimer's hand was tapping a jittery, restless pattern against his leg. "Farid found another leakage in the privies—thaumic leakage, that is. Very messy. Need to get back to the vaults before something explodes."

"Wait, but—what exactly do we do with these artifacts once we get to Shpelling?"

"It's not that complicated, Novice. Identify the artifacts and their enchantments, label and record them, store them away, and make sure they're safely warded at all times."

He jostled her and Mage Aurelia out of the way as he reached into the wagon to grab hold of a thick, leather-bound tome and wave it under their noses. "Here's the book of records. Already has some notes I'd started. They're incomplete, obviously, but you can use them as a starting point, though you also ought to verify my entries while you're at it. I was in a bit of a rush. Too much to do, not enough time—" He dropped the tome back into the wagon with a thump; it sent little clouds of dust flying.

"And are we to liaise with a Guild contact at the village? Where are we to store the artifacts?" interrupted Aurelia.

Certainty resisted the urge to roll her eyes. *Liaise.* Mother and Sons, she talked like an instruction manual.

"The High Mage sent a fast courier on ahead to purchase a suitable building from the local lord of the province," Fanya said, swinging the wagon door shut. It latched with a secure-sounding *thunk*. "By the time you arrive, the storehouse should already be prepared for you. You'll just need to unload the artifacts and cast appropriate wards of protection. Make sure you check them often."

"Of course," Aurelia said, sounding offended. "And our supplies?"

"All loaded in the wagons already. Spell components, food and water for the journey, and so on. Magic-resistant gloves, too, for handling the artifacts—don't want you to activate any enchantments accidentally." The quartermaster tossed Mage Aurelia a fat coin purse. "And here's plenty of coin to pay for inns and anything else you may need—though if I were you, I wouldn't expect the kind of comforts you're used to here in the Guildtower."

"Ah yes, the famously luxurious life of a novice," Certainty said, grinning. "I'm sure I'll miss my kitchen chores. Maybe they'll even let me do my own laundry if I'm feeling homesick."

Fanya snorted, but Aurelia didn't even crack a smile. "I'm sure the accommodations will be adequate, quartermaster."

"Look, the important thing is to get these away from here as quickly as possible, yes?" said Mage Mortimer. He made an impatient shooing gesture with his hands—as if they were unwanted strays on the Guild's doorstep—and Certainty felt a jolt of indignation. "Go, go. Once the artifacts are all cataloged and stored away in Shpelling, your job's done."

Mage Aurelia seemed equally eager to be gone. "Fine," she said. "If that's all, then Novice Certainty and I will set off." She strode to the front of the wagons, hoisted up her traveling pack, and climbed onto the driving perch.

"Finally," muttered Mage Mortimer. He turned to leave the stables, shouting over his shoulder as he did so. "Just try not to set the whole village on fire!"

Certainty, hesitating, looked over to where Aurelia was waiting for her with poorly hidden impatience. Perhaps she thought that the sooner they left, the sooner they could get the assignment over with. Then she could return to the Guildtower to do . . . whatever it was, exactly, that she did here.

This assignment was the single best chance Certainty had ever had at advancement, and she still felt thoroughly unprepared for it. But what else could she do?

There was Fanya, she supposed. They were friendly with her, and well trusted in the Guildtower. That meant they might know things. Useful things.

"This assignment," she said to them quietly. "The High Mage said that if it goes well, I could finally earn my magehood. I *need* it to go well, Fanya. Do you have any advice for me?"

The dwarf put their thumbs in their belt loops and looked at her thoughtfully. "You're a good one, Cert. I've no doubt you'll do just fine. But . . ." They lowered their voice conspiratorially, leaning in. "I've heard some rumblings from the senior mages lately. They're saying that the Guild is on thin ice with the Crown. Ordinary folk don't trust mages, even more now than ever, and there's all this talk about how best to appease the lords, you know?"

Certainty nodded. The Guild and the Council lords were always at loggerheads over something or other. The Guild of Mages might be Eshtera's greatest military and economic asset, but it still bowed before the Crown, in accordance with the ancient pact that had ended the Mage Wars and maintained peace for generations. Still, the Crown had its royal hands full managing the delicate balance between the Guild and the Council of Ministers. There was a reason why hawks weren't kept in the same kennels as hunting dogs. Especially when the dogs weren't actually dogs, but enormously wealthy old men with a generational mistrust of uppity spellcasters.

"So if you want my advice," continued Fanya. "Go to this village, keep your head down, and do the work you've been asked to. But do it quietly. Keep things boring. The loudest pick brings down the mine, see?"

"Got it."

"And . . ." The dwarf's eyes flicked over to Aurelia. "Be careful with that one, aye? Sometimes polished gems crack the easiest."

Certainty's brow furrowed. "What do you mean, be careful—"

But Fanya hushed her quickly, looking around at the mostly empty stable. "Look, just be careful. That's all I'll say. Now be off already; the Guild isn't paying us to stand around gossiping."

The Guild wasn't paying *her* at all, other than in room, board, and instruction, but now didn't feel like the right time to point that out. Certainty nodded. She took a deep breath, rolling her shoulders as if preparing for a fight. For all she knew, this assignment might be one. *Be boring, and be careful.* She could manage that, couldn't she?

"Thank you, Fanya. Really."

The dwarf waved her off brusquely. "Oh, go on then," they said as they turned away, but Certainty saw the ghost of a smile somewhere in their beard.

Grinning to herself, she joined Aurelia on the wagon bench. "Sorry. I'm ready to leave now." Certainty expected her to say something snippy about dawdling. But instead, Aurelia merely nodded.

"Then time to go to Shpelling, Novice."

The mage rapped three times on the side of the wagon, invoking its enchantments, and it thrummed to life beneath them. Certainty thought she detected a sense of eagerness in the wood beneath her. Then Fanya threw open the gates and forward they lurched, out of the Guildtower courtyard and onto the cobbles of Margrave's High City.

Behind them, the second wagon followed closely as if tethered on an invisible chain, and the sight of two horseless traveling wagons bearing the Guild circles was noteworthy enough to ensure that those few Margravians in the streets at this early hour gave them a wide berth. Certainty couldn't resist looking over her shoulder as the Guildtower shrank behind them. How long would it be until she saw it again?

Novices were permitted to leave the tower for family visits, festival days, and city errands, but Certainty did so relatively infrequently. Her family lived just a bit too far from Margrave to make regular day trips, and even if she occasionally joined Dav and Saralie for nights out at taverns, she more often found herself choosing to stay back at the tower—to cover for their chores (*Oh thank you, Cert! You're such a dear—I owe you one—*), do extra reading, or practice her spellcasting. Not that that helped much. She'd just sit in her room staring at a rock and trying to levitate it; to transform it into an ant; to do something useful, for Mother's sake.

But it felt different, leaving the Guildtower this time. Going on an official assignment—one for which she'd been specifically chosen by the High Mage, no less.

Her heart lifted, and she looked over at her companion. She

wished she knew what Fanya meant by *be careful with that one*. Aurelia didn't look particularly dangerous to her. Uptight and stern, and pretty in the sharp-edged way of a finely crafted dagger, sure, but there were worse things.

Certainty probably ought to try to get to know her better. Even if they'd never be friends, it'd be nice to not have to spend the next two months navigating the awkward tension between them. She cleared her throat.

"Mage Aurelia, have you traveled much within Eshtera?"

Aurelia's jaw ticked, and too late, Certainty realized that may have been a poor opener, given all the gossip about her being tower-bound. "Sorry, I didn't mean on assignment—I meant, um, in general. Are you from Margrave? I'm from Potshire, just a little ways west. A little farming village, you know; my da grows pears, mostly, except he said in his last letter that he's also trying some cherries this year—"

With effort, she stopped herself from babbling. *Nobody cares about the cherries, Cert.*

Aurelia gave her a sidelong look. "Yes," she said stiffly. "I was raised in the Paper Quarter. My father is a Minister's aide, and my mother is a royal alchemist."

"Ah."

A very different sort of childhood, then.

Certainty always assumed she'd be following her parents into farming. Until her magic showed up—and then, all of a sudden, there had been something bigger and grander to hope for.

Aurelia, on the other hand, had likely never milked a cow in her life. She'd probably had fine tutors, dancing lessons, music classes . . . cityfolk things. The Paper Quarter was in the Middle City, but the scholars who lived there were well respected and wealthy. Not nobility, but wielding enough coin and influence (which were one and the same, really) that they may as well be.

Certainty cast Aurelia a surreptitious glance. The morning sun lit her golden hair from behind, foregrounding sharp cheekbones and a proud chin. It was a profile that wouldn't have looked out of place stamped onto a coin, or framed and hung in a gallery.

"So, Shpelling," she said as the wagon rattled beneath them. "I suppose it'll be a very different sort of place. Not what you're accustomed to, I mean."

"I'm a mage, not a spoiled lapdragon." Aurelia's words were clipped, but her tone was cool, not angry. "I will do the work before me, whatever that entails, Novice."

Not a great start. But Certainty was nothing if not persistent.

"My friends all call me Cert, by the way," she offered.

Aurelia glanced at her, then away again. If Certainty didn't know better, she'd have said the mage looked discomfited. She wondered if Aurelia was thinking about what Certainty's friends had called *her*.

They rode silently for a short while. The wagon wheels clattered energetically through the streets of the Middle City. Shops were just opening, and apprentices and hired workers called out jibes and greetings to each other, some pushing heavily laden carts across the cobblestones. One portly shopkeeper—a wine merchant, Certainty thought—shouted imprecations at the men carrying heavy barrels into his store.

It wasn't until the wagons had made their way through the fragrant Flower Quarter and down the gated ramp to the Lower City that Aurelia spoke again.

"Interesting name."

"Pardon?" Certainty was looking around at their passing surroundings. The Lows, with its drinking alleys and ramshackle sleeping-houses, really wasn't meant to be seen during the daytime—or when sober. Unless, of course, you were one of the thousands of laborers or servants who had no choice but to live there, in the hopes that working in the Middle City might one day lift you out of such poverty. It was always shocking to remember that this place, too, was part of the great and enlightened capital city of Margrave. Certainty always thought that she'd much rather be poor in the countryside than poor in the Lows—but luckily, it wasn't a choice she'd have to make. Not while she was still fed and sheltered beneath the Guild's wings, anyway.

Aurelia cleared her throat. "Certainty, I mean. Your name. It's . . . interesting."

"Oh. Yes. My parents liked the idea of naming their children after virtues they wanted us to have. A first birthday gift to us, of sorts."

"Us?"

"My little brother and me. He got Aspiration, but everyone just calls him Asp."

"Ah. Charming."

"You think so?" Cert grinned at Aurelia. "Well, it fits him well enough. He wants to be an apothecary, of all things . . . Not a knight, not a soldier, but an *apothecary*. Decided it at six years old when a traveling master came through Potshire with all his little bottles and vials and healed Ellie Haspen of her ague."

"How old is he now?"

Certainty's smile faded. "Fifteen." Which was quite nearly too old to be any kind of apprentice at all. Most masters only took on younger apprentices so that they'd get enough years of work out of them before they'd be tempted away by a pretty girl or a paying job.

But she shoved the thought away. She just had to finish this assignment and collect her circles; the first year of a mage's stipend was always paid out immediately. One and a half months, the High Mage had said the assignment would take. There was still plenty of time for her to keep her promise.

"And does your name suit you, too?" Aurelia asked.

"Not really." She laughed a little self-consciously, swaying as the wagon turned toward the city gates. "I'm not certain of very much at all. But I suppose Doubtful and Questioning didn't quite have the same ring to them."

Aurelia's lips quirked at that. Only for a moment, and then her face went back to the same composed formality as before—but not until Certainty had already seen it. *So you* can *smile*, she thought triumphantly. But her victory was short-lived.

"Novice, I understand that your ability allows you to speak with objects. If we're to work together, I'll need to understand the nature—and the limits—of your magic. What exactly can you do?"

"Um. Well." Certainty fiddled with her robes. "I can touch something—just objects, nothing living—and understand it. What it is, what it does, what its purpose is. And I can convince it to do things, sometimes."

"Transformation?"

"Not quite." Certainty wrinkled her nose, thinking of the time she tried to talk a hand mirror into becoming a salad bowl. It'd been so offended that it cracked right down the middle. And she'd certainly never managed to transform anything into gold, or Asp would already be a master apothecary, and she'd be wearing much nicer boots.

"Enchantment, then? Can you embed spells in objects?"

"Er, no." She wished she could; skilled artificers could make a fortune crafting magical trinkets for the nobility, even outside of their official Guild work.

Aurelia was frowning. Certainty seemed to have exhausted the mage's ideas of useful applications of her ability. *Tell me about it*, she thought crossly.

If Certainty were a competent enough spellcaster, the weakness of her specialization might have been fine; Eshtera always had a need for generalist working mages, even if they got the least-glamorous postings and were treated more like well-paid workhorses than elite sorcerers. And if she'd had a more powerful specialization, then she could have built her mage career upon that instead, weak spellcasting be damned. But here she was with neither—so becoming Deputy Keeper beside Mage Mortimer was as high an ambition as she'd ever dared to have.

Of course, to someone like Aurelia, it probably sounded like a fate worse than death.

"Well, I suppose being able to quickly identify the enchantments on these artifacts will be helpful for completing our assignment . . ." said Aurelia slowly. *But not much else* was the unspoken rest of the sentence. "Can you demonstrate?"

Certainty blinked. "What, now? Here?"

"Why not?"

By then, they had already passed through the outer gates of Margrave; their wagon jounced along the wide gravel road leading south, and Certainty squinted against the brightness of the morning. It was strange to be confronted with the wide-open expanse of fields and roads after having grown used to the comfortable confines of the Guildtower. Even when she left the tower to venture into the city, she was still surrounded by noise and activity, market stalls and shopping strangers. Here, there was only space. Distance. She inhaled deeply, savoring the way the air tasted, unfiltered as it was by the presence of other people.

"All right," she said. She tried to sound nonchalant. "What should I talk to, the wagon?"

"No, you already know its enchantment. Try this." Aurelia's hands went behind her neck, brushing aside her braid, and she unclasped a fine silver chain that Certainty hadn't noticed her wearing. A small pendant dangled from it: a silver charm, finely wrought, in the shape of a closed book. "Tell me about this necklace."

Certainty took it hesitantly, rolling the chain between her fingers. It was still warm from Aurelia's neck. She pooled it gently in her palm and closed her fingers around it, trying to hide her nervousness. This was her chance to prove to Aurelia that she wasn't entirely useless. Feeling self-conscious under Aurelia's gaze, she shut her eyes, blocking out the glare of the sun and the movement of the wagon, and let her magic trickle into the necklace.

"What is your purpose, necklace?"

The necklace's object-voice, when it responded, was a delicate whisper. It sounded like the clink of thin glass, the spritz of a perfume bottle, the shimmer on a watersilk gown. It sounded expensive.

"I am an enchanted necklace. I adorn. I distinguish. I enhance."

"And what's your enchantment?"

"I bear a spell of focus. I ward my wearer against distractions of body and mind. I remind them of what it is they strive for."

Certainty frowned. *"Distractions of body and mind?"*

"Hunger. Thirst. Loneliness. Exhaustion. I dull their edges."

She thought she could see how that might be useful. *"Show me,"* she thought.

The necklace complied.

Certainty felt the bloom of its magic first within her hand, then flowing through her body. The spell felt like being immersed in cool, still water; the world was suddenly quiet around her. Her body became distant, as if she were a being of intellect rather than anything so crude as a living, breathing thing. Like a knife on a whetstone, her mind sharpened itself against the spell, and her thoughts grew unusually clear. She considered what it'd be like to train her magic under such conditions. Which exercises she'd go through, in what sequence; how she could optimize their effectiveness...

Then the whispers began to snake through the channels of her mind.

"You need to work harder," murmured a voice that sounded strangely like her own. *"Your magic is too weak. You're not good enough. You'll never be good enough."*

"Stop that," she thought at the necklace.

"Cert, I'm disappointed in you." Her father's voice now. *"We were all counting on you, you know."*

"That's enough—"

Then came Asp's voice, as clear as if he were sitting right beside her.

"But Cert, you promised me..."

"STOP!"

The whispers ceased immediately.

Certainty's eyes shot open. Her heart was thumping hard, and her breaths felt ragged and short. The necklace's enchantment was as powerful as any Cert had ever felt. It frightened her.

Aurelia was watching her intently. "Well?"

She swallowed. "It's... it's enchanted with a spell of focus." Her expression must have said more than that, though, because Aurelia's eyes tightened.

"Do you disapprove, Novice?"

Yes! It's awful. Who wouldn't? She was still reminding herself that the voices weren't real. But Aurelia owned the necklace—had been wearing the blasted thing, presumably by choice, although what that said about her Certainty didn't know—so she hedged.

"Not entirely. I'm just trying to understand... If you don't mind my asking, why do you want to have a voice always criticizing you inside your own head? Do you really need that just so you can—what, get more work done?"

"My work is important." Aurelia's voice was stiff again. "This necklace helps me be the best mage that I can be." She took it back and clasped it around her neck once more, where it vanished beneath her robes.

Huh. Certainty searched for something safe and inoffensive to say.

"Um. The craftwork on it is lovely. Did you commission it from a Guild artificer?"

"No," Aurelia said. "It was a gift from my parents."

"I . . . see." *Mother and Sons.* What sort of parents would inflict such a horrible gift on their own daughter? Rich ones, obviously, but more than that . . .

"It doesn't speak constantly." Aurelia's tone was carefully neutral. "The voice of the necklace, I mean. Only sometimes."

"Oh."

Certainty didn't know what else to say.

She couldn't help but think of the fine carriage horses she often saw in the High City. Immaculately groomed and wearing tack that gleamed with silver and jewels, they high-stepped through the streets in perfect synchronization. The purebred horses were as much a symbol of their passengers' wealth and status as the family crests inlaid on the carriage doors.

They always rode blinkered, of course, with cups of dark leather attached to the bridle such that they could only see straight ahead. The blinkers were meant to prevent the horses from startling, but Certainty had always felt bad for those fine, beautiful horses in their fine, beautiful harnesses, whose worlds were shrunk in half by scraps of leather, and who learned to only ever walk in the direction where they were pointed.

Certainty shuddered lightly and put all thoughts of the necklace out of her head. She held her hands in her lap, looking out at the landscape rolling by. She turned her face up to the sun and let her thoughts drift along with the breeze, imagining what the village of Shpelling would be like. Wondering what Dav and Saralie were up to back at the Guildtower, and thinking of her family, and whether her father had begun the season's planting yet.

But all the while, as they traveled on, Mage Aurelia looked only straight ahead.

FIVE

AFTER LEAVING MARGRAVE, their wagons rolled southward and then east, passing merchants and other travelers along the wide dirt roads. The weather was fine and clear, and the farmlands to either side were busy with the work of spring planting.

The sound of shovels striking earth and the damp scent of freshly turned soil were familiar and comforting to Certainty. Back home in Potshire, she'd helped her father tend to their crops since she was barely tall enough to lift a spade. But all that was before her magic had been discovered. Once it was, she'd left to apply to the Guild before that year's pears had even begun to warm from green to gold.

Thanks to the wagons' enchantments, Certainty and Aurelia had very little to do during their journey besides look properly magerial to any passersby. The wagons (and Aurelia) bore the Guild's circles, so Certainty was conscious of being seen as an official representative of the Guild despite her novice's whites. Every so often, Aurelia would unroll the map that Fanya had given them, squinting at its markings and then up at whatever signs or landmarks were visible. Occasionally, she'd mutter an invocation and twist her fingers to cast a basic wayfinding spell, and after the fourth or fifth such occasion of this, Certainty decided to say something.

"You don't need to do that, you know." She nodded toward the map in Aurelia's hands. "Fanya said that the wagons are enchanted to know the way. They'll take us to Shpelling by the best route."

"'It is a poor mage who relies on another man's magic over his own wits,'" quoted the mage. "Mage Freinar, during the reign of Queen Lisbet the First, from his treatise on—"

"—on elemental magic and the proper uses thereof," finished Cert. "Yes, I've read it."

Aurelia looked at her with enough surprise that Certainty might have been offended if she were someone more like Aurelia.

"Yes, well." The mage cleared her throat. "Then you should understand why I'm checking the map, even if the wagons are spelled. I'm the ranking mage on this assignment, and it's my responsibility to make sure all goes as planned."

Certainty didn't love the phrase "ranking mage," but she also felt a twinge of guilt. Aurelia was just being diligent, she supposed. A little excessively so, maybe, but she wasn't entirely wrong. And she hadn't even asked Certainty to help her monitor their route—she'd just taken the task on herself. *My responsibility*, she'd said.

But it was Certainty's advancement on the line, not Aurelia's. If anyone should be wholly focused on making sure that their assignment went off without so much as an unintended detour, it should be her. So, contrite, she held out an open hand.

"You're right. I'm sorry. We can take turns—may I?"

After a moment's hesitation, Aurelia handed over the map. Cert scanned it, trying to gauge their progress—the mapmaker seemed to have prioritized artistry more than legibility; what were those swirly symbols even supposed to *mean*—but when she looked up again, she found Aurelia watching her with a guarded expression.

"What is it?"

"Nothing," Aurelia said abruptly. Then: "I've just found that other mages don't always agree. With me, I mean. How I approach my work."

"Oh. Um." Certainty thought it far more likely that the other mages just didn't like Aurelia herself rather than her methods, but she wasn't about to voice that theory. She rummaged for something to say. "I can't promise I'll always agree with you, either. But if not, I'll at least listen to your reasons and tell you if I still don't. If that's all right?"

"I . . . yes." Aurelia smoothed the end of her braid. "That would be acceptable."

"Good," said Cert, nonplussed.

". . . good."

And as they traveled on, if the mage snuck occasional puzzled, sidelong glances at her as if she were an unfamiliar new problem to be solved, well, Certainty was perfectly content not to notice. Things were already awkward enough as they were, thank you very much.

WHEN DUSK FELL, Certainty wondered how the wagons would know when they needed to rest, but she needn't have—the thought had hardly passed through her mind before they rolled to a gentle stop in the courtyard of a prosperous-looking three-story inn. They were met there by the inn's anxious and obsequious proprietor, a man with a forehead rather too large for the rest of his face.

"Welcome, mages, welcome. The Crimson Rose is always honored to host our fine patrons from the Guild." If he noticed that Certainty was in novice's whites rather than a mage's robes, he didn't seem to care, as he bowed low to them both.

"Thank you," said Aurelia, declining his offered hand as she stepped down. With a creak, their wagon lowered itself and obligingly tipped to one side. Aurelia somehow made dismounting from the wagon look elegant; Certainty followed behind with much less grace and a suppressed wince. The enchanted transports might be efficient, but it had still been a long day full of very bumpy roads. It was too bad they couldn't have requisitioned some flying carpets instead; she'd heard that those were a far smoother ride.

"The wagons are warded and can remain outside," Aurelia said to the innkeeper. "But we do require meals and two rooms for the night."

The innkeeper, who had been eyeing the wagons with curiosity, snapped his attention back to her. "Oh! I'm sorry, lady mage, but we only have one more room available. It's a busy time for the silk merchants, you see, they're traveling to Margrave for the season's auction—"

"Then we'll take it," Aurelia said impatiently. "I assume you're not down to one bed, as well?"

The innkeeper looked offended. "Of course not! What sort of respectable inn doesn't have any extra beds? I'll have a second one brought to the room presently. Please, come in, come in."

AT LEAST THE food was good. As their packs were carried up to the room being prepared for them, Cert and Aurelia sat down at a round table beside the roaring hearth of the inn's common room, and a serving maid promptly brought over two heaping plates of beef and barley stew along with tankards of fresh cider.

The room was crowded with merchants, it seemed, all

dressed in an unusual abundance of colorful silks. The two women attracted stares from the other patrons—some curious, some nervous, one or two verging on hostile—but nobody approached their table. As much as Aurelia's mage robes drew attention, they also served as an effective deterrent against unwanted company; Eshterans usually preferred their mages either on the front lines of battle or hidden away behind Guild-tower walls.

Certainty tucked into her stew with pleasure and Aurelia did the same, albeit with better table manners. Certainty watched surreptitiously as the mage used her fork to fill her spoon, then lifted each bite with care to her lips. By the time Certainty had cleared her plate, Aurelia was still only halfway through hers, so she sipped at her cider while the mage ate.

Once they'd both finished (Certainty noticing that Aurelia had left behind the crispy brown chunks of fat that were really the best bits), the serving maid returned to take their plates and replace them with a pan of what looked like soggy apple crisp. Burnt sugar and buttery brown crumbles were scattered over gooey chunks of preserved apples that had half melted into the honey sauce they bathed in.

"Chef's specialty," the serving maid informed them. "Best to eat it quickly 'fore it cools."

Certainty needed no further urging. She was four forkfuls in before she noticed that Aurelia hadn't taken a bite. "You don't like apples?"

"I don't eat sweets," said the mage.

"Oh. All right." She took another bite and an involuntary, almost indecent noise came from somewhere deep inside her. It really *was* good. Cert felt Aurelia's eyes on her as she chewed.

"I used to. When I was a child," said Aurelia suddenly. "Eat sweets, I mean."

"Oh?" Certainty didn't point out that most children ate sweets. It was something of a defining characteristic of being a child, wasn't it?

"But my mother discouraged it. Said it'd ruin my figure."

Ah. Certainty had never been too concerned with her own figure (if she had to describe it in one word, it'd be "bouncy"), but she knew that some of the other female novices fretted over fitting into their dresses whenever ball season came around. It seemed to be a uniquely Margravian anxiety, or perhaps just one endemic to the upper classes. Growing up in Potshire, a healthily rounded figure was always seen as a fine trait for a future wife. It was a sign that she enjoyed her food, and *that* was a sign that she'd be a good cook.

"Well, your mother's not here," she said. And without thinking—lulled into complacency by the warmth of the fire and the fullness of a good meal—she added: "Besides, I think your figure's just fine."

Aurelia's eyes widened. *Oh. Oh no.* Certainty desperately tried to backtrack. "I mean—I didn't mean—not that I was *looking*—"

Aurelia's face went through a complicated series of motions. Her mouth opened and closed. Then Certainty saw her raise one hand, subconsciously, to touch the necklace around her neck.

"I think I'll go up to our room now, Novice. I would suggest you do the same once you've finished. We'll make another early start tomorrow." And before Certainty could even respond, Aurelia stood up, gave her a businesslike nod, and left.

Certainty watched with perplexity as the mage wound her way through the common room toward the stairs, surrounded by a radius of empty space where the inn's patrons edged out of her path. Even though she knew what the necklace did now, she still couldn't bring herself to understand why anyone would subject themselves to it. But at least Aurelia hadn't been offended by her thoughtless comment. Or had she? It was so hard to tell beneath all those layers of enchantment and professional composure.

Still, the rest of the apple crisp lay waiting in all of its sticky goodness, and Certainty was not one to waste a perfectly good dessert. She picked her fork back up and carried on alone with the very taxing and important Guild business of demolishing the remainder of the pan.

FOR THE NEXT several days, their journey proceeded without incident while their wagons rolled on through the bucolic farmlands of southeastern Eshtera. As Fanya had promised, they remained unbothered by bandits. One dodgy-looking fellow rode a little too close to them, but Aurelia narrowed her eyes at him, and their wagon rattled its wheels menacingly and emitted a wooden sort of growling noise, all of which promptly convinced the rider that, actually, he'd meant to be traveling very quickly in the opposite direction. Certainty thought she detected a hint of smugness in the way their wagon bounced over the road while the man fled.

So without any real threat of being attacked or getting lost, their greatest difficulty was staying awake on the bench during monotonous stretches of travel. Or at least, that was Certainty's greatest difficulty. Aurelia seemed to be capable of staying awake and upright—with annoyingly perfect posture, nonetheless—to scan the roads for hours at a time. Certainty wondered how much of that was the necklace's doing.

She tried at times to make conversation, but as they neared their destination, Aurelia grew more curt and monosyllabic in her responses. Certainty wondered if Aurelia was thinking about where she should have been instead: the White Palace, perhaps, or in a foreign capital. Not rattling around the Eshteran countryside with a novice and two enchanted wagons full of next-to-useless trinkets.

The weather seemed to turn, along with Aurelia's temperament. As they traveled on, the sun retreated behind lumpy clouds to sulk, and they soon found themselves beset with a half-hearted drizzle that suggested the sky couldn't even muster the energy for a proper storm. Certainty drew her cloak more tightly around her, huddling beneath the wagon's slim overhang, and as mud splattered against the wagons' sides, she thought longingly of the warm, dry novice's quarters in the Guildtower.

It was, all in all, not a particularly pleasant journey. Really, it ought to have at least been exciting and dangerous to make up for it. That was how it worked in stories, wasn't it?

"Pass me the map," Certainty said when she spotted a far-off, blurry shape in the distance. "Is that the Lesser Moot we're supposed to be turning left at?"

Aurelia squinted through the sleeting rain. "I think that's just a haystack, Novice."

"Oh." Certainty sighed and went back to feeling damp and discontented. Seventeen point four leagues was a much greater distance than it had seemed on parchment.

IT WAS WITH a great deal of relief that on the afternoon of the fifth day, Certainty looked up from the map and saw, through dribbling rain, the twin hills and forked streams that meant they were nearly at their destination. Their enchanted wagons crested the western hill, and finally, the village of Shpelling came into view—but not before the pungent, unmistakable smell of raw garlic washed over them.

"Mother and Sons." Certainty's eyes watered, and beside her, Aurelia made a small choking sound. "At least we'll be well defended against any vampyres here."

"Don't be frivolous. Eshtera hasn't had any confirmed vampyre sightings in ages." Aurelia's voice was muffled behind her cloak, which she was holding over her nose and mouth. Certainty doubted it helped; the smell of the garlic was nearly thick enough to chew. "I did read that the region was a significant exporter of produce, but honestly—*this* place is really where we're meant to store the artifacts?"

Shpelling looked as though the gods had picked up a handful of cottages and shops and trees, shaken them in their fists, and rolled them like dice over a game board of hilly fields. Clusters of wood-and-brick buildings dotted the valley below, and small, limp puffs of smoke could be seen rising from a number of chimneys. The main village road did not run straight, but instead wound through the sloping hills from building to building like a ribbon through the hooks of a bodice. From the hilltop where they sat, Certainty could spot a few moving figures—a farmer kneeling beside rows of green plants (the aforescented garlic, presumably); a handful of sturdy-looking cows at pasture; someone pushing a wheelbarrow uphill along a curved path. She assumed that the rest of the villagers were sheltering indoors from the wet weather.

"I think it looks nice," Certainty said uncertainly. "Just . . . a little quiet, is all."

But as the enchanted wagons took them lower into the valley and they drew nearer to the buildings, the sun fell behind the hills, and Certainty began to notice what they had not seen from a distance: the village's glory days, if it'd ever had them at all, were clearly far behind it. Many of the homes were in disrepair; only one in every three seemed to show signs of habitation, and these, too, had missing shingles, or faded and worn brickwork. There was something forlorn about the place, like a wilting flower whose petals had already begun to brown. And once within the village boundaries, Certainty began feeling the slightest, vaguest sense of discomfort, like she had eaten something questionable for lunch instead of the inoffensive cheese biscuit from their supply pack.

Aurelia must have felt it, too; the mage shifted a little on the bench. Certainty lowered her voice. It felt right to do so, even if she didn't know why.

"Do you feel . . . a bit off, too? Is that the lack of magic?"

Aurelia fidgeted with the end of her braid. She did that sometimes when she was worried, Certainty had noticed. "I think so. Mage Lacrima has done research into thaumic voids. She wrote that entering one can feel like a sudden illness and the dulling of all your senses." Aurelia's voice was equally hushed. "This seems like a weaker version of that. I don't think non-mages would feel it as strongly as we do, though."

The village road narrowed as it took them between homes and a few shops, most of them shuttered. The sky grew darker as they rolled on. Ruts and holes in the path sent jolts up Certainty's spine, to the point that she worried whether any of the artifacts jostling within their boxes were at risk of breakage. She gritted her teeth and hung on.

Finally, the wagons squelched to an apologetic halt in what must have been Shpelling's central square, though the stone well and drinking trough beside it looked disused and filled with rainwater. Apart from the well, the square was just a flat patch of dirt half churned to mud in front of a large, rectangular building.

The building was made of thatch and timber, two stories tall though somehow still squat-looking. Its mismatched window shutters dripped with rain. A crooked sign bore the symbol of a plough where it hung, creaking disconsolately, above rough-hewn double doors. Certainty thought the plough might have been painted yellow at one time, but it was hard to tell under its worn, chipped varnish of bird droppings.

It might have been the least welcoming place Certainty had ever seen.

"The local inn?" she asked doubtfully.

"Must be." Aurelia drew her hood up and stepped down off the wagon, holding her robes up and looking around in distaste. There didn't seem to be anyone waiting to receive them. "I hope they have a bath to wash this mud off. Not to mention the smell."

Just then, a short, white-haired woman with deep wrinkles and sharp eyes emerged from the wooden doors. Favoring her right leg, the old woman came to a stop just before the building's dripping eaves, and from there looked them up and down. She looked thoroughly unimpressed. "You two the mages, then?"

Aurelia drew herself up. "We are. Is this the village of Shpelling? We'll be taking rooms at the inn."

"This is Shpelling, all right. But this isn't an inn. Hasn't been for years."

Aurelia squinted up at the building's sign. "But isn't this—"

"What, the Golden Plough? Pah! It's just a tavern now. Ferdinand's turned all the rooms into garlic storage."

"But then where are we meant to stay?" The rain had strengthened, and Aurelia's cloak grew increasingly sodden as she stood exposed in the muddy square. She made an impatient gesture with one hand, and a translucent sphere popped into existence around her head to deflect the falling rain. "What arrangements were made for our arrival?"

The old woman, dry beneath the tavern's overhang, eyed Aurelia's magical bubble for a moment. Then she shrugged and crossed her arms. "Lord Godfrey's secretary sent word that the Guild bought the old stable and carriage house, and that we were to expect some mages to show up. He didn't say anything about needing any rooms. I figured you'd be staying across the way in Ruggan, like he does."

"Ruggan?" Certainty asked. "How far is that?" She'd been desperately looking forward to a nice warm bed.

The old woman sucked on her teeth. "Would take you the best part of a day, weather like this. Half that when it's not raining."

Ugh. Certainty and Aurelia looked at each other. "It's nearly dark," Aurelia said. "We can't travel that far tonight. And we can't do so twice a day, either—we have work to do here in Shpelling."

"We-ell, like I said, the old stable and carriage house belong to you and your Guild now, don't they? You could always sleep there. Just up the second path and to the left."

Something in the old woman's eyes made it clear that her words were a challenge. Certainty's heart sank.

"I see. Thank you for the welcome." Pointedly, Aurelia wrung a few drops of water out of her sleeve, and her tone was icy. "Maybe I shouldn't have expected any better of a backwater place like this."

Too late, Certainty realized that perhaps she should have been the one to do the talking here, not Aurelia.

"Take it up with the secretary if you like," said the old woman, her eyes narrowing. "He'll be back here tomorrow. If you need food and drink, you can find it in the Plough. But Shpelling's not a place meant for visitors. I'm sure you'll soon see why."

And with that cryptic farewell, she disappeared back into the tavern, leaving Certainty and Aurelia behind in the muddy square.

Aurelia hauled herself back onto the wagon's bench, her disgruntlement clear in every motion. Certainty scooched over to make room for her.

"So no inn. What do we do now?"

Aurelia let her magical bubble evaporate. "I don't know." The grudging way she said it made Certainty think that it wasn't something she said often.

Certainty mulled things over. "Well . . . could you use your farspeaking to send a message back to the Guild? Ask the High Mage or Fanya what we ought to do?"

"No." Aurelia's answer was immediate.

"But . . ."

"The High Mage gave us a task and expects to see it done," snapped the mage. "We can't go crying back to the Guild for every minor obstacle."

"Having nowhere to stay seems like a bit more than a 'minor obstacle.'" Certainty had never been sent on assignment before, but even so, she didn't think Guild mages often had to sleep in stables.

Aurelia didn't look like she relished the prospect, either. "Maybe we could requisition rooms at one of the villagers' homes, under the Guild's authority. There are precedents for that, in times of need . . ."

Certainty tried to imagine how her neighbors back home would have reacted to Guild mages showing up one day and demanding to sleep in their beds.

"No," she said very firmly. "Aurelia, we can't force them out of their own homes. If we're to do our work here, we need their cooperation—or at the very least, we need them to not actively hate us."

Aurelia hesitated, considering this. Then she nodded reluctantly. "Fine. If a stable and a carriage house is what we have, we'll have to make do with them. Let's go see the state of the buildings."

Following the old woman's instructions, they directed the wagons along one of the paths stretching uphill. They found the stable easily enough, but the sight of it only deepened Aurelia's glower. Like many of the houses they'd seen on the way into the village, the building was in a sad state of disrepair. Long and rectangular, with square windows cut into it all in a row, the stable had holes in its thatched roof that were visible even from outside. Clinging to its side like a barnacle to a ship was a smaller stone structure: a carriage house with a wooden door and two shuttered windows, all covered in a tangled drapery of thin, leafy vines.

"Fanya would throw a fit at the sight of this place," Certainty said. These buildings were a far cry from the immaculately kept Guildtower stables.

Aurelia, her jaw set, pushed open the wide wooden doors. They creaked open slowly, revealing nothing but darkness.

"Mages first," Certainty said.

With a look, Aurelia swept past her to enter the stable, and Certainty followed, peering around with trepidation. The interior of the stable was just as dark, damp, and musty as it had appeared from outside: It was an open space on one end, with the remainder split into ten stalls, five to a side. The stalls were all empty save for cobwebs, rain puddles, and a truly prodigious number of rodent droppings; above them, the wind whistled in through ragged holes in the thatched roof. Abandoned nests crowded the rafters, the ground below stained white. Certainty walked around, wrinkling her nose at the smell. She spotted a stack of lumber leaning in one corner; someone had probably meant to make repairs but decided it wasn't worth it.

The best that could be said for the place was that it was definitely large enough to hold all of the artifacts they had brought.

"I suppose they didn't have much time to clean the place up before we arrived..." Certainty said doubtfully. But she couldn't help but be dismayed. They'd never have tolerated an eyesore like this back home. They might not have much coin or many fine things in Potshire, but they had pride and brooms aplenty. There would have been no shortage of willing hands, either, if the stables' owner had needed help to get it cleaned up. How could Shpelling have let the place fall into such disrepair?

"'*The storehouse will be prepared for you—*'" Aurelia muttered. "This place is hardly even fit for animals."

Gingerly, Certainty brushed aside some cobwebs and opened the door connecting the stables to the carriage house. She stepped through it.

The carriage house was the size of a large bedroom, with coarse stone walls and floor. One wood-framed door connected it to the stable, while another led outside. It smelled of old garlic and, strangely, peppermint tea.

With effort, Aurelia unbarred the windows and threw open their shutters, letting in dusty rays of fading sun that didn't quite reach to the back of the room. There in the recesses was a large woodstove that at least seemed to be in working order, judging from the woodpile in the corner.

Aurelia prodded at the stove. An alarmed squeak came from within, prompting an even more alarmed squeak from Certainty as several brown field mice fled chittering from the stove's crevices to escape underneath the door. Aurelia gave her a look that said *Really?*, and Certainty shrugged one shoulder to hide her embarrassment. "I don't like mice."

And just like that, their examination of the small carriage house was done. Certainty and Aurelia turned in a slow circle, their muddy boots squelching on the stone, taking in their new and hopefully temporary shelter. The overwhelming impression was one of neglect. Of abandonment. It was fitting, in a way, given what they were supposed to be doing here.

Certainty glanced at Aurelia. Mice notwithstanding, she

knew she'd be able to handle these ramshackle accommodations; it'd be no worse than the nights she'd spent in the barn with their calving cows as a child. But Aurelia . . . how would a mage raised in the polished comfort of Margrave's Middle City react to staying in a place like this?

Aurelia was silent, and her jaw was tight.

"We'll make do" was all she said.

THEY LEFT THE wagons outside the stable and retraced the muddy path back to the Golden Plough on foot. At least the rain had finally stopped.

The sun was hardly visible behind soggy tatters of cloud, and the growing dimness suggested that it had already begun to set. It seemed like most of the village's inhabitants were gathered within the tavern on this wet evening. Candlelight flickered in its smudged windows, and Certainty heard a steady murmur of voices as they approached its doors. But the moment they stepped foot inside, heads turned toward them, and conversations halted abruptly.

"Hello," Certainty said.

Nobody said anything back, so she took the opportunity to look around.

The tavern had several small tables scattered around the fringes of its great room, but in the center was a long communal table surrounded by mismatched chairs and stools. Fewer than half the seats were presently occupied, though it was a rather different sort of crowd than that of the Guildtower dining hall; blinking at her in surprise were middle-aged farmers in muddy boots fresh from the field, sitting beside women in patched and practical-looking frocks; over in the corner were old men with protruding nose hairs, nodding off over their mugs.

Despite the lack of welcome, Certainty took all this in with something approximating relief. Here, finally, was something that reminded her of home. The tavern patrons looked as though they could just as easily have been her family's neighbors—though there were fewer of them here than she would have expected in a village this size. She tried a tentative smile on those closest to her and got only bemused stares back.

At the far end of the room was a hearth where a large fire crackled, and nearer to the doors, a burly old man with the bushiest mustache Cert had ever seen was holding court at the bar. Behind the barman and his counter was a doorway through which the sounds of banging and clattering could be heard—the kitchen, presumably.

The barman was wiping at a plate with a dirty-looking cloth. Certainty also noted the incongruous sight of a massive, rusted pike mounted high on the wall behind him. Perhaps he'd once been a soldier.

Ignoring the chilly reception, Aurelia lowered her hood and strode over to the bar. Clearly, she had decided to take charge here; Certainty followed close behind, more than a little apprehensive of what the mage might say.

"Tavernkeep. Two meals, please. And cider or mead, if you have it."

The barman's arm paused mid-wipe as he looked them up and down. Then the wiping resumed. "Name's Ferdinand. Ale's all we got, and it's garlic-and-bean stew tonight. Four silverpennies."

Aurelia's nose wrinkled. "Are there any other options?"

"Could fix you up some bread with roasted garlic spread."

"Anything without garlic?"

Ferdinand gave the plate one last, aggressive wipe (not that it looked any cleaner than it had before) and finally set it down. He squinted at the two of them. "What've you got against garlic?

Finest garlic in all of Eshtera's grown here. Keeps you strong and healthy; it'll put some hair on your chest."

Aurelia raised one eyebrow at him.

"Figuratively speaking," he said.

"I have nothing against garlic," Aurelia said. "Or any other allium, for that matter. I just wondered whether you might have a bit more . . . variety in your dishes." Her tone did a poor job of hiding her distaste, and the tavernkeep clearly took note of it. His expression grew even surlier.

"What do you expect, stuffed venison and silk tablecloths? This isn't the High City, no matter what you fancy Guild folk may be used to. Got to have pride in something, so why not garlic?" He threw his cloth onto the counter beside the plate and leaned forward, arms spread. "Look, do you want to eat tonight, or not?"

"Yes," interrupted Certainty quickly—before Aurelia could make things worse. Gods, had she never interacted with anyone outside of Margrave before? But Ferdinand's image of their lives there wasn't quite accurate, either. She'd only ever had stuffed venison once at a Guild Winterfair feast, and found it too rich for her taste anyway. "Yes, we'll have the stew, please. And ale. Thank you."

"Hmph." But the man—Ferdinand—swiped her coins from the bar and jerked his head toward the long table. "Out in a bit."

Aurelia wasn't done, though. "Tavernkeep, we'll also require assistance in repairing the stable and carriage house."

"That so." Ferdinand's tone suggested a lack of inclination to provide such assistance.

"We'll pay for the labor, of course. And pay well."

"Aurelia—" Certainty said in an undertone, but the mage ignored her. She heard a snort from somewhere behind them; she looked over her shoulder and saw the old woman from earlier, seated at the head of the long table.

"Sorry. Too busy," said Ferdinand, picking up another dirty plate to wipe. "Got a tavern to run and all, see? Just a simple *tavernkeep*, I am."

"Well, is there anyone else in the village we might be able to hire?"

"You're welcome to ask them yourself," he said, gesturing at the other tavern patrons with his rag, and the old woman behind Certainty snorted again. "But it's planting season soon. Folk are busy. There used to be old Jasper the carpenter, but he and his family up and left for Forlinet last fall. Per'aps if you tried down in Ruggan, you might find someone there who knows his way around a hammer and a saw. If they're inclined to take Guild coin, that is."

This was not going well. *"Aurelia,"* Certainty hissed.

"What?" The mage spun on Certainty. "Repairing the buildings is our first priority. We need to secure assistance."

"We can eat first and figure it out later—I'm sure Master Ferdinand is busy—"

"I believe he's being intentionally unhelpful," Aurelia snapped. "Master Ferdinand, our coin is just as good as any other."

Ferdinand only glowered at them silently from behind his mustache. The moment swelled, and for an instant, Certainty worried that Aurelia would force the matter; her eyes were flashing with anger and her chin was high. Though what she could do, Certainty had no idea; it wasn't as though a Guild mage could go around challenging tavernkeeps to duels—not if she didn't want to be laughed out of the Guild. And if she did, Certainty wasn't entirely sure whose side she'd be obligated to take—not that she'd be of much use in a brawl. She supposed she could always throw a mug of ale in someone's face. Seemed a waste of perfectly good ale.

Then someone in the room coughed, and Aurelia seemed to realize the ridiculousness of the situation. With a sharp exhale through her nose, she spun on her heel, and Certainty followed her to the table with relief.

Certainty tried another smile on the villagers already seated there, to little effect. The ones closest to her shifted farther away on the bench, and the old woman simply continued to watch them with unfriendly eyes.

"Don't bother," Aurelia muttered. "They've clearly already decided they don't want us here. Probably just uneducated rustics who hate mages for no reason. Even as they reap the benefits of the Guild's work, of course."

Certainty blinked at her, taken aback. Then she felt the slow roll of anger. It simmered up from the parts of her that still remembered what it'd felt like to show up to the Guildtower with Potshire mud on her boots, to be seen as one of those *rustics*. To hear the difference in how her classmates spoke and what they spoke of, all crisp vowels and upper-class ambition.

But anger wasn't productive, so she pushed it aside for now, even as she noted that the old woman's eyes had narrowed even further. Not good.

She leaned over the table and kept her voice low and level, hoping Aurelia would take the hint.

"Aurelia, it's not about education. People are always afraid of what they don't understand." Her own parents had been the same, at least until her magic showed itself, and even still, it'd taken them a fair bit of getting used to. Though even then, they'd have treated any strangers to Potshire—mages or no—with more kindness than what she and Aurelia had gotten so far in Shpelling. "And if that's the case, perhaps we can change their minds? You know—get to know them, so they can see that we're just like them."

"We're *not* just like them, Novice."

"Well." Certainty's brow furrowed. "In some senses—"

But Aurelia shook her head as if to clear it, and the silver chain of her necklace danced against her neck. "Let's just focus on completing our assignment as quickly as possible. The sooner we're done and can return to Margrave, the better. I'll have *words* with this so-called secretary tomorrow about his arrangements."

Certainty sighed.

"Fine."

Even if she wanted to argue, she wasn't going to do so within hearing of the villagers. The garlic-and-bean stew arrived shortly (heavy on the garlic), and the two of them forwent further discussion in favor of eating quickly so that they might escape the tavern's hostile atmosphere and the dozens of eyes that watched them while they ate.

AFTER DINNER, THEY trudged back up the dirt path to the carriage house to see what could be done with it. It seemed like Aurelia had decided to put aside her anger in favor of focusing on the problem at hand. The mage glanced at the darkened sky and rolled up her sleeves. "We just need to do the minimum necessary to make this place habitable for the night." Aurelia flicked her fingers outward, wordlessly summoning an orb of light that lit the inside of the carriage house with a soft glow. "Novice, you sweep the carriage house out and sort out our bedding; I'll find some dry wood and get a fire started in the stove. We can handle the rest tomorrow."

Certainty nodded, and the two women went to their tasks. Fortunately, Fanya—Mother bless their dwarven heart—had included warm, thick woolen bedrolls in their supplies. Certainty rolled these out on clean stretches of floor along opposite walls, near but not too near to the stove that would hopefully be keeping them warm through the night.

However, her search for a broom turned up empty. Fanya could be forgiven for this oversight, given that the two women were mages and not witches, but it still posed a dilemma. Any proper mage would simply cast a sweeping spell and blow all the dirt and dust out of the place, but Certainty... well. She considered asking Aurelia to do it, but reminding her of her spellcasting deficiencies this early on probably wouldn't help their partnership, not to mention what remained of her pride. Surely there must be a broom somewhere...

"Hello?" A male voice, cracking on its syllables in a way that implied adolescence, called to them from outside. "Lady mages? Are you in there?"

Aurelia's face took on a *what now* expression. They emerged from the stable to find a lanky red-haired boy, exactly as awkward and pimply as his voice suggested. He was holding a broom in one hand and a very large milking bucket in the other. He gawked at them for a moment before recalling he'd come there with a purpose.

"Old Gertha sent me. Figured you'd need to clean the place up a bit 'fore it's fit for sleeping in, so she told me to bring over a few things."

Certainty took the broom and the bucket and peered inside; there were folded blankets and pillows at the bottom, in addition to some kindling and several squat tallow candles.

"Thank you," she said, surprised by the unexpected kindness.

"Old Gertha?" Aurelia asked.

The boy nodded. "The one who went out to talk to you when you first showed up. Shpelling doesn't have a headman anymore, but if we did, she'd be it. Or, uh, headwoman."

"I see. And what's your name?"

"Oh." The boy blushed, face nearly matching his hair. "I'm Orrin, miss."

"Well, Orrin, perhaps you could tell this Old Gertha that if she means this gesture as an apol—"

"Thank you!" Certainty interjected quickly. "Tell Old Gertha we said thank you, please, and it's very nice to meet you, Orrin."

The boy ducked his head, still blushing. "Yes, miss. I will. And, uh . . . welcome to Shpelling," he mumbled, before fleeing back down the path.

Certainty and Aurelia watched him go.

"See? Maybe they don't hate mages after all."

Aurelia sniffed. "The old woman probably remembered that we could demand the use of her house, if we really wanted to."

Certainty bit her lip. It was quickly becoming clear to her why Aurelia had such a reputation back at the Guildtower. But if they were to live and work in this village for over a month, they couldn't afford to make enemies of their neighbors. It'd be counterproductive—and just plain unpleasant, besides. She didn't know how many more tense tavern dinners she could sit through.

But Aurelia was a mage, and she was just a novice. She'd have to tread carefully.

"Mage Aurelia, I know you don't really want to be here, but we are. And the people here may not be the friendliest, but if they don't trust outsiders, well, maybe they've got good reason not to. And maybe . . . maybe we ought to try not to antagonize them any further?"

"I haven't antagonized them, Novice."

Certainty gave her a look. "In my experience, folk don't particularly appreciate being called uneducated rustics."

Aurelia hesitated, looking discomfited for a moment. But then she shrugged one shoulder. "If the shoe fits."

If the shoe—

Certainty felt her face grow warm. The anger she'd managed to silence earlier returned, hot and heady. Did Aurelia forget that Certainty's parents were farmers, too? She swallowed hard, reaching for calm, reminding herself that everything depended upon the two of them being able to work together.

"All I'm saying," she said, proud of how reasonable she sounded, "is that you might want to take more care with your words here. Or people might think that you think you're better than them."

"I—well—" Aurelia drew herself up, high cheekbones stained pink. "Whether or not that's true depends on how you define better, Novice. Isn't my time and my ability of greater value than theirs?"

For one incredulous moment, Certainty just stared at her. Did she really believe that? Is that what being a farspeaker raised in the Middle City had taught her?

"It must be lonely to be you," she said at last.

Aurelia's eyes tightened and her jaw tensed, but she didn't reply. Instead, she seized the borrowed broom and went inside the carriage house to sweep it out herself, leaving Certainty standing outside in the sodden darkness.

SIX

THE NEXT MORNING, Certainty stretched in her blankets, stomach rumbling. Hopefully the dining hall would have eggs at breakfast—proper fried ones, all crispy round the edges, and not just that healthy porridge nonsense. Why people insisted on putting birdseed into perfectly good food, she'd never understand . . . She squinted blearily against the sunlight. One of the other novices must have left the curtains open again last night. Probably Helga; she liked to sigh dramatically out of the window sometimes. Reading too many courtly romances, in Certainty's opinion, which always seemed to feature handsome knights waiting underneath windows for beautiful maidens. She didn't understand why they couldn't just meet on the same floor.

Certainty sat up, brushing some bits of hay off herself, then blinked down at the hay, wondering where it had come from and why her back hurt.

Right. She wasn't in the Guildtower anymore. She'd slept on the floor of a mouse-infested carriage house.

"Good, you're up."

Of course Aurelia was already awake. She looked like she had been for hours. The mage stood in the outside doorway, wielding a broom and framed like an artist's model by the soft morning light.

Aurelia's voice was brusque and businesslike. "I stopped by the tavern and bought us some breakfast. It's just bread and butter, but at least there's no garlic in any of it. Brought fresh water from the well up the path, too; it's all over by the wagons. Wash up and eat, but try to be quick about it. We have lots of work to do today."

Certainty's groggy brain struggled to keep up. It seemed like Aurelia was pretending that their argument last night had never happened, which suited Certainty just fine. Maybe fetching breakfast was her version of an apology. Hopefully she hadn't started any fresh feuding with Ferdinand when she did so.

"Right." She rubbed at her eyes, and Aurelia strode purposefully back out the door, presumably to do something productive and efficient. Morning people were the worst. But Certainty, yawning, proceeded to do as instructed, changing into fresh clothes from her pack before heading out. She helped herself to the water and a chunk of grainy bread, and as she leaned against one of the wagons, chewing meditatively, she took the opportunity to take fuller stock of their surroundings.

Their stable and carriage house sat upslope from the village square and tavern. From here, she had a good vantage of the village and the hills beyond, all of which looked more welcoming in the light of day.

Unseen birds chirped somewhere nearby, and a chorus of clucking hens and lowing cattle drifted up from the farms and fields. It helped, too, that the skies had cleared overnight. Even if the sun shone weak and pale, it at least wasn't ashamed to show its face, though it wasn't strong enough yet to burn away the morning mist.

Poking through the limned haze were neat little rows of green plants (garlic, Certainty assumed), and farther upslope to the east was a grove of what looked to be apple trees coming into bloom. Northward, the twin hills that they had crossed yesterday rose gently to meet wispy clouds, and a forking stream cut across one of the slopes.

Looking at it all, one could almost forget that the place was entirely devoid of magic.

Other, of course, than the Guild mage, Guild novice, and two enchanted wagons full of low-grade magical artifacts that had recently arrived.

There was a scuffling noise from somewhere behind her. Certainty turned around to find that a large orange rooster was perched on the stable's roof and looking down at her.

"What are you doing up there?"

It puffed its chest out and *bokk*-ed at her. She supposed she deserved it, asking a silly question like that; she grew up on a farm, for Mother's sake. Roosters liked climbing to the highest perches they could find. Something about asserting dominance over their territory; not all that different from men and big towers, when you thought about it. Certainty tilted her head. She couldn't see how it had managed to get up there, though—there weren't any large tree branches near the roof. Was she going to have to climb up there and rescue it?

The rooster took a few deliberate steps toward the edge of the roof, head bobbing and wattle wattling.

"Roosters can't fly," Certainty informed it.

It ignored her and jumped off the roof. There was a sudden frenzy of loud flapping noises and madly fluttering wings, an inelegant collision with the ground—but then the rooster was strutting in the dirt in front of her, resettling its feathers with what Certainty felt was a certain smugness. When she leaned down to stroke it, it pecked at her hand in warning and let out a loud and imperious *bok*.

Great. Even the livestock didn't want her there.

Certainty sighed, wiped the crumbs off her robes as a peace offering, and went back inside to find Aurelia.

In Certainty's absence, Aurelia had cleared the cobwebs, thrown open the shutters to air, and cast sweeping and freshening spells on the entirety of both buildings. The buildings were already looking much better—or at least more like habitable human dwellings than the central headquarters of several multi-generational rat colonies. The mage nodded briskly to her.

"I've left instructions at the tavern to send the secretary to us as soon as he arrives. But while we wait, I think we should start off-loading the artifacts. Once we have them inside the stable, I can cast our own warding spells, and we can send the wagons back to the Guildtower."

Certainty nodded, tying back her curls with a ribbon. Aurelia's own willingness to get her hands dirty felt like a challenge. "I'll start bringing them in."

"Don't forget to wear the gloves," the mage called after her.

It felt a little strange to pull on the fitted calfskin gloves, but better to be safe than accidentally turned into a cooking pot. Certainty cracked her knuckles and threw open the first wagon's door. Time to get to work.

⁓

THE SUN WAS only slightly higher in the sky when Lord Godfrey's secretary arrived at the stable. Certainty put down the box she was holding and straightened when she saw a cloaked figure climbing the path toward them. Aurelia looked up from the stable floor, where she was busy sorting out the components for a warding spell—a large jar of salt, short iron stakes, and a walnut-sized crystal that looked clear but glinted purple in the sun.

"Finally," the mage said, rising to her feet. She dusted her robes off and strode forward to meet their visitor. "You're the secretary who acted on the Guild's behalf here?"

"Indeed. Master Tobias, secretary to Lord Godfrey, at your pleasure."

The man was carrying a large leather satchel that looked out of place with his attire. He was dark-haired, very well-dressed, and younger than Certainty had expected—perhaps just a handful of years older than her—and he might even have been good-looking, if not for the oiliness of his voice, and the way his lip curled as he looked at them.

Aurelia didn't waste time with pleasantries. "I'm Mage Aurelia, and this is Novice Certainty. Master Tobias, I understand that you may not have had much time to see the Guild's instructions carried out before we arrived, but even so, these arrangements are unacceptable. We require you to hire a carpenter at once, and—"

"My most sincere apologies," interrupted Master Tobias. He sounded anything but sincere. "Did the villagers not tell you? Shpelling no longer has its own carpenter, I'm afraid."

"Surely the town nearby, Ruggan, has tradesmen—"

"Indeed, but the tradesmen in Ruggan are far too busy with their work to travel here."

"Offer them double the coin, then," Aurelia said through her teeth. "The Guild will pay."

Certainty looked between the two of them worriedly. Why did it feel like she was witnessing a duel?

The secretary flashed Aurelia a smile that didn't reach his eyes. "I'm sure they would. But it's not a simple matter of coin. Ruggan's tradesmen are all engaged in the construction of a new water mill, contracted by Lord Godfrey himself. A very important project for the region, and currently behind schedule due to the rains. Sadly, they cannot be spared to . . ."

He glanced pointedly at the holes in the stable roof and their bedding on the floor. "... to build furniture for two Guild mages performing inventory work in a farming village."

The derision in his voice was hard to miss. Aurelia bristled visibly, and this time Certainty couldn't blame her.

"Lord Godfrey may feel differently," gritted out Aurelia, "if the Guild expresses their dissatisfaction to him."

"Oh, indeed? Well of course, if you wish to write to your High Mage, and tell her that you require the Guild's assistance in surmounting the very dire threat of a drafty bedroom and a few rats, that is certainly your right." Tobias assembled his features into a thoughtful expression. "I'm sure the High Mage of Eshtera has no greater demands on her attention, aren't you?"

Certainty looked at Aurelia and saw that a muscle in the mage's jaw was ticking dangerously. Time for her to step in.

"Perhaps," she said hastily, before Aurelia could respond, "you have an alternative solution to suggest, Master Tobias?"

The secretary glanced at her then, his gaze seeming to linger contemptuously on her novice's robes. "I do, in fact."

He dropped the satchel he was carrying at their feet. It clanked.

"The previous village carpenter left behind an old set of tools. You're quite welcome to them—if you're not afraid to sully your hands like us lowly non-magical folk, that is."

He gave them both another snide smile, and Certainty found her temper rising. At least the villagers had the decency to be rude straight to their faces, instead of hiding it behind fancy words and pretty manners.

"Or," Tobias said brightly, as if a fresh thought had just occurred to him, "you could always return to your Guildtower and choose somewhere more suitable to store your artifacts."

Certainty thought about the reception they would get at the

Guildtower if they returned so quickly with the wagons still full of problematically magical artifacts. Her first assignment, an utter failure, thwarted by—what, a few unfriendly villagers? A dirty floor? She'd never get a chance like this one again.

Aurelia must have had a similar thought.

"We'll manage," Aurelia snapped. She picked up the sack of tools.

Master Tobias's smile hardened. "Wonderful. I look forward to seeing your progress. My duties to my lord require me to visit Shpelling often—though, fortunately, I don't have to actually *stay* here; can you imagine?—so I'm sure we'll see each other again."

He turned to go, then paused as if he'd remembered something.

"Oh, and you should know—Lord Godfrey has heard some concerns recently about the dangers of having mages carrying out magical activities on his lands."

Heard from his weasel-faced secretary, no doubt.

"Should there be any evidence of magic causing harm to life or property in Shpelling . . . well, I'm afraid I simply wouldn't be able to dissuade him from lodging an official complaint with the Council. You understand, of course."

Aurelia smiled back like a wolf baring its teeth.

"Perfectly. Good day, Master Tobias."

Still smiling, he gave them a mocking little half bow and headed back down the path.

"What an odious man." Aurelia looked as if she were contemplating a few choice spells.

Certainty watched with distaste as the secretary disappeared from view. Somehow, *he'd* managed to be the dismissive, supercilious one in that conversation. An impressive feat, given, well, Aurelia.

"I wonder why he dislikes us so much," she said half to herself. The way that he had looked at her robes, and at Aurelia's circles, too... "I mean, we only just met the man."

"We're mages. Lots of people don't like mages." If Aurelia recognized the irony in parroting Certainty's own words from last night back to her, she didn't show it.

"I know, but that felt..." Certainty scrunched up her nose. "Personal, somehow."

"As long as he doesn't interfere with our work, he can be as unpleasant as he likes, and when we're done and back in Margrave, we can lodge our own complaint." Aurelia rummaged through the sack of tools and pulled out a handsaw. "Have any experience with woodworking, Novice?"

CERTAINTY'S EXPERIENCE WITH carpentry extended only so far as knowing which end of a saw to hold, but it turned out that Aurelia had a reasonable grasp of it. Apparently, she'd once read a scroll on the parallels of woodworking with spellcraft and was eager to put the theory to the test.

They decided that Aurelia would begin the work of repairing the stable while Certainty was to continue unloading the artifacts from the wagons. It was hard and physical work for both of them, but the memory of Tobias's smirk was sufficiently motivating. Still, Certainty couldn't help but wish for a levitation spell or two to help with the boxes; a proper physical mage would be able to float all the artifacts in without even needing a lie-down afterward.

But shortly after midday, they were interrupted by the arrival of yet more visitors.

Certainty, now sweating, blew a few misbehaving curls out of her eyes and set down the box of artifacts she was carrying.

Old Gertha and another villager came up the path slowly, Gertha's walking stick making *thuk-thuk* noises in the dirt.

"Good day," Certainty said cautiously.

"Hm," said Gertha, neither confirming nor denying the goodness of the day. She squinted at the box on the ground, and then at the others within the wagon.

"See, Hull," she said to the man beside her. He was an older man, slightly stooped, but still appeared to be in wiry good health. "I *told* you the Guild was up to something funny. Buying the old stable, and then sending these two lady mages here with their magic wagons."

Aurelia came out of the stable then, drawn by the sound of their voices, and Certainty felt obligated to correct the old woman.

"I'm not a full mage yet, mistress—just a novice. My name's Certainty."

"Is it?" Old Gertha's voice was dry. "My condolences."

"And this is Mage Aurelia." Certainty nodded at Aurelia, who—with arms crossed—inclined her head the tiniest of fractions.

"Hmph. Orrin's already told you that I'm Gertha, I suppose, and this here's Hull. We brought you lunch, seeing as you're still here for some reason."

Hull nodded at them after Gertha's rather ungracious introduction, and held out a wicker basket containing a wedge of cheese and a round loaf of bread.

"Oh! Thank you." Certainty took it from him; the smell of the fresh-baked bread reminded her that she was, in fact, very hungry. Carrying heavy boxes worked up an appetite.

"And how much coin do we owe you for it?" Aurelia asked.

Gertha looked insulted. "We're not yet so desperate here that we need to take coin for simple hospitality."

Aurelia's brow was furrowed in confusion. "The tavernkeep, Ferdinand, was happy enough to take our coin for supper last night..."

"Of course he was! You were customers at his tavern, weren't you?" Gertha looked at Aurelia as if she were an idiot. "Hull and I aren't selling you anything."

"But..."

"Apologies, Gertha—things work a little differently in Margrave," Certainty said hastily. It would take more time than they had to explain to Aurelia the difference between hospitality and custom in a place such as Shpelling.

"I should say so! Trying to *pay* us for a welcome basket..." The old woman gave a loud and indignant sniff.

"Well, then—thank you," Aurelia said slowly. Certainty gave her a meaningful glance, jerking her head unsubtly back toward the stable; Aurelia took the hint. "And thank you also for sending us the supplies last night."

"Well." Gertha looked slightly mollified. "Couldn't have you sleeping on the bare ground, getting rained on and such. I reckon the Guild would come down hard on us if we let you freeze to death. But you're not actually planning on staying here, are you?"

"Of course we're staying. We have a job to do."

"Tobias didn't convince you to leave?"

"If that was his intent, then yes, he failed." Aurelia lifted her chin high.

"Slimy fop," Certainty muttered, and Gertha's lips twitched upward.

"He is that, isn't he," she said. "I knew him when he was just a boy from Ruggan. He wasn't so bad then, but then off he went with all sorts of grand ambitions. Came back with pretty clothes, fancy quills, a stick up his arse, and a chip on his shoulder big enough to lame a horse. Seems a common thing among folk who spend too much time in Margrave, hm?"

Aurelia narrowed her eyes as if trying to decide whether to be insulted or not, but—wisely, in Certainty's opinion—kept her mouth shut.

"So why has the Guild sent you two here?" Hull leaned forward, blinking at the two of them eagerly. "Are you here to lift the curse?"

"The curse?" Aurelia's voice was suddenly sharp. "What curse?"

"Why, the one on my family's apple grove!"

Gertha whacked him lightly with her walking stick. "Don't be daft, Hull; nobody's cursed your fruit trees specifically," she said irritably. "It's the whole village that's cursed." She gave them a measuring look. "So. *Are* you here to help us lift it?"

"No," Aurelia said.

Hull's face fell, and Gertha's hardened.

"Then what are you here for? What is it you've brought in these wagons of yours?"

Aurelia hesitated. "We've been tasked with storing some Guild artifacts here."

"Magical ones?"

"Very minorly," Certainty said quickly.

"But why here?" Hull asked, bewildered. "Shpelling is such a small village that I'm surprised the Guild's even heard of it."

Gertha's expression darkened. "I'd bet that's exactly why, Hull. Because we're small and unimportant. Dispensable, in case anything goes wrong, which magic always seems to do."

"There isn't any danger to Shpelling from what we've brought here," Aurelia said firmly. "And I don't know what curse—"

But Gertha spoke over her in a voice that rose with anger.

"You ought to know! It's your kind that laid it on us, isn't it?

My grandparents told me the whole story. Mage fought mage here in Shpelling, and one of 'em called fire up from beneath the ground and destroyed everything around us for leagues. Aye, sure, the grass grew back eventually, and folk rebuilt their houses, but it was never the same.

"We didn't notice it, not for a long while, but eventually the misfortunes all added up such that it had to be more than just bad luck. First the bees left, they said. Then the cats, too, and rats moved in to take their place, and disease with them . . . and with no bees, Hull's apple trees stopped fruiting. Everything did. That's why we grow all this garlic, you know. It's the only damned thing that thrives here."

"Gertha," Hull said quietly. He put one hand on her arm, but the old woman shook it off.

"Enough small things went wrong, and *kept* going wrong, that all the young folk left to find their fortunes elsewhere. And I can't hardly blame them for it! They say Shpelling's stuck in the mud while the rest of Eshtera moves forward.

"Thanks to you mages, our village is dying, slow as a drip. So you'll forgive us if we're not so eager to welcome the Guild coming to store its things here, like we're nought but a *spare closet*."

Gertha glared at them with her chest heaving and walking stick wobbling beneath her gnarled fist.

"I am very sorry for your hardships," Aurelia said, after a long pause. "We are . . . aware that what happened here during the Wars may have had unanticipated effects, but that is neither our concern nor our responsibility."

"Not your responsibility." The old woman made a contemptuous noise. "Typical Guild cowshit."

"The Guild of Mages serves the Crown and all of Eshtera with honor," Aurelia said. Her voice was low and dangerous, and she drew herself up to her full height, green eyes flashing.

"Mages work every day to safeguard and improve the lives of Eshterans—"

"Aye, and you collect fat bags of silver for the trouble, don't you? What do you mages know of our lives, living high in your whitestone towers and looking down upon the small folk—"

"If you knew even a *little* of what we mages sacrifice—!"

Certainty's eyes flicked back and forth between the other two women with growing alarm. This was going very poorly indeed. The villagers' anger might be misplaced—the Guild hadn't even existed during the Wars, after all—but she understood, too, how the resentment had festered over time, a scab passed down and picked at from generation to generation. And Aurelia's over-starched defensiveness wasn't helping. So she put out a placating hand.

"Look, we're not here to cause the village any more harm," she said. "We have a job to do, but if there's anything that we can do to help you and the other villagers . . . we will." She looked at them, meeting Hull's resignation and Gertha's anger, willing them to believe her. "I promise."

I promise. When had she last said those words? Had they always felt so heavy?

Old Gertha gave Certainty a long, hard look. It was a look of someone who'd lived a lifetime of hoping for things and being disappointed, over and over again, until she'd finally learned not to hope anymore.

But Hull . . .

"Thank you," he said, eyes crinkling at her. "That's something, at least."

AFTER GERTHA AND Hull left, Certainty and Aurelia took a break to eat the food they had been given. They sat outside near the stable, using tree stumps as both chairs and table. Certainty thought that it was much nicer to be in the fresh air and sunlight than in the confines of the carriage house—and, to her relief, the bullying rooster from earlier didn't even strut by to accost them.

Certainty half expected Aurelia to chastise her for promising to help the villagers, but the mage was quiet as they made their way through the bread (airy, delightful) and cheese (sharp, middling). Certainty sighed, missing the loud, boisterous meals of the novices' dining hall. She thought about making conversation, but it seemed that every time she did so with Aurelia, she ended up planting her foot firmly in her mouth. Safest to just keep things professional.

But then Aurelia cleared her throat.

"You were right, Novice."

"About what?"

"What you said last night. That I was rude to the villagers. I . . . apologize."

"Oh." Certainty was pleasantly surprised. "Um, thank you. But maybe you should apologize to them, and not me?"

Aurelia's nostrils flared. "The old woman was rude to me first!"

Certainty just looked at her, and the mage held her gaze stubbornly for a second before looking away.

"Right. Well. I . . . that is, I'm not very good at people." Her speech was uncharacteristically halting. "Especially when I feel that they already dislike me. Like I'm not wanted somewhere. I can be . . ."

"Prickly?"

Aurelia shot her a look as if gauging whether or not she was mocking her—but Certainty smiled to take the sting out of it, and she seemed to relax.

"Maybe a little."

Certainty nodded, thoughtful. "I can understand that. But the people here, they aren't really our enemies, you know. They just have no choice but to accept our being here, and not having a say in matters makes people feel small."

Aurelia tilted her head. "I suppose I see what you mean. And I'll try to be better, Novice. I'll . . . follow your example. With them, I mean."

Well, that was something. Maybe they could find a way for everyone to get along after all. "Thank you, Mage. I appreciate you trying."

"But . . ." Aurelia straightened her back. Of course there was a "but." "What you promised them, about us helping— Novice, you know that our assignment must come first, right?"

"Yes, I know." Certainty sighed. "But if there's any way we can help them, it'd go a long way toward how they see us, don't you think? How they view the Guild, and our work here, too."

Aurelia mulled this over. Below them to the north, a farmer wheeled a cart full of garlic scapes across his fields; to the east, a gangly figure that might have been Orrin scrambled down the slopes holding two wooden buckets.

"Maybe, but I'm not sure how we'd even begin to help. It sounds like all of their troubles stem from the loss of the land's magic. That's not the sort of thing any individual spell can fix, not even a very powerful one."

"Could just us being here help? Or the presence of all of these magical artifacts?"

"It's possible . . ." The mage picked at her bread thoughtfully. "Proximal magical transference is a known phenomenon. But it depends upon the duration and the power of the magic at play. I'm not sure we'd generate enough magical residue to change things noticeably."

The power of the magic used. Anything Certainty could do wasn't going to be very helpful, then. She sighed again.

Aurelia looked like she wanted to say something more. But then a rooster crowed, somewhere in the distance, and the moment was gone. The mage stood, wiping off her robes, and ducked a quick nod at Certainty.

"Back to work?"

TWO AND A half more hours of gloved carrying, and the stable was newly crowded with dozens of boxes and magical miscellany while the two Guild transports finally stood empty.

Certainty was exhausted. She wiped one hand across a forehead plastered in sweaty curls and looked at Aurelia. It was deeply unfair that after all that physical labor, the mage still looked so good. She was *glistening*, for Mother's sake.

Aurelia didn't notice her envy.

"Time to cast the wards," she said. She looked sidelong at Certainty. "The High Mage said that I'd need to do all of the spellwork while we were here, but I could use your help with drawing the boundaries, if you're willing . . . ?"

Certainty nodded wearily. She knew the *theory* of spellcasting well enough; her problem was mustering sufficient magic to cast them. She'd make an excellent mage's assistant—but somehow, that seemed even worse than remaining a novice forever. At least a novice could still hope to eventually be something more.

She picked up the large earthenware jar of salt, put the iron stakes and hammer into her belt, and followed Aurelia outside.

Together, they walked in a slow circle around the stable and the carriage house. As they walked, Certainty poured out a continuous stream of salt to mark a narrow white border. Every half dozen paces or so, they paused so that she could also hammer one of the rods into the ground, deep enough that the metal was barely visible above the dirt.

Once the ward's boundaries had been drawn, they returned to the inside of the stable so that Aurelia could seal the warding. They looked out from the doorway, and Aurelia's hands danced gracefully in the air while she spoke the words of protection. Certainty watched her cast the spell with a dull, familiar sort of envy.

Then Aurelia knelt and, with the curved side of the hammer, dug out a small hole in the very center of the stable's packed dirt floor. Into the hole went the small, purple-tinged crystal that would serve as the focal point for the warding spells. Aurelia spoke the final incantation in a quiet, steady voice, and Certainty patted loose dirt back over the crystal to bury it.

"There," said Aurelia, sounding tired but satisfied. While warding spells weren't particularly complicated, they required a good deal of magic to establish and maintain. "That will stop anyone who tries to enter with ill intent."

"What will your wards do to them?"

"Oh, nothing lethal." But the mage smiled in a way that Certainty found a little alarming. "But it's remarkably difficult for a thief to run away when their limbs have been rearranged."

***

THE TWO GUILD wagons were standing empty outside the stable, so they saw to those next. Certainty detected an air of restlessness about them; perhaps, like borrowed horses, they were eager to return to their proper masters.

Aurelia gave the wagons one final checking over to ensure they hadn't missed any loose artifacts, then closed the doors and stepped back. She rapped three times on the wagon closest to them.

"Return to the Guildtower in Margrave," she said crisply. The transports thrummed into life immediately and, without further farewell, took themselves off down the village path at a brisk speed—although they did pause politely to allow a villager to cross in front of them.

Certainty and Aurelia watched the wagons go in silence. It wasn't long before their emblazoned Guild crests disappeared behind the distant hills, and it was then that the sense of isolation struck Certainty with an almost physical pang.

She was stuck here in Shpelling—in this remote, unwelcoming, bafflingly garlicky place—for the foreseeable future. Away from her family, away from her friends, away even from the simple luxury of the Guildtower dormitory.

And what did she have in place of those things? The company of Aurelia—a mage she couldn't remotely begin to understand—and a handful of villagers who'd already made it quite clear that they wanted them gone.

"Now our real work begins," Aurelia said quietly.

SEVEN

THE "REAL WORK," as it turned out, was exceptionally dull and repetitive, but Certainty applied herself to it with the same dogged cheerfulness with which she tackled any of her novice chores. At least with this assignment, there might be a magehood—and a promise to her family fulfilled—at its end.

While she sat cross-legged on the stable floor (now strewn with fresh straw, grudgingly sold to them by Ferdinand) and sorted artifacts into neat rows, she imagined donning silver mage's robes for the first time. As she removed one calfskin glove to carefully touch each artifact, speak with it, and understand its enchantment, she mulled over how she might word the news in a future letter to her parents. She wasn't one to count her chickens before they hatched, of course, but when this assignment was over, and she became Deputy Keeper . . .

Would she write it at the very top? Or would she save it for the end of the letter as a surprise? A casual, offhand mention—*by the way, I'm a mage now; tell Asp he'll be an apprentice by summer.*

Certainty grinned at this delicious thought as she put a sheathed dagger carefully off to the side. She jotted down its entry (*No. 17, dagger enchanted to give victim papercuts in vulnerable areas*) in Mortimer's tome.

Aurelia, thankfully, didn't notice her daydreaming; the mage was presently occupied with the hard work of carpentry. She'd joined Certainty for the first hour of artifact identification, but it quickly became clear that (a) there wasn't much Aurelia could contribute when Certainty was the one with the ability to speak with the artifacts, and (b) Certainty communing silently with inanimate objects was a very boring thing to watch.

So Aurelia had armed herself with the old woodworking tools as if preparing for battle, and set about turning the empty stable stalls into organized storage. This necessitated shelving. Hammering, sawing, and the occasional muttered imprecation came from her direction. Certainty might have been concerned if not for the fact that Aurelia had already managed to assemble a perfectly serviceable work desk and two benches from the pile of spare lumber.

Of course, she'd had the benefit of using spellwork as an aid; while floating the heavy wood into place would have been a massively taxing effort, Aurelia hadn't been shy about using levitation spells to hold nails in place while she hammered them, or summoning a very small and localized sandstorm to smooth the planks for her. The whole place smelled like sawdust now, which was frankly a significant improvement over the original scent of old horse and rat droppings.

Certainty brought the tome of records over to the magically sanded desk and plopped herself down on the bench with a sigh. Her chin rested on one hand as she flipped through the records, running her finger down its dusty pages. She had to make an effort to keep her eyes from drifting to the open window even though there was nothing more interesting to be seen there than a willow shivering in the breeze and the occasional passing cloud.

The day was sunny and crisp, a welcome reprieve from the spate of spring rain that they'd had lately. If she didn't have work to do, Certainty would have loved to be walking in the fields and the hills, inhaling the scent of damp earth and enjoying the openness of it all.

But she did. *Focus, Cert.*

Then she thought again of Aurelia's necklace, and shuddered.

More out of boredom than curiosity, she stroked one finger along the spine of the tome and let a tiny amount of her magic slip into it, willing the book to open its object-mind to hers.

"Greetings, knowledge-seeker. I am a Book. I am a holder of knowledge."

The voice of the tome was a brittle whisper. The sound of a turning page, a finger brushing against parchment. There was a sly knowingness to it, too, an intelligence that was the telltale sign of a magical object. Perhaps it had also been enchanted in some way, or had simply absorbed magic over time upon its shelf in the Guildtower vaults.

"What knowledge do you hold?"

"I am a Book. I hold things written. I hold things forgotten. I hold names, and purposes, and failings."

"Can you show me . . . something interesting? Something useful, maybe?"

There was a shivering, thoughtful silence from it. Certainty felt a gentle probing in her mind—as if the book itself were feeling out the shape of her, and judging her.

It vibrated beneath her fingers. Slowly, without her doing anything at all, its pages began to turn, sending small dust clouds up as they did. Then it stopped abruptly. It had settled back into stillness, open to a page near the end that Certainty hadn't reached yet. For reasons unknown to Certainty, Mortimer had made his own scant entries seemingly randomly throughout the tome, rather than in the usual front-to-back order. She meant to ask him about it when they returned.

"What is it?"

But the book had lapsed back into silence and refused to respond.

Certainty let her eyes run down the page. There didn't seem to be anything particularly noteworthy on it, just a half dozen or so artifact records written in Mortimer's scratchy hand: a ring that, when twisted, rotated its wearer counterclockwise; a brass spoon that unmixed baking ingredients; a fancy hat that sprouted a different-colored feather each time it was worn . . . but then Certainty's gaze snagged on one particular entry.

Mortimer's penmanship was scragglier than normal, as if the description had been written in a hurry:

> No. 5, a wand of infestation. Enchanted by Mage Festor during the Wars; ineffective for military use. Summons honeybees which refuse to attack on command. Festor improved subsequent versions to summon appropriately aggressive wasps. Activated with spoken command "innundo." Do not test indoors!!

Certainty stared down at the page, the gears of her mind shifting slowly. *Summons honeybees.* She looked out the window again. Shpelling's apple grove, already flowering, was just visible in the distance, behind the clusters of houses that dotted the land like currants in a scone.

Technically, she was perfectly within her rights to test any of the magical artifacts they'd brought with them, wasn't she? Her task wasn't only to see them stored away safely—it was also to ensure that their records were thorough and accurate. And who was to say that old Keeper Mortimer hadn't gotten mixed up? Maybe it wasn't even a wand of infestation, but instead a wand of . . . of rain-summoning. Or of teleportation.

She stood abruptly, pulled her gloves back on, and began rummaging with purpose through the open boxes of artifacts, looking for a matching label.

"Aurelia," she called. "I'm going out for a bit; I need to test something."

The only reply was the sound of hammering and a muffled swear that somehow still managed to sound prim. Certainty hesitated for a moment, six years of obedient novicehood dragging at her limbs—but blast it, she wasn't in the Guildtower anymore. Moving quickly so as to outpace the part of her that was still wringing its hands, she scribbled a quick note and left it on the desk for when Aurelia found her gone.

Yes; surely it would only be diligent of her to make sure the wand wasn't a far more powerful artifact than what Mortimer's notes said. Nobody could fault her for being thorough. And she may as well do her testing somewhere safely outdoors, at a healthy distance from Aurelia and all the other artifacts.

Somewhere like in Hull's sad, fruitless grove of apple trees.

THE WAND WAS a crudely carved rod of beechwood roughly the length of Certainty's forearm. She wrapped it carefully in a spare shawl, then stowed it away in a pocket of her cloak before she hurried up the village path, nodding politely to an elderly villager who squinted at her suspiciously along the way. She didn't have to ask directions to Hull's home, as the grove was clearly visible uphill to the east. She hoped he was home.

When she arrived, she paused to take in the wood-beamed cottage in front of the grove. It was a small home, charmingly square and squat, and looked as though it had been patched and built upon with a hodgepodge of materials: some brickwork here, some wood and plaster there, and a roof thatched with straw and reeds. Two windows were open, although their view was partly obscured by the ivy growing thickly upward from window boxes to climb along the walls and roof of the cottage.

It looked, above all, like a home that had been well and thoroughly lived in. Certainty smiled and knocked on the cottage door.

She only had to wait a few moments before it opened and Hull's sun-wrinkled face peered out at her.

"Hello again!" She spoke brightly, feeling the outline of the wand in her cloak. "I was wondering if you'd mind showing me your apple trees, please?"

"Oh! Well . . ." said the older man, taken aback. He opened the door wider, and Certainty saw Gertha standing beside him with her hands on her hips.

"Why do you want to see them?" the old woman asked suspiciously.

"I just—I had an idea."

"An idea." Gertha pursed her lips. "How nice for you."

"It can't hurt to let her see, can it?" Hull said to Gertha.

The two villagers looked at each other, having some sort of wordless argument while Certainty waited on the doorstep and tried to look helpful. Evidently Hull won, as Gertha gave a huff of displeasure and turned away.

"Come with me," he said to Certainty. "They're just this way."

He led Certainty around the back of the cottage, Gertha following behind them with her walking stick. The first thing Certainty noticed as they came around the corner was the riot of color. Blossoms in white, pink, and red crowded her vision.

Small, five-petaled flowers had burst into bloom on a dozen or so mature apple trees that stood proudly in a semicircle. The trees all looked healthy enough; they had wide, sturdy trunks, and their branches were heavy with leaves and flowers that rustled in a pleasing way when the breeze flowed through them.

"My father planted them," Hull said, looking around at the grove. "Granda gave him the seeds, said they were a family heirloom. Claimed the seeds were enchanted by a traveling hedgemage, and that's why the apples were so sweet. His heart would've broken to know that they've stopped fruiting."

"They're beautiful." Certainty reached out to touch one of the blossoms, then lifted her fingers to her face. They smelled of honeysuckle and spring.

"Yes, they flower wonderfully still, but . . ." Hull's words broke off.

"And you said you've tried different methods to bring the bees back?"

"Tried everything. Flowering bushes, woven skeps and water basins . . . I even sent Della's boy to buy a few hives off of the beekeeper down in Ruggan two years back. Brought them back all careful-like, wrapped in skins, had some nice beech boxes made special for them, too."

He gestured at two layered wooden boxes resting on slats to the side of the apple trees. "But the next day, I went to check on them, and they'd all disappeared. Flown off somewhere, and never came back."

Certainty knew perfectly well why the bees hadn't stayed, of course: Shpelling was a magical desert.

Bees, like cats, were creatures of magic. They needed it in the same way that humans needed sunlight. Sure, one could *survive* without it, but it would be a stunted, pale, and unhappy existence—not a life one would ever willingly accept, not if they had any choice in the matter.

She felt that funny little twinge in her stomach again. Sunlight brought warmth and growth. Magic brought... well, *magic*.

"I see" was all she said. No point elaborating on theories of apicultural thaumaturgy. "Hull, Gertha, I'd like to try something here, if that's all right with you?"

"Something magical?" The old man straightened, looking simultaneously excited and nervous.

Gertha snorted. "Thought you weren't even a proper mage."

Ouch. "Yes, something magical, and no, I'm not. But I found an artifact that might help. I can't promise it'll work, though, so you may not want to get your hopes up. It's just an idea."

Hull nodded, eyes wide and eager. "Well, that's fine, miss. It means a lot just that you're willing to try."

"Suppose so," muttered Gertha.

"Right." Certainty exhaled. "Then... you both may want to go back inside for this. Just as a precaution."

"A precaution against what?"

Against the likelihood that a swarm of magical attack wasps comes out instead.

"Um... just in case."

Gertha eyed her suspiciously, but Hull hurried her back inside his cottage. Certainty could still see their faces—one hopeful, one mistrusting—watching her through a window.

She took a deep breath, removed her calfskin gloves, and took out the wand.

"Wand?" She sent a trickle of magic into it.

At the Guildtower, she'd rarely had the chance to use magical artifacts in her lessons, but it was always a thrill when she did.

Since they were enchanted to be used by anyone—regardless of the strength of their magic—using them almost helped her forget about her magical shortcomings. A pity she couldn't simply raid the Guild vaults and equip herself with an array of artifacts for every spell she'd ever need to cast.

"Are you ready to summon bees for me?"

She sensed a responding magic awakening. A light wind played with her hair as she stood in the center of the grove, and instead of object-speech, there was suddenly a low and gentle buzzing in her mind.

It sounded . . . friendly?

Good enough.

Certainty steeled herself and lifted the wand, pointing it in the direction of Hull's empty bee boxes.

"*Innundo*," she said, enunciating each syllable.

At first, nothing happened, and she thought that perhaps she had mispronounced the incantation—but then a single honeybee, fat and yellow and fuzzy, sprang out from the tip of the wand. It buzzed around in curious, wobbly circles, the sound of its vibrating wings waxing and waning with its nearness, and Certainty laughed out loud in delight.

"Is it just you, little friend?"

It dipped among her curls, perhaps mistaking her for a large flower of some odd and fuzzy variety, and she stood very still and let it explore. But then the buzzing grew louder and louder in her mind, and then—her breath caught—a *stream* of bees erupted from the wand.

The rod vibrated in her hand as bees poured out of it, and Cert fought to hold it still, holding her breath without realizing it as the air in front of her filled with fuzzy, flying bodies. A black-and-yellow swarm danced in the center of the grove, swirling in little currents and eddies, and there was something joyous and wonderful in its flight. One bee landed on her hand, another joined the first explorer in her hair, but Certainty wasn't afraid. She somehow knew that these bees would not hurt her. She thought, in fact, that they might be thanking her.

"Free, free, free," the swarm buzzed in her mind.

Then, in one synchronized motion, the swarm swung and forked in two. One elongated cloud of honeybees descended upon the apple blossoms, bathing themselves in pollen and making the pink and white petals shiver as they nestled among the flowers. The other half of the swarm flew over to the bee boxes, investigating their nooks and crannies.

"They're for you," Certainty called out to them, too flush with giddy triumph to feel foolish about talking to bees. "You're very welcome here! Why don't you stay awhile?"

"Oh!" Hull had come running out of his cottage; Gertha followed a short distance behind. "Oh, oh, oh—" It seemed the old man had lost the use of his words. He whirled from the sight of bees feasting in the flowers, to the newly buzzing bee boxes beside them, and back again. "Gertha, look! Do you see?"

Gertha was staring at the bees. "I see them, Hull."

Her gaze swung to Certainty, and there was still distrust in those sharp eyes—but there was something else there now, too.

Hull, though, had no reservations. Not anymore. The old man laughed as he stood there in his family's grove, alive again with the soft buzzing of bees and the scent of apple blossoms. He turned to face Certainty, and for just a moment, she thought she could see a glimpse of the boy he had once been, for the wideness of his smile removed years from his face.

"Will the bees live in my boxes, do you know?" he asked. "Will they stay?"

Certainty looked down at the beech wand in her hand. It felt still and empty. She sent another pulse of magic through it, inquiring. A faint, buzzing echo was her only response.

"I don't know for certain," she said. "But I think so. I think they're glad to be out of the wand. I'll leave it here with you, just in case they change their minds."

He blinked at it, then at her. His eyes shone, and when he took her hands in his own, they were warm and steady.

"Thank you," he said. "From my heart, miss, thank you."

EVEN AFTER SHE'D gotten back to the stable and returned to the inventory work, Certainty couldn't stop smiling. Aurelia noticed.

"You seem cheerful," she said with narrowed eyes while she checked the wards again. "More so than normal, I mean."

"Ah . . ." Certainty suspected that Aurelia wouldn't approve of what she'd done. She decided to go with a half-truth. "It's just the test I ran earlier, on one of the artifacts that I wasn't sure of. It worked. I was able to confirm Mage Mortimer's notes."

Aurelia looked puzzled for a moment, and then her expression cleared. "That's . . . good. I'm glad you've come to care so much about our work, Novice. I have to admit that I was afraid you wouldn't take our assignment seriously."

"Right," said Certainty, feeling a twinge of guilt. "Yeah. Yeah, I do."

She did care about her work, really, it was just . . . seeing Hull's joy had been so much more rewarding than knowing that the Guild's records were accurate. Especially when she knew that nobody cared about these particular objects, outside of wanting them stored a safely large distance away from the artifacts they *actually* considered valuable. Surely nobody from the

Guild would care—or even notice—one missing wand of bee-summoning?

Certainty shoved away these thoughts and looked around instead at the progress they'd made that day. Most of the boxes and loose items were still piled in the middle of the stable, but a few dozen of the artifacts that Certainty had already checked against the record book were now stored neatly away on newly built shelves in the leftmost stall. Aurelia blew sawdust off her hands, looking pleased with herself.

"I think we've made a good start of things today, Novice. More than *Master Tobias* expected us to achieve, I'm sure. I spotted a bakery down in the square earlier. Want to go see what they have?"

AS THEY WALKED through Shpelling, Certainty watched Aurelia's eyes roam over the dilapidated houses and the empty storefronts.

"It must be a hard thing," the mage mused. "To grow up somewhere and watch it fade around you."

"I suppose." Certainty looked around, but there were no villagers nearby to overhear. She couldn't imagine they'd have been pleased to hear the two of them discussing Shpelling's sad state.

"The village you're from—Potshire, was it? Is it much like Shpelling?"

Cert shook her head as they rounded a bend. "In some ways, maybe, but mostly not. Potshire was always full of life. I grew up with a flock of other children to play with."

They had seen barely a handful of children younger than Orrin in Shpelling so far. Part of what contributed to the village's unusual quietness, Certainty realized.

"Potshire's a farming village, too, but people there grow all sorts of different things, not just a single crop. Nobody back home is rich, but we all had enough to eat and a little extra besides. Enough to put a little bit of coin by, enough to buy a few nice things on market days . . ." Not quite enough for a younger brother's apothecary apprenticeship, though. She bit her lip.

"Anyway, our village square was always loud and busy, not like this. But I think I understand what Old Gertha meant when she talked about the village dying slowly. In a small village, you can't help but be afraid of being left behind. You hear of all the exciting things happening in the cities—new inventions, new goods, new styles—and it makes you worry that your whole life is . . ." Certainty shrugged a little. "Just another old-fashioned thing. Something that the world will cast aside and forget."

Aurelia glanced sideways at her. "But you escaped it, didn't you? Thanks to the Guild accepting you as a novice."

"Potshire wasn't something I wanted to escape from," Certainty said, a little too sharply.

It wasn't strictly true, of course. There was the small, selfish, guilty part of her that had been excited to leave for Margrave—to have a chance at a different sort of life, to be a mage, to be special. But there was a difference between acknowledging that in the privacy of her own mind and hearing it said out loud by someone else. Potshire was *her* home. Outsiders like Aurelia didn't get to put it down.

But she was being unfair; Aurelia was just making conversation. An effort to be rewarded, since it clearly didn't come naturally to her.

"Sorry. I just mean that—" Certainty turned the words over in her mouth, trying to find the right way to convey her thoughts. "Margrave folk always assume that living in Margrave is better than living anywhere else. But I think it's not necessarily better, just different. And there's times when I miss Potshire and my family very much."

In Potshire, Certainty never felt like she had to earn the right to be there. Never felt inadequate or useless, or like she was letting everybody down.

But she'd been younger then. All that had been expected of her was to learn the best ways to prune a pear tree, how to patch clothing without wasting thread, and perhaps, eventually, to marry well and produce more little Bulrushes. Funny how differently she looked at her future now, on the other side of six years.

"I see," Aurelia said quietly, and she still seemed deep in thought when they came to the bakery. It was a homey little shop near the village square, with the scent of yeast rising from its chimney and a few shingles missing from its roof. They ducked inside where a brown-haired woman in an apron startled at their entry.

"Oh, hello—!"

"Hello." Certainty smiled at her. "I'm Certainty, and this is Mage Aurelia. We're conducting some Guild business here in Shpelling and will be staying in the old carriage house and stable for a while. We thought we'd come by to introduce ourselves, and . . ." She sniffed hopefully. "Purchase some bread?"

The baker's elbows slumped onto her counter. "Oh, miss, it's good to meet you both—I'm Brienna—but I'm afraid I've nothing to sell you at the moment. I only had enough flour to make a half batch of loaves today, and they're all gone already." She threw her hands up in exasperation, showering the counter in flour. "Lost half of it to the damp from all this rain, and the rest of it to all the blasted mice! I just can't keep them out of my storeroom."

Aurelia looked around the small bakery, her nose wrinkling.

"An infestation, is it? We saw them in the carriage house as well."

"Practically a plague, I'd call it!"

"Mice tend to show themselves more after rainy weather," said Certainty.

But the baker shook her head in frustration.

"They've been running amok in Shpelling for years and years now, nothing to do with the weather. We've tried traps, of course, and poisoned cheese, and sealing all our food away—anything else you can imagine, too—but nothing ever takes. We just can't catch them as quickly as they breed."

"Grimy little pests," said Certainty with sympathy, thinking of the mice that had startled her in the carriage house that first night. The Guildtower was the one place in Margrave that was reliably rodent-free, thanks to the High Mage's particular magical abilities. It was said that she could speak to rats and command them to do her bidding—which included spying on foreign emissaries from within the walls of the White Palace, eating through enemy granaries, and keeping well clear of the Guildtower kitchens. Certainty had a great appreciation for this last fact.

The baker heaved a resigned sigh. "In any case, I'm sorry not to have any bread to sell you today. Maybe tomorrow. But if you're hungry, the Plough ought to be serving dinner soon enough. You could pop over there for a meal?"

DINNER AT THE Golden Plough, alas, meant a choice between garlicky greens or garlicky turnips, with a side of garlic-and-salt pork. To her credit, Aurelia ate her meal without complaint this time, although she did so with the determined air of a soldier doing her duty.

Certainty was making her way through her turnips (which weren't all that bad, really) when Ferdinand stopped by their table holding two small cups and a bottle half-full of golden liquid. "Apple mead," he said gruffly, pouring it out for them. "Compliments of Master Hull."

Aurelia looked surprised. "Mead? I thought you said you only had ale here."

"Aye, normally we'd have to buy a fresh cask from Ruggan, but this bottle's from Hull's private stores. From the last bottling before his trees stopped fruiting."

"That's kind of him. But we must pay for it . . ."

The tavernkeep shook his head at Aurelia, sending the ends of his mustache aquiver. "He won't take coin from you two. Not after what you've done for him."

"What we've . . . done for him?" Aurelia looked at Certainty.

"It was really nothing," Certainty said weakly. "Please tell him thank you."

Ferdinand grunted. "Might've been wrong about you two. Hope so, anyway. We'll see." And with those cryptic words, he returned to his bar, leaving Certainty alone to face Aurelia and her raised eyebrow. *Blast.*

"Care to explain?"

Certainty swallowed. "Well, that artifact I went out to test earlier . . ."

"Yes?"

"It was a wand of infestation," she said, lowering her voice. "It summons bees, and I remembered what Hull and Gertha had said about his family apple grove, and figured that I may as well test the wand there, and . . . and it worked, Aurelia! There's a whole swarm of bees now, living in his boxes!"

Aurelia set her fork down emphatically. "You—you *used* an artifact? On one of the villagers' homes? Novice, we're meant to take inventory of these artifacts, not experiment with them for our own purposes!"

"But it wasn't for my own purpose, it was to help restore an old man's livelihood! His da had planted those trees, Aurelia."

Aurelia looked like she didn't know whether to be more worried or angry. "That may be true, but the misuse of magical artifacts for personal purposes is prohibited for good reason. Imagine if something had gone wrong? That secretary would be reporting us in an instant."

Drat. Certainty had forgotten about him. But . . . "He's back in Ruggan now; he won't find out! And besides, the use of magical artifacts is only restricted because some are too powerful and dangerous to be used safely. Whereas the objects we brought here are here specifically because they are *neither* of those things."

"We can't know that for sure without individually confirming each item's powers—"

"—which I did, in this case. By talking to the wand before I used it." Certainty stuck her chin out, and the two women glared at each other across the table.

But Certainty wasn't going to back down. What she did with the wand might have been against the Guild rules (she maintained that it was technically a gray area, and very much a matter of interpretation), but even so, she knew that what she did was *right*. She just needed Aurelia to see that, too.

Without breaking eye contact, Certainty reached for her cup and took a sip of Hull's mead. It was delicious: crisp and floral, with tartness cutting through the honey-sweetness, and a gentle touch of spice in the finish. Aurelia's eyes flicked to the cup.

"It's good," Certainty said, keeping her voice carefully neutral. "May as well not let it go to waste."

The mage squinted at her suspiciously, but relented and

picked up her own cup. Eyes still on Certainty's, she drank, and Certainty could tell from her expression that she was savoring the taste, too. They each sat there sipping their mead for a few moments, saying nothing.

"Did the wand have any other effects?" Aurelia asked abruptly. "Any injuries or damage of any kind?"

Certainty shook her head. "Just the bees. Who were perfectly obliging guests, mind you."

Aurelia's tongue darted out to taste the mead still on her lips, and Certainty found her eyes tracking the motion. She yanked them back up to Aurelia's face, flushing, but luckily the mage hadn't noticed. Aurelia's eyes were on Ferdinand as the tavernkeep busied himself behind his bar. There was something uncertain in her gaze, as if she were being confronted with a test she hadn't studied for.

"I . . . I suppose there's no harm done," Aurelia said slowly. "This one time."

Certainty grinned in triumph, and for a moment Aurelia's lips twitched upward, too. But then Aurelia's eyes went back to Certainty's, and they were steady and serious. "Still, Certainty, remember what we're here for. Finishing our assignment takes priority above everything else. I need to send a progress report to the High Mage soon. So no more . . . *experimenting* . . . with the artifacts unless strictly necessary. Agreed?"

Certainty knew the mage was only being rational, but that didn't mean she had to be happy about it. She sighed, thinking of Fanya's advice when they'd taken leave of the Guildtower. *Keep your head down. Be the quietest pick that ever picked.* But where was the fun in that?

"Yes," she said reluctantly. "Agreed."

At least she'd helped Hull and his apple trees. That would have to be enough.

EIGHT

THE NEXT MORNING, Certainty woke up (wincing, because they *really* needed to find a way to get some beds into the carriage house—she'd agreed to a stint in a farming village, not a prison cell) to an empty carriage house.

"Aurelia?"

Certainty wandered through the door to the stable, rubbing at her eyes blearily and looking for her wayward partner. She found her in a rather odd position: sitting cross-legged atop a folded blanket in one of the disused stable stalls, palms on her knees, and eyes closed. She was ringed by lit candles.

"Morning," Certainty said. "Are we making an occult sacrifice today?"

"Hush," Aurelia said without opening her eyes. "I need to focus. The High Mage told me I should take advantage of the peace and quiet"—this last said rather pointedly—"in Shpelling to . . . advance my personal studies. I thought this morning would be a good opportunity to do so."

"What personal studies?"

Aurelia shifted on her blanket. "Farspeaker exercises. You wouldn't understand."

Certainty narrowed her eyes. She knew that farspeakers were rare and highly valued, of course. While other mages could be trained to receive a farspeaker's communication over great distances, only farspeakers themselves could *open* those channels of communication—which naturally made them vital to any military campaign, trading association, or intelligence network. Knowing an enemy's movements or the falling price of lamp oil in Lindisi days before others did was worth more than gold could buy. (Not that the Guild was above trying to find out exactly how *much* more.)

Honestly, it seemed like a terrible waste of resources for the Guild to have sent one of their few farspeakers with Certainty to a farming village of no strategic importance at all. But she wasn't one to question the High Mage's decisions. Surely she had a good reason, and hopefully it was something other than a lack of trust in Certainty's ability to get the job done alone.

"Is farspeaking hard to do?" Certainty always wondered that about other mages' abilities. For her, speaking with objects felt as easy and natural as thinking—though it *did* lead to terrible headaches if she did so for too long.

Aurelia heaved an exasperated sigh and finally opened her eyes to look up at Certainty.

"Yes, it's hard," she said. "And it is proportionally harder the farther you are from your recipient, so opening a channel across the vast expanse of the kingdom requires a great deal of concentration. And silence."

"Fine." Certainty pouted. "I'll just get dressed and leave you to your fancy, very advanced farspeaking exercises, the likes of which a mere novice like me couldn't possibly understand."

"I didn't say—"

Certainty could practically hear Aurelia's teeth grinding. But the mage took a deep breath. "I'm sorry, I didn't mean to imply that. But I do need to be alone to do my exercises. Will you be all right carrying out your inventory work without me today?"

Certainty shrugged. "Sure."

Aurelia nodded, and closed her eyes again. "Don't forget to wear your gloves."

Yes, Mother. Certainty huffed in exasperation as she left the carriage house in search of breakfast and better company.

She decided to take the long route to the village tavern, wanting to explore more of Shpelling while she had the opportunity. The path wound uphill and eastward to Hull's home and apple grove, and continued up past a field grown wild with weeds. A patch of dandelions had chosen to flower early, their bright yellow blooms swaying on hollow stalks in the breeze beside their cottony siblings. Certainty liked dandelions. She'd always thought they were beautiful, and as a child hadn't understood why her mother had made her pick them out of the flower beds. *Aren't they flowers, too?* she'd asked. But no, bright and pretty as they were, dandelions were weeds, good only for pulling out and throwing away. They didn't belong where they had grown, her mother said. But Certainty liked them anyway. She liked to think they kept the real flowers on their toes.

Beyond the overgrown field, the path led into a copse of green saplings. She walked along the path there, enjoying the early spring coolness contrasting with the warm, dappled sunlight while she touched a supple leaf here, let her hand drag against smooth bark there.

"What are you doing here?"

Gertha's voice broke her reverie. The old woman was coming up the path behind her. She held her walking stick in one hand and a wooden bucket full of water in the other, and Certainty rushed to assist her.

"Here, let me help you—"

Gertha batted her off. "I'm old, not helpless. Wouldn't be carrying it if I couldn't manage it on my own, would I?"

"I know you can, but you don't have to. Please, just let me take it—"

Gertha grudgingly allowed her to take the bucket. Certainty nearly dropped it as soon as she realized how heavy it was.

"Don't spill it," Gertha said irritably. "I don't want to have to walk all the way back to the well. Bah, if only the old well in the village square were still working . . . somehow things are always easier in your memories, aren't they? I remember when we'd all gather there in the mornings to fetch water and chat. Well's gone dry now, and so's all the gossip, so here I am fetching water from half a league away and uphill, even with my knees. But that's why *I'm* here. What about you?"

"I was just out for a walk. Exploring the village."

Gertha kept walking, so she followed the old woman up along the path. The water in the bucket sloshed against its sides, and she took care not to let any spill out, even as it knocked painfully against her knees.

"It's lovely here," she ventured.

"Hmph. Was even lovelier before you lot ruined it."

"Gertha, the Mage Wars were decades before Aurelia and I were even born," Certainty said patiently.

The old woman grunted, her stick *thuk-thuk*ing against the path. "I know that, girl. I know it's not you or her blond highness who caused all this. But sometimes folk need someone to blame. Easier to be mad at the person in front of you than to be mad at the whole wide world."

They walked in silence for a bit, which was probably for the best, as Certainty needed all of her breath just to keep carrying the blasted water bucket. Gertha paused to examine a fat brown slug crossing the path in front of them, and Certainty gratefully seized the chance to put down the bucket and catch her breath. "How's Hull?"

"The bees are still there, if that's what you're asking. He checks on them constantly, like a doting father."

Certainty grinned at the image. "Good." She'd been slightly worried the bees would leave again, but had hoped that the residual magic from the wand would be enough to sustain them.

Gertha began walking again, and Certainty hefted the bucket back up with a groan.

"Where are we going exactly, Gertha?"

"Just a bit further. Come. Since you're here, there's something I want to show you."

Gertha led her through the copse for several more long minutes, ignoring Certainty's wheezing, and the two women picked their way over roots and between branches before emerging into a small clearing surrounded by trees. Certainty slowly lowered the bucket to the ground.

"This is where it happened," said Gertha.

Before them was a perfect circle of bare land, just large enough for Certainty to lie down in—not that she had any wish to. The ground might have been called dry, or blackened, or barren—but *dead* was the truest descriptor. Despite the green vibrancy of the forest around them, within the circle, Certainty couldn't see any signs of life. No seedlings thrust up from the ashy gravel; no insects explored the surface. It was strangely silent in the clearing, and Certainty couldn't help but feel as though she were standing before a gravesite.

"This is where the magic was drained?"

The old woman nodded. "Been like this since I was a child. We've tried to restore it over the years—digging it up, replacing it with fresh soil, covering it with sod and dung and what have you—but nothing ever takes. It always comes back just like this."

Certainty stared at it. Such an ugly thing, to be here in the center of such beauty. A sore that wouldn't heal.

"I come here every week to remind myself," said Gertha. "And to try."

"Try what?"

In answer, Gertha picked up the bucket of water—with such little visible effort that Certainty thought the old woman must be far more robust than she seemed—and strode into the center of the circle.

She took a small spade out from somewhere inside her robes, knelt down with some effort, and dug a hole in the lifeless dirt. From one pocket came a handful of tiny seeds, which she scattered into the hole before covering it again. Then Gertha lifted the bucket and gently poured water onto the mound, and all around it, too.

She returned to Certainty, who looked at her with a question in her eyes.

"Folk need someone to blame," said the old woman. "But they need something to hope for, too."

HOURS LATER, CERTAINTY found herself distracted by thoughts of the clearing and Gertha's words as she worked through one of the boxes of artifacts. She stared at the paper label attached to the artifact in front of her (an enormous iron vambrace enchanted to shrink to fit any arm that wore it and was then impossible to remove) with eyes that blurred. Had she already recorded this one? She couldn't remember, and she couldn't muster the energy to check.

She sighed, giving up for the moment; it was already lunchtime, anyway.

She stripped off her gloves and poked her head into the stall. Aurelia was still sitting on her blanket. The mage looked as if she hadn't moved a muscle since Certainty had left her that morning, though her brow was furrowed with concentration and her lips were twitching slightly. Farspeaking, presumably. Certainty wondered with whom.

She left the mage alone to fetch lunch, but returned shortly from the Plough with her arms full of two loaves of bread, a jar of garlic preserved in herbs and oil, a generous hunk of soft cheese, and cold ham slices wrapped in a waxed paper packet. She plopped it all down on the table and mulled over the situation at hand.

Aurelia had explicitly asked her to carry on their work alone today. It was therefore implied that the mage didn't want to be disturbed for the remainder of the day. But . . . it was lunchtime. And the mage clearly hadn't eaten anything yet, which couldn't be healthy.

Certainty made up her mind.

"Mage Aurelia," she said, crouching down in front of her. Nothing happened.

She tried a little louder. "Aurelia!" Still nothing.

So she reached out and touched her hand, and suddenly found herself lying on the dirt floor with a very thin knife at her throat, a knee on her chest, and Aurelia's face taking up the majority of her vision.

"Hey!"

Aurelia blinked, and the knife vanished back into her robes. The mage lifted her knee and stood, and Certainty's face heated up as Aurelia lifted her bodily back onto her feet. She must be stronger than she looked. Certainty brushed her robes off, hiding her indignation at being manhandled—*womanhandled*—with such ease.

"Why did you touch me?" asked Aurelia abruptly.

"Why did I—" Certainty sputtered. "Why did *you* attack me with a knife?"

"I have basic training in arms and combat. A mage cannot always rely on her magic, as Mage Freinar wrote."

"I've read Freinar and had basic training, too, but you don't see me going around slashing at my colleagues willy-nilly," muttered Certainty. "And we have defensive wards up, anyway!"

Aurelia's face was flushed, too, though whether from exertion or embarrassment, Certainty couldn't be sure. "I apologize, all right? Now, what's so urgent that you had to interrupt me?"

Certainty eyed the mage, trying to decide whether or not to accept her apology, but then her stomach decided for her with a loud rumble.

"Lunch," she said grudgingly. "I thought you ought to eat something."

"Oh. I'm not hungry."

"Why don't you take off your necklace and check?"

Brow furrowed, Aurelia slowly unclasped her necklace and dropped it into a pocket. "It hardly matters, Certainty; I won't starve if I miss one meal . . ."

"You ought to take the necklace off more often. You don't always need to be as focused as possible, you know."

"Laziness and negligence are self-feeding contagions. One must strive for excellence at all times."

That sounded like a quote. "Is that Freinar, too?"

"No," said Aurelia, somewhat unwillingly. "My mother."

Huh. Certainty ignored this questionable nugget of parental wisdom in favor of piling cold ham and cheese slices on top of a thick slab of crusty bread already smeared with preserved garlic. She waved her creation under Aurelia's nose.

"Are you very sure you're not hungry?"

The mage, sniffing, tracked the bread with her eyes. "I . . . well . . ."

With her other hand, Certainty exaggeratedly wafted the savory scents toward Aurelia.

Aurelia capitulated.

"Oh, very well."

She grabbed the food from Certainty and sat down on the bench. Cert grinned and joined her, making her own stacked slice from the food laid out before them.

"So, any good tower gossip from whichever mage you were farspeaking with?"

"I—we don't—" Aurelia stumbled over her words. "No." She avoided Certainty's eyes as she took a careful bite of her food, trying not to topple the precariously stacked ham and cheese slices.

"Oh, come on; I don't believe you. There's got to be *something* interesting happening in Margrave."

"Shocking as it may be, not everyone in the Guildtower is preoccupied with other people's business."

That was categorically untrue, based on Certainty's own experience there. But she rolled her eyes and resorted to the cheap, yet effective, persuasion tactics she'd learned from Asp in childhood. *"Pleeeease—"*

"Fine, fine! I suppose . . ." Aurelia dabbed delicately at her lips with a handkerchief. "I did hear something interesting in the Guildtower just before we left. Mage Cassia told me that the High Mage has been summoned to many Council sessions recently. Apparently, the Minister of Trade and the Minister of

Justice are both working to reduce the Guild's influence. They've been arguing that Eshtera is too reliant on its mages and insinuating that the Guild could pose a threat to the Crown if it grows too powerful."

Certainty frowned. "Queen Lisbet won't believe that, will she? I've heard that she trusts High Mage Melea a great deal."

Certainty had never had a head for politics, but living in Margrave for six years made them somewhat difficult to avoid. The constant machinations of the Council, the guilds, and the lords seemed to her to be very much like the gears and wheels turning in one of those newfangled gnomish devices that the artificers delighted over: a great deal of fuss and noise and movement, with very little actual output to show for it.

"She does, but she also can't simply ignore her Ministers. And the High Mage is in a delicate position, since she's just expended a great deal of political capital getting the Council to agree to the establishment of a kingdom-wide healer network. Many lords who'd resisted having Guild stations in their fiefs were overruled."

"But shouldn't they be glad to have Guild healers in their lands?"

Aurelia shrugged one elegant shoulder, her robes slipping slightly with the motion. "Folk are always happy enough to have the services of a mage when they need them. But that doesn't mean they want the mages there when they don't, and they certainly don't want to be paying out of their own coffers for it."

"Huh." Certainty mulled this over while the two women ate in companionable silence (or semi-silence, given the crunching and chewing noises coming from both). As working lunches went, it was quite good; the ham was thick and salty, balancing out the milder cheese, and even the garlic spread enhanced the flavors rather than overpowering them.

"Tasty, don't you think? Beats most of the meals at the Guildtower, I'd say." Certainty wiped off an errant bit of garlic spread that had made it onto her chin. "Though the whitefish pie with gravy that the kitchen makes on Scholarsdays is in its own class, of course."

Aurelia gave her an amused look. "Missing Margrave already?"

"Not so much Margrave as the Guildtower." Certainty propped her chin up with one hand, head tilted over the table. "But a little bit, yes. I miss my friends. And my bed." And, surprisingly, she found that she missed her classes and chores, too. The comforting routine of it all. "I've just been there long enough that it feels like home to me. Six years is a long time."

The majority of her adult life, in fact. Who would she be, if not Novice Certainty of the Guild of Mages? It was hard to imagine, and that, too, was discomfiting.

"I've been at the Guildtower for years, too," Aurelia said. She picked up a piece of ham that had fallen off and nibbled at it pensively. "But I don't think time is enough, on its own, to make a place a home."

"Then what do you think does?"

Aurelia didn't respond right away. After a moment's thought, Certainty answered her own question. "Silly question, I suppose. It's the people, isn't it? Friends, family, folk you care for, and who care for you . . ."

Something in Aurelia's expression shuttered at this. Silently, she finished her food and wiped the crumbs off her hands. She clasped the silver necklace back around her neck without meeting Certainty's eyes.

"I need to get back to my work," Aurelia said quietly. She stood and turned away, then hesitated. She looked back at Certainty.

"Thank you for bringing me lunch," she said, before vanishing back into the empty stall.

NINE

"**CERTAINTY! I NEED** you!"

Aurelia's voice rang through the rafters, and Certainty nearly toppled off of the beam on which she was precariously balanced.

"What is it?" she called back, trying not to drop the handful of nails she was holding.

Needing a break from object-voices in her head, Certainty had volunteered to help Aurelia with the repair work for a bit—though she was quickly realizing that hammers, heights, and her own lack of coordination were a nonideal combination.

"Can you come here, please?"

The mage's voice was clear and authoritative—as usual—but a hint of a quaver in it got Certainty's attention. Slightly worried, Certainty dropped the nails into her apron pocket and shimmied carefully down the ladder.

"What do you need?"

A small wooden box lay on its side in the middle of the stable. The mage herself was standing several paces away and wielding a broom like a rapier. Certainty noted her stance—legs apart, knees bent, torso angled. She must've had dueling lessons growing up in Margrave. There was the faint shimmer of a defense spell surrounding Aurelia, too.

"There's something wrong with that box," Aurelia said tightly. "I need you to check what its enchantment is."

"What happened?" Certainty edged closer. The box just looked like a box to her.

"I was carrying it over to the shelves, but it—it *vibrated* at me. Rumbled. I hadn't even done anything to it, and I was still wearing my gloves."

Certainty circled the wooden box warily. It didn't move.

"Does it have a label on it? A number?"

Aurelia shook her head. Her broom, still leveled at the box, didn't waver.

Certainty couldn't see any label, either, which meant it must be one of the unidentified artifacts. There was only one way for her to assess the box's powers. She steeled herself.

"All right. I'm going to touch it and ask it what its enchantment is. If anything bad happens, knock it away from me quickly."

Aurelia hesitated, but must not have been able to think of any better solution. She nodded and used her free hand to cast a second defense spell on Certainty as well.

"Be careful."

Certainty swallowed and lowered herself to her knees beside the box. Gingerly, she laid one palm against the smooth wooden surface.

Nothing happened.

Bracing herself, she channeled just the tiniest bit of magic into the box. It was like tapping gently at the door of its soul, if objects had souls—she wasn't entirely clear on the theology of it all.

"BOX." Its response was a hollow echo in her mind.

"What is your purpose, Box?"

"BOX. CONTAIN."

Certainty frowned. Its object-voice was dull and wooden, with none of the awareness that an enchanted artifact should have.

"What do you contain, Box?"

"CONTENTS."

"I'm not sure it's magical," she said to Aurelia doubtfully.

Then a sound came from inside the box itself, perfectly audible to both of them.

The box said: *"Meow."*

Certainty blinked down at it.

"Is . . ." The tip of Aurelia's broom-sword lowered. "Certainty, is there a *cat* in that box?"

"I don't know. How do we open it?" Certainty ran her fingers over the edges of the wooden box, but couldn't find any hinges.

The defense spells vaporized with a faint sizzle. Aurelia flung her broom aside, stalked back into the carriage house, then reemerged with a crowbar and an air of grim determination.

"Move aside," she ordered.

Certainty scrambled out of the way. "Don't hurt it!"

"I'm not going to. I'm going to let it out!"

Levering the crowbar beneath one side of the box, Aurelia placed a foot on the opposite side and shoved down hard. With a loud creak, the wooden slats popped off. Aurelia nudged them off with the crowbar, and the two women leaned over the box to look.

"Meow."

A cat, black with white-stockinged paws, looked up at them placidly. It seemed entirely unconcerned that it had just been freed from a sealed wooden box.

"Now how did you get in here?" Aurelia dropped the crowbar and reached into the box to lift the cat up gently. It tolerated this, hanging limp in her grip as she examined it this way and that. "You look like a perfectly ordinary cat to me. Certainty, there wasn't anything in Mortimer's notes about an artifact enchanted to look like a cat, was there?"

"Definitely not." She'd have remembered, if so. "But if it's really just a cat ... how did it get in there?" It looked perfectly healthy and far too well-fed for a cat that had theoretically been trapped in a box for at least a week.

"Yes," said Aurelia, frowning. The cat was now curled comfortably in her arms. It seemed to be purring. "The box was tightly sealed; you saw how much force I had to use to open it. And there's nothing else in there—no food, no water. You're sure the box itself isn't a magical artifact?"

Certainty shook her head. "I'm sure. No enchantment in it that I could detect. It's just an empty box ... or rather, a box with a cat in it, I guess. Maybe Fanya and Mage Mortimer loaded it onto the wagon by mistake?"

"But then ... how did the cat ..."

Aurelia's eyes unfocused, and she seemed to go somewhere far away. Then her eyes widened.

"Oh my ... Mother and Sons and the Silent Daughter, I think I've read about this. I wrote a *paper* about this—" The mage gesticulated with one arm, the other still clutching the cat against her chest. Blond strands fell loose from her braid, which she ignored. "It must be the feline paradox of magical superpositionality!"

"The feline ..." Certainty didn't even bother trying to repeat it. "What?"

Aurelia flapped a hand at her impatiently, practically hopping with excitement.

"Mage Deswagones postulated in his 'Treatise on Experimental Magic' that cats have access to a unique magical plane, superimposed upon our own earthly plane at specific points. He theorized that that's how cats travel seemingly impossible distances, at times appearing to teleport from one place to another. He spent most of his life studying cats, living among them, trying to classify those points of paradox and prove his theory—"

"—so one could say he *cat*-aloged them?" Certainty grinned. She was proud of that one. But Aurelia didn't even seem to hear, or perhaps merely chose not to dignify that with a response.

"—yet he never succeeded. But what if you combined the feline paradox with Scholar Olde's theory of unobserved manifestation? Oh, that would make so much sense—such an elegant solution—"

Aurelia dropped the cat (which landed on its feet, of course, albeit with an irritated hiss) and grabbed Certainty's shoulders. Her eyes were only a little mad.

"Certainty, everyone knows that if you have an open container and a cat, the cat will soon occupy the container. But if you have a *closed* container..."

Certainty was thoroughly distracted by Aurelia's sudden nearness, but still tried her best to follow along. "Then... the container may or may not... contain a cat?"

"Yes!" Aurelia made a small, excited hopping motion, still holding on to Certainty. "Oh, we must conduct further research. In the name of magical knowledge!"

"Um..." Certainty had never noticed before just how vivid a shade of green the mage's eyes were. "Sure?"

Then she shook herself mentally. "Wait, research. That requires experiments."

"Yes—"

"The same sort of experiments you said I shouldn't be conducting?"

Aurelia only then seemed to realize that she was still holding onto Certainty; she dropped her arms to her sides and cleared her throat awkwardly. Certainty tried not to pay attention to the sudden lack of warmth where Aurelia's hands had been.

"Well, you said this box isn't magical," Aurelia said, sounding uncertain. "So it wouldn't really be misuse of an artifact..."

"I *think* it's not magical, but I really couldn't say for sure." Cert blinked big, innocent eyes up at Aurelia. "It was on the wagon with the others, after all. Maybe I'm wrong."

Aurelia hesitated, then narrowed her eyes. "Are you attempting to manipulate me?"

"Maybe. Is it working?"

The mage looked at the box longingly, then back at Certainty. "... a little."

Certainty grinned at her, and Aurelia capitulated.

"Fine. I suppose it's only fair that we can both carry out some minor experiments, then. But *carefully*. Nothing risky. Nothing that might bring any unwanted attention or, Mother forbid, give that insufferable secretary a reason to complain to the Guild. Agreed?"

"Yes, Mage!" Certainty snapped off a sloppy salute, still grinning. "Only very safe and boring magical artifact experimentation, Mage!"

Aurelia rolled her eyes, but as the mage turned away, Certainty could have sworn she saw the barest hint of a smile.

THE CAT HAD made its escape from the stable during their conversation, but Certainty wasn't too worried. In her experience, cats were perfectly capable of managing on their own, and really only kept humans around for the sake of their egos.

Aurelia set the empty wooden box just outside the entry of the stable, very carefully replacing its wooden lid. Certainty watched in bemusement as the mage proceeded to do some odd things—squinting into the sky, measuring the box's dimensions with a string, even sniffing it—before recording her notes on a parchment.

There was something endearing about Aurelia's sudden scholarly enthusiasm. It was almost as if an entirely different person had been lurking underneath that mask of polished competence. Certainty wished she would let this side of herself out more; it certainly made for better company. What exactly was she hiding it from?

She said none of this, of course, and only smiled at Aurelia when the mage finally finished doing whatever it was she was doing.

"All set?"

"Yes! We'll just need to check it every twelve hours for a fresh cat, to start, and it's possible that the witching hour will be when it's most susceptible to superpositionality—" The mage cut herself off, biting her lip. "Never mind. It's just a theory, of course. But don't worry, I'll handle monitoring everything. It's my experiment, after all, and I wouldn't want it to distract you."

"Oh, I wouldn't worry about that."

Aurelia gave an embarrassed cough. "I suppose my interest in it must seem very dull to you."

"Not at all. I think it's..." Adorable? But Certainty didn't want to sound patronizing, not to mention inappropriate. "... very commendable. I'm sure the High Mage would approve of such intellectual curiosity." *Nice, Cert. That doesn't sound forced at all.*

But Aurelia blinked at her in surprise, a rather attractive pink dusting her cheeks, and Certainty thought she might have said the right thing after all.

"Oh. Thank you."

"You're welcome."

Awkwardness fell between them, but it was the pleasant sort

of awkwardness where both parties are trying to think of something nice to say to the other, but hesitating for fear of being *too* nice, which would of course amplify the awkwardness. An impossible impasse. Out of sheer desperation, Certainty was just about to ask Aurelia to explain what "superpositionality" meant when Orrin arrived.

"Hi," the boy said, panting slightly. He'd clearly jogged up the hill and was wearing a knapsack with what looked like tools sticking out from it.

"Hello, Orrin."

"Hi," he said again. He was standing just outside the line of salt, looking down at it with a nervous sort of fascination. "Gosh. This is a magical ward, isn't it?"

"Yes," said Aurelia. "But don't worry; it won't hurt anyone who's not trying to break in and do something bad. You can tell the other villagers that, too. But, er . . . may we help you with something?"

He immediately turned the shade of a ripe cherry tomato.

"Right, yes! I mean, no—I thought I could—I was wondering if you needed . . . maybe . . ."

Certainty took pity on him. "Are you perhaps here to offer *us* your help?"

"Yes," he said, seizing upon this gratefully. "With the repairs and all." He gestured vaguely toward the stable, being very careful not to cross the warding circle. "Since you've been trying to fix up the place by yourselves. It's probably a lot of work, and I'm handy with tools. I helped my uncle fix up our family's barn last fall."

"Well . . ." Aurelia looked at Certainty. Perhaps she was reluctant to involve any of Shpelling's residents in anything magical? But Certainty shrugged back at her. There couldn't be *that* much risk in it, particularly if she and Aurelia were there to supervise the boy. And another set of hands (especially hands that knew their way around a saw) would be useful.

Aurelia hesitated for a moment longer, then nodded. "Thank you, Orrin. We'd appreciate it."

"Really? I mean, great!" He looked delighted.

"We can pay you ten silverpennies a day," said Aurelia.

"Oh, um. I couldn't take your coin, miss, and I can't work full days." Orrin rubbed at his neck awkwardly. "I'll still be needed back on the farm. I just meant to do a favor or two, like."

"Thank you, Orrin," said Certainty, cutting in firmly. "That's very kind of you, and we'll take as much of your help as you're willing to spare—but how about instead of coin, we make you a nice cup of tea, and whenever we can do you or your family a favor, you be sure to call on us?"

The boy looked relieved. "Yes, miss! Cup of tea sounds nice, thanks."

Certainty grinned and gestured him into the stable, but he looked down again at the line of salt.

"Do I just step over it? Do I have to say anything, or . . . ?"

"Just walk over it. You'll be completely fine," Certainty reassured him.

"Unless you're trying to steal any Guild artifacts," Aurelia said.

He shook his head fervently and, looking like he was holding his breath, stepped across the line. Nothing happened, and he gusted out a sigh of relief.

"See? Nothing at all to be worried about," said Aurelia. "But one more thing—please make *very sure* not to touch any of the items inside without gloves on, Orrin. Or terrible things will happen, and you'll put everyone in the village and possibly the entire kingdom at risk."

Orrin went pale, and Certainty glared at Aurelia. *Really?*

"Bad things," the mage amended. "Moderately bad things might happen."

Certainty gave the boy her most reassuring smile and tossed him a spare pair of gloves. "You'll be fine."

"Um, all right." He tugged on the gloves uncertainly, but looked like he might be starting to regret his offer. Still, with an encouraging nod from Certainty, he hefted his bag of tools and followed them in.

Once inside, Orrin boggled at the shelves in the stalls, the piled boxes, and the labeled and unlabeled artifacts laid out in neat rows in the straw.

"What are all of these things?"

"Guild business," said Aurelia primly.

Certainty rolled her eyes at the mage. The boy wasn't an enemy spy, and what they were doing here was hardly a secret. "They're magical artifacts, Orrin."

"Oh." The boy eyed the nearest pile. "That looks like a pair of dirty knickers over there."

"*Magical* dirty knickers."

"What do they do?"

"Well . . ." The knickers didn't have a label on them yet. "We don't actually know. But that's what we're doing here, you see? Mage Aurelia and I are taking inventory of all of these artifacts. We're checking what their enchantments are and entering them into the Guild's records so that the artifacts can be safely stored here and retrieved should anyone ever, er, need to use them."

Orrin nodded, but his expression suggested a great deal of doubt that anyone would ever want to use a pair of stained undergarments that may or may not be enchanted to do something mysterious. He pointed at a small pewter statue of a chicken sitting on a shelf. "What's that one do?"

"Makes your enemy's food always taste of eggs."

"What about that one?" He pointed at a chipped teapot with a floral pattern.

"Conversational teapot. Makes perfectly brewed tea every time, but will talk your ear off as it does."

Certainty had taken special note of that one; she had very high standards for tea and thought that they might be able to make use of it while they were here.

"Oh." Orrin sounded distinctly unimpressed. But then he saw the rusty sword lying across the work table and his face lit up. "Wow! Is that a magic sword?"

"Well, yes," Certainty said. She'd just finished identifying it earlier. "Sort of."

"Neat!"

"What's its enchantment?" Aurelia asked, curious. "I'd have thought that any magic swords would be classified as second-degree artifacts, at least."

"Not this one." Certainty walked over to it, pulling off one glove and picking up the weapon by its worn leather hilt. "It's meant to be a flaming sword, but the enchantment's almost completely worn off, so . . ." She gave it a quick slash through the air and felt its magic kindle.

Ffft. A tiny, cheeky spurt of flame flicked out from the sword tip. It was rather like seeing a giant blow a bubble.

"That's it?" asked Orrin, clearly disappointed.

"Ah," said Aurelia. "I see."

"It could still be useful," Certainty said, feeling oddly defensive of the sword. It was doing its best! "I thought maybe we could use it to light the stove, instead of your having to cast a fire spell every morning."

Aurelia thought about it for a moment, then nodded. "I suppose there's no harm in that, if we're careful."

Orrin cleared his throat, his interest in the scattered artifacts clearly diminished by Certainty's demonstration.

"So if you two are busy with all of these . . . things . . . then how can I help?"

Aurelia and Certainty looked at each other.

"The leaking roof?" suggested Certainty.

"The drafty windows?"

"The door sticks sometimes when it's damp—"

"—and some furniture, maybe; it'd be nice to sleep on proper beds."

"Right," Orrin said hastily. "Maybe I'll start with that."

Certainty looked at him with surprise. "Do you know how to build beds?"

He shrugged. "Can't be that hard. They're just long tables that you lie on, aren't they?" And with that, he hefted his tools and entered the carriage house, whistling as he went.

The two women looked at each other.

"I told you they don't hate us," Certainty said smugly, and went to put the chatty teapot and flaming sword by the stove.

IT TURNED OUT that Orrin might have had an ulterior motive for volunteering his help. As he hammered and sawed, he peppered the two of them with questions—about the Guild, about what it was like to live in Margrave, about whether they'd ever met the Queen . . .

There was a wistfulness and a hunger beneath his questions that Certainty recognized. She knew what it was to grow up somewhere small and unimportant—even if it was a place you loved—and to wonder whether if only you lived somewhere *grand* instead, your life would broaden and stretch to fit its new boundaries.

But her own life had disproved that theory, hadn't it? She thought of the comfortable repetition of her chores-lessons-gossip days at the Guildtower. Hardly the stuff of legend. No, it was more like familiarity and routine shrank your surroundings, no matter how glorious they were, to fit snugly around the contours of what you already knew.

Then again, maybe it was different for other people. Maybe princesses and adventurers and beautiful, wealthy mages like Aurelia got to live lives of glamour and excitement, and it was only Certainty—plain, useless, perpetual novice Certainty—who could not escape the gravity of her own ordinariness.

"Is it true that the roads of the High City are paved in silver and gold?"

Orrin was perched on a beam as he hammered a plank into place. Having constructed two beds (slightly wobbly, but sound enough that Certainty wasn't worried about hers collapsing in the middle of the night), he was now working on the roof.

"Not quite . . ." Aurelia sounded distracted. She was busy ordering all the labeled items. They were saving the unidentified artifacts for last, judging that those would require more time and greater caution. "They're made of whitestone, but if it's any consolation, I believe some of the lords' estates in the High City have silver on their gates."

The boy sighed dreamily. "I'd give anything to go there someday."

"Why don't you?" asked Certainty. "It's not so far from here. Just a handful of days' travel by horse."

"My parents don't want me to. They think I won't come back if I do, and they want me to stay here in Shpelling and take over the farm."

"Ah. Well, farming's a fine occupation. There's plenty of lads who would count themselves lucky to inherit a farm."

"I guess," Orrin said. He jumped to the ground from halfway down the ladder; Certainty's knees twinged in sympathy. "It's just . . . that's *all* that's here for me, see? I dunno if I want to be a garlic farmer for the rest of my days. What girl wants to walk around on the arm of a garlic farmer?"

"Your father's a garlic farmer, isn't he? And he's clearly managed to find himself a wife."

Orrin looked aghast. "Yes, but she's my *mum*! That hardly counts."

Certainty swallowed a laugh. He sighed again, full of youthful frustration.

"Girls aside, Shpelling is just a nowhere village full of nobodies. Even the folk over in Ruggan laugh at us." He kicked at the straw on the stable floor. "Think they're better than us, just because they've got a big fancy inn, and a new water mill, and their own resident bard . . . they always hold their Fair the week after ours, you know, just so they can show off how much better they are."

"They sound obnoxious," Aurelia said.

"Rude," Certainty agreed.

The boy looked somewhat mollified. "We ought to tell them we've got two Guild mages now, see how they like it. They don't even have *one*."

Aurelia cleared her throat. "Well, Novice Certainty and I are only staying here temporarily, Orrin. Until we've completed our inventory."

"Oh. Right." He deflated again. "Well . . . you'll be here for the Fair, at least? It's in a few weeks."

"Sure," Certainty said. It'd take them at least that long to get through all of the artifacts; she couldn't speak with more than a few dozen or so each day before the headaches became intolerable.

Orrin nodded morosely. "Maybe ours will be even better than Ruggan's this year. Maybe things will finally start looking up for Shpelling soon."

But he didn't really sound like he believed it.

INTERLUDE

DUSK.

A cat prowled silently outside the stable-turned-warehouse, yellow eyes unblinking as it hunted. It had already caught three mice that night, but one or two more would make for a nice nightcap.

It had come to this strange land through a small, dark place that smelled of long-dead trees. It had come because those two humans had called out with their magic and unbarred the Way. But the air, when the cat emerged, had tasted odd. Flat and stale, as if it had been stagnant for a long time.

Still, there didn't seem to be anything wrong with it now. And besides, it was swarming with mice.

A fine place, the cat thought.

It paused with one paw raised, sniffing curiously at the line of salt before it. Then, delicately, the paw dipped over the line. There was a brief moment of resistance where the magical wards wavered, uncertain whether or not the moral indifference endemic to all cats counted as "ill intent"—but then the cat passed through unharmed and padded into the stable.

It leapt gracefully onto a wooden shelf. Half-unpacked crates and their contents were arranged there in an attempt at order. The cat's nose twitched in disinterest. None of these objects smelled edible.

For no particular reason aside from the fact that it could, the cat batted the closest item off the shelf, and a small silver triangle fell to the ground with a tinkle.

Next went a pair of spectacles. As its paw touched them, for a fleeting second, the cat saw the world in vivid shades of pink. How interesting. It licked its paw and continued exploring.

Behind the spectacles lay a very odd feather. Its barbs looked soft but gleamed black like obsidian, and the tip of its quill was curved into the shape of a long claw. Tied to this strange feather was a small strip of paper. If the cat could read, it would have seen that on the paper was written:

> No. 61. Spell of draconic flight. One-time use: consumable upon contact with magic. Intended to permanently transform user into a fearsome winged being, but enchantment is underpowered. Do not use.

But it could not read, on account of being a cat. And even if it could, it would likely have done exactly what it proceeded to do next anyway.

The cat sniffed at the clawed feather.

The small pink triangle of its nose made contact.

Pop.

The feather vanished—and, with mild surprise, the cat unfurled its new wings.

They were a deep black, scaled and leathery, with an almost imperceptible sheen—and perfectly sized for a cat. The cat gave its new wings an experimental flap, sending itself briefly aloft before landing back on the wooden shelf in a puff of sawdust.

It blinked slowly, pleased, and settled its new wings comfortably against its sides.

This village was a fine place indeed, the cat decided. Perhaps it would stay awhile.

And with a graceful extension of its wings, it glided noiselessly down, out the door and back over the line of salt, then launched itself into the night sky to begin an unprecedented campaign of terror against the local rodents.

TEN

AURELIA LOOKED DISAPPOINTED when she lifted the lid on her experimental cat box the next morning.

Two tree stumps away, an inquisitive squirrel stood on its hind legs to chitter at them; Certainty immediately tore off a piece of bread and tossed it over as a peace offering. She'd learned from her encounter with the rooster.

"No new cat?"

"Nothing yet." The mage sighed, but resettled her shoulders with a determined air. "We must be patient. Mage Purnell waited eight years to prove his theory on the magical viscosity of dragonsap, after all."

"I don't think we have eight years here, Aurelia."

"I certainly hope not." The mage prodded gently at the box and made a few more notes on her parchment. "Well. On with our work, then."

SEVERAL AFTERNOONS AND many dozens of identified artifacts later, another of the villagers made an appearance at the stable. A voice from outside interrupted Certainty just as she was crossing out an incorrect entry in the artifact records. Aurelia was seated across from her, taking a "break" by burying her nose in a thick book of advanced magical theory that she had brought along for some light reading. They went to see who their visitor was and found a stocky, middle-aged man wearing an exceptionally thick and fluffy white jacket standing just beyond the warding line.

"'scuse me," he said, his voice gruff. "Are you two the Guild mages?"

"I'm just a novice," Certainty corrected automatically. "But yes. You're welcome to cross the warding circle, by the way; it's just there to protect us from anyone with bad intentions. Thieves, spies, and the like."

The man eyed it with some wariness. "Huh. Wouldn't expect many thieves or spies in Shpelling." But he still stepped over it gingerly. Then he shrugged off his jacket, which turned out to be two massive, shaggy rugs.

"Brought you this. Gertha said you'd been sleeping in this old carriage house, and, well, I imagine it's a bit drafty at night. Sorry we don't have an inn anymore. Thought this might make it a little bit more comfortable for you. Cozy, like."

"Oh!" Aurelia removed her gloves and took the rugs from him, rubbing the thick wool between her fingers. "Thank you very much, Master . . . ?" Certainty was relieved when the mage didn't reach for her coin purse or say anything about paying him; maybe she was learning.

"Murph," he said, ducking his head awkwardly. "Just Murph, miss. I'm Orrin's uncle. Sorry if he's been bothering you two."

"Not at all," said Certainty. "He's been a big help to us. And thank you for loaning us these! My feet are always freezing in the mornings." (It was true; she'd spent half an hour yesterday paging through the record book in search of anything that might be useful for heating the floor stones. The closest thing she'd found was a doormat enchanted to burst into green flames when stepped upon; she'd decided not to try it.)

He nodded, waving away their thanks, but didn't make any move to leave. He just shoved his hands into his pockets and shuffled his feet a little in the straw.

"Can we offer you some tea, or—?"

"Gertha also told me you helped Hull with his apple grove," Murph said abruptly. "Summoned some bees with a magical thingummy, she said. They think they'll get the trees to fruit this year."

Of course. Certainty should have guessed that the news would have spread.

"And I thought . . ." He scratched at his beard. "I wondered if you might have something to help my wife Brienna with her bakery."

"What sort of help?"

"The rats, miss. Eating all her stores, they are, no matter what we do. Do you have any . . ." He waved his hands about, mimicking a spell being cast and looking deeply uncomfortable about it. "You know, a spell? To magick them away?"

Certainty and Aurelia looked at each other, and then at the experimental cat box just outside the doorway.

"Not as such . . ." said Aurelia slowly. "But we'll see what we can do."

THEY DIDN'T HAVE to wait very long. The next day, Certainty was just lifting her hands from an overly chatty enchanted pillow (*No. 132, pillow imbued with a frost spell: cooling effect activated by flipping it over*) when she heard a small noise from the doorway.

"Meow."

Certainty froze. "Aurelia?"

"Yes?"

The mage poked her head out from the carriage house where she'd been making a pot of tea—with the assistance of both the enchanted teapot and the barely flaming sword, much to Certainty's gratification. She could hear the faint burble of the teapot from behind Aurelia, its prattling voice resembling that of a gossipy and slightly judgmental aunt.

"—*do mind you wear your cloak today, dearie; my spout feels a bit of a drizzle coming on. Might be a good time to curl up with a nice book, hmm? And me, of course, though it's always a good time for tea, I say—*"

It was fairly clear to both of them why the teapot had been relegated to this remote storage site instead of being requisitioned by a senior mage for their personal office. And yet . . . it *did* make excellent tea, so allowances must be made. (Thankfully, it fell silent whenever it was not in use, so one only had to put up with its one-sided conversation while waiting for a pot to brew.) Certainty did her best to ignore the teapot's chattering and jerked her head toward the stable entrance.

"I think you should check on your experiment."

"Oh!"

Aurelia dashed out ("*—why, excuse me! How rude to leave in the middle of a conversation—*"), Certainty joining her, and the two women hovered over the wooden box just outside the doors. Carefully and with great anticipation, Aurelia lifted the lid.

"Meow."

A brown tabby looked up at them.

"Yes!" Aurelia did a little jig of excitement. "It worked!"

The tabby hopped nimbly out of the box. It looked around

at its surroundings with interest, sniffed once, and then sauntered off in the vague direction of the village bakery. Aurelia returned the lid to the box and made furious notes in her parchment.

"You're trying again?"

"Of course! One trial is insufficient to prove the repeatability of the phenomenon. Besides, the more cats we attract, the faster Brienna's rat problem will be solved."

Certainty grinned. "Excellent. Soon we'll have a whole clowder running around the village."

Aurelia wrinkled her nose. "A what?"

"A clowder! Have you never heard of a clowder of cats before? It means a lot of them."

"Oh. What a ridiculous word. I love it." Then Aurelia's smile faded. "Certainty . . . we're not being irresponsible, are we? Using artifacts to make tea, and conducting magical experiments to attract cats?"

She seemed so worried and crestfallen that Certainty rushed to reassure her.

"No, of course not! It's not hurting anybody, nor is it getting in the way of our work. And besides, it's all in the name of research and scholarship, isn't it? You're proving your . . . unobserved . . . superparadox . . . thingy." And the tea was simply necessary; what sort of mage didn't drink at least two cups a day?

Aurelia nodded hesitantly, then with growing enthusiasm. "Yes . . . you're right. The artifacts are still safe with us, and the advancement of magical knowledge is paramount . . . surely the Guild couldn't disapprove. And we're not causing either the local residents *or* the cats themselves any harm—in fact, the learnings we'll obtain may be of great benefit to all!"

Everyone except the local rodents, perhaps. But Certainty

didn't feel the need to point that out, not when Aurelia was finally seeming to unbend a little.

"That's the spirit," she said cheerfully.

THE NEXT SEVERAL days sauntered lazily past, the early spring weather began to warm, and Certainty began to enjoy herself in their new routine. The work was going smoothly, and they made steady progress through the boxes of artifacts on the stable floor. Aurelia's shelves continued to fill up with ordered and labeled items, the book of records accumulated many new pages of entries, and Certainty only shrieked just the once when a mouse ran over her foot. Progress.

The carriage house was also far cozier than it had been when they'd first arrived, thanks to the addition of the thick wool rugs and Orrin's raised beds stuffed with straw. The occasional mindless nattering of the conversational teapot was easy enough to ignore, and the place even smelled nice now, too, thanks to Aurelia's freshening spells and Certainty's own discovery of a healthy patch of lemon balm halfway up the hill to the well. They kept a jar of it growing on the windowsill, where the leafy cuttings gave off a gentle and citrusy fragrance, and occasionally Aurelia added a few leaves of it to their tea. Certainty was of a mind to add jars of thyme and rosemary, too, and make it a proper little herb garden.

And in an even more welcome change, it seemed that the residents of Shpelling had finally thawed to their presence. Instead of glares or wary glances, she and Aurelia now received polite nods and good-days when they walked by, and communal meals at the tavern were no longer uncomfortable affairs (although Certainty *did* long for a little more variety of produce;

there was only so much pickled garlic a girl could eat). Aurelia's experimental box had even produced two more cats, and these roving guests stopped by the stable from time to time to rub up against their legs and collect a scratch or two.

And yet, even as Certainty relaxed, Aurelia seemed to be growing more tense and distracted. Certainty wasn't sure why until the mage finally said something at lunch one day.

"We're due to send our report to the High Mage, and Ferdinand said the mail courier will be here in the morning to take our message. Is there anything you'd like me to say about our progress?"

Right. The report to the High Mage. Certainty had nearly forgotten about that.

"Well, I'm about halfway through the inventory," she said, mentally running through the pages of artifact records. "I've gone through and confirmed all of Mortimer's existing notes, and I've just started on the unidentified artifacts. Those are taking longer, of course."

"Good. Hopefully we'll be able to stay on schedule." Aurelia's fingers tapped a nervous pattern against her thigh.

"I'm sure the High Mage will be satisfied with what we've managed so far," reasoned Certainty. "She can't possibly expect us to have finished yet, and she wouldn't have known we'd have to spend so much time repairing the buildings ourselves, either."

Aurelia pressed her lips together. "I've learned to assume that people will always expect more of you than you think," she said quietly.

Certainty frowned. She still didn't understand why Aurelia was so hard on herself. She was already a mage and a farspeaker; what more did she have to prove?

Speaking of which . . .

"Wait—why are we sending our report back to the Guild by messenger? Can't you just farspeak with the High Mage and tell her directly?"

Aurelia looked away. "No. That's . . . not an option, at the moment."

"Why not?"

"That's irrelevant," said Aurelia abruptly. Certainty narrowed her eyes, and would have pushed for further explanation if not for the tavern doors swinging open and Master Tobias walking in.

They watched as the secretary spoke a few words to Ferdinand. Then he turned, and his glance swung over to them. Certainty thought she saw his expression darken for just a second before smoothing back into the supercilious smirk that seemed to be its default resting state. He strode over to their table, well-shined boots clicking against the wooden floor.

"Mage Aurelia, and Novice . . . Surety, was it?"

"It's Certainty."

"Indeed." His mouth curved upward. "I confess I'm surprised to still find you both here. I would have thought Guild mages such as yourselves would have been eager to return to the pleasures of Margrave. Are you lodging in the old stable after all, then? I suppose the cart horses used to find it comfortable enough . . ."

"We've converted the carriage house into adequate accommodations, yes," said Aurelia. She matched his tone with her own, inflecting each word with the sort of genteel disdain that all Margravian nobles seemed to master by age ten. "And as we made clear upon our arrival, we've no intention of leaving until our work is complete."

"I see. And how goes that 'work'?" Tobias looked pointedly around the tavern, where a handful of old men had already gotten a head start on that night's drinking. "I've heard there have been a few interesting occurrences in Shpelling since you've settled in. I wouldn't have expected the Guild to take such an interest in Farmer Hull's apple trees, for example."

"Fortunately, it's not really your concern what the Guild takes an interest in, is it?" Certainty smiled sweetly at him. It really was a pity that Guild mages were forbidden from casting offensive spells on other Eshterans, other than in self-defense. Not that she'd be able to cast them anyway.

He gave her his own tight smile. "Not unless that interest causes any harm to my lord's lands or their inhabitants. I hope you've ensured that your artifacts are all well-secured."

"Of course we have. We've warded both buildings." Aurelia's tone was cool and dismissive.

"Ah, yes. It's just that magic can be so *unpredictable* sometimes, don't you think?"

"Perhaps it only seems so to those who don't understand it." Aurelia drank the rest of the water in her cup, then stood up. Certainty did the same, marveling at the mage's poise and trying for the same nonchalance. "Your concern, Master Tobias, is noted. Should you hear of any such harm being done, you know where to find us. In the meantime, we wish you the best of luck with your secretarial duties. I hope your, hm, *tax records* are well-secured."

Tobias looked like he'd swallowed a mouthful of mud. But before the secretary could say anything more, Aurelia strode out of the tavern and Certainty followed, leaving Tobias to glare at their backs with an animosity that she still couldn't comprehend.

AURELIA'S REPORT WENT out as scheduled the following morning, and the High Mage's reply came less than a week later via a Guild messenger. With it came a pleasant surprise: two letters for Certainty—one from Potshire, and the other from Dav and Saralie.

"Some mail for both of you," said the messenger cheerfully as he handed the letters over. The sight of Saralie's looping cursive and her da's scratchy handwriting made Certainty smile. "And if you've any responses, you can just send them along to the outpost in Ruggan; someone there will see to it." His duties thus discharged, he gave them a nod and a tip of his cap as he headed back out onto the road—bound for a proper inn, no doubt.

When they returned to the carriage house, Certainty plopped herself onto her bed to read her mail. First, she read the letter from her friends; it was filled with enthusiastic gossip and cheerful teasing about her missing out on such exciting Guild-tower happenings as a group of novices being caught pillaging the wine cellars. There hadn't been any further thaumic spillage incidents, thankfully—it seemed that removing the excess artifacts from the kitchen pantry had indeed solved that particular problem.

Then she turned her attention to her father's letter.

My dearest Cert,

We were all so excited to read your last letter! Being sent out on an official Guild assignment—that's big, that is. I'm not sure where this Shpelling is, but the messenger assured me this letter would get to you in good time.

In any case, you've no need to fret about us (though I know you always do)—we're all doing just fine at home. Ma's leg keeps bothering her when it rains, but besides that, we're all in good health, Mother and Maker Son be praised. The pear trees are starting to bloom nicely, too. Oh, and Asp—I don't know what that boy has been eating, but he's had a strong growing season of his own! Almost as tall as me now, and very nearly as good-looking. He'll have to beat the lasses off with a stick soon.

There is some other news, I suppose. Master Jamison—the apothecary over in Leffin, you remember?—told us that he'll be traveling out east before midsummer. If Asp is to join him on the road, then we'll need to pay his apprenticeship fee by summer's start. Apothecary materials have gotten more expensive, he says, and an apprentice goes through a lot of them while learning, so... Jamison says he can loan us some, but even so, we're short by a good bit. This is the last year before Asp's too old to apprentice, so we're seeing what we can sell to make the difference, but—

Well. Never mind all that. Asp may just have to set his sights on a different path, that's all. But don't worry yourself about it, Cert. He's been a great help to us on the farm, so it's not all bad.

Good luck with the assignment! Write us again soon, won't you?

Sending you all of our love,
Da

Certainty stared down at the parchment, blinking away the sudden blurriness in her eyes. She could almost hear her da's voice. Practically felt his arms around her, and his beard against her cheek ... Mother and Sons, she missed him. She missed them all. How different might her life be at this moment if she'd never left Potshire? Would she be happily married and living in her own cottage somewhere just down the road? And Asp ...

There was a heaviness deep down in her stomach, like she'd swallowed a seed and it'd grown into a rock. If not for her joining the Guild, Asp would never have truly hoped to become an apothecary in the first place, because she wouldn't have promised him that future. Perhaps that would have been the kinder thing.

But ... *by summer's start*. There was still hope, however faint. If she and Aurelia could finish the inventory on schedule, and if the High Mage awarded her a mage's circles and stipend immediately afterward ...

She heard a slow exhale from Aurelia, who sat across from her on her own bed. The mage was looking down at the paper in her hands.

"Well? What did the High Mage say?"

"That our progress is satisfactory."

"... that's it? Let me see it—"

"Yes, that's it. The message was addressed to me, Certainty." Her voice was curt.

"If that's all it says, why do you look like she personally insulted your grandmother?"

Aurelia sighed and folded the scroll into a small, tight wad, which she squeezed between her fingers. "The High Mage also referenced other topics besides our assignment."

"What sort of topics?"

"That's none of your concern, Novice."

"Oh. Fine. My apologies, *Mage* Aurelia."

Certainty couldn't help but feel stung. Yes, Aurelia outranked her, but their distance from the Guildtower had blurred the lines of hierarchy over the last few weeks. Or at least, she'd thought it had. There didn't seem much point to observing rank when, mage or novice, they both spent a good portion of their days occupied with tasks as grand as sweeping out a stable and fetching water from a well. Besides, it seemed to Certainty that Aurelia's presence was practically a formality. Certainty was the one with the ability to speak with and identify the artifacts. Aurelia was just there to cast some spells and be officious, wasn't she?

"I didn't mean—" Aurelia blew out a heavy, frustrated breath and tossed the folded letter aside. "Look, I'm sorry, Certainty. In the report I sent, I'd also asked her if she had any other assignments in mind for me, once we've finished here. And we discussed my . . . my farspeaking studies."

"Oh." Certainty looked down into her cup. Of course Aurelia's preoccupation would be with her own career and getting something more useful to do than babysitting a novice and some junk artifacts. "What'd she say?"

"She said no. Not yet. She said we could discuss it once we return to the Guildtower."

A moment of silence stretched between them.

"I'm sorry," Certainty said eventually. She spoke quietly, but her voice still sounded too loud and forced in the dimness of the carriage house. "I know you don't want to be here. I know this isn't the assignment you would have picked."

"No, it's not." Aurelia looked away, and Certainty saw her throat move when she swallowed. She picked at a fraying thread on her sleeve, winding it tight enough that Certainty saw her fingertip whiten underneath. "But it's not your fault. It's mine."

You know very well why, the High Mage had said to Aurelia in her office.

Certainty burned to know the truth. Why hadn't Aurelia—brilliant, overachieving Aurelia—been given a more important assignment? Why had one of the fastest full-fledged mages in a generation and a valuable farspeaker, no less, been held back behind Guildtower walls for so long?

Certainty hadn't dared to ask before, but Aurelia looked softer and more vulnerable, somehow, sitting there on her wobbly bed of straw. More open. It almost seemed like she wanted to be asked.

"Aurelia, can I ask..." Certainty hesitated, then plunged on. "Why were you sent here with me? Even though you're a farspeaker?"

Aurelia looked at her for a long moment then. Finally, she spoke.

"I *was* a farspeaker." Her lips twisted, as if she were dragging up the words from somewhere painful. "But my farspeaking... Certainty, it doesn't work anymore."

Certainty leaned back, stunned. "What do you mean?"

Aurelia unclasped her necklace and held it between her fingers. She stared at it, letting the little silver book slip and dangle between her hands. Her green eyes shone a little too much in the reflected firelight.

"There was an incident." Aurelia kept her eyes on the necklace as she spoke. "Very shortly after I passed my mage trials, I made a... a mistake. A bad one. I was farspeaking to another mage—trying a new technique, one where I could send images to my recipient, and not only words—but... but he hadn't had enough training to safely receive them. And I pushed too hard."

Aurelia looked back up at her. Her lips worked tightly as if she were fighting for control, and her eyes glittered like brittle crystal.

"I burned him out, Certainty. He lost his magic, all of it. He's a blacksmith now."

The fire in the stove flickered and dimmed as the wood burned down. Embers pulsed orange, then faded, and in the stillness of the carriage house, Certainty felt suddenly cold.

She remembered what Fanya had said in the Guild stables: *Be careful with that one.*

"I didn't do it on purpose," Aurelia said. There was a quiet urgency in her voice, as if she desperately needed Certainty to believe her. "I swear, Certainty, I didn't mean to do it. But I understand why people might think that—I never hid my ambition, he was an academic rival, and I even wondered myself, afterward, whether part of me really *had* meant to do it. And maybe that's why my farspeaking stopped working; I don't know—"

Aurelia took a slow, shuddering breath. She was gripping the necklace tightly; her knuckles made pale, sharp angles around it.

"There was an inquiry. The High Mage believed my innocence. It was kept quiet so as not to cause conflict; the other mages don't really know what happened, only that Yanni left, and I stayed. But you know what the Guildtower's like. There are plenty of stories. Rumors."

Certainty sat very still, taking this in. Although being burned out was exceptionally rare, mages still talked about it in hushed voices—a fate almost worse than death, to many. To know that you had done that to another mage—a friend, a classmate . . . She couldn't imagine the crushing guilt that Aurelia must have felt. The loathing that she would have been the target of, had the others had any idea at all what had happened.

She swallowed and wet her lips. "And . . . and your own powers? You weren't burned out?"

"No. But I couldn't farspeak again after that. The High Mage thinks it's not a magical problem, that I just have some kind of—of *block* in my mind now. That I'm doing this to myself. But she also thinks I can overcome it, if I try hard enough. Focus more."

"That's what you've been doing during your isolation sessions," Certainty said slowly.

Aurelia gave a jerky nod. "But even if she thinks so, I'm not sure I'll ever be able to farspeak again. And it doesn't really matter, does it?" She looked down at her hands. "I'll always be tainted by what I've done. The other mages never liked me anyway, and now they don't trust me, and I—I'm not sure I even trust myself."

The carriage house was silent except for the soft crackle of the dying fire and the sound of their breaths. Aurelia's was shaky with suppressed feeling, and Certainty's was far too loud.

But she looked at Aurelia, and she knew—she knew, from her ears down to the cold tips of her toes—that it had been nothing more than an honest mistake.

I believe you was what she wanted to say.

But instead, what came out was, "Why didn't the other mages like you?"

Aurelia blinked. Then she gave a derisive sort of laugh. Too harsh a sound to be coming from her mouth, Certainty thought.

"Why do you think? I'm too uptight, too rigid, abrasive even when I don't mean to be . . . I never liked drinking in taverns, was too busy studying to go to their parties, never knew how to have fun . . ." She made a helpless gesture. "I'm just not a likable person, Cert."

Certainty opened her mouth to protest—*no, that's not true; of course you are*—but then she closed it again. Aurelia noticed; she raised an eyebrow wryly, as if to say *There; you see?* It made Certainty's heart hurt.

"*I* like you," she blurted.

Aurelia's fingers stilled. Her eyes lifted to Certainty's, searching. "You do?"

"Yes." And as Certainty said it, she realized it was true. Her cheeks were on fire, but she didn't look away. Aurelia needed to see her *mean* it, to see her thoughts and feelings laid bare. "And I believe you, too. I believe you didn't mean to do it."

"Oh. I . . ." Aurelia's voice hitched. She sounded almost disbelieving, as if Certainty had given her a gift she hadn't expected. And maybe she had, after all. "Thank you. I . . . I like you, too, Certainty."

And then she gave Certainty a shy, timorous smile. It was a smile that softened all of her sharp angles and edges, and gave her face a soft glow from within, and it made Certainty want to reach out and touch her to see if Aurelia's lips were as soft as they looked, and—

Oh.

Oh no.

Certainty was in trouble.

ELEVEN

FOR OBVIOUS REASONS, Certainty decided to keep her somewhat alarming attraction to Aurelia to herself. And really, she could hardly be blamed for not realizing it until now. Aurelia was about as far as possible from her usual type—namely, strapping Guild stable boys who were good at lifting heavy objects and making her laugh.

But relationships between novices and mages of the same gender weren't uncommon. Even if some parts of Eshtera (particularly the more rural towns west of the Saltpeaks) still viewed such relationships with discomfort, Margrave was a far more cosmopolitan sort of place, and the Guildtower itself, even more so. When she first took office, High Mage Melea had made it clear that she didn't care what they all got up to in their bedrooms so long as it didn't affect their studies or their work—a policy Certainty found eminently reasonable.

Still, Certainty had no idea what Aurelia's romantic inclinations were . . . whether she had a sweetheart back home, whether she was secretly engaged to a foreign prince (she'd be just the type), or whether she didn't even have those messy sorts of feelings at all. And it certainly wouldn't do for Certainty to make any advances while they were working together. Frankly, she wouldn't even know where to start. If she had any feminine wiles—whatever those even were—they were very well-hidden indeed.

No, while this was a very interesting personal finding, it was also one best shoved into storage like a low-grade artifact, until she had the time and distance to investigate it further and catalog it properly. In the meantime, she'd just ... avoid standing too close to Aurelia. Ignore the way her hair shone in the sunlight. Pay no attention to the little dimples that appeared whenever Aurelia held back a smile.

Easy.

CERTAINTY DISTRACTED HERSELF by writing a response to her father's letter, in which she told him of Shpelling (*"never seen so much garlic in my life"*), of Aurelia (*"not quite what I'd expected"*), and of her very real hope of earning a magehood before the start of summer (*"tell Asp he's not allowed to give up just yet"*). Once this was done, she buried herself in their artifact work, ignoring the fact that Aurelia's constant proximity posed a very real threat to this strategy.

With the storage shelves all fully built, the mage had volunteered herself to take down Certainty's dictated notes on each artifact. They'd become a well-oiled machine: sitting opposite each other at the work desk, a gloved Aurelia would hand Certainty the next artifact to identify; Certainty would pick it up and speak with it using her magic, then describe to Aurelia the details of the item's enchantment. Aurelia would attach a label, record their notes into the book, and shelve the artifact appropriately.

With this method, they could get through thirty, maybe

forty, artifacts per working session before Cert's headaches became too severe. Soon, the pile of boxes on the stable floor dwindled as their contents were processed and stored in the appropriate stall—categorized, per Aurelia's insistence, by the nature of their enchantments.

But one morning, just as Certainty was settling herself down to the desk, Aurelia returned from rechecking the boundary wards with a determined look on her face.

"No inventory work today, Cert. I'm exercising my ranking authority here to declare that we have a bigger priority. One that requires our immediate attention."

Certainty was puzzled. She hadn't heard any shouting or other alarming noises. "What's going on? Did one of the villagers say something? Have we had a letter?"

"No, it's a conclusion reached from my own observations."

"What is?"

"We need to bathe." The mage had an enthusiastic glint in her eye.

Certainty gave herself a surreptitious sniff. Was it really that bad? They'd been in Shpelling for nearly three weeks already, but it was hard to tell how dire the personal hygiene situation was when everything around them already smelled so . . . agricultural.

"We are *exuding* garlic, Certainty. You may not have noticed, but we are presently well-seasoned with it, inside and out. And we've been sleeping in a stable, besides."

"Carriage house," Certainty corrected. She ran one hand through her hair, feeling the accumulated oiliness in her curls that quick morning rinses with well water hadn't been able to dislodge. "But point taken."

"Excellent! I've been thinking about how best to achieve this." Aurelia straightened her shoulders, practically vibrating with purpose. "The Golden Plough doesn't have a bathhouse, but it ought to have a bath*tub*—it used to be an inn once upon a time, after all. If we can convince Ferdinand to lend a tub, then all we need is a way to fill the tub with hot water. I already have soap that I brought with me."

At a proper inn, maids or servants would be sent up with pails of hot water for the bath. Sometimes, they'd even help soap and scrub you. Certainty smirked at the thought.

"Somehow I don't think Old Gertha would be willing to be your bath maid, Aurelia. Now, Orrin, on the other hand . . ."

But Aurelia paced between the stalls, barely listening.

"We could heat water on the stove, but that would be terribly slow—even if we managed two pots at a time, the water would never keep warm long enough to fill the tub. Casting a warming spell on the water is another option, of course, but maintaining it for the duration of both of our baths would be a draining task that I don't particularly care to take on . . ."

Certainty grinned. She could see the direction that Aurelia's logic was heading.

"You want to use a magical artifact to heat our bath, don't you?"

Aurelia stopped pacing. "It's only practical, Cert. Wouldn't you agree?"

"Oh, absolutely! I'm all for being practical." And a bath *did* sound nice, she had to admit. There were few things more enjoyable than a good, long, sudsy soak. "I just didn't expect you to be the one suggesting we—how had you phrased it, again? 'Misuse Guild artifacts for personal purposes'?"

"We're not." Aurelia crossed her arms defensively. "It's temporary use in service to our assignment, like the teapot and the flaming sword. We can hardly be expected to be optimally productive when we reek of garlic and livestock."

"Of course not," Certainty said, still grinning. "So where do we start?"

CERTAINTY WAS DISPATCHED to the Plough to beg a tub off of Ferdinand. Annoyingly, as with so many of her other theories, Aurelia's supposition had been correct. The tavernkeep led Cert into a dark side room that adjoined the main great room.

"Here it is," he said cheerfully as they both batted aside the braids of drying garlic that hung throughout the room. A plump white cat emerged, meowing, from behind some of the garlic and slunk between Certainty's legs as it left the room. One of the more recent arrivals from Aurelia's box. "You're welcome to take it; Mother and Sons know we haven't been making use of it here."

A large wooden washtub, oval-shaped and bound with thick iron bands, lay abandoned in the corner. It was, of course, full of more garlic, but this was remedied easily enough. Two sturdy handles jutted out from either end, which would make it easier for Certainty and whomever she conscripted into helping—Orrin, probably—to carry it back up to the stable. She could tell by looking at it that it would be just large enough to contain a rather short Guild novice, or a rather tall Guild mage, if Aurelia were willing to bend her knees a bit.

"Perfect," she said with satisfaction.

BY THE TIME Certainty managed to find Orrin and recruit him into helping her lug the washtub up the path, Aurelia had already prepared its new home. Since only some of the stable stalls were being used for artifact storage, she'd decided to repurpose one of the empty ones into a private bathing room.

A large bedsheet hung like a curtain from two nails hammered into the stall's outward posts, providing privacy for the intrepid bather. Within the stall, another nail was hammered in at eye height ("For hanging your clothes!"), and one of their two wool rugs had been dragged in to cover the floor. A lantern and a small butter dish lay on the floor beside the tub. In it was a bar of pink, lavender-scented soap and a small bunch of freshly cut lemon balm tied with twine.

Aurelia hovered behind Certainty anxiously.

"What do you think?"

It looked . . . ridiculous. It also looked perfect. Certainty's mouth suddenly went dry at the thought of Aurelia taking a bath mere steps from her, separated only by that thin bedsheet.

"Lovely," she croaked.

Aurelia beamed at her. "And I've already reviewed the entries in the record book, and believe that I've found a possible solution for heating the bathwater! Come take a look—"

They sat down at the work desk, Aurelia flipping through the book eagerly.

"Numbers 215 and 216," she said, pointing them out. "What do you think?"

"'Stone of boiling,'" Certainty read dutifully. "'Drop into castle moat during enemy siege action. Stone of freezing, drop into river or lake to form ice bridge for troop crossings. Effective range and potency severely diminished due to weakening of enchantments over time.'"

She looked up at Aurelia. "I'm not sure what sort of baths you like to take, Aurelia, but I generally prefer to be neither boiled alive nor frozen during mine."

"Obviously not," said Aurelia impatiently. "But what do you think the effect would be if we used both stones together?"

Certainty squinted at the book, trying to recall her past lessons in basic alchemy, before realizing there was no point. Aurelia would surely know better than she did.

"I suppose it might work," she said, and was rewarded for it by the sight of Aurelia's smile.

IT TOOK BOTH of them several trips to the well to fill the washtub (Orrin, sadly, had returned to his actual farmwork) and by the time they were done, if Certainty hadn't needed a bath before, she certainly did then.

"Right," said Aurelia, panting as they stood in the entrance to the bathing stall, watching water slosh gently against the sides of the tub. She'd taken off her outer robes after the first few trips to the well, and Certainty did her brave best to not notice the rising and falling of her chest, or the gleam of sweat on her well-toned forearms. "Now time for the artifacts."

Certainty was glad for a reason to escape. She retreated to the next stall down where she pulled on some gloves, sternly reminded herself of all the reasons she shouldn't be ogling her partner, and retrieved the two artifacts from their shelf.

They were unassuming things: perfectly spherical and roughly the size of her palms. One was made of a coarse reddish stone, and the other of smooth white. They were unusually heavy.

She brought them back to Aurelia. "Their enchantments activate on contact with water," she said, offering them up. "Should we drop them in one after the other? Or at the same time?"

Aurelia, now also gloved, took the red sphere from her. "One after the other, and the stone of boiling first, I think."

They stood on either side of the washtub holding their stones. Anticipation was thick in the air, and the women smiled at each other. There was something thrilling about experimenting together, even for something as silly as this.

"Ready?"

Aurelia nodded. She dropped her sphere. It entered the water with a soft *plup*, sinking rapidly to the bottom of the tub. They held their breath.

The water stirred gently...

Small bubbles began to rise. Then they expanded in size, and the surface of the water started to roil and seethe. The stall grew warm and humid, and moisture beaded on Certainty's forehead.

"Quick, the other stone—"

Certainty dropped the white sphere in, flinching back from the splash of boiling water, and it, too, sank to the bottom.

There was an odd sizzling noise, and the roiling bubbles calmed. But steam still rose, thick and inviting, from the water's surface.

Aurelia pulled off a glove. Very carefully, she lowered one finger into the water. As soon as it passed one knuckle, a smile spread across her face, creasing her eyes in a way that Certainty found devastatingly attractive. Gods, she had it bad.

"I claim the first bath," Aurelia said, sounding deeply satisfied. She reached for the tie of her robes, then hesitated. "Unless you'd rather...?"

"No," squeaked Certainty, fleeing from the stall hurriedly enough that she nearly knocked over the soap dish. "Go ahead—all yours!"

TO CERTAINTY'S EQUAL relief and disappointment, both of their baths went without incident, and she discovered that a freshly scrubbed and lavender-scented Aurelia was even more distracting than an unwashed, garlicky Aurelia. Every time Aurelia reached across the table, a soft and feminine scent wafted toward Certainty, and she had to focus all of her willpower on not breathing in deeply. She was new to Guild assignments, of course, but sniffing your colleague's hair didn't seem like professionally acceptable behavior, mage or not.

On a sunny Scholarsday afternoon, just as Certainty was beginning to flag, Aurelia plunked a small contraption onto the desk before her. Made of brass, it had three fat metal cylinders, two smooth and one ridged, all secured together with fiddly little bolts and screws. A wooden-handled lever jutted out from one side.

Certainty looked the artifact over, intrigued.

"What do you think this one is supposed to be?"

Aurelia tilted her head to peer at it from different angles. "It almost looks mechanical rather than magical. Some sort of device."

Certainty's curiosity was piqued. Closing her eyes, she laid both hands on either side of the device and gave it a gentle prod with her magic.

Then her eyes shot back open in surprise.

"What? What is it?" Aurelia looked at her anxiously, seeming ready to summon a defensive bubble, but Certainty shook her head, trying to make sense of what she'd heard.

The device's object-voice was unctuous and jolly; it buzzed in her mind like the din of a busy kitchen, the bubbling of a pot, the scrape of a fork. But it was also speaking in what sounded like . . . Lindisian?

"What are you? What is your purpose?" tried Certainty.

The artifact's response was once more unintelligible to her. She got the vague impression of fingertips held together in a point above a palm, and an emphatic bobbing gesture.

This had never happened to her before. Clearly her magic was functioning well enough; she was still able to communicate with the artifact—but why wasn't it speaking Eshteran? Certainty tried to convey her lack of comprehension through the bond, and only the artifact's exasperation came through loud and clear.

Then images, fleeting and blurry, poured into her mind. She blinked furiously, taking them in, until—with what felt like a needlessly dramatic flourish—the artifact fell silent, and the bond was severed.

She shook her head again, trying to dislodge the ache behind her eyes, and looked at Aurelia.

"Well, that was interesting."

"Are you all right?" Aurelia sounded anxious. "What happened?"

"I'm fine. I think . . ." Certainty set the artifact back down on the desk. "I think this artifact *makes food*."

The mage blinked at her and picked up her quill. "Yes? I need more detail than that for the records."

But Certainty was thinking hard. "Forget the records for a moment, Aurelia . . . we could bring this over to the Golden Plough!"

"Why? What even *is* it?"

"It's a . . . well, I don't really know what it's called, because it only thought Lindisian at me and I don't speak Lindisian, but the gist of it was that it makes something tasty!"

"It *thought* in Lindisian?" Aurelia's eyes went distant. "Fascinating—that suggests a far greater degree of connection between the origin of the maker, or perhaps the location in which an object is made, and—"

Certainty waved a hand impatiently. "Yes, yes, must be a foreign artifact. Very interesting scholarly implications, you can write a paper about it later. Back to the important bit: *food*."

Aurelia sighed. "So it's an artifact from Lindisi that makes food. And you want to do what with it, precisely?"

"Lend it to the Plough, and teach Ferdinand how to use it so that we can eat something that's not stew, for a change!"

"But do you even know how to use it?"

"Of course." At Aurelia's skeptical expression, Certainty amended her statement. "Well, sort of. It showed me! You mix flour, water, and raw egg into a paste, and then feed it through this thing while cranking the lever. I think the food is called *paste-a*." Certainty bit her lip, looking up at Aurelia with a pleading expression. "Please?"

Aurelia's eyes seemed to be caught on Certainty's mouth for some reason. "Uh."

"Think of it as more research . . ." Certainty said, coaxing.

Aurelia relented. "Fine. We can take it to Ferdinand and see what he makes of it. I suppose a change of menu wouldn't be the worst thing."

FERDINAND WAS AT first offended, then suspicious, and then offended all over again as Certainty explained her proposition, but he reluctantly agreed to at least test what the artifact could do. Just to satisfy their curiosity, of course.

The three of them crowded round the artifact in the Golden Plough's cluttered kitchen. An enormous pot of something thick and brown gurgled away on the stove, and more braids of garlic hung from all parts of the ceiling and rafters. Plates and tankards fought for space on the small kitchen counter, but Ferdinand simply swept up an armful of them and deposited them unceremoniously in a corner to make room for the device.

Certainty concentrated on recalling as much as she could about what the artifact had shown her. As Ferdinand mixed flour, water, and egg in a bowl to her instructions, Aurelia hovered beside her with a skeptical and slightly anxious air. Soon, the bowl held only a yellow blob of thick paste.

"Basically a very dense dough, innit," Ferdinand said, prodding at it doubtfully. "You sure this is right?"

As a proud Eshteran, he had an innate resistance to anything foreign, and Certainty's implication that the Lindisians might have come up with something tastier than garlic-and-bean stew had put his back up. (She'd mollified him by assuring him that some variety in menu would surely only increase his patrons' appreciation for the stew. *Distance makes the heart grow fonder, Ferdinand. I'm sure it applies to stomachs, too.*)

"I'm positive," said Certainty, trying to sound confident. "Now we just roll it out to be a flat sheet—like so—and feed it into the artifact, slowly, while one of us turns the lever."

As this required some rather awkward positioning and more hands than the two of them possessed, Aurelia was conscripted into turning the lever while the others grappled with the sticky, misshapen sheet of dough. While the brass cylinders rotated, Certainty spoke the incantation that the artifact had communicated to her, enunciating very carefully.

"Bone-Apple-Tea!"

"Really? That hardly sounds like a proper incantation . . ." But Aurelia kept turning the lever nonetheless, and the flattened dough was drawn into the device. Suddenly, the dough beneath their hands began to glow, and then it shot violently through the bladed cylinders and landed on the other side with a *thwup*.

They all looked at the tangle of perfect, wide golden ribbons that lay there.

"Aha!" said Certainty in triumph. "Behold, paste-a!"

"Now what?" Ferdinand picked up one of the limp strands and gave it a dubious nibble. "Don't taste like much."

"It's not done yet. You boil it in salted water, drain it, then stir in a load of cheese shavings and cream, or other sauces."

"Hmph. Foreign nonsense."

But at her pleading look, Ferdinand did as she asked, grumbling the whole time, and shortly thereafter the three of them were staring down at a steaming plate full of cooked pasta drenched in a creamy sauce. Certainty picked up a fork and made to taste it.

"Wait. It needs one more thing." Ferdinand grabbed a small earthenware jug and poured a careful stream of golden liquid over the food. "Roasted garlic oil. Wouldn't be a Golden Plough meal without it."

Aurelia grinned at Certainty's look of despair. "Go on, then, Cert. Tell us whether this magical Lindisian food is everything you hoped for."

Certainty stuck her tongue out at the mage, but lowered her face to the plate. She had to admit—even with the garlic oil (or *especially* with the garlic oil, her traitorous nose suggested)—it smelled divine.

She twirled a few of the glistening ribbons around her fork and lifted it to her mouth as the other two watched. She took a bite. Chewed.

Oh. *Oh.*

Mother and Sons, she was ready to renounce Eshtera and board a ship for Lindisi then and there. Where had this food *been* all her life? Who wanted mushy brown stews and bland pork pies when there was *this*?

Each salty, creamy strand was smooth and buttery, soft and toothsome at the same time; each bite introduced new and miraculous textures that were somehow familiar and deeply comforting. The pasta spoke to something deep within Certainty, something primal and hungry that craved starchy foods drowning in melted cheese, and she felt as though she could devour the entire plate then and there.

Certainty found that her eyes were closed, and someone in the kitchen was making a very inappropriate noise. She opened her eyes. Aurelia was staring at her, eyes wide and cheeks flushed; Ferdinand had edged away. Ah. So it was her.

"Well?" the tavernkeep demanded. "Was it worth all the fuss, then?"

Wordlessly, Certainty handed him the fork. Still bearing an expression of deep skepticism, Ferdinand scooped up a few strands of pasta dripping with melted cheese and garlic oil, and, with the manner of someone doing a friend a great and unpleasant favor, took a bite.

He talked as he chewed, mumbling around the mouthful.

"I don't see what y—"

But then he stopped talking. His eyes went unfocused, and he stood very still.

It was Certainty's first time witnessing a religious awakening. If the roof and sky above were to open up just then to let a pillar of the Mother's golden light shine down upon that crowded kitchen, and if a chorus of faerie fiddlers were to burst into rapturous song, she wouldn't even blink. It would have been appropriate to the occasion.

Ferdinand chewed, swallowed, and slowly emerged from his fugue state.

"Maker Son be praised," he said, his voice slightly hoarse. He handed the fork to Aurelia. "Ladies, I'm going to need to borrow this device of yours for a while. And somebody fetch me some more flour."

TWELVE

THEY ALL KNEW that as soon as word got out, folk would come from leagues around for just a taste of this, this—this *pasta*. "Need to spread the news," Ferdinand said, in between mouthfuls. Aurelia's and Certainty's forks went in for more at the same time, and a silent, pitched duel over the plate ensued.

Orrin was summoned, converted to the cause with his own plate of pasta, and sent to fetch any villagers who might be interested in trying this new addition to the Plough's menu.

Within the hour, the tavern's great room was packed wall to window with eager customers, and both Certainty and Aurelia were pressed into helping Ferdinand make as much of the Lindisian pasta as they could. Even with three sets of hands, it was difficult for them to keep pace with the orders that came flying in for second and third helpings. Still, it was worth it. Even Gertha had stuck her head into the kitchen to demand another plate of "that foreign nonsense."

It was utter chaos, but it was also *fun*, a welcome diversion from the tedium of identifying and labeling all those artifacts. Besides, Aurelia looked utterly adorable with flour all over her face.

It was late by the time the two women left the Plough and

walked back to the carriage house together. Lacking competition from glowing magelamps, the moon and stars shone brighter overhead here than they ever could in Margrave, and Certainty let her head dangle a little, looking up at the twinkling shapes they made. Her headache had returned as soon as they were out of the noise and warmth of the tavern, but the cool night breeze flicking through her curls eased the pain a little.

There was a quiet meowing sound from the side of the path; they looked to see a cinnamon-colored kitten crouched like a tiny loaf of bread among the dandelions. Another recent arrival, courtesy of Aurelia's experiment box. Aurelia reached down, and the kitten accepted her pets before stretching playfully and bounding once more into the shadowed grass.

Cert smiled at the mage, and they continued on.

The two women walked side by side in silence, but it was a thoughtful, comfortable sort of silence. It was clear that Aurelia had enjoyed their unexpected culinary excursion, and Certainty felt a little thrill inside of her at the thought that she'd made that happen.

Calm yourself, Cert. It was cooking, not foreplay.

When they reached the stable and carriage house, Aurelia's steps slowed. She stopped before the door and took a deep breath, looking up at the night sky.

"This place," she said, her voice quiet to match the humming crickets. "It's so different from Margrave. So different from everything I've known."

Certainty looked at Aurelia's face, open and lit only by the moon. "Different good?"

"Different good." Aurelia smiled softly at her. "Because of you, mostly. I don't think I'd have seen it—really seen it, I mean—without you to show me. Thank you for that."

Certainty flushed, suddenly warm despite the cool night air.

"I didn't really do anything. I'm just more used to places like this than you. I fit right in here—not like in Margrave, where everyone's fancy and important, and I'm just . . . me." She felt a sting of bitterness, thinking of Brannon and all the others who had left her behind, but played it off with a laugh.

Aurelia saw right through her, though. "Don't do that."

"Do what?"

She faced Certainty. Her eyes were green and serious. "Don't say that you're not important. Don't make yourself smaller than you are. Other people will always try to do so, but don't do it for them. You *are* important. And you belong there as much as anyone does."

Certainty's heart stuttered. "Oh," she said. "I . . ."

How did Aurelia *do* that? Her attention felt like sunlight; Certainty wanted to bask in it, to wrap herself in Aurelia's words and buckle them on like armor. Aurelia spoke of such things so straightforwardly, so easily, and just like that, Certainty was made a little bit more whole.

Then an owl hooted nearby, and Aurelia looked away. "We should get ready for bed."

"Right," said Certainty. *Thank you*, she wanted to say, but didn't. She followed Aurelia into the carriage house.

Once inside, Certainty couldn't help watching Aurelia. She moved with a dancer's grace, even when all she was doing was poking at kindling with a slightly flaming sword. A vision of poise, of elegance, of . . .

Then Certainty smirked. "Aurelia, you still have flour on your face."

"Where?" Aurelia set the sword down to wipe at her cheek, but succeeded only in smearing the flour onto her chin. "Did I get it?"

"No, you've made it worse—here—"

Certainty closed the distance, reaching up a hand to help. Too late—far too late—her brain began ringing alarm bells, but her hand wasn't taking orders from her brain anymore.

It lifted and gently wiped away the flour, thumb running over the soft point of Aurelia's cheekbone, the slope of her chin. She heard Aurelia's breath catch, just a tiny hitch, but she was near enough (so near) that even just that whisper of a sound filled her senses.

The universe was frozen in that moment—Aurelia's lips parted slowly, so slowly—

But then the silver chain on her neck shifted slightly against her collar, and Aurelia seemed to suddenly become aware of how close they were.

They both stepped back hastily. Certainty cleared her throat.

"There," she mumbled. "All gone."

"Um, thank you."

"No problem."

Certainty lay down on her bed, staring blankly at the ceiling. Gods. What was she thinking? Aurelia was the last mage who would ever entertain any sort of . . . fraternization. Especially while on assignment.

She closed her eyes, imagining what might have happened if she'd actually tried to kiss her just then. An expression of shock, of disgust, or—worse yet—of pity on Aurelia's face. She probably didn't even think of women that way. No, far better to leave things as they were. She and Aurelia had come a long way since they first set out from Margrave together. Certainty thought she might even call her a friend now. That was something, wasn't it?

It would have to be enough. No matter how good it felt to see Aurelia's smile, and to know that she had been the one to put it there.

THE NEXT MORNING, when Certainty sat up groggily from her nest of pillows and blankets, Aurelia was already awake and redoing her braid.

"Good morning," she said, and gave Certainty a soft, radiant smile that immediately revived last night's inconvenient urge to kiss her senseless. It didn't help that while she braided her hair, her head was tilted at just the right angle to expose the soft curve of her neck to the sun streaming in through the window.

"Morning," Certainty said, glancing aside before her blush could give her away.

Luckily, Aurelia didn't seem to notice. "I need to spend this morning on my farspeaking exercises again," she said. "I haven't been spending nearly enough time practicing."

"*Practice makes perfect! Even the finest leaves take time to steep, don't they? Speaking of which, I do think we could do a bit better, ladies; not to be a snob about it, but I must say I'm used to a finer quality than—*"

Oh good. The tea was already brewing. Certainty picked some hay out of her hair as she swung her legs out of bed, ignoring the teapot's commentary.

"How do your exercises work, anyway?"

"Well . . . mostly, I try to do all the things I would do if I were actually trying to farspeak to someone. Clear my thoughts, focus my magic, imagine opening the channel within my mind."

"But you're *not* actually trying to farspeak to anyone? Wouldn't that be more effective?"

Aurelia gave a little shrug as she tied off the end of her braid. "We tried that in the beginning. The High Mage had one of the other farspeakers working with me for a while. But I couldn't open the channel at all, and that farspeaker was needed elsewhere, so . . ."

"What if you practiced with me?" The idea came out of her mouth before Certainty could consider what she was proposing; Aurelia's eyes snapped onto hers in surprise.

"You're not trained to receive farspeaking, are you?"

"No, I'm not, but . . . couldn't you teach me?"

Certainty felt a stab of guilt even as she spoke. She really shouldn't be offering to join Aurelia in her farspeaking exercises when there were still more boxes of artifacts to be identified. The sensible thing would be to focus on getting the inventory done in time to pay Asp's apprenticeship fee, but . . . they still had some weeks, didn't they? And what if she really *could* help Aurelia?

"I suppose I could show you," said Aurelia slowly. "The basics, anyway. But . . . aren't you afraid? The last person I farspoke to—I told you what happened, Cert."

"I know you'd be careful. I trust you." She kept her voice casual, even though they both knew it was no small thing she was offering.

"You—" Aurelia swallowed, looking down at her lap. "Are you sure?"

She was. Even if she *weren't* suddenly and vexingly attracted to Aurelia, she'd want to help her with this. She knew all too well how it felt to be seen as deficient, at least in the eyes of the Guild. But unlike Certainty's spellcasting, Aurelia's ability hadn't always been lacking . . .

Still. Not the sort of thing she wanted to talk about before they'd even had breakfast, so she opted for the easy way out instead.

"I am absolutely, entirely, positively . . ." Certainty leaned over to give the mage her best shit-eating grin. *"Certain."*

Even the teapot let out a groan. The brief sight of Aurelia's expression was her only reward, right before a feather-stuffed pillow smacked her in the face and obscured her view of it.

AFTER A QUICK breakfast, Certainty followed Aurelia into the stall that had become her practice area. The women both sat cross-legged upon folded blankets in the cramped space, and Aurelia seemed nervous as she lit the candles between them with a spell.

"We'll try just the absolute basics. And if you change your mind—if anything at all doesn't feel right—we'll stop immediately. All right?"

"Sure."

Aurelia took a deep breath and launched into her lecturer mode (which Certainty was growing quite familiar with).

"Right. So. Receiving a farspeaker's communication is essentially just recognizing when a farspeaker is attempting to open a channel to you, then allowing their magic to join with your own. It's a simple enough thing, but can be difficult because it feels so vulnerable. A mage's instinct is often to resist such intrusions, so it takes training and willpower to relax your mental barriers.

"The first step for a recipient is to clear away their thoughts and attune their magical senses to any external outreach. Since you haven't done this before, we'll attempt to simply open the channel for now."

"What will it feel like?"

"It depends on the recipient. Some say it's like someone knocking on the door of your mind. Or the ringing of a bell, or like someone calling out to you from a distance, but you can't quite hear the words yet. If it works, that is—which it likely won't." Aurelia rolled her shoulders and set her palms on her knees. "Are you ready?"

Certainty mirrored her. When the mage began taking deep, steady breaths, she did the same. But when Aurelia closed her eyes, Certainty just watched her silently for a moment. The mage's lips were slightly parted, and her skin glowed softly in the candlelight. Seen like this, with her face open and unguarded, Aurelia was as beautiful as she had ever looked.

Stop it, Cert. Focus!

Certainty squeezed her own eyes shut and set about trying to clear her mind of all thoughts, particularly distracting ones about pretty blond mages sitting an arm's-length away. It was something of an uphill battle, but eventually, she found herself in a state of relaxed awareness. Her senses took note of fresh hay and old damp beneath the scent of lemon balm, the firmness of packed earth beneath scratchy wool, the slide of her sleeves against her arms. Took note of them, then let them drift away. Her breath came slow and steady without her controlling it, as if the air around her were breathing for her, filling and emptying her lungs like a gentle bellows. Her mind was open; her magic was warm and swirling within, ready to greet Aurelia's.

She listened intently for the calling Aurelia had said would come, and waited.

And waited.

And waited.

Long minutes passed, and eventually she heard a rustling and a sigh. She opened her eyes and was met by Aurelia's downcast expression.

"I didn't feel any knocking or calling," she said apologetically.

"No. It didn't work, as expected." Aurelia's lips pressed together thinly, as if trying to contain her disappointment.

"I'm sorry, Aurelia. It might have been my fault, not yours. Other than talking to objects, my magic's always been weak—"

"No, Certainty. It's just me; it's always just been me." Aurelia closed her eyes, exhaled, and opened them again. She gave Certainty a rueful smile. "Ironic, isn't it? Your magical talent works perfectly fine even though you struggle with general spellcasting, and I can cast all the spells I like but can't make my farspeaking work anymore. If you combined the two of us, you might even get one fully functional mage."

"Maybe that's why the High Mage sent us here together."

Aurelia's smile faded. "I don't think so. I think she sent *you* because you were the best person for the work that needed doing. But I think I'm only here because she didn't know what else to do with me. Because she thought getting me out of Margrave might help fix whatever's broken in me."

Broken. Certainty hated that Aurelia saw herself that way. Only *things* could be broken, not people.

"Well . . . perhaps we can try again tomorrow?" Certainty gave Aurelia a small, hopeful smile. "And in the meantime, Orrin says that the honeyberry bushes down by the streams have started ripening; maybe we could go for a walk, take a break . . ."

Aurelia hesitated, looking tempted, but then she shook her head. "You go without me. I'm going to keep working at it on my own for a bit."

"Well, at lunch, then. You'll need to eat—"

"I'm fine, Certainty. Please." Aurelia's words were clipped.

Certainty sighed as she stood and stretched. There would be no budging Aurelia, not when she was like this. She couldn't help looking over her shoulder as she left.

"You made one mistake, Aurelia," she said gently. "You don't have to punish yourself for it for the rest of your life."

But Aurelia's eyes were closed once more as she sat still and straight-backed on the floor, and she did not respond.

A FEW DAYS later, Certainty groaned and let her head drop into her hands, grinding both palms against her eyes. It seemed wholly unfair to her that her particular magical talent was both minimally useful *and* exhausting.

"That bad?" Aurelia asked with sympathy.

Spurred on by the thought of Asp's apprenticeship slipping away, Certainty had been pushing herself, trying to identify and record as many artifacts as she could each day, but hadn't yet found any solution for the nagging headaches that resulted. Aurelia brewed her pots of mint-and-chamomile tea, but while the hot tea was soothing, it only eased the pain slightly. Still, the vision of the High Mage pinning Guild circles onto her robes drove her on.

"What? No, it's not too bad yet." Certainty nodded at the artifact on the desk. "Just finished with that one. Will you mark it down for me? Number 283, enchanted handkerchief. Prompts uncontrollable sneezing in its user. Activates with spoken incantation 'sternutatio.' Oh—oh, blast, I shouldn't have said that—"

Aurelia ducked out of range of the subsequent sneezing fit. In between eye-watering sneezes, Certainty managed to grab hold of the handkerchief.

"*Stop that!*" she thought very sternly, and the sneezes subsided. The handkerchief fluttered sullenly in her grip.

"Sounds like you've caught a cold. Comes from going to bed with your hair wet, you know."

Gertha had walked into the stable unannounced, her walking stick shuffling among the straw as she peered around without any trace of self-consciousness. Certainty supposed that despite her crotchetiness, the old woman must not have any real ill intent toward them, given that the wards hadn't stopped her and all of her limbs still seemed to be where they ought to be. "Looks like you've just about fixed this place up, hm? I suppose Orrin's been helping you. I hope you haven't filled that fool boy's head with grand tales about the Terraced City."

"Hello, Gertha."

"Hmph. Brought you this."

The old woman dropped a cloth-wrapped bundle onto the desk. Certainty unwrapped it to find a dark, dense loaf and a small jar of butter.

"Honeycake. Baked it myself, now that Hull's got bees again. And the butter's from Murph and Brienna."

"Oh," said Certainty, touched. "Thank you! That's very kind."

"It is. But you two have done as you said and helped us some, so it's only proper that we thank you." The old woman nodded in an ungracious sort of way. "Humble as we may be here in this backwater place."

"Gertha . . . it's long past time I apologized for that," Aurelia said. She straightened, hands clasped in front of her. "I'm very sorry I said those things when we first arrived. It was rude and unkind. Will you forgive me?"

"Hmph," said Gertha again. But her eyes were a little crinklier around the edges as she regarded the two of them. "Suppose I've got to accept your apology, don't I? Can't have the big, fancy Guild mages holding a grudge against Old Gertha. I don't suppose you had something to do with the rats and mice, too?"

"Um . . ." Certainty and Aurelia exchanged a guilty glance. Gertha saw it, of course, and cackled.

"Hah! I knew it. Brienna said she hadn't seen a single mouse dropping these last few days, and the bakery used to be overrun with them! Couldn't leave a sack of nuts out without half of them disappearing by the next morning. Did you summon the cats with a magic wand, too, like you did those bees?"

"Not . . . a wand, as such," hedged Certainty, looking at Aurelia. She hoped the mage didn't feel the need to launch into an explanation of her theory on cats and boxes and paradoxes.

Gertha snorted. "Doesn't matter how you did it, just that you did. Nice to see cats round here again, you know; I've started leaving out a little dish of cream for them every night."

"Actually, cats shouldn't have dairy. Their stomachs don't—" Certainty caught Aurelia's eye, and the mage course-corrected admirably. "Uh. That is, I'm sure the cats appreciate the gift."

Gertha nodded with satisfaction. "As *you* should, too. That honeycake's a secret family recipe. I always used to make it for the Spring Fair. Suppose I will again this year. I assume you two will be joining the festivities? It's just a week from now, on the day of the full moon."

Certainty paused. Had it really already been a month since they'd first arrived in Shpelling? Somehow it didn't feel like that long, even though they were already on the last several boxes of artifacts. She should be thrilled. Finishing the job early meant an apprenticeship for Asp. It meant returning to the Guildtower and becoming Deputy Keeper. Then she'd be put in charge of proper artifacts, not just these dusty trinkets and novelties. She'd get to sleep in a real bed again, rather than in Orrin's wobbly, straw-filled contraption. She'd finally be back in the heart of the kingdom's capital instead of whiling away her youth in a sleepy village full of garlic farmers.

. . . the problem was, she kind of *liked* the sleepy village full of garlic farmers.

She liked Hull's optimism and Ferdinand's mustache; Orrin's blushing self-consciousness; and Murph and Brienna, too. She liked how quietly loud the mornings were here, full of birds singing and hens clucking and cows lowing, and also the way the land glowed gold when the sun set behind the hills. Mother and Sons, she even liked Gertha, despite the old woman's best efforts.

And of course, there was Aurelia. Here in Shpelling, the two of them had become a team—working together, eating together, constantly sharing the same small, lemon balm–scented space.

They'd tried a few more farspeaking practice sessions together, too, and while they still hadn't managed to open a channel between them, Certainty thought she'd felt the faintest niggling at the edges of her mind during the last attempt, which had cheered both of them immensely. She'd begun to feel like perhaps the two of them were helping each other, as opposed to Aurelia only being here to help her. It was a good feeling.

In a way, Shpelling was their own little bubble, a place to rest and breathe away from the pressures of the outside world. But bubbles popped, and Certainty knew that everything would change the minute they stepped foot back in the Guildtower. That was the way of things, wasn't it?

Certainty blinked herself back into the moment.

"Yes, we'd be happy to take part in the Fair," Aurelia was saying. "Is there anything we can contribute?"

"Ha! Not unless you can magick us up something to make Shpelling look more like Margrave. Those show-offs from Ruggan'll be here for the Fair, and they always have something to say about the chipping paint, or the fields left fallow . . . Especially Tobias. The man likes to pretend he's cityfolk now, as if I can't remember when he was just a sticky little boy stealing hand pies off of windowsills." The old woman gave a loud, disapproving sniff.

Certainty found it hard to imagine Tobias as a boy, let alone a sticky and larcenous one. "Why is he so . . ." She rummaged in her brain for the right words, but Gertha beat her to it.

"Puffed up and pissy?"

"Yes. And he seems to hate Aurelia and me especially!"

Gertha shrugged. "All I know is what I heard from the Ruggan folk, but he grew up—not *poor*, really, but having less than his neighbors. His pa passed young, see. The boy left for Margrave soon as he was old enough, and told everyone he'd become rich and important and never come back. But whatever his grand plans were, they fizzled out, and he ended up becoming a scribe, then a secretary to Lord Godfrey. Most of us would call it a fine station, but he's always seemed to think himself above it. No idea why when he's grown in the same soil as all the rest of us."

"Some people just always want more," said Certainty, shrugging.

Gertha sniffed again. "Seems a good way to keep yourself unhappy, if you ask me."

"It's not always easy to see that, though," Aurelia said quietly. "Even if it seems obvious to others."

Certainty looked at Aurelia in surprise, but she avoided her gaze.

"In any case . . ." Aurelia cleared her throat. "I'm not sure what we could do to help spruce the village up, but we're always happy to lend a hand with a sweeping spell or two."

Gertha waved off her offer. "Don't bother. I'm sure you've more important Guild things to be doing, although I can't imagine what in the Mother's name they might be. I'm off to the Plough; I'll see you two at dinner, yes?"

And without waiting for a response, she left.

"A proper Spring Fair!" Certainty beamed at Aurelia, who smiled back. She'd been smiling a lot more, Cert had noticed. Or rather, had determinedly tried *not* to notice.

"I've never been to one, you know. It should be quite educational."

Certainty sighed. "Fun, Aurelia. It's called fun."

WHEN THEY STROLLED together to the tavern that evening, they passed by Ferdinand the tavernkeep, sweaty and panting as he leaned on a large wooden barrel beside the path.

"Evening," he wheezed. "Don't suppose you two might be free for just a moment . . . ?"

"Good evening," said Aurelia. "Of course, can we assist you with . . ."

". . . with whatever it is you're doing?" finished Certainty.

"Yes indeed, thank you." He smoothed his mustache. "That'd be very kind of you. Just trying to get all this water down to the Plough, but it's funny how the same barrel seems to be getting heavier as I get older."

Together, the three of them tipped over the barrel and rolled it toward the tavern, taking care not to let it tumble down the slope. The water sloshed vigorously within, and soon enough they'd managed to get it all the way to the Plough's double doors without flattening any villagers, cats, or crops along the way.

"I miss the days when I could just fetch water from the well here," said Ferdinand, wiping his forehead and nodding toward the dusty well in the center of the village square. "But I suppose that'd just be too easy, hm? The gods like to keep us Shpelling folk on our toes. In any case, thank you both for the help. I'll take this barrel in now. We've got forty-clove chicken for dinner tonight; I'll fix you up two plates?"

"Yes, thank you," said Aurelia. He tipped an imaginary hat at them and disappeared into his tavern.

"You know," Certainty said, looking at the well. "It would also be convenient for us to be able to fetch our water from here, instead of having to walk all the way over to the other one by Hull's place."

"I suppose so." Aurelia leaned over the empty well to look. "Dry as a bone, though. Must have run empty ages ago."

Certainty hesitated, then lay her palm against the coarse stone of the well. It couldn't hurt just to check, could it? She sent a trickle of magic into it.

"Water well, can you tell me why you're dry?"

There was a long, despondent silence in her mind. Certainty was about to give up when, finally, the well responded to her, in a hoarse whisper like gravel on sand.

"Trapped, trapped," it wheezed, the words echoing strangely in her mind. *"Below, below. Parched, parched."*

Certainty's brows drew together. *"What is trapped? What do you mean, below?"*

She felt a frisson of despair from the well. *"My water! Trapped below, below, below. I was full, once. I gave it freely. People came to me each morning, but they come no longer. I am dry, dry, dry. Failed, failed, failed."*

Water... trapped below. Certainty leaned as far into the well as she could, listening intently. She thought she could detect just the slightest whisper of running water, faint and barely audible.

"Certainty?" Aurelia, watching with concern, lifted one arm as if to grab her in case she fell. "What is it saying?"

"It said that its water is trapped below. And I think I can hear it—can you?"

Aurelia tilted her head, also listening. "You're right! There must be an underwater river below it. Probably just too far below the well's current depth, unfortunately. Maybe Lord Godfrey can hire some stonemasons to deepen it."

"Remember the state the stable was in when we arrived? Lord Godfrey doesn't seem in any rush to spend coin on making improvements to Shpelling. I think it's up to us, if we want to do something about it."

Aurelia nibbled at her bottom lip. "You're right. I suppose I could try a water-summoning spell, but elemental magic was never my strong suit... We'd need a proper water mage for that. I could draw a bit of rain out of the air, but I can't pull a geyser out of the ground."

"Do you remember if we came across any water-generating artifacts in our inventory?"

"Well, there was that charm of underwater breathing that fills your mouth with seawater . . . and that staff of dousing that's meant to drown your enemies but just makes their socks damp . . ."

Certainty shook her head in frustration. "Well, it was worth a thought. Maybe we'll find something in the last few boxes."

There was a sudden *whoosh*, and a shadow crossed over them. Certainty pushed herself away from the well to squint up into the darkening sky. "What was that?"

Aurelia was looking up, too. "I thought I saw . . . maybe a very large bat?" But her voice was doubtful.

Certainty shrugged. Probably just a bird of some kind. Which reminded her that she was getting hungry. "Time to go have some forty-clove chicken?"

LATER THAT NIGHT, they split a slice of Gertha's sweet honeycake (Aurelia hesitated before eating her portion, but only briefly) and Aurelia reviewed the tome of records by candlelight ("I'm sure you've been very thorough, Cert, but it can't hurt to have a second pair of eyes—") while Certainty sat on her bed sewing a tear in her cloak. The woodstove burned merrily, the teapot was blissfully silent, and fresh bunches of lemon balm and mint were hung up to dry in the window. One of the more recently summoned cats—a plump tabby—was stretched out on the rug between their beds, thoroughly asleep and snoring softly.

It was altogether a cozy, quiet evening of the sort Certainty thought she might miss once they left Shpelling.

"Hmm," said Aurelia.

"Hmm?"

"Number 318. Do you think that might work?"

Certainty took the needle out from between her lips. "I haven't memorized every entry, Aurelia—I'm not you. Which one is that?"

Aurelia flicked a piece of straw at her. "The portable battering ram."

Certainty screwed up her nose, thinking. "Yes. What about it?"

"Do you think we could use it for the well?"

"How would that work? I thought its enchantment's nearly worn out. It only has enough power left to blast holes far too small for any—*oh*. Oh, I see."

If there was an underground body of water already flowing beneath the floor of the well, all they'd really need was to penetrate the rock layers just enough to release the pressure and give all that water a way up. It wouldn't matter whether the hole was small or large.

"Clever."

"I know," said Aurelia smugly.

Certainty tossed some straw back at her. "Didn't Mage Freinar have something to say about humility in his treatises, too?"

"I can't remember. Maybe it was only in the section written for novices." Aurelia smirked at Certainty—honest-to-gods *smirked*—and heat rushed to Certainty's face (and possibly a few other parts) as she instantly forgot whatever witty rejoinder she had planned to make. It was simply unfair the effect that the woman managed to have on her, even while being completely and utterly unaware of it. Certainty attempted to hide her reaction by reaching out for another piece of honeycake. The tabby awoke instantly and bounded up onto the bed beside her, eyes wide and interested as it focused on the cake. Distracted, she let it have a piece.

"I suppose the battering ram is worth a try," she said weakly, and then was punished for her sins by the sight of Aurelia licking sticky cake crumbs off her long fingers.

THE NEXT MORNING, Certainty and Aurelia carried the worn-out artifact, which was little more than a small, squat log with handles on the side and a hammered iron cap on one end, between them to the well. After some awkward lifting and positioning, and a great deal of huffing, they decided that the simplest method would be to tie a rope onto the handles and then drop the ram repeatedly down the well, iron-side down.

Certainty was sure they looked like fools, but fortunately none of Shpelling's residents—or, Mother forfend, *Tobias*—were nearby just then to witness it. Once the ram was rigged into place, she removed her gloves and placed one palm against the stone rim of the well.

"We're going to try to help you," she thought at it. *"We'll try to free the water."*

The well did not respond, but she thought she could feel a shiver of hope through their connection. She grabbed the handles of the log while Aurelia gripped the end of the rope that held it.

"Battering ram," Certainty thought next, sending fresh magic through her fingertips and into the artifact. *"Are you ready to ram?"*

"CHARGE! ATTACK!" The voice of the battering ram sounded like rusty metal drowning in ale. She got the impression of a drunken sergeant, roaring as he staggered toward the enemy; the log twitched violently beneath her hands, and she held onto the handles more firmly.

"No! No charging! We're not laying siege to anything today."

"No . . . charging?" The ram's voice was plaintive. *"I am an Enchanted Battering Ram of Might!"*

"*Yes, you are, and a very good ram you are, too. But I need you to blast a hole in a well, not a wall.*" Too late, Certainty realized how confusing that might be. "*I mean—in rock. Underground. To open a hole, so that water can fill a well.*"

"*But . . . I am a mighty weapon, not a shovel! Is there no glorious war? No enemy castle?*"

"*The ground is the enemy,*" she thought sternly at it. "*And you'll be helping these villagers get fresh water more easily, which is definitely more glorious than killing people.*"

"*Fine,*" said the ram, although it still sounded sulky. "*I will blast the ground. I will lay waste to all foes!*"

"*Just the one foe today, thank you.*"

Certainty took a breath, made sure the ram was positioned properly, and then spoke the enchantment's incantation out loud. "Perditio."

As soon as she felt the magic thrum to life beneath her fingers, she dropped the log and stepped back; propelled by its enchantment, it barreled downward with immense force to hit the hard, dry rock below. There was a massive, echoing *whump* from the well.

"Did it work?" Aurelia peered down into the darkness as she hauled the rope up. Eventually, the battering ram came back into sight, and the two of them balanced it on the side of the well. Alas, there was no sound of rushing water, and the well still looked as dry as it had before.

"Damn." Certainty chewed on her lip. "The magic took— I felt it—but . . . should we try again?"

Aurelia shrugged, and they made to position the battering ram for another attempt. Then the doors to the Golden Plough swung outward, and Ferdinand and Gertha emerged from within.

"What in the name of the Mother and the Maker Son are you two doing?"

"Aye, all that ruckus sounds like someone trying to knock a building down!"

"Er," said Certainty. "We thought we might be able to get this well working again."

The two villagers approached, eyeing the iron-capped ram dubiously.

"With that child's toy of a siege weapon?" Ferdinand asked.

"A *magical* siege weapon," said Aurelia indignantly.

The tavernkeep shook his head, his mustache bobbing at the ends. "It's a good idea, but it won't work. We've tried dropping heavy stones and the like before, see. Just compresses the dirt below. No, what might work is something like a big needle, if we could stab down with enough force to pierce through."

"I don't think we have anything like that," said Cert, mentally sorting through the artifacts in the stable.

Gertha snorted. "Of course you don't. Why would anyone own a giant blasted needle?"

But Aurelia's eyes were narrowed and thoughtful. "They might if they were a soldier. A pikeman, in fact. Ferdinand, am I correct in recalling that there's a very large pike hanging above your bar?"

Ferdinand looked surprised. "Aye, there is, but it'd never reach all the way down to the bottom of the well."

"Not on its own, maybe." Aurelia smiled, a glint in her eye. "Can we borrow it?"

IT TOOK A short while for Ferdinand to find a ladder, and longer to wrest the pike off the rusty brackets holding it to the wall, but eventually they managed to carry it out to the well. While this was being done, Aurelia returned to the stable to fetch *No. 180*, the enchanted shrinking vambrace sized for a giant.

Brienna happened to be walking by as Ferdinand carried the spear out of the tavern's doors, and her eyes widened in alarm at the sight of the tavernkeep wielding the half-rusted old weapon.

"Hello, Ferdinand," the baker said uncertainly. "Are you expecting to need that spear today, then?"

He waved one hand at her. "The lady mages want to try something with it, that's all! Won't be attacking anyone. Not in my old age, anyway."

This didn't seem to reassure Brienna particularly, but she wished them good luck all the same as she left the square. Aurelia took the pike very carefully from Ferdinand and laid it on the ground beside the battering ram.

"You see, if we can combine the pike with the battering ram," she said, placing the enormous metal vambrace over both the pike's shaft and the iron cap of the battering ram, "then the ram's force can be applied to the pike's iron point. Simple physics. Theoretically, anyway." She looked up at Certainty, eyes alight with scholarly enthusiasm. "Will you do the honors?"

Certainty eyed the arrangement dubiously, but shrugged. It was worth a shot. She knelt beside the vambrace and pulled off her glove, touching one finger to its metallic plates.

"*Prepare for battle*," she commanded it.

There was a chiming noise, and the vambrace suddenly glowed red beneath her finger; she pulled her hand away hurriedly, but it wasn't hot. It simply glowed, and then, as the four of them watched, its thousands of tiny plates shrank in, molding the metal around both the end of the pike and the end of the battering ram to pull them together into one deadly-looking contraption.

"Well!" said Aurelia, pleased. "That ought to do it, I think."

She, Ferdinand, and Certainty angled the unwieldy apparatus

into place in the center of the well while Gertha stood several safe paces away, muttering about foolish ex-soldiers turning the village into an armory. As Aurelia and Ferdinand held the rope, Certainty took a breath and touched the battering ram once more.

"*Let me at them!*" roared the siege engine in her mind. "*I'll pulverize the—wait. What has been done to me? What is this pointy thing stuck on my end??*"

"It's an upgrade," Certainty thought quickly. "*A weapon! To make you even more, er, fearsome and deadly.*"

"*I was already fearsome and deadly.*" The battering ram's voice was petulant.

"*Before, you could only knock down doors and walls! With the pike, now you can also impale people.*" Certainty tried to be encouraging. "*Anyway, we need you to attack again. It didn't work last time.*"

A spike of indignant alarm came through her magic. "*Our foe still lives?*"

"*Yes, but you can help us achieve victory by piercing it!*"

The battering ram vibrated eagerly where it hung above the well, ready to attack. Certainty grinned.

"Perditio," she said once more, and the makeshift spear-cannon blasted itself down into the well. There was a sharp cracking sound, like rock splintering—and then, blessedly, the eager hiss of water spurting upward, and the well began to fill.

Ferdinand whooped, and Aurelia gave a small cheer. Gertha deigned to shuffle closer, peering down as if to verify for herself that the well had water again.

"Hmph," she said, for once at a loss for anything more critical to say.

They hauled their magical contraption back up to the surface and laughed when it swung on the rope and dripped water on them. The well was already nearly half-full of clean, clear water; Certainty could even see the blurry outlines of their reflections in it.

As Ferdinand carefully untied the rope, Aurelia smiled at Certainty—there were those blasted dimples again—and flicked a drop of water at her.

"Well, I'd call that a success." The mage looked very pleased with herself. "Wouldn't you?"

THEY WERE GIVEN extra-large servings of pasta with meat sauce at dinner that night, and even Gertha, sitting at the head of the communal table, lifted her mug grudgingly when Ferdinand raised a toast to the saviors of the central well. Something about the tavern was different, though, Certainty thought as they sat down to their meals. The place felt . . . brighter. More cheerful.

She looked around, only then noticing the many small changes that Ferdinand had made. He must have sanded down the long table, which no longer bore its previous stains and divots, and at some point had also swapped out the mismatched stools for new chairs. There were fresh rush mats on the floor, too, lending the air a scent of sweet spices and hay, and all the dribbly old candle stubs around the room had been replaced with new ones that stood tall and proud in their carved wooden candleholders. The dusty windows were wiped clean, and even the hearth looked like someone had scrubbed all the soot off.

All in all, it was a remarkable difference: The Golden Plough now looked like a respectable inn rather than a deteriorating relic.

It was also far busier than it had been when Certainty and Aurelia had first arrived in Shpelling—there was hardly a free chair, the room was so tightly packed with customers. Most were Shpelling folk whom Certainty recognized from around the village, but some faces were unfamiliar. People visiting from Ruggan, perhaps, or the odd traveler stopping for a meal. Regardless, it was a large and attentive crowd to whom Ferdinand told the story of the well that night. He told it over and over, gesturing emphatically at the battering-spear contraption (which had been put back into its pride of place on the wall) while his audience oohed and aahed in all the right places. Villagers came by Certainty and Aurelia's table to clap them on the back and say their thank-yous, and Certainty observed how Aurelia seemed to glow under the light of their praise.

She noticed, too, that Aurelia wasn't wearing her necklace. And it *wasn't* because her eyes were drifting along the lines of Aurelia's collarbone—not at all.

It was good to see the mage so relaxed in this setting—such a stark difference from how tense her shoulders had been the first night they'd arrived; how she'd held herself rigid and braced, as if always under the threat of attack. Certainty's eyes lingered on the battering-pike above the bar, and her thoughts turned to the items that they'd spent the last several weeks cataloging.

"Have you noticed how many of the artifacts we brought with us are weapons?" she asked Aurelia. "Or are intended to be, anyway. The battering ram, the wand, all these magical daggers and arrows and so on—they were made for fighting. Even if they're not very useful for it anymore."

Loose hair fell over Aurelia's eyes as she tilted her head. "Well, the Mage Wars were a dark time. Eshterans needed magic to protect themselves against magic."

"Yes, but these aren't items for protection. They're things made to hurt people."

"And that's its own form of protection, isn't it? If someone's coming at you with a big stick, you wave about your own, bigger stick to scare them away." Aurelia gestured with her fork. "Deterrence."

Certainty frowned. "But then everyone's running around with very big sticks, and tripping over them, and dropping them in places where the big sticks cause a lot of unintended damage, like killing the plants and chasing away the cats and bees, and . . . this metaphor is getting away from me." She blew a breath out.

But Aurelia seemed to understand what she was trying to say.

"These artifacts are mostly very old, Cert. Relics of a darker, worse time. I think the Guild has made a lot of progress, expanding the ways in which magic can be used for good. Just look at what our harvest mages do, or the network of healers that the Guild is putting into place."

"I suppose," Certainty said. "But it still feels as though all those things come second to the Guild's main value to Eshtera. Which is being the biggest stick." She tapped her own fork lightly against Aurelia's; the mage smiled but looked thoughtful.

"You're not wrong. The mages considered most powerful are often still the ones who can do the most damage, like the fire mages. And if Eshtera were to go to war again, all of us farspeakers would serve alongside the generals, because that's where the Crown would want us. To coordinate the movements of armies and plan attacks. But . . . it would be nice if we learned to value other, quieter kinds of magic just as much." Aurelia put her fork down on her plate, but her hand stayed close enough to Certainty's that she could feel the warmth emanating from it. "Like yours."

Certainty swallowed.

"My magic isn't just quiet, it's practically useless," she said, trying for flippant but landing somewhere near bitter. "I don't do anything that a few well-written scrolls of identification couldn't do. I'm lucky that the Guild has let me hang around this long as a novice. Lucky that the High Mage thinks I might still be useful, helping Mage Mortimer in the vaults."

"It's *not* useless." Certainty was surprised at the sudden fierceness in Aurelia's voice. The mage gestured emphatically at the bustling activity around them in the tavern. "Look at what you've done for Shpelling already, in just a few short weeks! That wasn't just the artifacts, Cert, that was you. Nobody else would have thought to even try. That's—that's a different kind of power."

"Oh," said Certainty.

Her throat felt tight and prickly, and she had to look away from Aurelia's face for fear that her emotions were written too clearly on her own. They lapsed into silence again, but it was a warm silence, taut with tenderness and things unspoken.

And when she offered Aurelia the plate of garlic bread, the mage's fingers lingered just for a moment on hers, and left the slightest tingle in their wake.

INTERLUDE

NIGHT FELL, AND all in the village of Shpelling was silent and still.

All, that is, except the dancing fireflies. And the mice. And the bats, and the raccoons, and a solitary mole burrowing down beneath rows and rows of garlic shoots. There were the hunting owls, too. And the—

All right, so not everything was still. The village of Shpelling positively bustled with nocturnal activity.

Gangs of cats padded through shadows behind the tavern, eyes glowing and whiskers a-twitch. (One particular cat—if cat it still was—soared and swooped above the village on wings of night, practically invisible against the dark sky of a waning moon.)

In Hull's grove, the bees buzzed happily in their beechwood boxes, filling the cells of their honeycombs with sweet nectar. Not far away, a soft snoring could be heard from Murph and Brienna's barn as their cows dreamed merry cow dreams. And the old well in the village square sloshed and burbled, the hanging water bucket creaking softly where it swayed in the breeze.

Shpelling had been transformed. New, fresh magic had arrived. Carted in, unloaded, and released into the village like . . .

Well, like a swarm of bees.

And drawn by the buzzing liveliness of this new magic were streams of old magic, too, filling the gaps in between. The ancient, wild magic of the land had kindled and begun to return—but it came in bursts, as if it had been pent-up and was making up for decades of lost time. (It was.)

As it forced its way up through roots and pebbles, it produced some unusual effects:

A cream-colored hen accustomed to producing eggs of a lovely blue was mildly perturbed to find one morning that she hadn't been keeping an egg warm, but instead a fat golden acorn.

The wheat that Murph had optimistically sown in his empty field sprouted into spindly seedlings. This wouldn't have been entirely odd, except for the fact that they did so in a perfectly geometric zigzagging pattern.

A farmer about to shear his sheep was equal parts surprised and delighted to find that his sheep had not only shorn themselves, but also somehow contrived to spin the wool into neat stacks of balled yarn.

The yarn was pink.

These currents of wild magic, swirling and singing, eventually made their way into a wooded copse and a clearing atop a hill. They thrummed through desiccated tangles of roots, through layers of dry soil and sandy gravel, and found their path blocked by a circle of dull lifelessness. But the land was not dead, even though it may have seemed so to the world.

It was merely . . . dormant.

The wild magic encircled this strange clearing. Its tendrils prodded gently at it; sought entrance. *Let me in*, the magic seemed to whisper. *I am of you.*

And slowly, so slowly, the sleeping land awoke, and began to drink . . .

THIRTEEN

WITH ONLY FOUR days remaining until the Spring Fair, the village was in a state of frenzied preparation. Ferdinand had recruited Orrin to help fix the Golden Plough's crooked window shutters, and Hull stood outside squinting up and shouting largely unhelpful instructions at them. Murph and Brienna's cows, out grazing in their pasture, were suddenly and inexplicably wearing flower garlands around their necks. And Gertha—well, Gertha was nowhere to be seen, but word was that she'd barricaded herself in her kitchen, baking enough honeycake to feed all of eastern Eshtera. No matter where Certainty looked, there was a villager weeding, scrubbing, sweeping, or otherwise attempting to make Shpelling look its fairday best.

When she and Aurelia stopped by the well in the square to fetch water, a woman there—Doreen, a grandmotherly sort clutching a discontented goose under one arm—hinted unsubtly that perhaps the nice lady mages from the Guild might want to spruce up the old stable and carriage house for the fair, yes? So, feeling pressured, they retreated to the stable and stood outside evaluating its appearance with a more critical eye.

The vines that cascaded down from the carriage house roof

had bloomed practically overnight, covering the worn stone walls with a lush shawl of tiny purple flowers that stretched over the left side of the stable. A pair of butterflies, one yellow and one white, chased each other in fluttering circles between the flowers. The freshly patched roof and aged stone of the buildings might have looked motley, but somehow, seen under the bright blue sky, looked charmingly lived-in instead. (That blasted orange rooster was perched on the roof again, too, but Certainty thought that she might have finally managed to strike a tentative peace with it over crumbs of honeycake.)

Altogether, the place looked like something old and unwanted made beautiful again through use and care.

"I think it already looks wonderful," Certainty said.

"Yes," Aurelia said quietly. "I do, too."

"*Bokk*," opined the rooster from above.

They stood there silently, side by side. The two butterflies danced up and away, over and behind the hills. Then Hull shouted something unintelligible down in the square, and the sound rippled through the moment, breaking the surface of it like a leaf fallen onto still water. Aurelia cleared her throat.

"Anyway, it's a stable, not a dollhouse. What do they expect us to do, cover it in lace?"

"I suppose we could paint it? Or plant some more flowers?"

Then they heard a soft clattering sound from inside the carriage house. The women looked at each other in alarm—an intruder? Certainty looked down at the salt that encircled the building; it was still unbroken, from what she could tell.

Aurelia moved decisively, grabbing a fallen branch from nearby. Wielding it like a mace, she advanced grimly on the carriage house and threw open the door.

"If you think you can get away with stealing from the Guild of Mages, you have—"

But the words died on her lips. Impatient, Certainty edged around the mage to look for herself, and she saw . . .

A cat on the desk, casually eating the remains of their honeycake.

A cat with *dragon wings*.

"Certainty . . ." Aurelia's words were slow and careful. "Did you perhaps conduct any other magical experiments that you neglected to tell me of?"

"No!"

Unruffled by being discovered, the catdragon cleaned cake crumbs off its face and then delicately washed a paw. It unfurled black wings, flapped them once or twice, and glided easily to the doorway. Aurelia and Certainty took several hasty steps backward, but the catdragon only tucked its wings back and wound itself nonchalantly between the two women, rubbing up on their ankles.

"Meow," it said, blinking up at them. (The rooster, clucking in alarm, made a hasty escape.)

Maybe the creature was thanking them for the cake. Certainty reached down and tentatively stroked its back, dragging one fingertip gently along a folded wing. It felt like soft, scaled leather. The catdragon arched its back and purred, and a stifled noise came from Aurelia's direction. The noise sounded like a squee, but surely that couldn't be right.

"What do we do with it? Aurelia?"

But Aurelia only had eyes for the catdragon. She seemed utterly entranced. Certainty wondered if she'd ever had a pet growing up. Probably not—her parents didn't sound much like pet people.

"I suppose . . . I suppose it would be very irresponsible for us to keep her, wouldn't it?"

Aurelia's voice was wistful. She tossed the branch aside and reached down to scratch the creature under its chin. The catdragon closed its eyes in clear enjoyment, and it was hard to say whether it or Aurelia was more charmed with the other.

Certainty thought quickly.

"Couldn't it be argued that it would be equally irresponsible of us to *not* keep her? Releasing a clearly magical creature into the Eshteran countryside?"

Aurelia looked up, eyes glinting. ". . . an excellent point, Novice. Who knows what kind of threat she might pose to innocent villagers?"

"Exactly." Certainty grinned back at her. "We'd only be doing our duty to the Guild and to Eshtera. Keeping the kingdom safe from unknown monsters and ferocious beasts. Honestly, the Guild ought to give us a medal."

The ferocious beast meowed again, pawing at Aurelia for more pets, and Cert knew from the look in the mage's eyes that the war was won.

"She'll need a name. What should we call her?"

Aurelia hesitated, looking down at the creature with soft eyes. Then she looked back up at Certainty. "Hope. Let's call her Hope."

Certainty's breath hitched at the longing in Aurelia's voice. "Good name."

And when Hope the catdragon decided that she had had enough of the dusty ground and flew up to settle herself in Aurelia's arms instead, the mage could not hide her delight.

THEIR NEW COMPANION seemed perfectly content to be domesticated. After exploring the rest of the stable, she flew about in lazy circles for a while. Then she carried a few mouthfuls of straw to a corner of the rafters, made herself a nest, and curled up there in a purring ball, emerging only occasionally for more scraps of honeycake and attention.

Aurelia and Cert kept a close eye on the catdragon at first. Aurelia in particular was anxious about whether the creature might begin to breathe flame ("It's a common trait of dragons, Cert, everyone knows that!"), which would pose something of a problem given the flammability of their beds, the straw, the roof, and, well, everything. But Hope betrayed no further magical abilities besides draconic flight and feline adorableness, and soon became just one more piece of their lives in Shpelling. The villagers, too, took her arrival surprisingly in stride.

"I don't suppose this wee beastie belongs to you two?" asked Hull one day. He'd stopped by the stable with a fresh slab of honeycomb for them, and Hope was draped over his shoulder, pawing at the wrapped bundle and meowing furiously. The farmer had to stretch out his arm to keep the honeycomb away.

"Oh—oh dear! I'm so sorry, Hull—"

Certainty took the honeycomb and Aurelia snatched Hope off of the beleaguered farmer. The catdragon meowed petulantly, wriggling and flapping in the mage's grip.

"Found it in one of my apple trees, watching a nest of robins in a way I didn't like."

Hull rubbed at his shoulder; Certainty could imagine the scratches that Hope's claws might have left there. Her own arms already bore a crisscrossing of fine red lines from misjudging when Hope did or did not want to be stroked (although, in her defense, it seemed the catdragon often changed her mind on that subject mid-pet).

"Hope, we've talked about this," Aurelia said sternly to the catdragon that was currently mimicking an ill-tempered sack of potatoes in her arms. "You're to leave the birds *alone*, yes? No eating other flappy things? The gods know there are enough rodents here to keep you fed. And that awful secretary would love to charge us with unleashing a terrible bloodthirsty predator upon the village."

"*Mrao*," Hope said, clearly sulking.

Aurelia sighed and let Hope down onto the straw. The cat-dragon promptly hop-flew back out the open doors of the stable.

"I do apologize, Hull. I hope she didn't frighten you or cause any damage in your grove."

He waved an easy hand. "It's all right, miss, no harm done. In truth, I was more worried about the bees going after her than anything else."

They all looked out the stable window, where Hope could now be seen swooping in lazy circles above the village square. A few puzzled villagers squinted up at her, and one little girl squealed in delight as she pointed.

Hull grinned. "I think you'll find, miss, that Shpelling folk have come to have a more accepting view of all things magical than before."

ORRIN IN PARTICULAR fawned over Hope from the instant the two met, and could thereafter reliably be expected to have pockets full of cheese rinds whenever he visited the stable.

Even though the stable had been fully repaired and the carriage house made into comfortable lodgings, the boy still came by most afternoons to see if they needed his help with anything. Aurelia generally managed to find some sort of useful task for him—fetching more water, or chopping wood for the stove—and he seemed glad for any excuse to hang about.

"I've decided to go to Margrave," he proclaimed one day while sweeping fresh straw into one of the stalls. Hope swooped down to bat at his broom, thinking it an excellent game.

Certainty and Aurelia were seated at the desk, working their way through another box of unidentified artifacts, but they looked up at this.

"Oh?"

"Yes. I'm going to apply to join the Guildtower's guardsmen!" He puffed his chest out.

The two women exchanged a look. "Aren't you . . . a little young for that?" Aurelia asked carefully.

Orrin's chest unpuffed. "I don't know. How old do I have to be?"

Certainty didn't know the formal requirements, but she did know that every guard she saw in the Guildtower looked like they could easily bench-press Orrin. Several Orrins.

Aurelia was better informed. "Eighteen, at least, and there's an extensive set of physical tests. I think they generally like to recruit veterans from the Royal Army, or perhaps the Palace Guard."

Orrin slumped against his broom. "Oh. Well . . . maybe in a few years, then." Then a hopeful expression sprang onto his face. "Mage Aurelia, do you think I could use you as a reference when I apply? You know, so you could put in a good word."

"Sure," Aurelia said, smiling. "I'll tell them how helpful you've been to us."

The boy went pink. "Thanks, miss. I hope they accept me. So that I can see you around the Guildtower." Certainty hid her laugh behind a cough, and he glanced at her in embarrassment. "Both of you, I mean."

"I'm sure you will."

But Certainty looked at him in all his eagerness and felt a pang in her chest. She saw herself at seventeen, boarding a mail coach bound for Margrave. Saw her parents, anxious and proud, waving goodbye.

"Orrin . . . just don't be in too much of a rush to leave, all right?" She smiled a little, trying to lighten her words. "Everything will be different when you leave home. You'll come back to visit, I'm sure, and your family'll still be here, but it won't ever be the same as it is now. So just . . . try to hang on to it all for a little longer, if you can?"

He nodded uncertainly at her, but Certainty didn't think he quite understood. But maybe that was just how things were. Maybe that was what people meant by wisdom coming with age—like wrinkles and bad knees, it came whether you liked it or not, and only when it was too late to do anything about it. She was sure that in ten years, she'd be looking back at herself as she was now and thinking *What an idiot.*

Orrin left soon after, giving Hope a scratch behind the wings as he did so and blushing furiously when Aurelia thanked him again for his help.

Certainty couldn't hold back her amusement any longer. As she tied a label onto a pair of iron-plated mittens (No. 373, gauntlets of warming), she said, "Careful, Aurelia. That boy's likely to follow us home if you smile at him one more time."

"What do you mean?"

"Oh, come on, surely you're not that oblivious. He's smitten with you."

Aurelia gaped at her. "Orrin? He's half my age."

"I don't think he minds an older woman. Honestly, how haven't you noticed?"

It was the mage's turn to blush. "I . . . I wasn't really paying attention. I haven't had much experience with, uh, attracting attention. Of that kind."

Certainty scoffed. "What, you? Look at you, with your hair and your—your face—" She gestured vaguely at all of Aurelia, aware she was edging closer to dangerous territory. *Careful, Cert.*

"I'm sure you've left a trail of brokenhearted suitors halfway from the White Palace to here."

Aurelia snorted in unladylike fashion, then looked appalled at herself for doing so. "Hardly. I haven't had time for that sort of thing."

"Trust me, there's *always* time for that sort of thing." Certainty thought of Dav and other friends at the Guildtower. She'd covered more than one chore shift for a fellow novice who'd been getting too busy in a linen closet to actually fold any linens.

"Yes, well . . ." Aurelia cleared her throat and smoothed down her robes. "I suppose there was someone, several years ago."

"Who was he? Another novice? A scholar?" Too late, Certainty realized her questions might be intrusive. "Only if you want to tell me, of course; you don't have to. Actually, forget I asked."

Aurelia went quiet for a fraction too long. Certainty had the sense that the mage was wrestling with herself, but then suddenly she spoke again without meeting Certainty's eyes.

"She was a merchant's daughter."

A woman. Certainty felt a sudden, wild, irresponsible surge of hope—but *no, stop it, just because she might've kissed one woman once doesn't mean she wants to kiss* you! It took her a moment to wrestle these inconvenient thoughts down, and in the meantime, the silence stretched between them, tense and expectant. She panicked. *Shit. Say something!*

"Oh," Certainty squeaked, before swallowing and trying again in a more normal voice. "Of course. Not *of course* of course, just, um. I mean, that's fine. Absolutely fine. With me."

She wanted to strangle herself with her own apron strings. What was that? Mother and Sons, she wished she could slide right off the bench. Novice Certainty Bulrush of Potshire could cease to exist entirely, and she'd just become a drippy little puddle of melted awkwardness on the stable floor for the rest of existence.

But . . . she also couldn't stop herself from wanting to know more.

"So, uh." She tried to sound casual. Interested, but not *too* interested. "What happened? With her, I mean."

Aurelia was avoiding her eyes. "My parents found out. They . . . didn't approve."

"Because she was . . ." Certainty didn't know how to finish the question. A woman? Only a merchant's daughter? All of the above?

"A distraction," Aurelia said simply.

"Oh."

Certainty stared very hard at the silver hair comb she was supposed to be identifying. Aurelia did the same with the record book, seeming suddenly fascinated by a particular entry. After a few moments, without looking up, Aurelia spoke again.

"So do you . . ."

"No," said Certainty immediately. "I mean, I also—yes."

"Um," said Aurelia. "I see."

And that was when Certainty realized she didn't actually know what Aurelia's question was going to be. *Blast.* What had she just said no or yes to? No, she wasn't seeing anyone? Yes, she also was attracted to women, or at least one woman in particular? No, she didn't want any more tea??

Certainty stifled a groan. Why was she *like* this? It's not as if she were some blushing maiden who'd never been kissed before. She could make bawdy jokes with the best of them!

But perhaps the difference was simply that this was Aurelia, an unexpected source of attraction whom she'd at least been able to place on the mental shelf of "unattainable, not an actual prospect, don't bother fantasizing"—until now.

Now, of course, she could far too clearly picture the sight of Aurelia kissing this unknown merchant's daughter, of soft lips against the hollow of her neck, of slender fingers fumbling with skirts and bodices and . . .

Godsdamnit, and now it had been far too long for her to retract her response and ask Aurelia to repeat the question. *Brilliant. Well done, Cert.* She fought the urge to thunk her head against the table repeatedly.

So with that mutually unsatisfying exchange, the two of them returned to their work, although Certainty could barely focus enough to channel any more magic, and the rest of the afternoon flew by in a blurry haze of embarrassment.

And in the evening, when they retired to the carriage house to go to bed, Certainty couldn't help but be painfully, intensely aware of the fact that Aurelia was changing into her sleeping clothes just a few arm's-lengths behind her. She rolled over to face the wall, ignoring the sounds of clothing sliding against skin, the rustle as Aurelia climbed into her bed, the soft rise and fall as Aurelia's breathing eventually slowed.

Sleep was a long time coming for her that night.

FOURTEEN

THE NEXT EVENING, Certainty and Aurelia entered the Plough to discover that it was garlic-and-bean stew for dinner again. Ferdinand, alas, had entirely run out of the flour and eggs needed to make more pasta. He'd begun negotiations with a miller down in Ruggan for a steadier supply, and for the sake of her stomach, Certainty very much hoped that he managed to close the deal soon.

When Ferdinand finally brought their meals over, he was juggling two plates of stew along with a letter and a small, twine-and-paper-wrapped bundle. He dropped the mail onto the table in front of Certainty before setting their plates down.

"These came for you by messenger earlier," he said. "Oh, and Old Gertha said to ask you both to please meet her by the main road tomorrow morning, if you're not too busy then."

"Liar," said Certainty immediately. "Gertha wouldn't ask half so politely."

Ferdinand's mustache twitched. "All right, maybe she didn't quite use those words. Still, you get the gist. Said she wants to show you two something."

Then a customer called his name across the tavern, and he

made a noise of annoyance—the Golden Plough was a great deal busier these days—but Certainty could tell he was secretly pleased. He gave them a roguish wink before rushing off to whichever table had called for him.

"Is that from Margrave?" Aurelia tilted her head at the package.

"Potshire, I expect." Certainty turned the letter over in her hands; she recognized her father's handwriting. She pulled the twine loose from the package, feeling the shape of a jar, and smiled.

"What is it?"

Certainty unwrapped the jar and pried open its lid, closing her eyes to inhale from it. The scent of ripe pears was divine. It smelled like the essence of sunshine and sweetness, like laughter and sticky hands in the kitchen. It smelled of home.

"It's jam—pear jam. My ma makes it every fall." She dug her spoon in and pulled out a fat scoop. "Want to try?"

Aurelia accepted the spoon and took a hesitant nibble. Her eyes fluttered half-closed. "That's . . . delicious."

"Isn't it?" Certainty finished the bite, licking the spoon clean and trying not to think about the fact that Aurelia's mouth had also just been on it. "My da must've known I'd be missing it."

"I see."

They ate their meals in companionable silence then, but Certainty noticed that Aurelia seemed a little melancholic. When they returned to the carriage house after dinner, Certainty went to read her father's letter while Aurelia brewed them both a pot of rose hip tea ("—*rose hips, how novel! I shan't steep too strongly then, or the delicate flavor will be ruined. I refuse to be responsible for any bitterness; I have a reputation, you know—*"). She ignored the chattering of the enchanted teapot and tried to focus on the words before her.

Dear Cert,

I could hardly get a few minutes of peace and quiet to write back to you once we'd read your last message, it caused such a stir in the house. A magehood, at last—oh, Certainty, I know how hard you've worked for it all these years. And the idea of you earning it just in time for Asp to leave with Master Jamison—! The boy's beside himself.

Mother and Scholar Son watch over you, and may the rest of your assignment in Shpelling go smoothly and quickly. Do you think the Guild will give you leave to come visit us after you're made mage? I hope so; we all can't wait to see you in silver robes and those shiny Guild circles. My daughter, Mage Certainty. Imagine that!

We're so very proud of you, Cert. I hope you know that.

Sending our love (and a jar of your ma's jam),
Da

Certainty felt herself smiling as she folded the letter and put it beside the jar of jam. They could eat it with bread for breakfast. If they were careful, the jar might even last them the rest of their time in Shpelling.

Aurelia handed her a cup of tea, watching her with an unreadable expression.

"It's nice of him to think of you," she said.

"He's like that. He'd probably send me a full bushel of pears at harvest time, if the messengers would let him," Certain said fondly.

"Sounds like a good father."

"He is. He always put us first when we were growing up. Gave Asp and me the best bits at dinner, gave us pennies for sweets even when we couldn't really afford them..."

Aurelia looked down at her folded hands, and Certainty suddenly realized that the mage hadn't received any personal letters at all during their time in Shpelling—nothing from friends or family.

"He must love you and your brother very much," said Aurelia. Her voice was brittle.

For a moment, Certainty didn't know how to respond.

"But I'm sure your parents are proud of you, too..." Aurelia was an accomplished mage, after all—surely any parents, even Middle City aristocrats, would be pleased to have such a daughter.

Aurelia didn't reply immediately. She sat down across from Certainty on her own bed, ankles crossed. The carriage house was narrow enough that their knees were nearly touching.

"Not quite."

"But a Guild mage for a daughter—a farspeaker, no less!"

"They would've preferred that I had a high position at court, like them. And I'm a defective farspeaker, Cert. One whose ability doesn't work anymore. One who very nearly caused them the great embarrassment of having a daughter expelled from the Guild. They still haven't forgiven me for that."

"Forgiven you?" The image of a younger Aurelia, distraught, staring down at her feet while her parents castigated her for something she had no control over—it made Certainty want to have some *words* with Aurelia's parents, no matter what fancy court titles they might hold. "It's not as if you did it on purpose. You didn't *choose* to lose your farspeaking."

"That doesn't matter. Not to them." Aurelia's voice had gone clipped in that way again. "I thought for a time that if I made up for it in other ways—if I earned recognition for my scholarship, perhaps—that might be enough to compensate. But..." She gave a short laugh. "Clearly not. Mother and Sons only know what they're going to say once they learn the Guild has sent me here."

Suddenly, so many things about Aurelia made a great deal more sense to Certainty. She sat back against the wall, looking at Aurelia, seeing her in a new light.

"That's why you push yourself so hard, isn't it? You think that if you can restore your farspeaking..."

Aurelia met her gaze then. The yearning in her face—the desire for absolution, for love, for all of her sacrifice to have been *for* something—made Certainty's breath catch. Candlelight flickered in green eyes that carried their own spell of enchantment, and Certainty was helpless to look away.

"I push myself because I want to be... whole. Fixed. Because I'm not like other people, and this is my way of becoming someone of value, someone worth caring about. Isn't that what we all want?" Aurelia gave a despairing little laugh. "Sometimes I wonder—is everyone else just better at hiding it than I am?"

Certainty let out her breath in a slow exhale. "I think..."

It suddenly felt to her that this conversation was a crucial one. That how she responded to Aurelia would take the two of them down one forking pathway or another, and that her answer could change everything, or nothing at all. But what was the right answer? Certainty didn't know. So she spoke as honestly as she could.

"Aurelia... I think most of us just want to be happy."

"Oh." Each word from Aurelia's mouth was a small, breakable thing; a butterfly caught in a glass. "But I want that, too. I just haven't figured out how."

Certainty's heart ached at the longing in her voice. This woman—this brilliant, beautiful, magical woman—deserved so much more than what the world had given her.

More than tests and assignments, and never measuring up to the expectations heaped upon her. More than guilt and being defined by one terrible mistake. More than loneliness and isolation, than having to earn and re-earn the right to be loved, than believing the cup that held her worth was one with holes at the bottom, draining away as quickly as she could fill it.

Cert took a deep breath, looking into Aurelia's eyes. They were as green and still as the heart of a forest.

"Here's the how, Aurelia. If you find yourself feeling happy—and I don't just mean in a good mood, but really, truly happy... where it feels like everything that's ever happened, good or bad, must have been right because it led you to that moment. When you find yourself there, you need to figure out what it is that's made you feel like that."

"And then what?" Aurelia whispered. The air stretched between them, taut as a thread of silk.

"And then don't ever let it go."

There was no sound inside the carriage house but the soft crackling of the fire and Hope's rhythmic purring. Certainty felt stripped bare by Aurelia's gaze. When Aurelia spoke next, her voice was so feathery-soft that it nearly disappeared among the curls of steam rising from the tea beside her.

"Cert, I think I'm happier than I've ever been." Aurelia took a quiet, shuddering breath. "Here. With you."

Oh.

Intoxicating warmth coursed through Certainty's body. Her fingertips tingled as if she were channeling every drop of magic in her body. She could suddenly hear each breath she took, loud as thunder in her ears, and she discovered, too, that they'd been leaning in toward each other, and now the distance between her face and Aurelia's was both impossibly far and terrifyingly small.

This close, she thought she could count each blond eyelash, every sun-kissed freckle. Aurelia's eyes were lidded as they traced Certainty's face. Cert's mind was empty—no, it was full, she was drowning in Aurelia's nearness, and—

Aurelia kissed her. Kissed her with lips that were warm and tentative.

Certainty kissed her back.

She didn't let herself think. Couldn't, if she wanted to. She raised one hand to the curve of Aurelia's neck, where she felt the quickening of a pulse beneath warm skin. She let her fingers tangle in long golden hair, and her lips part, and all the while, Aurelia kissed her like she was everything she had ever wanted.

And all Certainty knew then was that everything that had ever happened to her, good or bad, must have been so wonderfully, extraordinarily right to have led her to this moment.

THUD.

They leapt apart, looking around. Hope had knocked over the jar of jam.

Certainty couldn't help it—she laughed, and Aurelia did, too.

Aurelia leaned back, flushed, and Certainty did the same, though she still felt a tingling warmth on her lips. The kiss had been so warm and soft, so full of yearning. All she wanted to do was return to it, but . . .

"We shouldn't . . ." Aurelia started.

"No, you're right," Certainty said quickly.

Aurelia swallowed, looking regretful, and Certainty tore her eyes away from the movement of her throat. This was a terrible, terrible idea. Of course they couldn't get romantically entangled.

Or physically entangled, as tantalizing as the images flitting through Certainty's head were.

Aurelia was still breathing heavily. Certainty desperately avoided noticing the way her chest heaved with each breath.

"I'm sorry," Aurelia said. Her voice was just a touch deeper and rougher than normal. "I didn't mean to—I mean, I *did*—but we . . . we shouldn't. We're on assignment."

"Right," said Certainty inanely. Gods, she could still smell the lavender scent of Aurelia's hair. How did she smell so good? They used the same soap! "Yes. That's fine. You're fine. I mean, you're right."

"We ought to . . . keep things professional." Aurelia seemed to be trying to convince herself as much as Certainty. Her hands twisted together in their lap.

"Absolutely." Aurelia's bottom lip was extra red where Certainty had nibbled it. "I'm sorry, too."

"Don't be. It was . . . I was the one who . . ." Aurelia's voice petered out weakly.

Certainty flapped one hand as if to wave the words away, even though part of her was screaming that she was being an idiot, an upright, self-denying idiot, when Aurelia was still right there and freshly kissed and so very beautiful. But also . . .

Rationality reasserted itself in Certainty. They were so close to completing the inventory. There was only one crate of unidentified artifacts left; they had to stay focused. Perhaps back at the Guildtower, after Certainty had received her circles and sent the money home for Asp, things could be different . . .

Hope meowed and they moved away, laughing awkwardly again, and as they busied themselves with preparing for bed, Certainty determinedly avoided looking at Aurelia. They didn't talk about the kiss. But the carriage house had never seemed quite so cramped as when they changed, each facing the opposite wall; Certainty could feel every electrifyingly small movement of air against her skin as Aurelia moved through the space behind her.

And when they slipped into bed (their *separate* beds, groused the less sensible but much more fun part of her brain), all that followed was a very loud silence in which Certainty's heart hammered hard enough to patch another roof, and each of them pretended not to be listening closely to the other's breaths.

FIFTEEN

CERTAINTY WOKE FIRST the next morning. She rolled over, taking in the sight of Aurelia asleep on the opposite bed. Some of her hair had fallen over her face, and yellow strands fluttered softly with each breath as her chest rose and fell. Aurelia's face was relaxed; her lips were slightly parted. Certainty lay there silently, thinking of what those lips had felt like against hers.

So soft and gentle, so different from the lips of any man she'd ever kissed. An offering, not a demand. *Here I am*, the kiss had said. *Do you want me as I want you?*

She did. Gods help her, she really did. But . . .

No! Stop it. Bad Certainty.

Certainty got up from bed as quietly as she could, trying not to wake Aurelia. She was unsuccessful; as she clasped her novice's robes over her undertunic, Aurelia stirred behind her and rose with a stifled yawn.

Her hair was unbound, flowing loose and golden down her back, and she was wearing only a linen nightgown. Her neck was bare of that terrible necklace. To Certainty, she was a vision.

"Good morning," Aurelia said softly. Shyly. Certainty wanted to kiss her all over again, but shoved the impulse somewhere deep down.

"Morning," she said.

They stood there looking at each other for a moment, and Aurelia looked away first, though Certainty saw the start of a blush creeping up along her neck.

"Shall we . . . shall we go get breakfast, then?"

"Yes." They were just going to pretend that the kiss never happened. That was fine. Everything was fine. She cleared her throat. "Um. Should we go see whatever it is that Gertha wanted us to see first?"

A SHORT WHILE later, Certainty squinted, tilting her head to one side. Behind her, Orrin gave an impressed whistle and said, "Gosh! It looks so proper and official, dunnit? We should have done this ages ago."

Gertha, Hull, Orrin, and Aurelia were all standing with Certainty by the twin hills near the outskirts of the village, just after the fork in the road. When the two mages arrived, Orrin and Hull were lifting Gertha's surprise into place: a large wooden sign on a stake, hammered into the ground before them, with heavy rocks laid round its post as support.

The sign proudly declared to any who might travel by that taking the rightward path would lead them to SHPELLING. The village name was painted in neat black letters, but Certainty was discovering that seeing it written down was somehow nearly as bad as hearing it spoken. It made her brain itch.

"It's like we're a real city, eh?" Hull beamed at Orrin and slapped the boy on the back. "Maybe they'll start actually marking us on the maps!"

Gertha scoffed at that, but her eyes lingered proudly on the new sign all the same.

"Do you think we ought to decorate it a bit more?" asked Orrin. "Like . . . I dunno, putting a line under it? Maybe a red squiggly one?"

They all tilted their heads, studying the sign.

"Nah," said Hull eventually. "Best leave it as it is, I think."

"So, lady mages, what do you think?" Gertha jerked her chin toward the sign. "Does it meet your Margravian standards?"

Aurelia hesitated. "It's lovely, but . . . I wonder. Have you ever considered changing the name?"

Everyone looked at her in horror.

"Changing it *how*?" asked Gertha, her eyes narrowing dangerously. *Oh no.* Certainty widened her eyes at Aurelia, trying to farspeak the word "STOP," but it was no good.

"Well," said the mage. "You could remove the *h*, for starters."

"But why would we do that?"

"Aye—" Orrin's nose scrunched as he drew letters in the air with his finger, puzzling it out. "What sort of name is *Spelling*?"

"Don't listen to her highness, boy." Gertha cast Aurelia a glare that could have pickled garlic. "She doesn't know the importance of history and tradition. Shpelling is Shpelling, and sho it'll shtay."

"I'm sorry, yes, you're all right." Aurelia threw her hands up in exasperation. "Shpelling is a fine name, very distinguished."

"Unique," added Cert helpfully. Aurelia rolled her eyes at her, though a smile played at the corners of her lips. Certainty couldn't help herself from smiling back, and Aurelia's cheeks went pink. Gertha looked suspiciously between the two of them, but said nothing.

The group traipsed back to the Plough (Orrin chattering

excitedly the whole way about everything he planned to eat at the Fair), and as they walked, Certainty looked around at the village's homes and shops.

Shpelling still wasn't close to being a city—no matter Orrin's enthusiasm—or even an upstart town, but it was in a much better state than it had been when Certainty and Aurelia had first arrived. Remarkable what a coat of fresh paint, the forcible cat-based eviction of multiple rodent colonies, and the arrival of spring—proper spring, with bees buzzing and flowers blooming and small, round birds singing come-hither songs at each other among the branches—had done to the place. Even the plough on the Golden Plough's sign had been scrubbed and restored to a merry yellow.

It was then that Certainty realized that the funny feeling of discomfort, the unease that she'd felt since they'd first arrived, was gone. In its place was a warm sort of satisfaction, radiating out from within her like the first swallow of mead on a cold winter's night. Shpelling had been dying. A slow, creeping death, one of neglect and misfortune rather than malice. But now . . .

Certainty grinned at the sight of several villagers planting colorful daffodils along the path. It was like seeing small, green leaf buds dotting the withered branches of a very old, very stubborn tree. Shpelling might one day be restored to its magic, and she and Aurelia had had a hand in making it so. That was something to be proud of, she thought.

They'd made it by then to the well outside the Golden Plough, and Hull turned the crank so that they all could take a drink from the pail. The water was crisp and cool in Certainty's hands. As she leaned against the rim of the well, she thought she heard a whisper of object-voice in her mind: *"Thank you, thank you, thank you."* She smiled. There was a sudden flapping from overhead, and then Hope descended upon them.

They'd seen somewhat less of the catdragon recently, though Certainty thought she knew what was keeping Hope occupied. The other day, she had discovered the creature fussing over a strange pile in the unused workshop that had once belonged to Jasper the carpenter. There, Hope had somehow accumulated a veritable hoard of shiny odds and ends—brass tacks, half-rusted nails, the head of a small spade, and miscellaneous rocks of varying degrees of sparkliness—and had draped herself over them like some ancient queen, looking very pleased with herself. Certainty hoped she hadn't stolen anything that anyone would miss.

Aurelia made a cooing noise, cupping her hands to offer Hope some water; the catdragon deigned to lap it up delicately before hopping up to the mage's shoulder and nuzzling her cheek. Certainty tried not to be jealous.

"A good mouser, that one," Gertha said approvingly. "An owl's vantage point and a cat's quick instincts! You two ought to breed more of them."

"We didn't breed her, Gertha."

"Well, enchant more of them, then. Hatch them."

Certainty blinked, her mind grappling with the image of Hope sitting on a clutch of catdragon eggs. How would that even work? Would the kittens come out scaled, or fluffy? Aurelia would probably have a better sense. She'd likely read several books on magical hybridization, or something.

"Only two days now," Orrin was saying, bouncing on the balls of his feet. "What else is there to be done before the Fair, Gertha?"

"Suppose it's finally time for a shopping trip, isn't it? May as well get it over with."

Certainty perked up. "A shopping trip?"

"Don't get your hopes up, city girl. It's just to Ruggan. They might be a bunch of hoity-toities down there, but they have more shops and suppliers than we do, and sometimes we need to restock from their merchants. We'll need mead and spices for the Fair, a great deal more flour and eggs for Ferdinand's pasta, and probably some other things, too. Orrin—can you run around asking everyone what they want and make a list? I'll have Ferdinand get the cart ready."

Orrin dashed off to carry out this task, and Certainty and Aurelia looked at each other.

"There's only half a box of artifacts left to identify," said Certainty. "And it might be nice to see more of the area before we leave . . ."

Aurelia bit her lip, hiding a smile. "I suppose we *could* use some more dried rose hips for tea . . ."

Gertha made an impatient noise. "Oh, go on, then. I'm sure Ferdinand won't mind the extra company."

WITHIN THE HOUR, Certainty and Aurelia were comfortably ensconced between Orrin and a caged hen in the back of Ferdinand's open wagon. ("Farmer Tully asked me to have the hen looked at by the animal doctor in Ruggan," Ferdinand explained. "Apparently it laid a *very* odd egg the other day.") Hope, alas, had been left behind in the stable, as it would have been inconvenient to have to explain to the townsfolk of Ruggan why they had a winged cat with them. Plus, Certainty wasn't sure she trusted Hope in a market full of shiny baubles just waiting to be added to her hoard.

The wagon was outfitted with two slim benches on either side, although "bench" was a bit of a stretch, in Certainty's opinion—they were really just two flimsy, unsanded planks of wood resting across some empty barrels. But Ferdinand assured them that the ride to Ruggan would only take a few hours in this fair weather, and that he'd previously transported pigs and milch cows that were *far* heavier than they were, so it'd all be perfectly fine. Certainty didn't particularly appreciate these comparative references, nor did she point out that his previous passengers probably had lower standards of comfort and safety than human women.

The wagon was pulled by Ferdinand's two cart horses, both of which seemed like they really ought to be enjoying their golden years sunning themselves in an open pasture instead of being put to work. One, a graying dun, bore an unimpressed expression that reminded Certainty remarkably of Old Gertha. But once they were ready to depart, Ferdinand twitched the reins and the horses plodded forward willingly enough.

It was a pleasant ride, even if the landscape of southeastern Eshtera failed to hold Certainty's interest for long (and even if the occasional brush of Aurelia's leg against hers was of far too *much* interest). There were only so many picturesque hills and sweeping farmlands one could appreciate before they all started looking the same. Instead, the four of them entertained themselves with vigorous debates on such heady topics as whether dragons or a Shinn invasion would be more difficult to repel (dragons, unless the Shinn had their own foreign dragons); which forms of baked good were superior (fruit pies over cakes, but cakes over biscuits); whether Old Gertha and Hull were more than just friendly housemates (obviously, though nobody wanted to linger overly much on the thought).

Eventually, they came to the town of Ruggan, as proclaimed by a hanging wooden sign much larger and more ornate than the one they'd just installed in Shpelling. Orrin let out an envious sigh.

It was immediately clear that Ruggan was a more populous

and flourishing place than the village of Shpelling. All along the wide avenues, tents and stalls with colorful awnings hawked a wide variety of goods, many edible. Multiple horse-drawn carts occupied the central road that ran through the market, and dozens of shoppers bustled through the spaces in between. Many held baskets full of purchased goods; others clutched the hands of small children looking longingly at the sweets sellers. Somewhere in the distance, a church bell was ringing, adding its own tenor to the clopping of hooves and creaking of wheels: a loud, cheerful chorus of bucolic prosperity.

Ferdinand brought them to a halt in front of what looked to be a prosperous inn several times the size of the Golden Plough. "I'll be inside negotiating for the mead," he said as he helped Aurelia and Certainty dismount from the wagon. "Might be a while—Old Corwin's a chatty one, and a tight-fisted bastard, too. But over there's a shop that sells tea and dried herbs, and over there are the grocers, and in that alley is a bookshop, which you learned ladies may find of interest. Have fun, but be back at the wagon within three hours, aye? Need to be getting back before the sun sets. Same for you, Orrin—"

The three of them professed their agreement to these terms, and he carried the caged hen with him into the tavern. Orrin dashed off with his list, and Certainty grinned at Aurelia. "When's the last time you went shopping?"

Aurelia tucked a lock of hair behind her ear. "I . . ."

"Aurelia. Please tell me you've gone shopping before."

"I have!" The mage's hand went instinctively to her neck, drawing Certainty's attention to the fact that she wasn't wearing the necklace again. "Of course I have. I just . . . can't recall a specific time at the moment."

"Oh, *Aurelia*," Certainty said with feeling, and grabbed the mage's arm to tow her in the direction of the tea shop.

She was just being friendly, of course. They were two young women going shopping together, which was a perfectly ordinary and colleague-appropriate thing to do.

Keep telling yourself that, snickered a voice in her mind.

THEY EMERGED FROM the shop a very pleasant hour later, stomachs full of tea samples and candied hibiscus (pressed upon them by the merchant, who was delighted by their custom—Guild mages being notable consumers of expensive tea) and arms full of their purchases, bundled into convenient sachets.

"Well, that was a productive stop." Aurelia was smiling. Her braid had come loose during their bouncy cart ride, and she hadn't yet seemed to notice. Her robes also slipped a little to one side as she juggled her purchases in her arms, and Certainty couldn't keep her eyes from the narrow patch of pale skin and collarbone that they exposed. "Cert?"

Certainty's eyes shot guiltily back up to meet Aurelia's gaze.

"Right. Yes. On to the bookshop?"

They made a quick detour to Ferdinand's wagon to deposit their purchases, then strolled through the market arm in arm as if they were two fine ladies on Margrave's High Street. Ruggan was nothing like it, of course, but with their own Spring Fair approaching, the town square was still a vibrant scene. There were stalls heaped with ruby-red cherries, shops with dolls and fine porcelain in the windows, and food vendors hawking sweetmeats in cones of waxed paper. Certainty saw Aurelia's eyes lingering on the treats, so she abruptly pivoted them mid-stride to face the vendor.

"How much for one?"

"Four pennies, milady."

Aurelia's hand shot out to grab Certainty's arm. "Cert, no, I don't need it. I was just looking—"

"Nobody *needs* sweets, Aurelia. Besides, who said I'm buying it for you?" She stuck her tongue out at Aurelia as she handed over the coins, and Aurelia gave her a look of exasperation but was smiling all the same. The vendor passed her the sweetmeat and Certainty took one small bite—it was a round ball of honeyed nuts, with some sort of sweetened seed paste in the center—before handing it to Aurelia. "Mmph," she said, trying to unstick it from her teeth. "It's good. Try it!"

Aurelia hesitated, then gave the sweet a delicate, ladylike nibble.

"Oh, come on," said Certainty. "We've been eating garlic-on-garlic for a month; I know you want it—"

Aurelia silenced her by shoving the entire rest of the ball into her mouth. "Mmf," she managed to say while chewing. "Oo appy?"

"Very," Certainty said, grinning. "More importantly, are you?"

She said it teasingly and without thinking, but the second after the words had left her mouth, she remembered what Aurelia had said last night. Just before she kissed her.

Aurelia was looking at her, eyes shining, and Certainty knew that she was remembering, too. It seemed as though she was about to respond (if not for her mouth presently being glued shut by a very large, very sticky ball of nuts)—but it was at that inopportune moment that they were interrupted.

"I say—is that you, Aurelia? Aurelia Mirellan?"

A portly middle-aged man wearing a green cloak, an expensive-looking doublet, and a palpable aura of self-importance shouldered his way through the market crowd to them. He peered over his spectacles at Aurelia, taking note of the Guild circles on her robes. "But it is! My dear, what are you doing here? Shouldn't you be in the Guildtower, or off on assignment?"

"Mmf," said Aurelia, and—with visible effort—swallowed the sweetmeat whole. "Greetings, Scholar Yorvick."

Her voice was slightly hoarse; Certainty wouldn't be surprised if the sweet had scraped her throat on the way down. The mage had straightened as the man approached, and now stood stiff and formal with her hands clasped in front of her body. She looked as if she were on trial.

Certainty looked between Aurelia and the scholar in question, waiting for an introduction.

"Apologies—Scholar Yorvick, allow me to introduce Novice Certainty, also of the Guild of Mages. We are both here on assignment." Her voice was suddenly formal.

"What, here? In *Ruggan*?" The scholar made the town's name sound like an indecency and ignored Certainty entirely.

"No, actually. In Shpelling, a nearby village."

"*Shpell*—what nonsense! But Aurelia, what assignment of any import could possibly have dragged you out to these hinterlands? *I'm* only here because there were reports of a rare new variety of bunnerfly in the area. My buffoon of an assistant wasn't able to bring me a live sample, so I've been forced to come myself, and—but never mind the bunnerfly. Do your parents know you're here?"

Aurelia looked like she wanted the ground to swallow her, and Certainty promptly decided that her initial impression of the man had been correct: He was an odious toad.

"The High Mage has tasked us with the transportation and storage of highly valuable magical artifacts," Certainty cut in. A slight stretching of the truth, perhaps, but what did it matter? "We're completing an inventory at a remote location so that the artifacts' powers can't pose any threat to the Guildtower or Margrave itself."

"Valuable magical artifacts?" Scholar Yorvick said, looking

down his nose at Certainty. "Why, all know that the *truly* valuable artifacts are all kept in the Guildtower vaults. I can't fathom why the High Mage would have sent one of Eshtera's only farspeakers on such a menial errand." Aurelia said nothing, her expression wooden and shoulders tight.

The scholar shook his head vigorously, setting the decorative silver beads on his doublet ajingle.

"Nonsense," he said again. "Never fear, Aurelia—I shall notify your parents when I return, and I'm sure they will take the matter up with the High Mage at once. They would be disappointed to know you're being wasted here."

Aurelia looked as though she were shrinking into herself, and Certainty wanted to say something, to invite this haughty scholar to kindly take his leave and self-pleasure, but he spoke again first.

"Well, while you're here, Aurelia, would you and this novice of yours care to join me for dinner? I've taken rooms at the inn here; it's a shabby sort of place—doesn't even have a bathhouse, if you can believe it—but they do a very passable roast . . . ?"

"No, thank you, Scholar Yorvick. My companion and I must be returning to our duties."

"Of course, of course. Well then, a pleasure seeing you, my dear, even if it is in such an unexpected place. May we both be back in Margrave's more civilized climes soon!" He gave them both a short, dismissive bow and left.

"What a horrible little man," said Certainty, watching him go.

Aurelia didn't respond, nor did she move. She stayed standing there beside the sweetmeat cart, staring fixedly at a point in space in front of her. Certainty glanced at her in worry.

"Um . . . shall we continue to the bookshop, then?"

"You go on," Aurelia said quietly. "I think I'll just go wait by the cart."

"Aurelia... That man is just a snobbish prick! Don't listen to him. Who cares what some aristocrat scholar thinks about—"

"*I* care," said Aurelia flatly. "My parents care. He's their friend. I come from aristocrat scholars, remember? I *am* an aristocrat scholar. No matter what pleasant fancies we've been playacting in Shpelling, this isn't our lives, Cert. And soon enough, we'll be back in Margrave, and I'll need to focus on earning my place. Living up to my name. My position."

Earning her place? *You have a place*, Certainty wanted to tell her. *Here! With me! Isn't this a good place? Haven't we made it one?*

But instead, she said, "Playacting? Is that what we've been doing? I must be mistaken, because I thought we were carrying out our duties for the Guild, and helping an entire village full of people, besides."

"Duties," said Aurelia bitterly. "Yes, and what have my duties here been? Casting a few wards? Woodworking? Making tea? Assigning me here was a farce, Certainty. I'm just another piece of unwanted junk the High Mage sent away."

Certainty felt as though she'd been hit. *A farce*. Was that what Aurelia really thought of their time here? What happened to *I'm happier than I've ever been*?

"I'm sorry you feel that way," she said, her voice small and wobbly and unlike her. "But to me, this is the most important thing I could possibly be doing. This is how I'll finally earn my circles, Aurelia. My family's future depends on it. So this matters to me. A lot."

"I know that, Cert. I know. I just..."

But Aurelia let her words trail off in frustration, and this time it was Certainty who looked away first.

The two women walked in silence through the bustling market and back to Ferdinand's cart. As they walked, Certainty couldn't help but reflect that there was nothing quite as heavy on one's mood as being unhappy in a place where others are joyful.

THE RIDE BACK to Shpelling was a far quieter one than the ride there (in part because Orrin, exhausted from running around Ruggan buying everything on his list, had fallen asleep on top of the chicken cage). Ferdinand seemed to notice that neither Aurelia nor Certainty were in the mood for conversation and left them to their thoughts, though Certainty saw him sneak a worried glance at them over his shoulder. Aurelia caught Certainty's eye once or twice, and opened her mouth as if to say something—but Certainty didn't want to hear it, so she stared out at the Eshteran countryside instead. It looked the same as it had several hours ago, naturally, but better to focus on rows of cornstalks and grassy hills than on what Aurelia had said.

Eventually Shpelling's new wooden sign appeared in the distance, and they turned off the road and rolled back along the narrow paths and into the village square.

The sun was low and the clouds were streaked with pink by the time they arrived back at the Golden Plough. Dismal as the homecoming felt to Certainty, they had at least achieved the outing's primary goal: The cart was full of purchased goods. Some, like the barrels of mead, were intended for the Fair; others comprised the personal shopping that had been done for various villagers. Certainty and Aurelia helped Ferdinand and Orrin unload the goods. When they finished, the others headed inside the tavern for an early supper, but Aurelia put a hand out to hold Certainty back from following them.

"Cert," she said quietly. "I'm sorry. I didn't mean it."

Certainty pressed her lips together. "Yes, you did."

Aurelia let out a long, frustrated breath. "All right, yes, I did.

That pompous ass Yorvick just reminded me of everything I'd begun to forget. I *do* think that this assignment is busywork for me, in a way, and that the High Mage just wanted me to finally be useful, for once..."

"What do you mean 'finally' be useful?" Certainty burst out. "You're an accomplished mage; you're a fantastic scholar—"

"I mean relative to what everyone expects of me—"

"And me? Nobody expects anything of useless Novice Certainty and her silly object-speaking, so it's all right that *I'm* here, right?"

"That's *not* what I said."

"It's what you were thinking, though, isn't it?"

Aurelia was angry now, too. "It wasn't, actually. Do you really want to know what I think, or do you just want to put words into my mouth?"

"Go on," challenged Certainty. "Tell me what you think, then."

"I think... I *think*, Certainty Bulrush of Potshire, that you're the best damned thing about this assignment. I think that you've made what we're doing here *matter*—and not just to the Guild, but to everyone here."

The sky behind her had shifted back to blue, but it was now the rich, inky blue of twilight, a lavish brushstroke across the hills. It made Aurelia's eyes look even greener as they held Certainty's gaze without flinching.

"So there. That's what I think."

The best damned thing.

Certainty's heart thudded loud and heavy in her ears. She swallowed hard. "Oh."

What Aurelia said didn't really change anything—didn't change the mage's resentment of her assignment here, didn't change the fact that they came from entirely different worlds, or that Aurelia was a farspeaker temporarily dispossessed of her talent while Certainty would at best be a Deputy Keeper and a minor footnote in the annals of the Guild—but hearing it aloud made all the difference.

It was as if Aurelia had painted with her words a picture of a woman who was better in all ways than Certainty knew herself to be—a woman who was kind, and determined, and strong—and then turned it around to reveal not a painting, but a mirror in which Certainty saw only herself reflected in Aurelia's eyes.

She saw Aurelia start to lift one hand as if to reach out for Certainty—but then the door to the Golden Plough swung open, releasing a sudden burst of cheerful noise.

"Let's go to dinner?" asked Aurelia quietly. Certainty nodded, and they returned to the safe familiarity of the warmly lit tavern, leaving unspoken things hanging behind them in the twilit breeze.

THEY SAT IN their usual seats in the Golden Plough but soon discovered one unfortunate drawback of the tavern's newfound success. As all the other tables were in use when Master Tobias walked in through the doors, Ferdinand pointed him to the only unoccupied chair in the room—the one directly across from Certainty and Aurelia. He didn't like this, either, judging from the grimace on his face, but he must have been hungry enough to tolerate their presence, for he pulled out the chair and sat.

"Thank you for allowing me to join you," he said stiffly.

"Not at all," said Aurelia, with an expression that said quite the opposite.

"And what brings you back to Shpelling, Master Tobias?" Certainty asked, joining in the pretense of polite conversation.

"I was just passing through on my way back to Ruggan, but

thought I'd stop to try this . . . *pasta* that Ferdinand has been serving recently. Apparently to great acclaim. Even my lordship is curious to sample it." His eyes flicked around the room at the bustling tavern, then back at her. "It seems you two have been busy here."

Aurelia crossed her arms. "Not everyone here is quite so mistrustful of magic as you thought. Turns out it can be useful after all. Who'd have thought?"

"It's not magic itself that I mistrust," Tobias said. His voice had an edge to it. "It's those who use it. Mages are not kings. Not divine beings, to be set above everyone else."

"We never claimed to be," said Aurelia, slightly bewildered.

"And yet your *Guild* is the arbiter of all magic in Eshtera," he snarled, leaning forward. There were points of red high in his cheeks. "You mages sit high and mighty in your Guildtower, passing judgment on who is worthy of joining your ranks. Who is worthy of magic itself, of learning to wield it, based on nothing more than—"

He broke off suddenly, and it clicked into place for Certainty. He'd left Ruggan for Margrave at a young age . . . he'd had grand dreams and ambitions, thwarted . . .

"You were an applicant, too," she said, realizing. "You tried to join the Guild when you were younger, didn't you? But they rejected you."

Tobias was abruptly unbalanced. His mouth worked for a moment before any words came out of it. "I don't see why that mat—"

"So that's why you've made things difficult for us at every turn," said Aurelia slowly. "You're just . . . jealous. But that's absurd—"

Tobias's face darkened. He pushed himself away from the table and stood, eyes cold with fury. "You two may be mages," he said, his voice low and dangerous, "but I am the voice in my lord's ear. I am the pen in his hand. And as soon as you take *one step* out of line here, I will have the weight of the Crown and its justice brought down upon you, and even your precious Guild won't want you then."

And without even waiting for his plate of pasta, he swept his cloak around him and stalked out of the tavern.

SIXTEEN

TOBIAS DID NOT reappear in the coming days, so they shrugged off his threat as empty and returned to doing what Certainty thought was an admirable job of ignoring their feelings for each other. Well, her feelings, at least, though she suspected (hoped) from Aurelia's uncharacteristic level of distraction that they were mutual.

Instead of doing anything so ridiculous as actually talking to each other about it, they turned instead to making their way through the very last box of unidentified artifacts, Certainty taking a great deal of satisfaction in watching Aurelia flip nearly all the way to the back of Mortimer's tome of records to find any remaining blank pages.

"Skyfire," said Certainty, wrenching her magic out of the semi-hollow tube in her hands. It had a tiger's head carved of wood capping one end, and a thick woven cord coming out of the other. Curiously, it had spoken to her in heavily Shinn-accented Eshteran; perhaps, unlike the Lindisian food machine, its components were of several different origins. "I think that's what it's called, anyway. This one's telling me that it's of Dashan make. From Shinara."

Aurelia looked up from the book with a furrowed brow. "What's skyfire?"

"Pretty much what it sounds like. You point the head at your enemy, or your enemy's castle, then light this fuse on the other end, and out comes magical fire: bang, boom, flash. There are different types, though—this one said it's meant to be used for public ceremonies and celebrations, not battle."

Aurelia snorted. "Ah, yes, I also like my civic events to come with the threat of immolation."

"They fire them at the *sky*, Aurelia, not each other. And the ceremonial skyfire doesn't burn for long, not like the battle kind."

Aurelia gave a skeptical hum, but recorded all of this dutifully into the tome. "Still sounds dangerous to me."

"I suppose so." Certainty turned the tube over, examining it. "Still fully functional, too. Might be something that ought to be in the Guildtower's vaults instead of here?"

Aurelia nodded, jotting something down on a label that she then handed to Certainty. "Let's put that one off to the side for now. We can bring it back to the Guildtower with us when we return."

Certainty tied the label onto the tube—*No. 404, DANGEROUS, handcannon of ceremonial Shinn skyfire*—and carried it carefully into an empty stall to lean it gingerly against the wall in the corner. They could wrap it safely for transport later. "Done. What's next?"

Aurelia, wearing her gloves, hefted the last artifact out of its box with a grunt. It was a large stone ball, which she dropped onto the table before Certainty with a thudding noise. It started to roll—it seemed that the table wasn't entirely level, Aurelia's woodworking skills notwithstanding—and Certainty shot one gloved hand out to stop it.

"Right, then. What are you?" She grasped it with her bare

hand, too, and sent her magic searching within. She closed her eyes, but the conversation with the artifact was brief.

"Cannonball," she said. "Enchanted to explode."

Aurelia frowned at her. "That also sounds like a dangerous enchantment . . . Shouldn't this one go back to the Guildtower, too?"

"Explodes into butterflies."

"Ah. Less useful," Aurelia acknowledged after a moment's consideration. She scribbled this final entry into the tome, then transferred the lepidopterous cannonball to an appropriate storage shelf. Certainty watched as she pulled out fresh parchment from her bag and began writing something.

"What are you doing now?"

Aurelia's quill didn't pause. "That was the last remaining artifact, so I'm drafting our final report to the Guild."

A growing excitement began to fill Certainty. "We're . . . done? All of the artifacts have been recorded?"

"That's what I just said, Cert." But Aurelia smiled at her over her quill to take the sting out of her words. "Perhaps you ought to write your own letter? To your family?"

"I . . ."

Somehow, Certainty couldn't quite believe it. She'd known it rationally, of course—had been counting the days until they were finished and she could return to Margrave to collect her circles and coin in a triumphant blaze of middling glory—but some part of her had always assumed that something would go terribly wrong. That she'd manage to muck it all up, and what she'd been working for all these years would be yanked away from her at the last moment.

But now, as she looked over the stalls full of hundreds of neatly ordered and labeled artifacts, all stowed away on their shelves, she finally allowed herself to believe the truth: They had done it.

Aurelia was grinning at her stunned expression.

"Here," said the mage, sliding over a piece of blank parchment and an inked quill. "Write to them."

Certainty took them, half-dazed.

Dear Da, she wrote. *I've done it.*

And then more words began to pour out, ones full of excitement and anticipation and plans for the future—*I'll make the trip home as soon as I can*—and for a short while, there was no sound in the stable but the scratching of both of their quills.

When she finished her letter, Aurelia had already blotted and folded the report to the Guild.

"I'll give these to Ferdinand for when the courier next arrives," she said, taking Certainty's letter as well.

"And what now?"

"What do you mean?"

"We've finished our work, and the Spring Fair is tomorrow. Then we have, what, at least a week before the Guild sends a carriage or horses to bring us back? What should we do in the meantime?"

Aurelia looked flummoxed.

"I . . . I suppose we could do more farspeaking practice?"

Certainty sighed heavily. They'd tried twice more together in the past week, but she still hadn't managed to feel anything more from Aurelia's efforts than an itching at the base of her skull. At this point, she doubted whether she'd ever be able to receive Aurelia's farspeaking, though she hadn't said as much to the mage, of course.

"Sure, but . . . I was more thinking about something fun."

"Fun," echoed Aurelia uncertainly.

Certainty thought for a moment, and then had a brilliant idea.

"What about the mirror? The one I identified a few days ago."

"Number . . . 361?"

"Probably. The one enchanted to transport soldiers, but that could only take them to a strange place, and nobody could figure out where it was?"

"Yes, but what in the Mother's name would we do with that? Cert, we can't send ourselves through a portal to nowhere—"

"Why not? We can come back after a few hours."

The excitement was building within Certainty. Something inside her felt as if it'd been knocked loose by the knowledge she'd soon—*finally*—fulfill her promise to her family. She felt happy, and free, and a little wild.

"Did you perhaps miss the part about an *unknown destination of terrible danger*?"

"I spoke with the mirror, Aurelia. I know where it'll send us, so it's not really an unknown destination."

"Where?"

"Well . . . I don't know its *name*, obviously. But it's a beach! Warm, sunny, pleasant—think of it, Aurelia, a massive ocean right there, sand you can dig your toes into—"

Aurelia wavered visibly.

"An ocean?"

Certainty nodded encouragement. "Don't you want to? Wouldn't it be good for, I don't know, geographical research? Magical . . . tides, and so forth?"

Aurelia chewed her lip briefly. Then something seemed to shift into place inside of her, and her eyes sparkled.

"All right," she said. "Just for a few hours."

THE MIRROR SEEMED delighted to finally be used for its purpose. Certainty leaned it up against the side of the storage stall, and the two women looked at their dusty reflections in it.

There was Certainty—short, soft, all rounded edges with quick laughing eyes and brown curls. And beside her, Aurelia—tall, regal, radiant. A lily in a field of asters. She wasn't wearing her mage robes today, and was instead clad in a simple blue linen dress with sleeves down to her elbows. Her hair was loose and lovely.

Certainty remembered how she had once thought that Aurelia looked like a beautiful statue, unfeeling and cold. The ice witch.

The moniker now seemed not only cruel, but simply wrong. Cert didn't know how she had ever missed the faint lines of thoughtfulness on Aurelia's brow, the way she nibbled her lip when uncertain. How had she not heard the depth of feeling in every word she spoke? Not seen the intelligence, the empathy, the unexpected mischief that sparkled in those green eyes?

Aurelia's reflection smiled softly at her then, and the spell was broken.

"Right," said Certainty, gathering her fragmented thoughts.

She touched the mirror's silver frame, ignoring the thick dust that coated her fingers. Running her hand down the edge, she found the carved symbol of a key that the mirror had spoken to her of. There. She felt the key with her fingertips, then pressed.

The mirror's surface shimmered and their reflections rippled away. In their place was a bright light that made Certainty squint. She saw nothing, but thought she could make out the faint sound of waves.

"Are you ready?" she asked, looking at Aurelia.

Aurelia took her hand, and the warmth of her skin sent shivers up Certainty's arm. "Yes."

Together, they walked forward into the light.

AURELIA GASPED AS they emerged, blinking, into a strange new world. Certainty cast a quick glance over her shoulder to make sure the portal was still there—it was, thankfully, begetting the incongruous sight of a full body-length mirror standing upright in white sand—before turning back to see what had stunned Aurelia into speechlessness.

It was . . . extraordinary.

It was a beach, yes, and there was a large body of water that could plausibly be called an ocean just to their right—but that was about all that was familiar.

In the sky, four small suns in varying shades of pink and orange sent warming rays of colorful light down to them. The waves that rose and fell onto the fine white sand looked ordinary enough, but riding their frothy caps were enormous, colorful flowers the size of rafts. These blooms dotted the surface of the ocean as far as Certainty could see, and these flowers, too, were rising and falling in their own way, petals fluttering open and closed to the suns as if breathing.

"What is this place?" whispered Aurelia, entranced.

The trees behind them—more like enormous leafy fronds than trees, really—whispered in response. A massive bird with crystalline plumes flew overhead, spiraling wide before diving sharply into the ocean itself, where it vanished in a puff of steam.

"I don't know," said Certainty. "But it's beautiful." She had never seen so much color, or such vibrancy, in one place. It was thoroughly wild—the very opposite of the Guildtower's austere whitestone walls. Aurelia bent and laid one tentative palm against the sand.

"You were right. It's warm." She smiled up at Certainty and

then removed her shoes, curling her feet into the sand. "It's nice, Cert, try it."

Certainty followed her example. The sand did indeed feel lovely. She wiggled her toes in it experimentally.

Aurelia led them over to a patch of sand partially shaded by one of the giant frond-trees. They sat there facing the waves, marveling at the strange, wonderful world to which they had been transported. The breeze was warm and scented with an unfamiliar spice.

"If only I'd brought paper to take notes with," said the mage. She touched the sand beside them in wonderment. "I could make sketches—observations—"

"Not everything has to be studied and explained, you know," said Certainty gently. "Sometimes, you can just . . . enjoy something."

Aurelia looked like she was going to argue for a moment, then laughed. "Fair enough. Well, I *am* enjoying it." She looked up, marveling at the vivid sky. "Almost makes you wish we didn't have to go back, doesn't it?" Her voice was teasing but held a wistful note.

Certainty bumped her shoulder lightly against Aurelia's. "Our own world isn't so bad. Besides, we couldn't leave Hope behind."

"You're right. And we couldn't possibly miss the Spring Fair, or Orrin would never forgive us."

The boy had reminded them twice already of when the Fair would take place, as if they might somehow miss a loud, festive gathering being held just down the path from their bedroom. Certainty half expected him to show up at their carriage house to personally escort them there.

Certainty picked up a small palmful of sand, letting the grains slide this way and that in her hand before they poured back out in a thin stream.

"Hard to imagine that we'll be back in Margrave soon." She kept her voice soft.

Aurelia went still beside her. "I know. It feels like going back to a different life entirely."

"So what will happen?"

"What do you mean? We'll leave Shpelling. Say our goodbyes to the villagers, check the wards one last time, and return to the Guildtower."

"Right. Back to the Guildtower."

Certainty tried to resummon the excitement, the *delight* she had first felt at hearing the High Mage tell her she might be made a mage. That moment in her office now felt so long ago. How much had changed since then? She imagined receiving her circles in that same office and pictured Asp's face when she finally returned home wearing them. It would transform her life, and her family's, too. Something warm and unfamiliar rose in her chest; she thought it might be pride.

"We still have some time before we go back, though," said Aurelia softly, interrupting her thoughts. Certainty looked up. "And the artifacts have all been recorded and stored away. As we were instructed to do."

"They have," said Certainty slowly. *Did she mean . . .* The stream of sand falling through her fingers jittered nervously. Aurelia said nothing, but the look in her eyes made Certainty plunge on bravely. "Our assignment is complete. So . . . perhaps we no longer have to be quite so . . . professional?"

Aurelia's breath hitched. "Perhaps not."

They were leaning toward each other now, drawn in by each other's gravity. Certainty felt hypersensitive to the physical world—noticing the grains of sand scraping against her skin, the drag of a warm breeze across her neck.

As if of its own accord, her right hand lifted to Aurelia's

shoulders, and—Certainty marveled at its boldness—traced the line of collarbone there with a finger.

Aurelia shivered. Certainty was close enough to see the goose bumps that rose on her skin.

"You don't wear your necklace anymore."

"No. My parents would be angry." Their faces were close together now; Aurelia's voice was a murmur. "For some reason, I can't quite bring myself to care."

Certainty allowed her fingers to drift down over Aurelia's shoulder, past where the fabric of her dress had slid to expose skin, then along Aurelia's forearm. She thrilled at the way the fine hairs there stood up underneath her touch; marveled at how soft she felt.

Aurelia's breath was coming fast and shallow now, and Certainty felt her own pulse thudding in her throat. Gods, she wanted—she *wanted*—

Then Aurelia's lips captured her own. They were soft and sure and hungry, and Certainty pushed back eagerly, winding one hand in hair that felt like smooth silk. She let her lips part, let her tongue slip past to taste Aurelia. Her mouth was hot and sweet—*pear jam*, some distant part of her brain noted—and it was all Certainty could do not to lose herself entirely.

Eventually, they had to resurface for air and, panting, leaned their foreheads against one another's. Somehow, they were lying down now; Aurelia's hands slid down Certainty's neck to the front of her robes, fingering the cord that held it tied. Just a flimsy piece of thread, really—so easily loosened . . . The spiced air around them was thick with anticipation and desire.

"I might have another experiment in mind," Aurelia whispered. Her breath was hot on Certainty's neck, making her skin tingle like some kind of reckless magic. "Do you—?"

"*Yes*," said Certainty. "Gods, yes—"

And then there were no more words, only *heat* and *need*, urgent mouths and arching backs and soft little gasps, and so was Certainty lost to the world, lost utterly and entirely to anything at all but the woman above her.

THEY LINGERED THERE in that peculiar paradise for another hour or so, paying far less attention to their surrounding geography than each other's—during which time Certainty learned, delightfully, that being a woman did not *at all* mean she knew everything about how women's bodies worked. Eventually, blissfully, Certainty lay on her side, her robes loose and crumpled beneath her, and marveled at the way Aurelia's skin glowed pink and amber beneath the light of the four suns.

"Now I *really* wish we didn't have to go back," said Aurelia, her voice lazy and sated in a way that Certainty couldn't help but feel smug about. (What could she say? She was a quick learner.) "Let's just stay here. Build a little cottage, plant some crops. Hope would like it here, I think."

"And maybe bring that pasta-maker."

"Yes," agreed Aurelia. "Ferdinand's allowed to visit if he makes us pasta."

Certainty nipped gently at Aurelia's shoulder, smiling at their imaginary life. They both knew it was only that, though. Too much waited for both of them on the other side of the mirror.

"At least we'll be going back to Margrave together," Certainty said.

But then her smile faded. When they went back . . .

Even if they would both be mages once Certainty received her circles, the two of them would still have a gulf between them. Aurelia was a Middle City Margravian, a daughter of aristocrat scholars; Certainty was a Potshire girl through and through. They might as well be from different kingdoms entirely. "Unless—is this—"

Aurelia must have heard the sudden uncertainty in her voice. The mage propped herself up on her elbows to look at Certainty. "What?"

Is this just a temporary distraction for you, a way to pass the time? What would your parents think of me? What happens if the Guild assigns us to different corners of the kingdom?

Certainty couldn't stop herself from picking at the loose threads of an uncertain future, from envisioning the various paths that could pull them apart. *Take your own advice, Cert, and just enjoy this.* But both her mind and her mouth refused to listen. All she could see were their reflections in the mirror, and how out of place she had looked beside Aurelia. Something plain next to something fine; a weed beside a flower.

"It won't be as simple back in Margrave, will it?" she said quietly. "Us."

Aurelia's smile faded; she clearly knew what Certainty meant. But did that mean she'd been thinking the same thing? The thought must have shown on Certainty's face.

"Stop that," said Aurelia sharply. Then, more gently: "Look, we'll figure it out. I promise."

". . . right."

Certainty tried to quash the doubt in her stomach, to silence the hateful voice in her head that whispered, *She wants more from this life than what you can give.* She tried to bring back the wonder she had felt in that moment when Aurelia had kissed her and opened up an entirely new world to her—much like the mirror had brought them here, to this marvelous beach.

I promise, Aurelia said.

She wanted to believe her.

THEY RETURNED BACK through the mirror before the lowest of the four suns had dipped down beneath the waves, and once back in the stable stall, Certainty helped Aurelia wrap the mirror carefully back up in its cloth, shedding grains of white sand onto the stable floor as she did so. Together, they carried it back to its proper storage stall—though Certainty did look back at it a little regretfully once they'd finished. Everything somehow seemed dimmer and less vibrant compared with the world behind its surface.

"I don't suppose we could just . . . borrow the mirror? Take it back to Margrave with us?"

Aurelia gave her an amused look. "It's Guild property, Cert. We can't just steal any artifacts we like. Even the ones you've loaned to the villagers will eventually need to be returned."

"Why? The High Mage only instructed us to store the artifacts in Shpelling—she didn't specify where. And they're all still in Shpelling, aren't they?"

Aurelia tried to look stern, but the dimples gave her away. "You're incorrigible."

"Pretty sure that's not what you thought on the beach."

Aurelia thwacked her on the arm, blushing furiously and adjusting her dress, and Certainty smirked. Maybe she'd finally located those feminine wiles of hers after all. But then she remembered the point she'd been trying to make.

"Look, I just think that the people of Shpelling deserve the Guild looking the other way if the artifacts are helping them. They've suffered a long time through no fault of their own, and besides, they've been kind to us."

They walked outside the stable, arms brushing against each

other, and looked out over the village. It was only a little past noon by then—time must work differently within the mirror—and Shpelling was as lively as Certainty had ever seen it. A group of villagers, Hull and Orrin among them, appeared to be using shovels to level the bumps and potholes in the main road, while others were piling bonfire wood, putting up colorful tents, and hanging flower garlands in the village square.

"They have," conceded Aurelia. "I misjudged this place at the start." She blew out a breath. "Really, I've misjudged a great many things, haven't I?"

"You weren't the only one. But we both came around to the right place in the end. That's what matters." Certainty squinted down at the decorations in the square, and an idea took shape in her mind. "Maybe we ought to give them all a thank-you gift before we leave . . ."

"A thank-you gift?"

"You heard what Gertha and Orrin said about the folk from Ruggan coming to the Fair and always looking down their noses at Shpelling."

"Yes . . ."

"Well." Certainty tilted her head. "What if we help them make tomorrow's Spring Fair the best they've ever had? Impress those Rugganites, and give Shpelling a farewell to remember."

"And how would we do that?"

Certainty turned to look pointedly at the stable behind them.

The stable that was full to bursting with shelves upon shelves of neatly organized, fully identified, minorly enchanted magical artifacts.

"*Ah*," said Aurelia. She hesitated for a moment, a shadow briefly passing across her face. Then she looked at Certainty again, and something within her seemed to resolve. She smiled. "Just tell me what to do."

THE CEREMONIAL SKYFIRE was the first thing that came to mind, of course, but she and Aurelia both agreed that it was much too risky to use. For one, neither of them had any experience with exploding things, and for another, it would be far too visible from surrounding towns—quite the opposite of *keep your head down* and *do the work quietly*. So instead, Certainty turned to the tome of artifact records for suggestions. With Aurelia watching, she opened the book and sent a tendril of magic into its pages.

"I am a Book," it whispered. *"You have filled more of my pages, knowledge-writer."*

"Yes. You helped me once, by showing me the wand of bees. I need your help again."

"What is it you seek?"

"I . . . I'm not sure. But this is what I'm trying to do." With immense focus, Certainty brought to the forefront of her mind images of the village of Shpelling—first the dismal scene of their first arrival, then its current state, much improved but still humble. She tried to convey envy and embarrassment, and the image of Ruggan, far finer and wealthier. *"Do you understand?"*

"Yes." A dry crackle. Laughter? She got the impression that the book found mortals like herself amusing. *"See."*

The tome thrummed, and its pages began to turn. It stopped first on one page, waiting for her and Aurelia to skim the lines and take note of a particular artifact (*No. 48, enchanted paintbrush, garish and unpredictable colors*) before flipping to another (*No. 182, enchanted watering pot, unexpected effects on Mage Hrivald's tomatoes*). Once it had shown them these two entries, the book spun around and slammed itself shut with a dusty, satisfied-sounding thump.

Certainty and Aurelia looked at each other. The mage's eyes were sparkling, and Certainty felt herself grinning like a madwoman.

Shpelling's Spring Fair this year would be one the villagers would never forget.

~

CERTAINTY CLAIMED THE watering pot while Aurelia took the paintbrush.

"You're sure there's no risk in using these?" Aurelia asked for the third time as they prepared to leave the stable. Habits were hard to break, and Certainty could tell that she was both exhilarated and terrified by what they were about to do. "They won't accidentally hurt anyone, or damage anything?"

"Yes, Aurelia. I'm sure. I spoke with both artifacts again to check—they won't do anything besides what's written in the book."

Aurelia nodded, still worrying at her lip. "I just don't want to give Tobias any reason to make trouble," she said, mostly to herself. "But some gardening and festive decorating . . . even he couldn't find a valid reason to take issue with that, surely."

"It'll be *fine*," said Certainty confidently.

(Had Certainty read more of the great histories, it might have occurred to her then that this phrase commonly preceded events that did *not*, in fact, turn out to be fine, and that several renowned linguistic scholars had recently proposed a joint investigation with the Guild of Mages to determine whether it functionally counted as a curse. But she had not, and neither had she or Aurelia noticed the small pile of unsettled dirt in the very center of the stable floor, where a small crystal that glinted purple in the sun no longer was, having instead been secreted away by a cat-dragon innocently building its hoard of shiny things . . .)

THEY PARTED WAYS then, and Certainty carried the watering pot to the well to fill. Despite what she'd told Aurelia, she still wasn't entirely sure what it would do—it had chanted something about growth and blooming when she'd asked—but the tome hadn't led her astray yet. She decided to try it first on the flowers that had been planted beside the village's main pathway. The watering can's enchantment was activated simply by using it, so she poured a stream of water onto some lovely little daffodils that were just beginning to poke out of their green sheaths.

The plants shivered lightly as the water soaked into their roots. Then, as she watched, they *shot* up in an explosion of white-and-yellow petals. The flowers grew rapidly until they were at a level with Certainty's face and about the same size, too.

"Oh my," she said, staring at the newly human-sized flowers.

She heard a gasp from behind her, and Certainty turned to see Brienna on the path clutching an armful of round, oat-studded loaves.

"Oh, hello, Brienna."

The baker's face tilted up to take in the sight of the enormous flowers.

"Hello, Certainty." Her voice wavered. "Er. Might I ask . . . ?"

"For the Fair," Certainty said, by way of an explanation.

"Ah. Yes, I see. They're very nice," Brienna said carefully. "Though perhaps a bit . . . larger than expected."

The two women looked up at the giant daffodils together. It seemed like the plants were done growing and had settled for waving slightly in the wind. Their stems were now as thick as Certainty's arm. They really did look quite nice, Certainty thought. And the perfume emitted by the flowers was lovely as well—it nearly covered up the smell of garlic.

"Well, don't let me keep you, then," said the baker. She looked at Certainty, and then at all the other, normal-sized flowers lining the path. "I'll see you and Mage Aurelia at the Fair?"

"See you there."

The baker bobbed a little curtsy, loaves wobbling, and continued on her way, stepping carefully over a well-fed-looking calico cat napping in the middle of the path. Really, the folk of Shpelling had adapted remarkably well to the sudden outpouring of magic in their daily lives. Certainty looked at the watering can, smiling to herself, and proceeded to water the rest of the daffodils.

When Certainty was done and two towering walls of giant golden blooms lined the pathway, she considered what to water next. Hull's apple trees, perhaps? But they were already so healthy; she didn't think they needed any magical help . . . The village's garlic farms? She shuddered. Absolutely not. She dreaded the thought of what Ferdinand might cook up if he had giant garlic bulbs at his disposal.

Ah, but wait—the clearing. Gertha's sad little pocketful of seeds, and the burnt, dead land . . .

Certainty refilled the watering can from the well and set off purposefully back toward the stable, then up around Hull's cottage to the forest path. Her anticipation grew as she pushed her way through the leafy branches, imagining Gertha's face at the sight of a living, growing plant thriving in the center of their ancient misfortune. When she at last emerged into the clearing, she found it just as she remembered: eerily still, silent, bare. The circle of soil looked unchanged; she could still see the little mound that Gertha had dug for her seeds.

Certainty walked out to the mound and knelt beside it. With careful hands, she lifted the can and poured water onto the mound. Then she sat back on her heels eagerly and waited for something to happen.

And waited.

And waited.

She tried pouring a little more water.

Still nothing.

Was there something wrong with the can? Had the enchantment petered out, somehow? Been used up on the daffodils? But no, when she touched it and opened her mind to it, she still felt the hum of the magic within. Then why wasn't it working?

"You can't always fix everything."

She turned in startlement, rising, and saw Gertha walking into the clearing behind her.

"I saw what you did with the flowers. Nice touch. Magic?" She nodded at the watering can in Certainty's hand.

"Yes. Aurelia and I . . . we, uh, thought we might help decorate the village for the Fair."

Gertha barked a laugh. "Well, it's decorated, all right. Those Rugganites will be frothing at the mouth to figure out how to buy their own giant flower seeds. And have you seen what Princess Mage has done with the houses and shops?"

Certainty shook her head.

"Painted 'em all. Every shade of the rainbow. My house is pink now, girl—*pink*. Shpelling looks like a gaggle of faeries and unicorns got drunk and set fire to a pigment stall."

"I don't think faeries—"

"Not the point, girl. What matters is that Shpelling looks alive again. Absurd, aye, but alive, and full of excitement, and—and *magical*." The old woman shook her head as if in disbelief at what she was saying. "As soon as word gets out about it all—about Ferdinand's pasta, the flowers, everything—folk'll start coming, mark my words. Most will come just to visit, but some will stay. They'll build homes, open shops, start families. Shpelling will be a proper village again." Gertha leaned on her walking stick, regarding Certainty. "Don't rightly know how you've done it, but, well . . . I'm glad that you did."

Certainty, embarrassed and pleased, looked down at her feet. "I'm glad, too," she said. "I'm glad that we've been of some use to you all."

But she looked again at the blackened patch behind her. Still no flowers; not even a little seedling. "I just thought the magic might work on this place, too. I'm sorry it didn't."

The old woman took her arm and began walking her back down the path to the village. "Never you mind. Like I said: Not everything can be fixed all at once, hm? These things take time. You've done enough, Certainty."

Certainty could only hope that was true.

SEVENTEEN

AURELIA WAS POSITIVELY glowing when Certainty found her in the Golden Plough.

"Did you see all the houses?" she burst out, even before Certainty had sat down to their usual spot at the communal table. "And the shops? The paintbrush—it was incredible, Cert! All I'd do is touch it to a wall, and color would spread over the whole thing in minutes. It would have been nice if I could control *which* color, of course, but the villagers don't really seem to mind..."

Certainty had seen the houses on her way back from the clearing. Even in the darkening blue of the spring evening, the village was an eye-catching marvel of contrasting color.

"It all looks wonderful, Aurelia. Did you see my giant flowers?"

"Ruggan's gardeners are going to fall over themselves trying to figure out how they're grown." Aurelia laughed, high and bright like the chime of a newly cast bell.

"Maybe a particularly enterprising mage could sell them some magic seeds..."

Aurelia was trying to look stern and utterly failing. "Cert, you know I can't condone swindling innocent Eshterans."

"Fine, fine. We'll just tell them that Shpelling's cows produce really excellent manure. Top-grade fertilizer, only ten pennies a bucket."

The Plough was as full of villagers as Certainty had ever seen it, and conversation was loud and cheerful in the great room. A heady sense of excitement and anticipation filled the air; there was something about a fairday that made everyone a child again. The power of tradition, Certainty thought. When something imprinted itself onto your earliest memories, you'd do anything you could to re-create it, to snatch at those fragments of remembered joy and bring them back into the present . . .

Certainty's musings were interrupted by Gertha plunking down into the seat in front of them.

"Ferdinand's already tapping into one of the mead barrels he just bought from Ruggan," groused the old woman. "Can't trust the hairy lout with his own merchandise; no head for business, that one."

"Hello, Gertha," said Aurelia.

Certainty peered into Gertha's cup. "Looks like you're sampling the mead as well, hm?"

Gertha sniffed. "Got to test it and make sure it's good, of course. Corbin's a snake; he'd as soon sell us watered product as cut us a deal."

"Oh, of course, *testing* it," echoed Aurelia, nodding. This earned her a hard squint.

"In any case, I just came by to say . . ." The old woman harrumphed. "The two of you haven't been entirely useless, I suppose. Shpelling is looking finer than it has in years, and you both have had a hand in that."

"Are you possibly trying to say thank you?" asked Certainty, grinning.

Gertha glared at her. "Don't get smart with me, girl. But . . .

THE KEEPER OF MAGICAL THINGS

as I said earlier, you've done some good here. And it's been noticed. That's all. Not like other young people these days..." She stared moodily into her mead, the lines on her face deepening. Certainty suspected it wasn't her first cup that night.

Aurelia and Certainty exchanged a glance.

"Gertha," said the mage carefully, "you don't speak much of your family. Do you have any children?"

"Aye. A daughter. A few years older than either of you. But you won't be meeting her tomorrow at the Fair. No, I just had a letter arrive from her. She'll be too busy, you see. Lady such-and-such is due for a fitting at her fancy embroidery store, and the weather might be poor, and Shpelling is much too far away from Forlinet to travel here for a simple village fair..."

Certainty heard the pain underneath the anger.

"I'm sorry, Gertha," she said quietly.

Growing up in Potshire, the Spring Fair had been the social event of the year, the village's equivalent of a royal ball. Even adult children who had moved away to the cities would do their best to return for the fairday, as it was considered a time for renewing family bonds (not to mention bringing gifts). For many, it was the *only* time each year that they'd return; Certainty knew it must sting that Gertha's only daughter didn't consider it worth the trip.

Gertha squinted at her over her cup. "S'not your fault, is it? It's the parents' job to make their home somewhere the child might want to stay. Suppose I've failed in that; she's well and settled in Forlinet now. She writes letters, sometimes, but they're all just news and facts. I know how the business is doing; I know whether she's healthy or not, but that's all. Sometimes, I feel like I don't know *her* anymore."

"Why don't you visit her?" asked Aurelia. Her hands toyed with the rim of her own cup. "Forlinet's not so far. You could go see her. Learn what her life there is really like. Talk to her."

Gertha scoffed. "An old village woman like me, in a grand city like that . . . I'd make a fool of myself. What would I even say to her?"

"I'm sure the words will come easy once you're together," said Certainty.

"Say that she can always come home, but that she doesn't have to. Say that . . ." Aurelia's voice frayed a little at the edges, like silk caught on unsanded wood. "That you're proud of her and the life she's built. That you love her, because she's your daughter, and that's enough. I promise she won't find that foolish."

Under the table, Certainty placed a hand on Aurelia's knee. The old woman nodded slowly, and if her eyes looked a little wet in the light of the tavern's lamps, well, Certainty wasn't going to say anything about it.

"Aye," Gertha said softly. "Aye, I suppose I could say something like that."

AT LONG LAST, the Spring Fair pounced upon the village like a catdragon upon a mouse. Certainty and Aurelia dressed quickly the next morning, and when they walked to the village square, they found a scene that could have been painted from a storybook. It was a bright and unseasonably warm day, and the sun shone down upon Shpelling as if illuminating a stage. Ribboned tents were propped up throughout the square, emitting scents of honeycake and mulled wine that mingled pleasantly with the perfume of the enormous waving flowers. A twig-and-flower effigy of the Mother had been constructed in the center of the square, and it towered benevolently over the village as if observing the festivities.

Certainty and Aurelia spent the morning strolling through the square, sampling sweets and complimenting the villagers' preparations as they went. Doreen, the old woman with the goose who had unsubtly suggested that they decorate the stable, beamed when they ran into her.

"Lovely daffodils we've gotten this season, eh?" She gave them an exaggerated wink and tapped her nose.

Certainty grinned back. "Sure are. Must be some very fine farmers who've grown them."

"And the new paint on all the houses! Why, the pigment seller in Ruggan must've had an excellent selection stocked indeed. I don't believe I've ever seen paint in quite that shade of orange before!"

"Indeed. I believe it was a foreign import," said Aurelia primly.

Doreen cackled in delight. "Ah, you two may have come here from Margrave, but I say that you're honorary Shpelling folk now, too." From her, it was clearly the highest of compliments.

The old woman patted them both on the arm when she left, and Certainty raised a teasing eyebrow at Aurelia.

"Foreign import? Mage Aurelia, I do believe I just witnessed you telling a lie."

"I beg to differ, Novice Certainty. The paintbrush must be pulling its paint from somewhere, and if not from another part of Eshtera—or, er, even our physical plane—then that would make it . . . foreign." Aurelia tilted her head. "In a manner of speaking, anyway."

"Scholars." Certainty rolled her eyes at Aurelia, but couldn't stop smiling. This woman.

THE FOLKS FROM Ruggan began arriving shortly after noon. Their wagons and carts rolled in on the freshly smoothed path, and Certainty thoroughly enjoyed observing their astonished gaping. She also spotted Master Tobias riding a dun horse, looking around at Shpelling in its fairday best with a glowering expression. Perhaps it was the thought that two Guild mages had been the ones to prompt such a change in the village, rather than anything he or his lord had done. *Maybe if you'd actually tried to help the people of Shpelling instead of just giving up on them*, Certainty thought. *You don't need to be a mage to be useful.*

Gertha leaned on her walking stick, waiting by the well to greet their visitors in her unofficial, self-declared position of village headwoman.

"Welcome," she called out as the Rugganites dismounted from their carts and stared around in wonder at all of the flowers and riotously colorful houses. Right on cue, Ferdinand began playing a jaunty tune on his fiddle, filling the square with music. "Welcome to our humble Spring Fair, neighbors!"

The Ruggan villagers' voices burst forth in a chaotic tumult.

"These flowers! How have you grown them so large?"

"But where did you get all of the paint—"

"I say, the place looks marvelous! And is that old well finally working again?"

"Ma, honeycakes!"

Old Gertha's face was the picture of satisfaction, smug as a catdragon with a dish of cream. And so the Fair began.

ALL WENT REMARKABLY well for the next several hours. Too well, in retrospect.

Ferdinand alternated between playing his fiddle and rushing into the Plough's kitchen to cook up more plates of pasta (which were met, as expected, with rapturous reception from the Rugganites). Orrin led a group of children in games of bluff-the-badger, drawing shouts of indignation as the younglings raced between skirts and underfoot throughout the square. Murph and Brienna had brought their florally decorated cows to the festivities, and they stood in the nearby field, mooing along happily to the fiddle music.

Certainty and Aurelia strolled through the Fair together, sampling Gertha's honeycakes and Ferdinand's pasta and thoroughly enjoying themselves. But when they joined the line for mead, they realized too late that they were standing behind Master Tobias. He gave them the barest of nods in acknowledgment.

"Mage Aurelia. Novice Certainty."

"Master Tobias. Are you enjoying the Fair?"

His lips tightened. "It's certainly *different* this year. Your doing, I presume. Typical of the Guild to presume it knows best and interfere with our local traditions so crassly."

"The people of Shpelling asked us to help decorate. They were appreciative of it, in fact."

"Perhaps they are tonight, but how will they feel about their homes still being pink and orange come the winter? And these absurd flowers . . ." His mouth curled in disdain.

"If they want the magic undone after the Fair, of course we'll do what we can to reverse it before we leave."

"Leave?" Tobias's eyes sharpened. "You've finished your work, then?"

"Yes," said Certainty. "We sent the final report to the Guild yesterday. We'll be out of your hair as soon as they send for us."

The secretary was silent for a moment—torn between pleasure at their impending departure and resentment that they'd succeeded, perhaps. Certainty would not miss the man in the slightest, but she also could imagine how it must have rankled, to have reminders of his past failure forced upon him constantly. So she tried to be kind.

"Look, I'm sorry things didn't turn out as you'd hoped when you tried to join the Guild." She kept her voice low so others in line would not hear. "I barely made it in myself, and it's not a good feeling to be the weakest of all your peers. But power isn't everything, magic or no."

Tobias looked at her incredulously.

"You know *nothing* about me. How dare you presume to know my feelings?"

"I'm sorry, I just meant—"

"I don't want your pity, Novice. I want nothing from you at all." He whirled on his heel, mead forgotten, and stalked away. Certainty sighed.

"Forget about him," said Aurelia. "Come on, let's go see how the pie contest is going, shall we?"

BY SUPPERTIME, WHEN the sun painted the hills gold and the warmth of the day finally began to seep into the ground, the villagers gathered round the Mother in the center of the square to prepare for the bonfire.

Gertha was supposed to do the honor of lighting it, but she paused with the flint and tinder in hand.

"Actually," she said, looking at Aurelia and Certainty, "perhaps our guests should do it this year. Their way."

Aurelia looked surprised. "You mean—with magic?"

A low, uneasy murmur rose among the visitors from Ruggan. They'd spotted Aurelia and Certainty in their Guild robes during the festivities, and many had surmised, of course, that the mages had had something to do with Shpelling's current state. But it was one thing to see harmlessly giant flowers and brightly painted houses, and another to witness a spell being cast right in front of them. Certainty looked around nervously at the muttering crowd, wondering if Master Tobias would object, but the secretary was nowhere to be seen.

"And why not?" Gertha sounded defiant as she looked around at the other Shpelling folk. "We've seen now that magic doesn't have to be a bad thing. That it can build and heal just as well as it destroys."

Ferdinand was nodding, and Hull beside him, too. "Aye. This year, the honor belongs to these two, who have done so much to help us."

Aurelia looked at Certainty, who smiled encouragingly back. "Go on. You know I can't cast worth a damn; you have to be the one to do it."

"We'll do it together, then." Aurelia took Certainty's hand.

They took a deep breath, looking at the stacked twigs beneath the towering effigy. With the hand that wasn't holding Certainty's, Aurelia pinched her fingers together, twisted her wrist, and flicked her fingers out. She whispered a few words—a basic spell of fire-summoning.

There was a cracking sound—everyone gasped—and then, suddenly, sparks danced and caught among the kindling. A loud *oooh* came from the crowd; they all watched as the flames spread and flew merrily up toward the Mother's skirts, her waist, her garlands of flowers. Certainty saw Aurelia smile at their reaction. For good measure, the mage flicked her fingers outward, and a half dozen orbs of light popped into being. These Aurelia sent floating out above the square, adding their warm glow to the light of the fire. The crowd cheered and clapped, delighted by the unexpected show.

With a cry of *ho!*, Ferdinand launched into his fiddling once more, this time a fast-paced springtime tune that prompted men and women both to grab their partners and swing them out into the square. The melody was lively and familiar, and Certainty couldn't help but think again of Potshire's Spring Fairs. The taste of pear cordial, cold and sweet; the firmness of her da's shoulders beneath her while she craned to see the dancers; the tickle of meadow grass on bare feet as she and Asp chased each other in the breathless joy of childhood.

"Cert," Aurelia said softly. The villagers were no longer paying them any attention now that the lighting was over. The mage touched Certainty's arm. "Is everything all right?"

Certainty blinked and found that there were tears in her eyes.

"Yes," she said, smiling back at Aurelia. "Yes. Everything is perfect."

Around them, the villagers had formed into pairs and circles, stepping and turning in a dance to welcome the coming of spring. Certainty looked up at Aurelia.

"Will you dance with me?"

Aurelia hesitated. "I don't know the steps." *And everyone will see.*

"It doesn't matter."

Certainty held out her hand, palm up. An offering. The mage looked at her hand, then at her. Slowly, she placed her own hand in Certainty's.

Closing her fingers, Certainty led Aurelia to the edges of the square, farther from the fire but where it was still warm. The music played. The bonfire crackled. The moon was fat and round overhead, outshining the stars glimmering faintly around it.

Beneath it, Certainty and Aurelia danced like fireflies in a meadow, and if Certainty could have cast a spell so that this perfect spring night would never end—so that this moment would stretch into an eternity, and they could forget the Guild and Aurelia's parents and such dull things as responsibility and duty, and simply bask in the joy of holding each other there by the fire, surrounded by friends—she would have.

She opened her mouth to try to express the feelings swirling within her, to somehow find the words to tell Aurelia that she wanted to choose this, to choose *her*—

And then the sky exploded.

A blinding flash suddenly lit the square and the surrounding hills, and with it came an enormous boom that shook the buildings nearby. Cries of terror rang out through the square as the stars themselves seemed to burst into terrible flame, raining glowing sparks of white and blue down over the village. They crouched, shielding their eyes, but through the gaps of her fingers Certainty watched as the sparks re-formed themselves into the shape of an enormous, monstrous tiger, which *roared* down at Shpelling in a voice of thunder and lightning.

More explosions followed, a relentless cacophony of light and sound and blue flame.

A tentpole collapsed, burying crying children underneath in folds of fabric; villagers struggled to free them even as they shielded their heads with one arm from the showers of burning sparks. A woman screamed somewhere; there was a crashing noise—mooing cows, their eyes rolling white in terror, pulled loose from their tethers and knocked over fences as they fled into the hills.

Aurelia spat out a defense spell, its bubble flickering into place around the two of them. Certainty whirled within it, panicked.

"The skyfire," she gasped. "It must have been set off—"

The villagers were shouting and calling out to each other in panic.

"Attack! We're being attacked!"

"The mages must've done it!" shouted a Ruggan man, his bearded face red and wild. "What dark magic is this?"

"It wasn't us!" cried Certainty. "We didn't do anything—"

There was another roar from the sky, and hot sparks sheeted down onto the thatched roof of the Golden Plough. The thickly packed straw, dry and brittle from the recent spate of sunny days, caught flame almost immediately.

"No," whispered Aurelia. She thrust both hands out before her in the beginnings of a water-summoning spell. The mage's eyes were wide and urgent. A rain cloud formed above the tavern, but its weak patter of raindrops only sizzled where they fell; the fire was already too strong for the shower to have any effect.

Ferdinand, his face white, raced to the well and flung a bucket of water onto the roof, sending up a plume of white smoke.

"Help me!" he shouted. "More buckets!"

Murph and Orrin ran to help, but others were too busy fleeing to their wagons, or rushing to pour water on their own homes and stores to dampen them against the flying sparks. Certainty whirled around, helpless, while Aurelia added her own efforts to theirs, her eyes screwing up in concentration as she shifted her water-summoning spell to instead draw a steady stream of well water and direct it toward the flames.

Shit. Certainty might not be able to cast any spells of her own, but there had to be *something* she could do.

"Protect the villagers," she shouted at Aurelia, before sprinting toward the tavern to join the men with the water buckets.

Aurelia's defense spell petered out around Certainty as she gained distance from the mage, but then she saw a larger one flicker into place around a huddle of villagers and children sheltering beneath the branches of a large maple. Certainty turned away from them, seeing the tightness in Aurelia's face and knowing that the mage would do all she could to keep them safe.

Instead, Certainty filled bucket after bucket with water from the well, passing them on to Orrin to heave onto the blazing tavern, but even with the combined efforts of multiple people and Aurelia's water spell, it was a losing battle. The flames simply spread too quickly, and soon the acrid scent of burning garlic filled the air.

As more thick smoke billowed out from the second floor, a dark shape suddenly swooped out of a window with a screech: *Hope*, thought Certainty with a stab of panic. But the yowling catdragon dove twice, prompting further screams from the panicked villagers below, before flapping up and away toward the hills.

The water buckets weren't working.

"Enough," said Ferdinand at last, as the heat of the flames pushed them farther back into the square. His voice was hoarse from the smoke and shouting. "Enough. We can't save it."

Certainty let the bucket in her hands fall to the ground; beside her, Murph tossed his aside with an oath. The steady, airborne stream of water from Aurelia's spell splashed to the ground as the mage let it go, slumping to her knees in exhaustion.

There was a loud cracking sound. Slowly, then all at once, the wooden post above the tavern doors fell, the roof began to cave, and the Golden Plough's sign—the one that had been so recently repainted—crashed to the ground in a pile of cinders.

At least the explosions in the sky had finally stopped. There was no sound except the dull roar of the flames and muted sobs of children being comforted. The village square held a stunned, disbelieving air. Everyone who remained simply stared, taking in the destruction in the aftermath of what had occurred.

It was into this fractured silence that Master Tobias stepped forward, breathing heavily and favoring one leg. His face bore gray smudges of ash and smoke; his cloak was torn and scorched at the hem. His eyes were like hard stones as he looked at Aurelia and Certainty.

"*What*," he said, his voice ringing loudly through the square, "have you done?"

EIGHTEEN

"WE DIDN'T DO this," said Aurelia, bewildered. "This wasn't us!"

"You expect us to believe that all that"—the secretary stabbed one finger at the now-darkened sky—"wasn't *magical*? The blasts, the skyfire? We may not all have your level of education here, mages, but neither are we fools."

"We didn't cast any spells like that—we didn't mean—"

"No," snarled Tobias. "You just carted two wagonloads of dangerous enchanted artifacts into Shpelling and treated them like playthings for your own amusement, as if nothing could ever go wrong. As if magic weren't a weapon!"

"It . . ."

Aurelia's shoulders were hunching inward against the accusations. Certainty's heart sank down to join the pit in her stomach; the secretary's words were all the more cutting for having some truth at their core. They *had* begun to treat the artifacts a little cavalierly . . .

"It may have been an artifact that caused it—but I don't know how . . . We were careful; they were all *warded*—" Aurelia's voice was faltering. Certainty tried to rescue her.

"This shouldn't have been possible," she said. "We would never have endangered the village like this."

She looked around the square at Shpelling's residents, the villagers she had come to know so well in the past month, willing them to believe her—but nobody would meet her eye. Instead, all she saw was the mess.

There were the honeycakes that Gertha had labored over for days, scattered in the dirt. Shards of broken plates and cups. Burning ribbons and broken flower garlands, strewn across the ground like so much rubbish.

"Ferdinand, I'm so sorry—"

Ferdinand seemed not to hear her. He simply stood, exhausted, his face lined and blank as he looked upon the burning wreck of his tavern. Brienna spoke instead.

"Are we still in danger?" Her voice was low and trembling. "Do we all need to leave the village now? This magic fire—the ashes have touched everything; our crops, our water . . ."

"No," Tobias said dismissively. "There's no reason to leave your farms. It's ordinary ash; Dashan skyfire isn't meant to do anything more than burn."

Certainty stared at him. "How do you know so much about skyfire?"

He gave her a cutting, scornful look. "Ever heard of books? Guild mages aren't the only ones with access to information, you know."

Aurelia narrowed her eyes at that, but then a windowpane fell and crashed, startling them all and sending up a fresh plume of sparks. Ferdinand made a soft, involuntary noise deep in his throat.

"I'm sure you didn't mean for it to happen," said Murph gruffly. "But . . ."

They all looked helplessly at the burning tavern.

But this is your fault. Certainty heard what they all weren't saying. *But we shouldn't have trusted you. But magic has ruined us. Again.* She blinked back hot tears of frustration. How could this have happened? How could they have let it?

At least it didn't seem like anyone had been badly hurt in the fire. Thank the Mother that Hope had escaped, and that the tavern had been otherwise empty when it burned.

Certainty took a shaky breath. "We need to go check the rest of the artifacts."

As she and Aurelia moved toward the edge of the square, the nearest villagers stepped back, away from the two of them. The silent accusation in their faces cut at Certainty like a dagger, but worse still was their fear.

"Go, then," Tobias spat at their backs. "See to your artifacts. Leave the rest of us to clean up your mess, as mages always do. Lord Godfrey will hear of this soon enough, as will your Guild, when he sends word to Margrave."

They had no response for him. "Come," Aurelia said quietly to Certainty, and they walked up the ash-covered path to the dark outlines of the stable and carriage house waiting above.

ONCE THERE, THEY found precisely what Certainty had feared: a whiff of sulfur in the air, splinters and scorch marks in the dirt, and the ivy leaves closest to the doorway burnt to a crisp upon their vines.

Certainty made to enter the building, but Aurelia held her back with one arm.

"Look."

The warding circle was still visible in the dirt in front of them, gleaming faintly in the moonlight. It was unbroken—and there were footprints leading across it, coming up the path and heading inside the stable. An intruder.

Someone—whoever it was who had come furtively in the dark while everyone else was at the bonfire; whoever it was who had sought access to the artifacts with malicious purpose—had simply stepped over the line, as if it were nothing more than ordinary salt.

Aurelia's wards had failed.

The two of them crossed the ring and entered the stable together, and at first glance Certainty felt a dull relief that at least all the other artifacts still seemed to be in place. The only items that appeared to be in disarray were the tome of records, which was open on the table, and—Certainty exhaled heavily—the tube of Shinn skyfire.

It lay on its side just inside the entryway, as if it had been tossed aside after firing. Its carved tiger head was gone, presumably blasted into smithereens. The scent of sulfur grew stronger when she leaned down. When Certainty picked up the tube, it was far lighter than it had been before. Empty. She sent her magic through her fingertips into it, searching, but the lack of any response only confirmed her suspicions: The magic within the artifact had been consumed. It was now nothing more than a lifeless shell of singed wood.

She brought it to show Aurelia, and found the mage kneeling in the center of the stable.

"It was definitely the skyfire," she said. "But who set it off? Why didn't the wards—"

Aurelia looked up at her. The mage's eyes were hollow and haunted. "Look. My focus crystal is gone. Without it, there *are* no wards. The artifacts were entirely unprotected tonight."

Certainty stared at the ground in front of Aurelia. Saw the little hole she had just dug out with her hands, and nothing but dirt within.

"How?"

"I don't know," said Aurelia dully. "It doesn't matter. It's my fault, my responsibility. I should have noticed. I should have checked the wards last night. I normally check them every night, but yesterday..."

"Aurelia, it's not your fault. It was just a mistake—"

Aurelia flinched as if hit. Certainty had chosen the wrong word.

"Just a mistake," Aurelia repeated, and Certainty knew she was thinking of the other time it had been *just a mistake*, and a young mage had lost his magic for it.

"That's not what I—Aurelia, don't—"

Aurelia was still kneeling, dirt between her fingers where they clenched the ground. Her other hand made a compulsive gesture, grabbing at the space where her necklace would have hung had she been wearing it. She shook her head as if to shake off Certainty's words.

"I shouldn't have gotten complacent. I should have stayed focused on our duties; I shouldn't have let you—" Aurelia stopped abruptly.

"Let me what?"

"Nothing. Never mind."

"Say it," said Certainty. Her voice was soft now, and a distant part of her was proud that it did not tremble and shake even though she felt like she was choking. "You shouldn't have let me what?"

Aurelia's eyes closed. She exhaled. "Shouldn't have let you distract me."

And there it is, Certainty thought. She was such a fool, such a godsdamned fool. She looked down at the empty skyfire tube in her hands. Nothing but worthless wood now. Evidence of their failure. Junk.

She let it fall to the ground.

THEY DID WHAT they had to do. Aurelia retrieved a second set of warding materials from her pack and redrew the ring of salt, burying a replacement focus crystal in the center of the stable once more. Certainty noticed she dug the hole far deeper this time, and set one of the empty wooden boxes on top of it for good measure.

While Aurelia saw to restoring the wards, Certainty picked up the tome and began making sure that each and every other recorded artifact was still within the stalls. Nothing looked to be missing (besides a highly specific clawed feather, which shed some light on Hope's origin), but given what had happened, she knew they had to be sure. It wouldn't absolve them, but she could at least see that no further incidents occurred to make things worse. If there *was* a worse.

Aurelia joined her once she had finished with the wards. They worked silently, side by side but feeling a world apart, until Certainty's eyes were blurry with the need for sleep, and the fragments of sky visible through the windows had faded into the subtle indigo that marked the small hours between true night and early morning. When the last artifact was confirmed to be on its shelf, they looked at each other, weariness and guilt and regret all warring for primacy. Aurelia opened her mouth, but closed it again after a moment. Certainty didn't blame her. What was there to say?

She turned away and went through the door to her bed in the carriage house. There, she sat, barely noticing the aching of her legs and thudding in her head, and leaned her head back against the stone wall, letting her body sag and her eyes close. She thought she might cry, except she felt too wrung out for tears. Too wrung out for anything, really. Only a numb, horrified sort of desolation remained.

Her mind still swam with images of the tavern in flames, of Ferdinand's expression, of the terror in the faces of the villagers as all their old fears of magic were justified and made real before their eyes . . .

Certainty didn't open her eyes as the door creaked open and shut again, nor when she heard Aurelia's soft footsteps and the rustle of the mage lying down upon her own bed. She wondered where Hope had gone. Whether the catdragon would ever return to them, or if it had decided that living wild and free in the hills was the better, safer option.

They had ruined such a good thing. And with it, everything else was ruined, too: all they had accomplished in Shpelling, Certainty's chances of magehood, Asp's apprenticeship, Aurelia's career . . . gods, they'd be lucky if they weren't expelled outright from the Guild. Mages had been stripped of their circles for less.

It was with these thoughts dragging at her mind that she finally succumbed to exhaustion and let sleep claim her. Maybe she'd wake up in the morning and find that it had all just been one terrible, vivid nightmare, instead of a night where everything she had ever wanted burned to ashes in her mouth.

MORNING CAME AND brought no such relief.

The first thing Certainty noticed when she woke was that she was still wearing her robes from yesterday, and that she smelled strongly of woodsmoke. Aurelia was washing her face from a bucket of water on the stove; she looked like she had changed clothes and re-braided her hair, but the lines of exhaustion on her face gave her away.

Aurelia gave Certainty a wan smile when she noticed that she was awake. "Morning."

Certainty got out of bed. "Morning," she said. A statement of fact.

"Tea?"

"Please."

Aurelia set the enchanted teapot on the stove to boil, but as soon it started to speak, she cast a silencing spell on it. They'd probably get an earful the next time they used it, but Certainty was grateful; she wasn't sure she could handle its chipper commentary this morning.

They went through their respective morning routines quietly, but the familiarity of it helped a little. They sat down at the table with their steaming mugs of mint-and-chamomile tea, and Certainty could almost pretend that everything was normal. Her hair still smelled of smoke, though.

"I think that we need to return to Margrave," said Aurelia.

Certainty looked blearily at the mage over her tea. "We were already going to do that. You sent your report to the Guildtower before . . . before last night."

Aurelia nodded, looking down at her hands. "But now I don't think we can afford to wait. They'll hear the news from Lord Godfrey's messengers at about the same time they receive our report, and the only course of action will be to recall us to the Guildtower immediately. It will look better for us if we've already gone back by then to report in person. It will show that we understand the gravity of the situation and are trying to take responsibility for it."

Certainty nodded slowly, digesting this. "What about the rest of the artifacts here?"

"I've re-cast the wards and put in place a number of other protections for good measure. Detection spells all around the perimeter; a dampening field for the artifacts' enchantments; locks on the doors that only other mages will be able to open. The artifacts will be secure here until the Guild decides what else to do with them."

"And what about—" Certainty swallowed. "What about Hope?"

Aurelia's expression crumbled. "She hasn't come back. We'll have to leave her here. I'm . . . I'm sure Orrin and everyone will take care of her, if she does return. I wish it weren't the case, but think of how it'd look, Cert, if we showed up with her in tow . . ."

She wasn't wrong, but that didn't mean Certainty had to like it. The thought of Hope flying through the window to greet them, and finding the stable and carriage house empty, and their scent gone . . .

Certainty pushed her tea away; it had gone cold now, anyway. Nothing good ever lasted. "I'll go pack my things," she said.

AURELIA LEFT TO procure transportation and supplies for their journey, and by the time Certainty had finished packing, the mage had returned with two horses and a sack of provisions in tow. "Hired them from Ferdinand," she said, tying their reins to a tree. "We can get remounts at the messenger stations along the way, but these will get us to the first one, at least. I asked him to make sure Hope's taken care of, too."

"How was he?"

"He was . . ." Aurelia gave a hopeless little shrug. "Tired. Still numb, I think. I promised him that the Guild would fully reimburse him for the damage. Told him how sorry we were."

"What did he say?"

"He said he doesn't blame us for what happened, but . . . well. I think everyone in the village will be more comfortable when we've gone."

Certainty nodded, looking down at her feet. "Probably best to just go, then. Let them rebuild without us. No need to say our goodbyes."

She knew she was being a coward, but truth be told, she wasn't sure she could manage looking them all in the face again. She didn't think she'd be able to say goodbye to anyone without guilt strangling her words.

Aurelia hesitated, then nodded. "Perhaps you're right. Better to leave sooner."

So they loaded up the horses, tying their bags behind their saddles. Aurelia stowed the tome of artifact records carefully within Certainty's pack, along with the spent skyfire tube. The Guild would want to examine it as evidence. The rest of the artifacts were left behind on their shelves, neatly ordered and painstakingly labeled either in Aurelia's careful script or Certainty's messier hand. Certainty led her mare over to the stump where they had eaten so many lunches, and then she mounted, watching as Aurelia double- and triple-checked the various wards and spells she had cast on the buildings. The damned rooster was back on the roof again, surveying their activities, and Certainty couldn't help but imagine that there was something reproachful in its gaze.

Eventually, the preparations were done, and they were ready to depart.

"Back to Margrave, then," said Aurelia quietly.

Certainty nodded. She didn't trust herself to speak. Aurelia gave the stable and carriage house one final glance, shame and longing and resignation written across her face, before spurring her horse down the sloped path. Certainty followed.

On they rode, kicking up ash as they went, along the winding path that led through and away from the village that had become a home, but would be no longer.

NINETEEN

THEIR TRIP BACK to Margrave was both shorter and rougher than their journey in the reverse direction had been, on account of traveling on horseback rather than in a wagon. Certainty wasn't an experienced rider, and her thighs were sore and aching by the second day, but she didn't complain. She just clung to her saddle and kept her eyes on the road, trying to keep pace behind Aurelia as the mage led them toward the Guildtower and whatever judgment was to come.

They rode through Margrave's outer gates before noon on the third day. After more than a month in Shpelling, the sudden bustle of the city grated on Certainty's senses. Had the city always been so loud, so crowded, so full of commotion?

Her horse snorted nervously as she guided it behind Aurelia's through the taverns and sleeping-houses of the Lower City, then the more genteel artisan quarters of the Middle City, before finally finding some relative calm and quiet along the wide, paved streets of the High City.

There, the Guildtower and the White Palace loomed over them like silent sovereigns, waiting to pass judgment.

When the walled base of the Guildtower came into sight,

Aurelia slowed her horse to a halt to let Certainty catch up beside her.

"Are you ready?" she asked quietly.

Certainty looked at Aurelia and saw an expression of grim resolve on the mage's face.

"Not really," she said. She half wished they could have just stayed in Shpelling and waited for the Guild to drag them back by their ears, even if she knew that returning immediately was the responsible choice. "But here we are anyway. Best to get it over with."

She squeezed her horse's flanks gently, prompting it on.

The guardsmen in Guild livery opened the gates readily for them after they identified themselves, and Fanya was the first to greet them in the courtyard of the Guild stables.

"Certainty! Mage Aurelia—I wasn't expecting you two back yet. Have you finished your work in Shpelling, then?"

"It's good to see you, Fanya. We have, but . . ."

"But there was an incident," said Aurelia, swinging herself off her horse. "One that we need to inform the High Mage of as soon as possible."

The quartermaster nodded, confusion plain on their gray-bearded face. "She's at the White Palace right now, but I'll send a page to her immediately. You can wait in her office until she returns." They gave Certainty a worried glance. "I hope everything is all right."

Certainty gave them a half-hearted smile. "I should have listened to your advice better," she said. "I tried to keep my head down, but . . . I suppose I couldn't even manage that."

Fanya frowned, clearly wanting to ask more, but she shook her head. The High Mage needed to know first. She and Aurelia pushed open the doors and began their long, weary climb to the High Mage's office.

THE OFFICE WAS just as Certainty remembered it, all polished wood and piled scrolls, softly lit by the sunshine filtering in through the enormous wall of windows. She and Aurelia sat in the cushioned chairs and waited for High Mage Melea.

"Do you think she's heard yet? From Lord Godfrey?"

Aurelia shrugged. "It's possible. If he sent a fast messenger who rode through the night, unlike us. He's not important enough to have a farspeaker posted with him, though."

Certainty swallowed. She wasn't sure which was better. If the High Mage had already heard the news, they wouldn't need to relive the details of the Fair; but if she hadn't, they would see her reaction firsthand.

The door to the office swung open, and they stood to attention as the High Mage strode in.

"Mage Aurelia, Novice Certainty," she said, settling herself into her own chair. "Sit."

They sat.

The High Mage regarded them for a moment, her expression giving nothing away. Then she sighed, removed her spectacles, and rubbed wearily at her eyes with one hand.

"A messenger from Lord Godfrey arrived this morning."

Aurelia lifted her chin slightly, as if preparing to take a blow. "High Mage, I take full responsibility for the incident," she said. "The wards were my responsibility, and I failed to—"

"Come off it, Aurelia; it was just as much my fault as yours—"

"I was the ranking mage—"

"I was the one who identified the skyfire—"

"Enough." The High Mage raised one hand, silencing them both. She sighed again and replaced her spectacles on her nose. "Some tea first, I think. For all of us."

She lifted the lid on a large teapot of hammered bronze, then muttered a warming spell. The golden-brown tea steamed as she poured it into three cups, but she looked them both up and down, taking in their appearances, and added several dollops of honey for good measure. She slid their cups across her desk. Aurelia accepted hers woodenly; Certainty took a long swallow.

The High Mage drank half of her own cup in one gulp. "Now," she said, regarding them over the top of her cup. "Here is the situation as I understand it.

"An unsecured artifact of considerable power caused the destruction of Shpelling's only tavern, and some other damage besides. No lives were lost or major injuries sustained, but this destruction was witnessed by nearly all of the inhabitants of Shpelling, Lord Godfrey's own secretary, and a large number of visitors from the neighboring town of Ruggan. There is no doubt that the fire was caused by one of the Guild artifacts in your care. Is this correct?"

"Yes," said Aurelia.

"Yes," said Certainty. "But someone else set off the artifact, not us. There was an intruder."

The High Mage's eyes sharpened on her. "Who?"

"Well, we don't know—"

But Aurelia cut in. "I have a suspicion, though. Lord Godfrey's secretary, Tobias; he hated us from the start. Hated what we were doing there, too."

Certainty and the High Mage both looked at her in surprise.

"The secretary?" The High Mage frowned. "Do you have proof?"

"Well." Aurelia hesitated. "Not as such, but . . ."

Melea's lips thinned. "I'm afraid a suspicion isn't nearly enough. Not to accuse Godfrey's own right-hand man of the disaster. No; unless we can *prove* beyond a doubt who the true culprit is . . . Godfrey is a proud sort, and now that he has the bit between his teeth, he won't be satisfied without a highly public resolution.

"Ordinarily, we might have been able to handle the matter internally, but this comes at the worst possible time for the Guild. Godfrey's made sure that the Council knows of this incident, and they're insisting that the Crown's Justice be involved in it, too." She rubbed at her temples. "Any progress we'd made in showing that the mages can win the trust of the general populace has been erased overnight."

Aurelia looked down at her lap. "I am very sorry, High Mage."

"*We* are very sorry," said Certainty, shooting Aurelia a look. "But also, High Mage—aside from this unfortunate incident, we did complete the task assigned to us. All of the other artifacts have been identified and stored safely."

High Mage Melea sighed. "Then there's that, at least. And removing those artifacts did stem the thaumic leakage problem here at the Guildtower. Mortimer's managed to reinforce the containment fields and expand our vaults for now, thankfully. But it remains to be seen whether we'll even be permitted to leave those minor artifacts in Shpelling at all, given the circumstances. It's possible that the Crown will order us to move them elsewhere."

"Oh," said Certainty, her voice very small. All of their work, undone. All of her hopes, unraveled.

"Mage Aurelia," said the High Mage. "Tell me—how did your individual studies progress in Shpelling? Has there been any development on that front?"

"Novice Certainty knows about my current farspeaking difficulties," Aurelia said quietly. "And no, High Mage. My abilities are still blocked, though it did feel like I made some progress . . ."

The High Mage pursed her lips. "I had hoped . . ." But then

she shook her head briefly, casting the thought aside. "Well. The fact of the matter is that there must be a disciplinary hearing now. A joint civil magerial court to determine your responsibility for the incident, and appropriate penalties. It's to be held three weeks from today.

"In the meantime, both of you are placed on suspension from the Guild, pending the results of the hearing. You will both return to your homes until then."

"Go home—" Aurelia's head shot up. "We can't stay in the Guildtower?"

The High Mage looked at them both regretfully. "No, Aurelia. I'm sorry. On suspension, both of you are no longer considered active Guild mages anymore, and as such you cannot stay here."

Aurelia looked devastated, and Certainty swallowed hard.

"High Mage, if I may ask," she said, stubbornly holding her voice steady. "What's going to happen to us? It seems to me there's not much doubt whether the tavern did or did not burn down, and neither is there any question of whether we're responsible. Why bother having a hearing at all? Can't you just give us our punishments and be done with it?"

"This isn't simply an internal Guild matter anymore; Godfrey wants to set an example. He wants a Margravian magistrate to pass judgment on the matter because he thinks the Guild shouldn't be permitted to sanction itself. But you're not wrong." The High Mage's gaze was regretful. "The outcome is already more or less known. We'll be able to shield you from criminal punishments like imprisonment or indenture, and the Guild's coffers will provide the coin to cover the costs of rebuilding the tavern, but . . . you both will likely be expelled from the Guild. Permanently."

A sick, hollow feeling spread throughout Certainty's stomach. Her chest constricted; she felt as though the very air was fighting her as she tried to breathe. She wouldn't even be a Novice anymore. Just Certainty, a nobody of nothing.

Gods—she shouldn't have told her da that she was finally going to become a mage; shouldn't have given Asp reason to hope again. What would they say when she told them it had all been just another empty promise?

Beside her, Aurelia's hands were clenched tightly in her lap.

"High Mage," she said. "My parents. Have they already been informed?"

"They have," said High Mage Melea. "They were both at court when I received Lord Godfrey's message, so I thought it best to let them know immediately. In fact, I believe your father is waiting on the floor below to receive you and take you home."

Aurelia's face went as still as whitestone.

"Though I have not yet sent a message to your family," the High Mage added, looking at Certainty. "And now that you've arrived, perhaps I will leave that to you."

"Yes, High Mage," said Certainty miserably.

The High Mage leaned back in her chair, regarding them both with clear regret. "That's all, then. You may both go, but return to the Guildtower by noon on the third Scholarsday from now for the hearing."

Certainty stood numbly and turned toward the door; beside her, Aurelia did the same, but the High Mage raised her hand slightly.

"Mage—that is, Lady Aurelia. Your circles, please."

Aurelia turned back. She slowly unpinned the golden circles from her robes and placed them on the High Mage's desk.

High Mage Melea's gaze was not unkind as she said, "Thank you. And I truly am sorry, you know. I wish this all had gone differently."

Yes, thought Certainty. *So do I.*

THE DOOR CLOSED behind them, and Aurelia and Certainty stood alone on the circular landing outside the High Mage's office, the great Guildtower stairs stretching out beneath them. They looked at each other, and Certainty didn't know what to do. *What now?* she wanted to ask. In Shpelling, she had fallen into the comfortable pattern of looking to Aurelia for guidance, for answers, for a plan. But now the mage looked just as lost as she did. There was no strategy, no work-around this time—just a time and a date three weeks in the future to seal their fates, locked out on the other side of the Guildtower walls.

"I'm so sorry, Cert," Aurelia said at last. Tentatively, she reached out and took Certainty's hand.

"I am, too." Certainty hesitated. "What will you do? After?"

"I don't know. I could . . . take up other forms of scholarship. Train in alchemy like my mother." Aurelia's hand tightened. "What will you do?"

Certainty could become one of those itinerant hedgemages, she supposed. She'd need to travel far from any Guildtowers, but she could perform small tricks, or use her object-speaking to fix tools and trinkets for coin . . .

Or she could always take up pear farming, like her parents. Like Asp would also likely have to do.

"I don't know," she said. "I'll figure something out."

Aurelia swallowed. "Maybe we could . . ."

But before Certainty could hear just what it was that Aurelia thought they could do, there were loud, purposeful footsteps from below, and a deep voice rang out against the tower's curved whitestone walls.

"Aurelia!"

They whipped apart, Aurelia dropping her hand like it

burned. A tall, silver-haired man in embroidered court robes strode up the last few steps toward them. He had high, proud cheekbones and green eyes that looked far too familiar.

"Father," said Aurelia, her eyes fixed on the floor. "I—"

But he spoke over her, looking Certainty up and down with a contemptuous gaze.

"And this is the novice, I presume? The one they sent you off with to that godsforsaken farming village. The one I have to thank for having my daughter returned to me in further disgrace, when I thought she had already fallen as low as she could have—"

"*Father*," said Aurelia again, but her voice was high and brittle and unlike her. "Please."

The man in fine robes—her father—looked back at her with cold anger. "Not wearing the locket, I see. That explains some of it. Where is it?"

"I still have it, Father." Aurelia pulled out the silver necklace from a pocket of her robes to show him. "I just—I thought I didn't need to always be wearing it—"

"Put it back on. We're leaving now, Aurelia. We'll discuss our options at home."

As Certainty watched, Aurelia slowly clasped the necklace back around her neck. She didn't meet Certainty's eyes as she did so, as if ashamed. "Cert—I'm sorry—"

"*Now*," said Aurelia's father.

And with one last look of despair at Certainty—of guilt, and apology, and so much else wrapped up in between—Aurelia let him turn her away down the stairs, and all Certainty could do was look numbly at her disappearing back.

CERTAINTY THOUGHT OF finding Dav and Saralie wherever they were in the Guildtower, but then she realized that she could not bear it: to see her friends again, only to tell them in person what had happened and what was to come. They would be shocked, she knew. Dismayed, sympathetic—but they didn't have the power to do anything about it. Nobody did, except the High Mage, and she had already made clear that she wouldn't put them before the Guild's greater interests. No; Certainty didn't want to see the pity in her friends' faces. She could send them a letter from Potshire.

She took a deep breath. There was no point in putting it off. She didn't even have to fetch her belongings; everything she owned was already in her traveling pack.

Certainty walked down the Guildtower stairs and made her way back to the stable. Fanya was still there, frowning over their papers, but they looked up as she entered.

"Certainty? What happened?"

"I need to borrow a horse," she said. "A fresh one."

"Why?"

"To go to Potshire. I'll bring it back in three weeks."

Fanya raised an eyebrow. "What's in three weeks?"

"Disciplinary hearing. They're going to expel me; I'm sure you'll hear all about it soon." Certainty went to her pack where it leaned against the wall and pulled out both the empty skyfire tube and the inventory book. "Give these to Mage Mortimer, please. He and the High Mage might need them."

She tightened the pack's straps and picked it up, waiting for a horse. She just wanted to be gone and away from here.

Fanya's face had fallen at the words "disciplinary hearing."

"Oh, Certainty," they said sadly. "I always liked you. I'd hoped that you were finally getting the chance you deserved ... You're good for the Guild, you know. Eshtera could've used a mage like you."

Gods. That hurt more than just about anything else they

could have said. Certainty fought the burning in her eyes, and Fanya seemed to realize they weren't helping things. They looked away, over at the horses resting in their stalls, and led a brown mare with gentle eyes over to the mounting block. "Take Jenny. Smooth gait; she'll carry you well."

Certainty swung herself up, ignoring the ache of her protesting legs, and Fanya tied her pack on securely behind the saddle.

"Thanks, Fanya," she managed. "For everything."

They only nodded regretfully, then gave the horse a hard pat on the rump. "Go on, then. Guards! Open the gates—"

The gates swung open, and out Certainty rode into the city of Margrave without looking back, knowing that it very well might be the last time she would ever see the inside of the Guildtower again.

TWENTY

POTSHIRE APPEARED OVER the hills first in the form of smoke. White puffs of it floated like cotton into the reddening sky, rising from the chimneys of her neighbors' houses.

They could have been any old chimneys, of course, belonging to any old houses in any old village—but even in the fading light, Certainty knew the sight of them like she knew the rhythm of her own heartbeat.

Here was the pasture where Daron the shepherd kept his sheep; there was the windmill with one sail torn and mended where the village boys had shot arrows at it (and had then been conscripted to haul wheat sacks for their troubles); over there was the well; and there—her breath hitched. There was her family's house atop its own little hill, with light in its windows and the grove of pear trees standing proud and lush behind it. The sight of her home settled around her shoulders like a shawl, comforting even when it had no right to be.

She rode up to the house slowly. She was grateful that few villagers were out and about just then, for nobody greeted her or stopped her to make conversation, even though she saw a few distant heads turn to look at the woman in white Guild novice's robes riding a horse into their village.

As she approached, the door to her home opened, and her father emerged.

"Cert!" His voice was just as she'd remembered—deep and warm, as if a laugh might be coming at any moment. He hastened to help her off the horse. "We weren't expecting you home just yet—though we've had your last letter, of course, and were all so excited to hear when . . . Cert? What's wrong?"

Certainty had managed to maintain a detached sort of stoicism up until then. But her father's delight to see her, the wide smile on his face—she just couldn't take it. Her heart crumpled.

"Da—" She let herself fall into his arms, let the tears leak out so that his rough linen tunic grew wet beneath her chin. All the emotions of the past week flooded out, past her walls, past the exhaustion. "Oh, Da, I've let you all down."

Her father's arms closed around her slowly, and she felt him exhale. "Oh, Cert. Let's go inside, shall we?"

He gently patted her on the back and separated himself just enough for them to walk into the house together. It smelled of baking bread, and her mother and Asp were there in the kitchen. They must have just been sitting down to dinner.

Either they'd heard what she'd said, or her tear-streaked face was enough of a clue, for her mother came swiftly to her and took her face in her hands.

"Cert, love. There now, it's all right—whatever has happened, it's all right. You're home now." She hugged her, and Certainty let herself be held.

"I'm so sorry," she whispered.

"Cert?"

Asp hovered uncertainly near her. Gods, he had grown, even

since Winterfair; instead of a boy with floppy hair, here stood a young man who hunched a little, as if unused to his own height.

"What's wrong?" he asked.

Certainty steeled herself. She wiped her tears away with her sleeve. She looked around at her family, who were watching her with concern. *Time to tell them all she'd failed them.*

"Something went wrong with our assignment. One of the artifacts caused a terrible accident. Aurelia and I are being held responsible, and . . . and I'm to be expelled from the Guild for it."

"Oh," said Asp. It was more an exhale than an actual word; the quiet sound of something deflating, and it made the shame well up fresh in her, hot enough to burn.

Certainty closed her eyes for a moment, shutting out the sight of her mother's worried expression. "I'm so sorry," she said again. "I know you all thought that . . . I know I'd given you reason to think, in my last letter—" Her voice wobbled.

"It's all right, dear," said her mother.

"No, it's *not*!"

Six years' worth of embarrassment, of dreams she'd tried to bury beneath patience and dogged cheerfulness, rose to choke her in their grip. She was a fool to think she'd ever be worth something. A fool to let her family think they could rely upon her.

"I'm a failure, ma! A disappointment. I know you all had such hopes for me when I left. I was supposed to become a mage, and Asp was supposed to become an apothecary—"

"Cert—"

"—and I was supposed to make something of myself, to send money home, to be the Potshire girl made good! But all I managed was to stay a useless novice for years, and now not even that—"

"*Cert!*"

She stopped abruptly. Her da had shouted. He *never* raised his voice.

But he came around now to look her in the face, and he lifted one big, calloused hand to her cheek. His brows were knitted in distress and bewilderment.

"Certainty Bulrush," he said. "You could never be a disappointment to us."

"But I—"

"*Never.* Do you hear me?"

Her mother touched her arm, too. "Listen to your da," she said softly.

Certainty's eyes were blurring with tears again. She looked over her parents' shoulders at her brother, standing a few paces away.

"But—your apprenticeship fee—I'm so sorry, Asp, really—"

She could tell he was disappointed; he was still young enough that his thoughts were written across his face, but . . . he didn't look angry at her. Why wasn't he angry?

"S'all right, Cert. It was always long odds; I knew that. And I know you worked really hard to try to make it happen." Asp ran one hand through his mop of hair and gave her a half shrug and a smile. "So maybe I won't be an apothecary, but I'll still be all right. There're other things out there for me."

"Like what?"

He shuffled his feet a little. "Remember Old Marigold, down by the river? The woman who knows about herbs and poultices and lives in the cottage with mushrooms all around it?"

"She's a witch, dear," their mother said patiently.

"Right, yes—well, back when I thought apprenticing for Jamison wasn't going to work, I talked to her. She said she'd be willing to teach me what she knows about healing. Without any apprenticeship fee, even! I'd just need to help her with her garden, and carry things, and run her errands—"

Certainty gaped at him, momentarily distracted from her own troubles.

"You'd become a witch's apprentice?"

"Why not?"

"I... well. It's just that I don't think I've heard of any men being witches before. Not that there's anything wrong with it, of course."

Asp shrugged again. "Then I'll be the first."

"And if it turns out witching isn't to his liking, there's always the farm," added their father helpfully. "You know what I always say: Pears never let you down!"

"*Da*," Certainty and Asp groaned at the same time, and she couldn't stop her lips from turning up when their eyes met. Asp grinned at her for a moment.

"Anyway, Cert, like I was saying. Thanks for trying so hard for my sake, but I'll still be all right. Really."

She nodded, and it felt like one layer of the sick, roiling ball of guilt within her slowly peeled away. She looked around at her parents and Asp.

"So you all really don't mind that I won't ever be a mage?"

Her parents looked at each other then, and her father spread his hands out wide.

"Cert, whether you're a Guild mage, a novice, or neither—if you stay home to grow pears, or if you run away to Lindisi to become a bard—none of that matters to us, you understand? All that matters is that you're happy."

"Yes," said her mother tearfully. "Though maybe we'd prefer it if you didn't run away to Lindisi. It's terribly far; I'm sure it'd make it hard to visit—"

"All right, not Lindisi, then," conceded her father, but Certainty hardly heard him.

All that matters is that you're happy.

The words vibrated through her, thrumming down to somewhere deep within her chest where they made themselves a nest, warming the breaths that flowed in and out of her lungs. For some reason, her cheeks were wet again; she wiped at them.

"I'd make an awful bard," she managed. "Can't sing."

Her father laughed, and the sound loosened something within her.

"Cert," he said tenderly, pulling her in again so that her chin rested on his shoulder and his beard scratched at her ear. "We love you. Loved you long before you started talking to the furniture; love you now. Always will. No matter what you are or aren't; no matter what you do or don't do. *We love you.* You hear me?"

"Yes," Cert whispered into his neck. His arms were warm and strong around her shoulders. They felt like understanding, and like love, too, which after all were very nearly the same thing. "Yes, Da. I hear you."

She had finally come home.

OVER THE NEXT few days, like cowherds reintroducing a lost calf to its barn, her family gently folded her back into the rhythm of daily life in Potshire. Certainty slept and ate, rested, and took on some light chores around the house—but just as important, she spoke, and laughed, and smiled. She quickly felt less bruised in both body and spirit, and she even managed to think about the Guild without getting that sick feeling in her stomach that made her want to shrivel up into a ball.

After her third day back home, she felt that she could finally write that long-due letter to Dav and Saralie, so she sat down at her father's desk and did so. In it, she apologized for not writing them sooner, and proceeded to summarize the events of the last few weeks. By now, they'd probably heard plenty of tower gossip about it already, but she thought she may as well tell them the story in full.

She debated how much to tell them about Aurelia, though—her heart ached even thinking of her—and settled for scribbling in *Aurelia isn't at all what she seemed at the start. We became close, and I care about her a lot. I think you both might like her, too, if you got to know her.* When she next saw them in person—*if* she saw them in person—she could tell them more. Somehow, it didn't feel right to simply write about what they had become to each other in a letter.

And as for what they were to each other *now*, after everything—well, Certainty couldn't even explain that to herself. Aurelia had made her a promise on a beach, then called her a distraction. Aurelia had said she was sorry, then had let her father take her away. Where did that leave them?

One thing at a time. Certainty rolled her shoulders and wrote on. She wrote to Dav and Saralie about the skyfire, the tavern burning, the hearing and its likely outcome—but her hand remained steady and her eyes dry, and she counted that as a small victory. She wondered if her friends would be at her hearing; if novices would even be allowed to attend. Honestly, she wasn't sure whether she wanted to see them there or not.

She signed and folded the letter, then pulled a clean piece of parchment toward her.

Now for the harder job. A letter to Aurelia.

Her quill hovered above the parchment, hesitant. What did she want to say?

She wanted to tell Aurelia that she was home now. That she had told her family what had happened, but the world hadn't ended, and life went on. That she missed her; that she hoped her own parents hadn't been too hard on her; that they would find a way to still see each other after the hearing. She wanted to tell her again how sorry she was that their Guild careers had been ruined, but also, that she didn't regret the rest of it in the slightest. That the time they'd spent together in Shpelling had been wonderful, and that one terrible thing didn't in any way negate or diminish the many good things that had come before.

It turned out there was quite a lot to be said after all. Certainty took a deep breath and dipped her quill into the inkwell. She began to write.

HER LETTERS WENT out with the mail courier the next morning, and Certainty let herself forget about them—about anything outside of Potshire's borders, in fact—for several days. She busied herself with helping her ma in the kitchen, and getting to know Asp the young man half as well as she knew Asp the boy. It was easier to talk to him now that the apprenticeship to Master Jamison no longer hung over them like some golden fruit just beyond their reach. Asp seemed to have accepted that that path had closed to him for good this time, and any lingering sadness he might have felt was chased away by his clear delight at having Certainty home again. So even as the date of the hearing grew nearer, Certainty let herself wallow in guilt only for brief moments and found that she was able to drag herself out of it by remembering what her mother and father and Asp had said to her in the kitchen the day she arrived. Nobody in her family could lie worth a damn—a Bulrush family trait, along with curly hair and a quick smile—so she knew somewhere deep within that if they said they loved her and were proud of her, it must be true.

She even managed some small talk with neighbors in the

village, letting her father deflect innocent questions about how her Guild studies were progressing. And as she grew reacclimated to the comfortable rhythm of home, Certainty tried to see Potshire with new eyes—to see what place she might carve for herself here. To see it as a possible future, and not only her past.

But even as she laughed, and smiled, and helped her father tie up pear branches with twine so that they wouldn't break when their fruit grew heavy come autumn, Certainty also grew more certain that this place, wonderful though it was, wasn't where she belonged.

She missed Aurelia, yes, but what was far more surprising to her was the discovery that she missed *magic*. It wasn't just the thrill of an object-voice in her mind, but the knowledge that her powers were being put toward some higher purpose. The sense that by being one of many who wore the Guild robes, she was part of something greater than herself.

"I think I still want to be a mage," Certainty said one night as she lay abed. She said it just to herself, quietly so nobody else in the house would hear, and to her great surprise, it didn't sound absurd at all. It sounded like a matter-of-fact truth. She blinked up at the ceiling.

For so long, she had sought to earn her circles for one purpose only—to try to make good on the hopes her family had placed on her. Now that she didn't have that to worry about any longer, she found that beneath that fog of purpose, another dream had been silently growing all the while: her own.

"I want to be a mage," she whispered again, then laughed a little at her own ridiculousness. Her amusement faded. *But how?* Such an ambition was more out of reach for her now than it ever had been. For Mother's sake, she was on the verge of expulsion from the Guild; in all practical terms, she *had* been expelled and was simply waiting for it to be formalized.

All that remained was the hearing. Was there any hope at all of persuading the magistrate to choose leniency? She mulled it over in the dark, ignoring the muted snoring of her father sleeping in the next room.

If Aurelia were here, they could strategize together—make a plan, prepare arguments . . . but Certainty hadn't yet received a reply from her. Maybe she'd write another letter to her tomorrow.

In the meantime, Certainty had just under two weeks to do what she could on her own. She was *Certainty Bulrush of Potshire*, godsdamnit. She would find a way. There were times for ordered and scholarly thinking, and there were times for being resolutely, pigheadedly stubborn—and she rather thought now was a time that called for both.

TWENTY-ONE

MAIL FINALLY CAME for Certainty the following day, but she frowned when she looked down at the letter in her hands. Saralie's elegant, looping handwriting looked back at her.

"Only this? Are you sure there isn't another for me from Margrave?"

The courier rifled through his messenger bag to check. "No, miss. It's just the one."

She nodded her thanks distractedly, turning back toward her family's home. Why hadn't Aurelia written back yet?

She pushed the niggling worry away as she sat down to her father's desk. Perhaps her friends might have news for her, either of the helpful or the entertaining sort; at this point, she'd happily take either.

Unfolding the letter, she read:

Dear Cert,

I hardly know how to begin. We, I should say—Dav is perched beside me like an anxious gargoyle and muttering suggestions as I write this—but I suppose we ought to start by saying we're so very sorry, Cert. It's terribly unfair that all of your hard work these past years hasn't earned you a little grace. What happened in Shpelling sounds like an unfortunate accident (I'm glad nobody was hurt!), and it's hardly your fault that you've been caught up in the royal mess that is Guild-Council politics . . .

But everyone in the tower seems to be talking about the upcoming hearing, and we've heard some gossip from someone I'd consider reliable. (Dav is telling me not to mention it here, but . . . I really think you ought to know, Cert.)

They're saying that Mage Aurelia's parents have struck a deal with the High Mage and the magistrate. Apparently they're making a sizable contribution to the restitution funds to appease Lord Godfrey, and have also convinced the High Mage that the Guild simply can't afford to lose one of our few farspeakers. Lord Godfrey will be satisfied as long as someone from the Guild is made an example of, and that someone . . . well, it's to be you. Aurelia has provided a signed affidavit attesting to your "poor judgment and irresponsible conduct" in Shpelling, and in exchange, she'll be allowed to keep her circles and continue her research.

Oh, Cert, I'm sorry—it's so infuriating!! I know you said that Aurelia's not the person she seemed, but . . . if she's willing to go along with this, then I'm having a hard time believing that she's someone you ought to consider a friend. (And Dav agrees with me on this, shockingly.)

If there's anything at all that we can do to help,

anything at all, we're here for you, Cert. Whether a Guild mage or not, you're still our friend. That won't change.

Faithfully yours,
Saralie + Davish

Certainty set the letter down, stunned. She read it twice again to make sure she hadn't misunderstood, but there it was, written plain as day—and Saralie wouldn't lie to her, not about something as important as this. But . . . Aurelia would never have agreed to such an arrangement! They had an equal amount of responsibility for the skyfire incident; Aurelia had even tried to take all the blame herself in the High Mage's office—

Then why hasn't she written you back yet?

Certainty tried to imagine Aurelia, back home in her Margravian family manor. Sitting on a finely turned chair in a finely appointed drawing room, wearing an elegant dress, surrounded by the familiar trappings of status and prestige instead of the straw and mud of a farming village. She imagined Aurelia's parents upbraiding her, chastising her, painting a vision with their words of the dismal future that awaited were she to be expelled from the Guild, all her studies and hard work for naught.

To be someone of value, Aurelia had whispered to her that one night in the carriage house. That was what she'd always wanted. And if she were offered a path back to that? A gilded path of little resistance, and all she had to do was walk it alone and leave Certainty behind?

She wouldn't. Surely she wouldn't. Not the woman who had hammered shelves beside her, and teased her, and danced with her around a bonfire. Not the Aurelia who had walked with her through a mirror and back again.

But the Aurelia who had stiffened and gone silent when that scholar in Ruggan had sneered at their work...

Certainty sat back heavily in her chair.

...was it possible?

Could she really have misjudged Aurelia so badly?

She rubbed at her eyes; there was a faint ringing sound in her ears, and she felt the beginnings of a headache.

She would just write Aurelia another letter. Yes, that was it; she would ask her directly about this rumor, and even if Aurelia was—was not who she thought, she was not a liar, and Certainty could hear directly from her whether there was any truth to it. The hearing was in a week and a half, and Certainty wanted to at least know what to expect before she arrived back in Margrave to face her fate.

She shook her head, trying to dislodge the fuzzy noise in her head, and picked up her quill.

TWO MORE DAYS passed. No letters came.

Certainty found herself increasingly sleepless. Late at night, she lay in bed staring at the ceiling and worrying at the fraying threads of her woolen blankets while all around her, the rest of her family slept peacefully. All the while, the bothersome whining in her head grew worse, and her headache simply wouldn't go away.

Despair tried to creep in, but she shoved it away and let herself be angry instead. Anger was more productive.

Whether Aurelia was or was not betraying her wasn't within her control. Instead, she'd focus on what she *could* control, which was preparing for the hearing as best she could. Grimly, she decided to assume that she would find herself standing alone.

What could she do or say that might have the slightest hope of persuading the High Mage and the magistrate to reconsider?

Well, she could apologize again to the Guild and to Lord Godfrey, of course. Profusely. Get on her knees and beg; express her very great remorse for what had happened.

Though really, it's not as though Lord Godfrey himself suffered anything at all, she thought bitterly. The loss of a single tavern in a village notable only for its garlic output must barely register in Lord Godfrey's provincial accounting books. All that had been damaged was his pride. His *secretary's* pride. The only people she really ought to apologize to were Ferdinand and the rest of the Shpelling folk . . .

She blinked as an idea shimmered into being. Was there time? She counted in her head—still nine days until the hearing. There might be.

She *should* apologize and beg forgiveness from the people of Shpelling, and she would. Not only for the skyfire but for leaving as she had, without even saying goodbye. But also . . . she remembered carrying Gertha's water bucket up the hill for her. Ferdinand, waiting beside the path with his heavy barrel for them to come along. Orrin showing up at the stable with a bag of tools in hand.

She was village folk, and so were they. And one thing village folk did—something carved deep on the mantel of their hearts, something taught to them by parents and friends and the simple fact of having neighbors who knew what it was to have a poor harvest one year, and a rich one the next—

They weren't ashamed to ask for help.

CERTAINTY ROSE WITH purpose the next morning, even before the rest of her family had woken, and sat down to write one more letter. But it wasn't going to Aurelia, nor to Dav or Saralie, either. In fact, it wasn't going to Margrave at all.

She began to write:

Dear Ferdinand, Gertha, Hull, Murph, Brienna, Orrin, and all the people of Shpelling . . .

CERTAINTY DIDN'T EXPECT a response before she left Potshire, of course; there wouldn't be time for one, and if her letter was successful, a response wouldn't be necessary. But there was no way of knowing until she arrived back in Margrave. So she spent her final week at home doing her best to enjoy the time with her family, reacquainting herself with old friends and neighbors, and breathing in the scent of pear blossoms and springtime as she read books about knights and explorers—old childhood favorites—in her family's grove.

It was a peaceful time, and she was grateful for it. It being only a temporary respite did not in any way make it less important or wonderful; if anything, she thought it was quite the opposite. You were always waiting for *something* to happen, after all. Life was a series of waits, of moments in between. You couldn't cram all your happiness and meaning into only the big moments, or you'd miss everything else that mattered along the way.

So it was with a newfound peace (but still that blasted headache, and the ringing in her ears, which had turned into a dull sort of murmur—she really ought to see a healer about it) that she rose not long after dawn on the final morning, packed a bag of clothes and quills and parchment, and went to the kitchen to find her family waiting for her.

"You're all up early," she said in surprise.

Her mother passed her a cup of hot, milky tea. "We all wanted to make sure we said goodbye before you left."

"And to see if you'd changed your mind about us coming with you," added her father. "I've told you, it'd hardly be any trouble—the pears will be fine without us for a few days—"

Her parents had wanted to travel back to Margrave with her to attend the hearing, but Certainty had asked them not to. She knew that leaving the farm, even for a short time, was no small thing; not during the height of planting season, when there were diseased branches to be pruned, promising young seedlings to be grafted, calving cows to be watched over. And besides, if the hearing resulted in her expulsion, she didn't want them there to watch; she'd have a hard enough time keeping her composure as it was.

"No, Da. Thank you, but I'm sure. I'd rather know that you all were back home waiting for me." She took a sip of the tea; it had been sweetened with a generous amount of honey, just how she liked it.

She could tell they were worried, but they didn't argue with her any further. Her mother reached out to fuss with Certainty's hair, where some curls were being particularly rebellious. "And take those sandwiches on the table there, in case you get hungry on the road—"

The journey would only take three hours at the most, but mothers would be mothers. Certainty smiled.

"Thanks, Ma."

"I saddled Jenny up for you," said Asp, yawning widely. "Gave her a good brushing, too; she needed it. You might want to do the same for your own hair—"

"Go back to bed, you lout," said Certainty affectionately. "I could've saddled her myself. And you're hardly one to talk about messy hair; you look like a sheep."

"Yeah, well." He gave an appropriately sheepish shrug, which Certainty interpreted to be teenage boy speak for *I love you, dear sister. Good luck, safe travels.*

And just like that, it was time for them to say goodbye. Her da smiled at her, awkward and fatherly and sweet. "We're all very proud of you, you know."

"You know I'm going back to the Guildtower to be expelled for accidentally burning down a building, right?"

But Certainty was grinning lightly as she said it; the words no longer held quite the same sting as they had two weeks ago. And besides, she still had the slightest of hopes that it wasn't too late.

Her father ignored this, threw his arms around her, and held her tightly. "Our little Certainty. You remember what your ma told you about why we named you that?"

"Because you wanted me to always be sure of who I was," she said, the words a little muffled by his shoulder.

He gave her a stubbly kiss on the forehead before releasing her. "And look at you now. It's almost like we had our own kind of magic, eh, love?" He led her outside, and once she had put her pack into Jenny's saddlebags, he hoisted her up into the saddle.

"I'll be back," Certainty said to her family. "I don't know when, exactly—" It depended on the outcome of the hearing, and whether the folks in Shpelling had read her letter, and had decided she was worth forgiving. "—but I promise you, I'll be back." She thought of Gertha's face as the old woman had spoken of her daughter in Forlinet, and added, "I'll always come back, you know."

"We know," said her mother.

"We'll be here when you do," said Asp.

Certainty nodded, not trusting herself to speak, and nudged Jenny into a walk and then a gentle trot. And when she rode again through the village of Potshire, she glanced over her shoulder as her home and her family disappeared from view, and found that she felt lighter somehow, as if she had left behind a weight she hadn't even known she was carrying.

TWENTY-TWO

MARGRAVE, THE TERRACED City, the silver-and-whitestone glory of Eshtera, did not seem to have been waiting for Certainty's return. As Certainty rode Jenny through the massive outer gates and navigated the crowded streets alongside farmers and merchants carting their wares in for the day, nobody paid her any attention at all. One plain young woman riding a horse poorly wasn't particularly worthy of notice, she supposed. And she wasn't wearing her novice's whites, seeing as . . . well. They were laundered and folded neatly within her pack, though. She hoped she might still need to wear them again.

But it felt odd to arrive in Margrave on what might be the single most consequential day of her life thus far and realize that to everyone else in this city, it was simply another Scholarsday. She smiled, laughing a little at herself; what else did she expect? The kingdom was hardly waiting with bated breath to learn the fate of Certainty Bulrush of Potshire. In a way, realizing just how inconsequential she was was liberating.

She directed Jenny up through the Middle City, then the High City, before finally arriving at the gates of the Guildtower courtyard. The guards in Guild livery there looked familiar; one of them recognized her, too.

"Novice Cert—that is, Miss Certainty Bulrush?"

"Yes," she said.

"We've been directed to take your horse and escort you to the courthouse."

"The hearing isn't in the Guildtower?"

He shook his head. "Afraid not, miss. Public hearings mean the courthouse. The High Mage is already there."

They helped her down off of Jenny, and the guard, a clean-shaven man with a nick on his ear, gave her an apologetic smile. Barlow, she thought his name might be.

She nodded, retrieving her pack from the saddlebags. It still had two sandwiches inside. "I'm ready."

One guard took Jenny's reins and brought the horse inside the gates, while Barlow led Certainty away from the Guildtower and east along the first ring road. They walked for ten minutes or so, and Certainty was grateful that the guard didn't try to make conversation. She was hard-pressed enough managing herself at the moment without also having to spill her anxieties to a stranger.

The guard stopped in front of an imposingly large building boasting two tall pillars with ornamental cornices in the Lindisian style. "Here we are," he said, nodding at it. "Just about noon now, too. You're right on time."

Certainty nodded, looking up at the double doors of the courthouse's entrance. She swallowed hard.

"Miss, Fanya also said to tell you good luck. From all of us who work at the Guildtower." The guard tugged at his forelock, and Certainty smiled gratefully at him.

"Thank you," she said. It was nice to think that there might be people in the Guild wishing her well. He nodded and turned to return to his post at the Guildtower, and Certainty was left alone.

She took a moment to master herself, and then climbed the whitestone steps toward the doors. They swung open; she entered, and saw:

A large room filled with strangers. Their faces turning toward her.

On the far end, an imposing figure who must be the magistrate, sitting at his elevated lectern in a high-collared black robe and a face made white with powder.

To his side, the High Mage, seated slightly lower and bearing a grim expression.

Facing them, two podiums: one manned already by Master Tobias, the other clearly intended for her. Certainty's throat closed.

No Aurelia. So that was that, then.

"Miss Certainty Bulrush of Potshire," called the magistrate. His voice was loud and authoritative. "Approach."

She put one foot in front of the other, and then another, and forced herself to walk down the aisle between the benches of observers. She was nearly halfway down to the podium when she heard Dav's voice.

"Psst! Cert!"

"Shush, Dav, we're not supposed to talk—"

She looked to her left and saw Dav and Saralie bickering. They brightened as soon as she looked at them; Dav gave her a furtive wave, and Saralie smiled encouragingly. All around them were other faces Certainty recognized, a mixture of mages and novices and Guild servants she had been friendly with. They nodded and smiled at her—*you're not alone*—and Certainty managed to smile back at them.

She continued forward, but just as she was about to reach her podium, she heard another voice to her right. It sounded sniffy and crotchety and deeply unimpressed. It sounded, in other words, like Old Gertha.

"So that's the High Mage up there, next to the old man in the wig?" Gertha wasn't even trying to keep her voice down. "You'd think she'd have, I dunno, some fancier robes, maybe. Or a staff with a big shiny gem on top."

The High Mage's lips twitched behind her lectern, and Certainty felt a rush of relief as she looked over her shoulder. There they were: Gertha, and Hull beside her, and Murph and Brienna, Ferdinand, and Orrin, too. They had gotten her letter! And they had come here, all the way from Shpelling to the grand High City of Margrave, for her.

Hull saw her looking and elbowed Gertha to be quiet. The villagers from Shpelling all looked at her then, and she smiled at them, willing them to feel her gratitude across the vast room. Orrin waved, and Gertha gave her a sharp nod, as if to say, *Go on, then. Stop dithering!*

"Miss Bulrush. Are you prepared to begin?"

Certainty turned back around and took a deep breath. "Yes, sir."

The magistrate picked up his gavel and cracked it sharply against his lectern. "Then let the hearing commence."

THEY BEGAN WITH the formalities. Certainty stood silent and dutiful at her podium as the facts of the situation were recited by the magistrate. How she and Aurelia had been sent on an urgent assignment by the Guild to safeguard a cache of magical artifacts in Shpelling. How an artifact in their care had led to the destruction of the village tavern and endangered the lives of the villagers. How Aurelia had sent the court a signed statement corroborating these facts, and had been excused for her own lesser role in these events in return. As the magistrate spoke, a court scribe seated in the corner dutifully scribbled down every word on a long scroll of parchment, and Certainty tried not to flinch every time Aurelia's name was spoken.

Tobias, too, performed his part in this theater, letting out little huffs of indignation as the burning of the tavern was described, but Certainty remained stoic. She imagined how Aurelia would comport herself if she were here—trying not to think about the fact that she was not—and lifted her chin high.

Then it was time for Tobias to speak.

"Your lordship," he said, turning to face the audience even though he was ostensibly addressing the magistrate. "I serve as secretary to my lord and patron, Lord Godfrey, in whose province the village of Shpelling lies. I speak today on his behalf.

"You have already heard of the terrible destruction wrought by the enchanted artifact in this woman's care. But it is possible that you may look at her and see a"—his lip curled—"naive young woman with a pleasant manner. You may be inclined to feel sympathy, to say that the burning of the tavern was simply an unfortunate accident.

"But as Lord Godfrey's representative in this matter, I am here to dissuade you of that notion. Lord magistrate, I am here to share with you what I observed of these women during their weeks in Shpelling."

Certainty stared at him. A gnawing fear took root somewhere in the vicinity of her stomach; the secretary was so confident, so smooth in his delivery. She knew she couldn't match him. The very same things that had made her take an immediate dislike to him were working to his favor here in the courtroom.

Tobias made eye contact with her briefly, and she saw that he was enjoying this. It made her loathe him even more.

"I am here," he began again, "to prove that the terrible burning of Shpelling's tavern was not merely an isolated and accidental incident, but the last and worst thread in Miss Certainty

Bulrush's pattern of misusing dangerous magical artifacts for frivolous and self-serving purposes."

There was a surprised murmur from the audience at this; Certainty closed her eyes. *Shit.*

"I have either personally witnessed or heard directly from the parties affected by the following instances: The use of an artifact to summon a swarm of bees. The use of an artifact to make tea. The use of an artifact to breed a dangerous beast as a pet." There were gasps and loud mutters now, and Tobias raised his voice to be heard as he went on, ticking off the examples with his fingers. "The use of an artifact to *warm her bathwater.* The use of an artifact to grow giant daffodils—"

"We didn't do it all for ourselves," burst out Certainty, unable to take any more. "We did it to help the village!"

"Order!" shouted the magistrate, banging his gavel amidst the din. *"Order!"*

The chaos settled somewhat, but Tobias's mouth was set in a small, satisfied smile. His arrows had hit their intended target; the magistrate's gaze when he looked upon Certainty was harsh. The High Mage simply looked resigned.

"Miss Bulrush, you will have your chance to speak once Master Tobias is done."

But Tobias was finished. His lip curled as he looked at her. "I thank you, your lordship. That is all."

The magistrate nodded. "Then Miss Bulrush. What do you have to say for yourself?"

Certainty swallowed, her mouth suddenly quite dry. "Your lordship, if I may . . . I would like to ask others who are here today to speak on my behalf."

The magistrate's brow knitted. "What others?"

There was some rustling and commotion from the observer benches.

"Us, sir," came Orrin's nervous young voice. "My lord. Your lordship." Tobias's head whipped around. Certainty looked behind her, too, and saw the villagers of Shpelling all standing up in a row.

"Who are you all?" the magistrate asked.

"We're the people who live in Shpelling," said Gertha, her tone acerbic. "I should think that means we know better than anyone what happened there, hm?"

"It was my tavern what burned down," added Ferdinand helpfully.

The magistrate looked perplexed, but beside him, High Mage Melea had straightened in her chair, looking suddenly interested in the proceedings. As Certainty watched, the High Mage leaned over and whispered something to the magistrate. The furrows on his forehead grew even deeper, but he nodded grudgingly and raised a hand to beckon the villagers forward.

"Very well, the court shall hear you."

As all watched, the unlikely party of witnesses shuffled out of their bench and into the front of the courtroom before the magistrate. But—Certainty narrowed her eyes in confusion—they each seemed to be carrying something in their hands...

Hull came forward first, and Certainty saw then that he held a small woven basket.

"Your lordship, we're here to give evidence of what Mage Aurelia and Novice Certainty did in Shpelling. So here's what they did for me."

He took another step toward the lectern and set the basket down gently so that the magistrate could lean over and see it for himself.

"Unripe apples," said the magistrate, and Tobias let out a derisive snort.

"Aye, apples," said Hull, undaunted. "That I plucked from trees in my family's grove, which hadn't grown anything at all for decades. Not until Certainty here"—he nodded toward her—"summoned the bees that made them start fruiting again."

The crowd murmured.

Hull stepped back, and Orrin stepped forward holding something dark and round in his arms. Certainty craned her neck to see; the dark shape moved, and stretched two paws up to climb onto Orrin's shoulder, where she perched primly.

"*Meow*," said the dangerous beast, and delighted coos were audible from several observers sitting in the front benches.

Something in Certainty's chest unclenched. Hope was fine; Hope was safe—and she had returned to Shpelling, after all!

The catdragon gave one cursory flap of her wings before settling them back down at her sides. Orrin scratched her under the chin, then looked up at the magistrate. "They brought us Hope. The catdragon, see, and I swear she's never hurt a single hair on any of our heads." (This wasn't *strictly* true, and Certainty knew that more than one villager bore some fading scratches on their arms or legs that would disprove it, but she certainly wasn't going to point that out.)

Murph and Brienna stepped up beside Orrin, too, and Brienna laid down a single, perfect-looking, round loaf of bread beside the basket of green apples. "Actually, Hope and the other cats helped get rid of Shpelling's rodent infestation. She saved my bakery," she said.

Certainty snuck a peek at the magistrate and the High Mage. The magistrate was frowning, but High Mage Melea was looking thoughtful; she took that as a positive sign.

Gertha hobbled forward next, leaning heavily on Hull's arm. Certainty hid a smile; Gertha was laying it on a touch thick. Everyone's eyes were on the frail, feeble old woman as she reached one trembling hand into her pocket and pulled out . . . a flower?

It was a single dandelion, its face fat and yellow as it craned upward from its stem, rooted only in a small sack of soil tied with twine.

"They grew this flower," Gertha said simply, and even though her hand shook, her voice was strong and steady. "In a clearing in the woods where nothing else would grow. This is what they did for us."

And even if nobody else in the courtroom understood, Certainty did, and she smiled at the old woman through sudden tears. Gertha nodded at her, bent down to place the little flower among the other offerings, and hobbled back to stand with the others.

Finally, only Ferdinand was left. He looked down at what he held as he approached the magistrate, not even seeming to notice the expectant hush of his captured audience as all waited to hear what the tavernkeep had to say.

"Aye, my tavern burned down," he said slowly, still looking down. "And I've already been given the coin to rebuild it and then some, and I will. But I won't just rebuild it as it was, m'lord. I'm going to build it better. It'll be the finest inn in all the province." He looked up now, and his mustache quivered with feeling as he addressed the magistrate. "And when I've built it, people will come, because this finally means something again."

He finally set what he held down on the ground, and turned it so that all could see.

It was the sign of the Golden Plough.

The last time Certainty saw it, it had lain scorched and cracked, its yellow paint melted off from the flames. But now, she could see that it had been lovingly repaired. The wood was sanded and polished where the flames had charred it, and the golden symbol gleamed proudly with fresh paint. A fat white bulb of garlic had been painted alongside the plough, too. Ferdinand gestured at the sign.

"This sign? Now, it means good food and drink. It means comfort. It means a place to rest in good company, and to share conversation and lighten the loads of the day.

"But it didn't—not when the mages first came to Shpelling. It wasn't a place to be proud of then. I'd let it fall into shabbiness because I looked at the village around me and thought, what's the point? But they changed all that, you see? Shpelling's *alive* again, alive and growing. They didn't take the Plough away—they gave it back to me. This is what Certainty did for me. Please don't punish her for it."

There was a moment of silence as eyes darted between the tavern's sign, Certainty, and Tobias; she looked up at the magistrate, daring to hope that he had been swayed. Surely, even if Ferdinand—the tavern owner himself—begged leniency for her . . .

"That's all well and good" came Tobias's sneering voice, cutting into the silence that had followed Ferdinand's speech. "But this sentimentality is meaningless, and an insult to the intelligence of his lordship the magistrate, besides." (Behind his lectern, the magistrate attempted to assemble an expression of appropriate offense.)

Tobias swung one arm out toward Ferdinand. "We all heard the man say so himself; his tavern was burned to the ground by magical fire! Well-intentioned or not, Miss Bulrush was responsible for creating a dangerous situation that risked lives and directly caused the destruction of valuable property. She *must* be held to account for it."

With dread, Certainty saw that the magistrate was nodding along with Tobias's words.

"Quite right," he said, leaning over the lectern. "Quite right, Master Tobias. The testimony of these villagers—while, er, fascinating—does not seem wholly pertinent. I have heard no evidence to disprove the fact that a tavern was burned, and this woman bears the greatest share of responsibility for it. And as such, I believe it appropriate to bring this hearing to its conclusion."

The magistrate leaned toward High Mage Melea to say something inaudible. Her expression was resigned, but she gave him a single tight, unwilling nod in return. His gaze turned back to Certainty.

"Certainty Bulrush of Potshire: In light of the facts laid before us, the joint court of this disciplinary hearing rules that you are responsible for the destruction in Shpelling, and that you are to be summarily expelled from the Royal Guild of Mages. Do you accept this judgment?"

There were shouts of protest from the Shpelling folk, but Certainty barely heard them. It was over; she could see that now. Certainty had done what she could in mustering the people of Shpelling to her aid—but she had no other plan waiting to be deployed. No other tricks or magical artifacts up her sleeve.

And as for Aurelia . . . well, her absence was answer enough.

There was nothing left to do but accept her fate, and to build a new future for herself—away from the Guildtower, away from her dreams both old and new. At least Certainty had tried. That was something, wasn't it? She could walk away with her dignity and the knowledge that she could not have done any more.

She only wished . . . well, she wished for a great many things, but in that particular moment, she only wished that her blasted headache would go away.

Certainty closed her eyes and inhaled deeply. She held her breath in. She pretended the pain in her temples didn't exist, and let her worries and thoughts fade away, if only for a moment, as she prepared herself to speak those simple words: *I accept the court's judgment.*

Slowly, she let her breath out, and just as the last bit of air squeezed itself out of her, she found a single, blissful moment of peace.

Her mind was finally still and empty.

And then—

The odd, niggling whine in her ears intensified into a roar...

Her magic flared in recognition...

...and a door somewhere within her mind opened—and through it came Aurelia's voice.

"I'm coming, Cert! Wait for me—"

The voice was indistinct, as if calling to her from the bottom of a deep well, but it was inarguably, miraculously Aurelia's.

Shock flooded through her. *"Aurelia? What is this? Are we farspeaking?"*

"Yes!" And there was definitely a note of triumph there, and relief, too, but Certainty didn't have time to dwell on what it meant that Aurelia could farspeak again. *"I'm on my way to the courthouse now—stall! Just stall for time; I'm bringing—"*

The voice faded back into unintelligibility. But through sheer force of will, Certainty pried the connection back open, pouring what remained of her magic through it to find Aurelia's.

"What, Aurelia? Bringing what?"

"Proof!"

And then the door slammed shut. Certainty was alone in her own head once more.

"Miss Bulrush," boomed the magistrate. "I repeat: Do you accept these facts and your permanent expulsion from the Royal Guild of Mages?"

"No," she said slowly. Louder, she said, "No, I do not." Heart pounding, Certainty turned toward Tobias. *Stall*, Aurelia had told her. She could do that.

"Master Tobias, I have a question for you. Why do you hate mages?"

"I—" For the first time she had seen during the hearing, the secretary looked utterly thrown. "What?"

"You hate mages, don't you? From the moment Aurelia and I arrived in Shpelling, you made that quite clear."

"Miss Bulrush, what is the relevance of this—" began the magistrate impatiently.

"But perhaps it's only women mages that you hate? Or women in general?"

Tobias looked murderous. "I do *not* hate women," he hissed.

"Mages it is, then," said Certainty cheerfully. "I just wanted to be sure of that point."

"*Miss Bulrush*, kindly explain this line of questioning at once!" The magistrate was furious, too; the powder he wore was losing its battle against the red in his face.

"Of course, your lordship!" Certainty's blood was rushing in her ears, and somehow the magistrate now just looked to her like an old man wearing rather silly robes. "I was merely thinking that if Master Tobias hates mages now, well, I imagine he's about to hate us even more very soon."

"And why is that?" snarled Tobias.

At that exact moment, the courtroom doors swung open with a bang, and—Certainty's heart soared, *yes, yes, yes*—a vision of tall, blond triumph stormed in.

Aurelia had arrived.

"I have proof that Tobias set off the skyfire!" she shouted, thrusting a thick sheaf of papers above her head.

"Because of that," Certainty said with a great deal of satisfaction, and tumult exploded in the courtroom.

TWENTY-THREE

AURELIA, PANTING AS she clutched the stack of papers like a talisman, was an utter mess. Her blond hair was a half-braided tangle, one sleeve of her cloak was stained, and she looked as if she hadn't slept in days. But as she stalked up the aisle like a lioness whose prey was finally within her sights, Certainty thought she had never looked more magnificent.

"Order!" shouted the magistrate, banging his gavel against the lectern in a futile attempt to contain the chaos that had erupted. "Someone restrain that woman—"

"*My name is Mage Aurelia Mirellan, and anyone who touches me is getting turned into a dung beetle!*"

The court guards nearest Aurelia had already begun to reach for her, but froze immediately where they stood. A few of them edged backward slowly.

"You will all hear what I have to say," Aurelia said, her chest heaving and eyes flashing as her gaze swept around the courtroom, challenging everyone there. "Because I had just as much part in all this as Certainty did. No matter what underhanded deal my parents struck with the Guild, no matter what—what *fuckery* they forced me to sign."

Certainty's eyes went wide; she'd never heard Aurelia swear like that before. Somehow, it still sounded prim.

"Cert, I'm so sorry I couldn't tell you," Aurelia said, turning to her. "I had to sign it; had to pretend I was going along with it all, or my parents wouldn't have let me out of the house. I needed the Guildtower library to find the evidence! I've been researching everything these past few weeks—I wanted to write you, I promise I wanted to, but I couldn't or they'd know what I was up to—"

"It's all right," Certainty said faintly. "But maybe we can talk about all that later?" She darted her eyes toward the apoplectic magistrate and the High Mage.

"Right! Yes!" Aurelia whirled back to them, waving her papers in Tobias's direction. "Like I said, I have proof that that odious little man was the one who set off the skyfire and burned down the tavern!"

"The woman is mad!" Behind his lectern, Master Tobias had gone from red to pale, and he stabbed one shaking finger at Aurelia. "She's just another lunatic mage; don't listen to her!"

It was a poor choice of words from a man surrounded by mages, many of whom were understandably touchy about having their sanity questioned. The courtroom burst into a cacophony; benches scraped and people stood; furious imprecations were flung. Shimmering bubbles of defense spells popped into existence around some of the more nervous members of the audience.

Then, suddenly, silence fell.

The High Mage was on her feet with a thunderous expression, and she had drawn one hand across her body, palm down, in a swift motion. A silencing spell, Certainty realized.

"Enough," said High Mage Melea. Her voice, the only audible sound in the room, was quiet with authority. "We will hear Mage Aurelia Mirellan's testimony. What proof do you claim?"

She lowered her hand, and there was a general exhale as everyone realized that the spell had been lifted. The magistrate cleared his throat, glancing uneasily at the High Mage. "Yes," he said, attempting to reassert some semblance of control over the proceedings. "Very well. We will hear her."

Slowly, everyone sank back into their seats. All looked at Aurelia, some warily, and some consideringly.

"Thank you, High Mage. Magistrate." Aurelia lifted her chin, once more the composed scholar, the state of her hair and attire notwithstanding. Certainty marveled at her; Aurelia exuded sheer competence the way a candle gave off light. "As I was saying—the burning of Master Ferdinand's tavern was no accident, but an act of sabotage.

"When Certainty and I returned to the stable where the artifacts were stored, there were footprints outside—clear signs that an intruder had been there, though we had no way then of knowing who. But there was something odd about the footprints... they crossed *directly over* my warding line. No shuffling around, no trying to break it first with a branch—whoever it was, despite clearly having malicious intentions, simply walked over it without fear.

"Now, my wards were inactive that night due to the focus crystal having been misplaced. But how would the intruder have known that?"

Aurelia held one unrolled parchment up in the air, turning in place so that all could see. Certainty squinted at it, but couldn't quite make it out.

"What is it, woman?" called out the magistrate irritably. "We can't see it from here."

"Why, this happens to be a page of the Guild admissions records from about fifteen years ago," said Aurelia brightly. "For an applicant named Tobias Smyde, of the town of Ruggan."

The crowd murmured again, and the High Mage leaned forward with interest. Tobias's shoulders had gone rigid.

"And this record," continued Aurelia as she handed it over to the High Mage, "states that Tobias Smyde, fifteen, displayed no magical talent when tested—but did demonstrate a weak ability to *detect* active magic. Tobias Smyde was rejected as a novice, but was offered a position as a magefinder, which he refused."

The High Mage, scanning the parchment, made a thoughtful noise. "Interesting. This is indeed a Guild admissions record. And the ability to detect magic... why, that might give someone the confidence to cross a visible warding line, even if they were an intruder with the intent to do harm. Because they would know if the warding had failed."

"Circumstantial," snarled Tobias, as everyone's eyes turned to him. "That was years and years ago; I haven't made any use of my ability since!"

The magistrate frowned, but Aurelia spoke again before he could intervene.

"I'm not done." Aurelia held up the rest of the papers. "There's this, too. Master Tobias, tell me again—how do you know what Dashan skyfire is? Because that's what you called it, isn't it? On the night of the fire."

"I read it in a book!" Tobias spat. "I'm a learned man; I read books. Is that a crime—"

"Which book? Because all of the texts that I could find on the topic of skyfire"—she shook the sheaf of papers—"state that the imperial government of Shinara has standardized its production so thoroughly that it's *impossible* to tell where a tube was produced simply by witnessing its effects!"

Tobias finally fell silent. His eyes were wide and wild as they darted between Aurelia and the High Mage.

"Of course, I suppose it's possible that Master Tobias, the

provincial lord's secretary, might have had access to more recent and sophisticated scholarship on foreign magic than what I could find in the Guild's libraries," Aurelia said with feigned thoughtfulness. "But it seems rather more likely to me that he simply read Certainty's notes on 'Dashan skyfire' in our book of artifact records while he was in the stable, looking for something to make trouble with. And if that's the case . . . Isn't it obvious? Master Tobias, who could tell that the wards had failed, was the intruder at the stable. Master Tobias, who resented our presence in Shpelling, was the one to set off the skyfire. *Master Tobias* is guilty of the tavern's burning. Not Certainty."

Aurelia looked back at Certainty then, with green eyes that glowed fierce and bright, and Certainty thought that she could very possibly love this brilliant, extraordinary woman.

The stunned silence of the courtroom was broken by a leathery flapping noise. Hope the catdragon launched herself from Orrin's lap to land, purring, on Aurelia's shoulder. There, she rubbed her whiskers against Aurelia's neck and made a contented purring noise, like a divine spirit anointing her chosen champion.

"*Liar!*" bellowed Tobias. He slammed a fist into his podium, rattling it. "These are all lies—your lordship, please, these mages cannot be trusted! The woman is lying; she lies to save herself—"

Hope hissed at him, swishing her tail in a warning familiar to anyone who had ever had the misfortune of provoking a cat's wrath. But the magistrate was already looking at Tobias with a troubled expression.

"Aurelia Mirellan was cleared of responsibility weeks ago. Her suspension from the Guild has already been lifted," the magistrate said slowly. "She gains nothing by coming here to lodge accusations against you; she has no reason to do so. No reason except for . . ."

"Except for the truth," said Certainty.

And for me. The thought made the cold, tight fear within her—the aching hollowness that had taken up residence in her chest ever since she'd read Dav and Saralie's letter—uncurl into something like relief. Aurelia had come here to help *her*, had plotted and lied and spent weeks in the library for *her*, had chosen *her* over whatever careful path her parents had tried to engineer.

"You know," said the High Mage thoughtfully, "we ought to be able to confirm whether Master Tobias set off the skyfire with just a few spells. You see, Aurelia and Certainty very sensibly brought the remains of the artifact in question back here to Margrave. Before, we had no hope of pinpointing the precise magical signature of its user, but if there's only one alleged culprit in question... well. Then it's just a problem of matching the signatures, which would be quite simple indeed."

Certainty's brows knitted in confusion. She wasn't a senior mage, of course, but what the High Mage was describing didn't sound simple to her at all. She looked at Aurelia; the mage, too, looked perplexed, but said nothing.

The High Mage leaned forward suddenly, and her gray eyes bored down upon the secretary like nails holding him in place. "So Master Tobias, if you would be so good as to provide just a few hairs from your head—any will do, no need to be fussy—we could clear up this whole matter quite painlessly. What say you?"

There was a sudden rash of whispers from the audience, particularly loud among the seated mages and novices, followed by a just-as-loud hushing from their neighbors. Everyone wanted to see how this play would end.

Tobias had gone very still. The guards nearest him tensed, hands moving toward their cudgels or sheathed shortswords.

Tobias noticed; Certainty saw the desperate calculation in his eyes as they flitted from side to side.

But the secretary was not a fighting man, and for all his failings, neither was he a stupid one.

Tobias slumped against his podium, head bowed. His knuckles were white and trembling.

"Fucking mages," he said. His voice had finally lost its polished sheen, and Certainty could hear the rounded vowels of a Ruggan farmer's son beneath the slipping mask. "If you'd just given me a chance back then. I could've . . . Cursed Daughter take you all, I could've been great."

Certainty heard in his voice an echo of Aurelia: *to be someone of value.*

If she could have traveled back in time to meet the young Tobias who had pulled on the bell rope of the great Guildtower doors with hungry ambition in his heart, she would have taken him by the hand, led him away for a bite to eat, and told him that he didn't need to be great. That to be good and to be kind was great enough. She would have told him that *he* was enough, and worthy just as he was, and that love wasn't something that needed to be earned like coin.

But she knew no spells to turn back time, and Tobias was not a brokenhearted farm boy standing before her, but a hard, bitter man in too-fine clothes who had done a terrible thing for a terrible reason, and then lied about it.

"How could you?" In the audience, Ferdinand was on his feet. His mustache quivered with incoherent rage. "You—you—"

"You're our *neighbor*," said Hull. The quiet disbelief in his voice was more cutting than any shout could have been. "We all chipped in coin and goods when your father died, Tobias. You were one of us. Why would you do such a thing?"

Tobias flinched and looked away, refusing to meet their gaze.

As the crowd murmured and shook their heads, the High Mage looked questioningly at the magistrate. "I think that rather settles things, don't you?"

The magistrate sighed and banged his gavel on the lectern.

"Guards," he snapped. "Seize him. This joint court hereby clears Certainty Bulrush of responsibility for the burning in Shpelling. This hearing is concluded, though it seems we'll now have to arrange a trial for Master Tobias instead. You are all dismissed."

There was a surge of noise and commotion as the audience rose to their feet, with some scattered clapping coming from the more enthusiastic among them. It had been a good show, after all. The guards moved forward to take Tobias by the arms, and a few benches behind, Old Gertha said in a voice that carried, "Always said he was a soggy lettuce of a man, didn't I, Hull?"

"I think it was 'slimy git,' dear. Or perhaps 'officious toadstool.'"

"Oh. Well, I was right, wasn't I?"

"You're always right, dear."

Above the din, the High Mage smiled down at Certainty and Aurelia from her lectern, gray eyes twinkling. She leaned down toward them.

"I think it's about time for a nice, calming cup of tea, don't you?"

TWENTY-FOUR

"WELL," SAID THE High Mage. She leaned back, taking a sip of her date-and-honey tea, and regarded them over the top of her mug. Her gravitas was compromised somewhat by the steam fogging up her spectacles. "That was an eventful afternoon, wouldn't you say?"

Certainty and Aurelia were once again in the High Mage's office. As the drama of the courtroom dissolved and Tobias was taken away by the guards, the High Mage had whisked them back to the Guildtower before they'd even had a chance to speak with each other or the villagers from Shpelling.

Aurelia's eyes were narrowed in thought as she sat down in the chair. "High Mage," she said as soon as the office doors had swung shut. "What you said in the courtroom, about being able to confirm whether Tobias was the culprit with some of his hair . . . that's . . ."

The High Mage raised one eyebrow as Aurelia trailed off. "Not strictly possible, at least not with our current understanding of individual magical signatures?"

"Well . . . yes."

A small smile played along High Mage Melea's lips.

"You lied," Certainty said, realizing. "It was a bluff to get him to confess. But that's—that's—"

"—*brilliant*," finished Aurelia, and Certainty looked at her in surprise. "What? It worked, didn't it?"

Certainty laughed. "I just didn't expect you, of all people, to approve of such underhanded methods." Aurelia grinned back at her. Her blond hair was still a mess, and with her rumpled cloak and relaxed air, she looked entirely the opposite of the rigid, polished mage that Certainty had met two months ago in this very same office.

"The general lack of understanding of—or lack of *desire* to understand—mages and our ways is often an impediment to our work. But when there's the rare opportunity to turn it to our favor . . ." The High Mage shrugged, smiling lightly. "I have no qualms about making use of it. Particularly not when it helps save the careers of two promising young mages."

Certainty shook herself mentally; *that* was what they ought to be talking about now, not how or why the High Mage had tricked Tobias into admitting his guilt.

"What happens now? Am I still being expelled?"

"High Mage, I'd like to formally retract my written statement," said Aurelia immediately. "The one my parents made me sign. It was made under duress, and I'd like to make clear that whatever punishment Certainty faces, I should face, too."

"Or no punishment," said Certainty. "Is no punishment an option? If so, I'd like to pick no punishment, please."

The High Mage was smiling behind her tea.

"Given the circumstances, I think that would be very reasonable, Novice."

Relief poured over Certainty's shoulders like a warm shower; her breath gusted out of her and she sank down into the chair.

"I also would like to apologize to both of you for the arrangement with your parents, Aurelia," continued the High Mage. "I was unaware that it had been done without your honest consent, or I'd never have allowed it. I recognize that it was unfair to Certainty, but—well, sometimes we must be pragmatic, and I thought it better to lose one of you than both."

Aurelia gave a stiff nod. "Thank you for the apology. But you should have known that I would never have wanted a deal like that."

"Should I have?" The High Mage tilted her head at Aurelia. "It didn't strike me as a compromise you necessarily would have disapproved of a few months ago."

Aurelia's shoulders shrunk inward; she looked down at her hands. But Certainty's light touch on her arm made her look up again and Aurelia's eyes softened, the shame in them giving way to something else entirely.

"Maybe you're right. Maybe I wouldn't have, before," Aurelia said to the High Mage. "But I want to believe that people can change. That *I've* changed."

The High Mage leaned back in her chair. "Well, from my limited perspective, you and Novice Certainty certainly have." She cocked her head. "*Novice* Certainty. Perhaps we can do better than that. You did complete the artifact inventory in Shpelling, did you not?"

Certainty blinked. Did she mean—?

"Yes?" she ventured, barely daring to hope.

High Mage Melea's smile broadened as she reached into a drawer to her left.

"Then I must inform Mage Mortimer that he has a new Deputy Keeper to train."

She drew her hand out of the drawer, and in it—Certainty's breath caught sharply—was a gold pin in the shape of delicately linked circles. "Congratulations, Mage Certainty. Normally, there's a bit more pomp and ceremony to this part, but I expect you don't mind, given the circumstances."

The moment swelled up in Certainty's throat. Feeling as though she were in a dream, she reached one trembling hand out to take the circles from the High Mage. She looked down at it.

Such a small thing it was, this pin—just a bit of gold and silver, held together by craftsmanship and time-worn enchantments. It was cold in her palm, and hardly weighed anything at all. And yet, if she were to place it on a scale, and pile up six years of hope and disappointment on the opposite side, the scale must surely balance, for that was the bargain that she'd made. Had it all been worth it?

Certainty didn't know, but she was ready to finally find out. She closed her fingers over the golden circles, too overcome to speak. She felt a warm hand on her wrist; Aurelia was smiling softly at her.

"And as for you, Mage Aurelia," said the High Mage. "The matter of your next assignment. Although you're not currently able to serve in a farspeaker capacity, I still believe there are opportunities for you to . . . yes?"

Certainty had made an involuntary noise in her throat, and the High Mage raised one eyebrow at her.

"What is it?"

"Uh . . ." Certainty looked at Aurelia. "Do you want to tell her, or should I?"

Aurelia only smiled and closed her eyes, taking a deep breath as she did so.

The High Mage looked perplexed. "Mage Aurelia, what are you—*oh*."

Her eyes went wide and unfocused for a moment, and Certainty looked between Aurelia and the High Mage, both of whom were as still as statues. Then Aurelia blinked her eyes open, and the High Mage seemed to come back to herself as well.

The High Mage beamed at Aurelia. "Oh, well *done*, Mage Aurelia! I stand corrected. That quite changes things. Tell me, how did you finally overcome your block?"

"It was Certainty," said Aurelia. Her voice was quiet but sure. "We practiced together in Shpelling. I've been trying to reach her for the past few weeks, but it wasn't until today that I— I finally was able to."

"My headaches that wouldn't go away," realized Certainty. "And the strange noise I'd been hearing— I thought I was going half-mad!"

Aurelia smiled at her and reached over to take her hand. "Like I said, I wanted to write you, but couldn't. I convinced my parents that I needed to access the Guild library to continue my normal scholarly work, but they were having me watched. I had to be careful. And even though I couldn't stand to think of you believing that I'd abandoned you... I knew I had to find a way to prove it was Tobias. It was a close thing, too; I only managed to dig up that admission record two hours ago. Incidentally, we both owe Librarian Korella a very generous gift. She likes chocolate."

Certainty squeezed Aurelia's hand, beaming back at her. Aurelia's eyes were soft and warm on hers, and it would have been so easy for Cert to let herself fall into their greenness and forget everything—forget that she was now a mage, that all their friends from Shpelling still awaited them below, that they were in the High Mage's office and she was right there watching—

The High Mage gave a polite little cough.

Certainty and Aurelia pulled away from each other sharply— when had their faces gotten so close?—but the High Mage had nothing recriminating to say, responding only with an amused, knowing "*hm*."

Aurelia cleared her throat, blushing.

"Sorry, High Mage, you were saying—you have an assignment for me?"

Certainty's heart sank a little; she had hoped the two of them might have some time together in Margrave. But it was a good thing if Aurelia was finally to be sent out on a proper farspeaker assignment, she reminded herself. It was what she deserved; more importantly, it was what she wanted.

"I had a particular posting in mind, yes. But now that your farspeaking has been restored, I rather think there's one other assignment that would suit you better."

"What is it?"

High Mage Melea paused to sip again at her tea, though Certainty rather thought that she was simply drawing out the moment for dramatic effect.

"The Queen has requested that a farspeaker be posted to her service in the White Palace."

Aurelia inhaled sharply. "The *Queen*—"

Being the Queen's personal farspeaker would mean becoming her trusted adviser and confidant. Cert knew it was everything Aurelia had ever wanted in an assignment. Everything *any* mage could ever want. It would mean influence—access—possibly even a pathway to becoming the High Mage's successor, if one played their cards right. It would *also* mean staying in Margrave, just a short walk away from the Guildtower, where Certainty would be serving as Deputy Keeper.

"A bit of a step up from warehouse duty, hm?" Certainty nudged Aurelia lightly.

But Aurelia was biting her lip. "I . . . Thank you for the honor, High Mage. But . . ."

High Mage Melea's eyebrows shot up. "*But?*"

"I'd love to accept the assignment, of course," Aurelia said hurriedly. "It's just that . . . there's also a—a scholarly experiment that I would like to propose to the Guild. An experiment I'd like to take part in."

"An experiment," repeated the High Mage, bemused. Her brow furrowed. "Go on."

"What are you doing?" Certainty hissed urgently at Aurelia. "Just say yes!"

But Aurelia only shook her head stubbornly.

"High Mage, what will happen to all of the artifacts we've left in Shpelling?"

The High Mage blinked, caught off balance by the sudden change of topic. "They will remain there," she said slowly. "Safely stored and warded. Perhaps we'll send a mage out every few months or so to reinspect them. Why?"

Aurelia took a deep breath, holding her hands tightly together in her lap.

"The Guild's greatest political challenge is gaining the trust of the common people, yes? Well, you heard the testimony of the Shpelling residents. High Mage, I think you would agree that our efforts—*Certainty's* efforts—were a success. With artifacts that the Guild viewed only as junk, we managed to revitalize an entire village. We've shown that magic can be used to help ordinary folk in a hundred small ways, and that magic need not be something that people fear. So . . . why stop there?"

"What exactly are you proposing, Mage Aurelia?"

Aurelia lifted her chin. "I'm proposing that the Guild try a new model of engaging with Eshtera, High Mage. We've never been able to deploy mages to solve people's everyday problems because there are simply not enough of us to do so. So we've prioritized the greater issues of the kingdom—defending our borders, improving our harvests, and so on. But there are *hundreds* of magical artifacts in that stable in Shpelling, High Mage.

And hundreds, maybe thousands more, in the Guildtower vaults—and you'd have them just sit on shelves gathering dust? I am proposing that the Guild share the magic it's hoarded with the very people it purports to serve!"

Certainty found that her mouth was hanging open. Aurelia's eyes glowed green and fierce; her voice was clear and impassioned.

"A *library*," Aurelia said, and the way she said the word made it sound like an invocation of something sacred. "A Royal Library of Magical Artifacts, to be managed jointly by the Crown and the Guild. With Certainty as its Master Librarian."

Certainty swiveled toward Aurelia in shock. "What—"

"Think about it, Cert," Aurelia insisted. "Do you really want to spend your life in the Guild vaults doing inventory with Mage Mortimer? I've never seen you as happy as when you're helping people, and this . . ."

This would make it her very purpose to do so.

The idea took root in Certainty's mind, stretching out its tendrils like a seedling hopeful for light. She could imagine it so vividly: people, ordinary people like her own family, journeying to the Library to ask for help. Her receiving them there. Making them comfortable, speaking with them in plain Eshteran to understand the problems they faced. And then she would use her magic—her small, silly magic, so easily dismissed before—to do what no one else could do. Among the endless records of the Guild's vaults, she would search for the forgotten artifacts, the ones once also dismissed as insignificant, that might yet change someone's life for the better.

The High Mage's expression was inscrutable as she leaned back in her chair, steepling her fingers before her.

"A library," she murmured, almost to herself. "Of magical artifacts. We'd have to take care with which ones are made available, of course, but . . . improving Guild–citizen relations. Hm. Lisbet would love it, I'm sure."

Her eyes resharpened, pinning both of them like butterflies under her gaze. (Certainty's mind snagged on the revelation that the High Mage was on a first-name basis with the Queen of Eshtera, and then dismissed the thought as unimportant to examine at that particular moment.)

"If we went forward with this experiment, Mage Aurelia, do you believe you would be able to contribute to it without neglecting your duties as the Queen's farspeaker?"

"I would, High Mage." Aurelia's chin was high, her eyes bright.

"Mage Certainty, do you support this? Would you commit to leading these efforts?"

"I . . . I do. I would."

High Mage Melea considered them both for one long moment, then nodded. "Then consider your proposal taken under advisement, Mage Aurelia. It won't be easy to muster enough Council support to pass it, but it has a fighting chance, if we prepare our arguments well. And if I can convince the Queen to speak in favor as well, of course."

Aurelia nodded, sitting even straighter in her chair than before. Certainty recognized the eager gleam in her eyes; Aurelia with a new project was like Hope on the trail of a mouse. She looked ready to throw herself into the chase without a moment's hesitation.

"Thank you, High Mage," said Aurelia, brimming with excitement.

"Yes—thank you, High Mage," said Certainty, still hardly able to believe how rapidly their fortunes had changed. Her mind was spinning with the possibilities, her thoughts and ideas for the Library tripping over themselves in a rush. But there would be time enough for all that soon.

The High Mage nodded. "In the meantime, perhaps the two of you ought to take a few days to . . . recuperate, hm? Your friends from Shpelling are waiting for you in the kitchens. Go speak with them; write to your families—I shall send for both of you once we're ready to discuss the details of the work to be done."

So Certainty and Aurelia rose, Certainty feeling a little unsteady on her feet as she did so. They walked toward the doors.

"Oh, and—" They turned back to the High Mage, who smiled at them again. "Well done, both of you. Perhaps I ought to have started with that."

THEY FOUND GERTHA, Hull, and all the rest of the Shpelling folk steadily making their way through a small mountain of roast chicken and potatoes in the heart of the Guild kitchens. The cooks all smiled and nodded as Aurelia and Certainty entered; perhaps they remembered Certainty's assistance with the unfortunate cabbage incident, or perhaps they were simply pleased to have visitors in their midst—particularly visitors as vocally appreciative of their cooking as the villagers were.

"Oy," Orrin called cheerfully to them as they entered. "The High Mage told us we could come have a bite here while waiting for you. Do you get fed this well *all* the time?"

"I dunno," muttered Ferdinand, sounding slightly miffed. "Think it could use a bit more garlic, personally." Gertha thwacked him on the arm, muttering something about rude houseguests.

"Thank you," said Certainty, beaming at them. "Thank you all, truly, for coming. I wasn't sure, when I sent you my letter, whether . . ."

Hull made a scoffing noise. "What? Whether we'd remember what you did for all of us? Whether we'd let them make you a scapegoat and ruin your future, just because the Plough got a wee bit scorched?"

This was a bit of an understatement, of course, but nobody bothered to correct him.

Gertha sniffed loudly. "Should've known it was that rotting turnip of a secretary who did it, anyway. Knew I didn't like him the moment I met him."

"Gertha, you never like anyone the moment you meet them," said Brienna.

"True," agreed the old woman. "Seems safest, as a rule. Most people are terrible."

Ferdinand set down his half-eaten chicken leg to scrutinize Aurelia and Certainty. "So they've reinstated the two of you, then? All's well, and you'll be back to your magery now as usual?"

"Of sorts," said Aurelia, smiling. "Certainty is now officially *Mage* Certainty, and we're being given an important project to manage..."

She told them then of her vision of the Library, and of how Shpelling itself had inspired it. There were many approving nods and exclamations as she did so, and Certainty felt a surge of pride as she watched Aurelia and the way she glowed beneath their friends' affection.

"Where's Hope?" asked Aurelia, looking around. Hearing her name, the catdragon poked her head out from beneath the wooden table, chicken scraps littering the floor around her, and fluttered onto her rightful place on Aurelia's shoulder. There, she curled her tail possessively around Aurelia's neck.

"I reckon she wants to stay here with you," said Orrin, a little sadly. "Do you think you two might still visit Shpelling sometimes? I've been keeping up the carriage house and stable for you. Just in case."

"You'll always have a place there," agreed Murph. "And once the new inn is built . . . We've already had a number of woodworkers come from Ruggan to start the work, you know. Some of them said they might even move their families to Shpelling to stay."

"I'm sure you hate that, Gertha," said Certainty, grinning. "All those new people to boss around." Old Gertha only gave her a lofty look in response.

"Of *course* we'll come visit," Aurelia said to Orrin. "Where else would we get our fill of garlic pasta?" Ferdinand made a scoffing noise, but Certainty could tell that he was pleased behind that mustache of his. "And Orrin, of course you'd always be welcome to come visit us in Margrave, too. See how you like it, and whether you really want to move here in the future."

"Oh!" Orrin rubbed at his neck. "Thank you, but I don't think I want to move to Margrave anymore."

"Why not?" asked Certainty curiously.

"He met a girl," said Gertha, waggling her eyebrows. "One of the woodworkers' daughters. Sings prettily and makes eyes at him by the well—"

"That's not why," Orrin protested, reddening. "Really, it's not! I've just . . . I've realized that Shpelling isn't so bad of a place, I suppose. It just needs people to care about it, and to want to make it better. So I want to do that. Even if I don't have any magic."

Certainty felt a lump in her throat as she looked at him. She rather thought Orrin did have his own brand of magic, after a fashion. They all did.

"Well," she said finally, once she'd managed to get her face back under control. "I think that's a very fine thing to want, Orrin. And Shpelling is lucky to have you."

THE VILLAGERS LEFT them shortly thereafter to begin their journey home, but only after many hugs and the promise of honeycake to be sent by courier soon. Certainty and Aurelia had also learned from them that Tobias was being summarily dismissed as Lord Godfrey's secretary and would be forced to contribute to the building costs for the new inn. Whether or not he would face an even harsher punishment remained to be seen.

"I almost feel bad for him," mused Certainty.

She and Aurelia were walking up the Guild's central stairs—Certainty toward the novice's dormitories to find Dav and Saralie; Aurelia to her room to write a curt message to her parents. Aurelia hadn't yet decided whether to cut them out of her life entirely, she told Certainty, but she couldn't forgive them for this. For treating her as though her only value was in her Guild rank, something to be preserved at all costs—no matter what it was that *she* wanted.

They'd always called what they did "love," of course. But it was losing Certainty that made Aurelia finally see it for what it really was: control. So she'd lied to them, and plotted, and searched for the proof she needed. And on her way to the courthouse, she'd finally thrown that stupid, horrible enchanted necklace into a gutter, because her choices and mistakes were all her own to make now. Certainty was proud of her.

"Tobias? I don't feel bad for him. The world is full of men like him," said Aurelia. "Men who believe they're entitled to greatness simply because they want it. Men angry at their own smallness, who tear down others when they can't rise. Men like him don't deserve your kindness, Cert."

"No," said Certainty, thoughtful. "But maybe we should give it to them anyway."

Aurelia looked at her in surprise. "I . . ." Then she laughed, her eyes crinkling in that way that Certainty found devastatingly beautiful. "I'll always have more to learn from you, won't I?"

Always. "I hope so," Certainty said softly.

It was the middle of afternoon lessons and all the other novices were busy in their classrooms. The landing where they stood now was empty. As Aurelia looked at her, Certainty suddenly felt shy.

They were still the same people they had been all those weeks ago. Aurelia was the same brilliant, determined, wholly unexpected woman that she had journeyed to Shpelling and back with. And she was the same old Certainty Bulrush, plus or minus a shiny golden pin and some emotional baggage.

But why did everything feel so different now?

"We're really going to do this, aren't we?" Certainty asked. "Together."

Aurelia took both of her hands, and the touch was grounding. Her long, warm fingers were the roots tethering Certainty to the earth, stopping her from floating away.

"Cert." Aurelia's voice was soft and sure, like a promise kept. "Someone very wise once told me to figure out what makes me happy, and to never let it go."

Like a flower drawn inexorably toward the sun, Aurelia leaned toward her.

"This is me not letting go," she whispered.

And when their lips touched, she tasted of lavender and honey, and Certainty thought she might never be able to taste either again without returning here to this perfect moment, holding and being held by a woman who looked at her as if she—Certainty Bulrush of Potshire, mage and soon-to-be Master Librarian—were the most extraordinary magic of all.

EPILOGUE

CERTAINTY PEEKED OUT from behind the counter at the people waiting just outside the wood-and-stained-glass doors. A line had already formed, but thankfully it was a short one; the midmorning bells were yet to ring, and the Library was generally busiest at noon or at the end of the day.

"Novice Geranium," she called behind her. The girl's mother was an avid gardener, poor thing—though Certainty really wasn't one to talk. "Are you ready to open the doors?"

Her assistant's head popped up from behind the towering stack of inventory books on her desk. "Just about, Mage Certainty! I'm just recording the return of the artifact brought back yesterday by the fisherman from Shellport."

Ah, yes, that was right. They had sent a representative back with the borrowed crab pot. He'd reported that they'd all been well-pleased with the results of its attraction charm, except that perhaps it was just a little *too* effective, and might the mages be able to adjust the enchantment before next season so that the crabs weren't quite so eager to leap into their boats and attempt to mate with them?

"Good," she said. "Please let in our patrons once you've finished, then."

Certainty readied herself by checking that there was a pot of tea brewing beside her (in a rather familiar chipped teapot, which had just finished telling her all about the differences between properly brewing a tisane as opposed to a tea) and an open notebook before her. *Library Requests on the Second Makersday of Highsun, 18th Year of the Reign of Her Majesty, Queen Lisbet the Second*, she wrote atop the page.

When she looked up, Novice Geranium was already opening the doors, and the first patrons of the day walked in.

The Royal Library of Minorly Magical Artifacts (there had been some negotiation with Mage Mortimer over precisely which Guild artifacts were too powerful to be loaned out, hence the addition of "Minorly") had only been open for two months, but already word of it had spread across Eshtera, and people came from near and far with their requests.

When it was being built, Certainty and Aurelia had insisted on making it a welcoming place for all, a place where either farmers or lords could feel comfortable. Still, it was located between (and symbolically equidistant from) the Guildtower and the White Palace itself, and the Crown required that certain standards of Margravian grandeur be met; as such, the Library's circular lobby was an interesting mix of practical and palatial.

Throughout the high-domed room, unfussy wooden tables and overstuffed armchairs offered patrons a place to rest as they waited their turn, but sunlight filtering in from the tall windows also lit up an enormous, gleaming inlay of the Crown's twin lions beside the Guild circles, both finely worked in gold and silver.

On the far side of the room, Certainty, her assistant, and other Library staff did their work behind a tall, wide counter of polished wood. On the counter itself rested the master artifacts register: an enormous tome, heavy enough that its covers were made of large wooden boards rather than leather or cloth. The master register had been the work of weeks, taking the efforts of Certainty, Mage Mortimer, and several assistants besides, yet it still wasn't complete; they'd needed to devise a system of adding small notecards between its pages every so often to record a newly identified artifact into the appropriate section.

And behind all this were shelves and shelves of smaller inventory books—some dusty, some tattered, some stiff and freshly inked—all waiting to be made useful by Certainty's magic.

The first patron to approach the counter was a young man wearing an exceptionally garish pair of ruffled purple pantaloons. "Sir Raffaello of Forlinet," he said to Certainty with a sweeping bow and an expectant smile.

"Hello," she said. "I'm Mage Certainty of Potshire. Welcome to the Library. How may I help you?"

The young man's face fell. "But . . . you do not recognize my name?" He spoke with a lilting accent—Lindisian, Certainty thought.

She shook her head. "I'm afraid I don't. Should I?"

Sir Raffaello sighed and hung his head. "Perhaps not, perhaps not. I am a poet, Mage Certainty. Of some renown, at least in some of the southern cities where I have traveled. But you see, that is what I have come to seek help with—I have lost my inspiration! It is gone!"

Certainty jotted this down in her notebook. "I see, Sir Raffaello . . . and you are looking for an artifact that might help you regain it?"

He nodded emphatically. "Does the Library have any such thing?"

"I'll have to check our records, but it's possible. Would you please wait for a moment? I'll just need to speak with the other guests first."

Novice Geranium guided the poet over to one of the chairs on the side, and the next patron stepped up to the counter.

"Good morning, Mage," said the middle-aged woman, ducking a curtsy. "My name is Celia of Winterburr."

"Welcome, Celia. What have you come to the Library for?"

Celia hesitated, worrying at her lip as her eyes darted from side to side. She bent over the counter, and Certainty leaned in to hear her.

"My husband's a grain merchant," she said conspiratorially. "He travels a lot. And he's always away for weeks at a time, sometimes months. And, well—I get lonely, you see."

Certainty's brow furrowed. "I'm not sure I—"

"*Very* lonely," said the woman. "If you catch my meaning? But I swore to be faithful, and I'd never break my vows . . ."

Certainty blinked. "Ah. Um, yes. That isn't ordinarily the sort of thing the Library helps with, but you might find, in a particular quarter of the Lower City . . ."

But then she recalled a particularly interesting entry from one of Mortimer's old record books. A mortar and pestle, except there was no mortar to be found, and the pestle had a rather interesting way of vibrating vigorously when its enchantment was activated.

Mortimer had been puzzled as to its purpose, of course. Certainty hadn't felt the need to enlighten him with her theories.

"Novice Geranium," she said thoughtfully. "Kindly look up any entries of enchanted pestles in the master artifacts register for me, if you would."

The novice nodded eagerly, flipping the enormous pages of

the book on the counter. She ran her finger down the list, looking for the section beginning with *P*.

"Three enchanted pestles, Mage Certainty. Shall I read off their enchantments now?"

"No," said Certainty hastily. "Thank you. I'll look through them myself shortly." To the waiting woman, she said, "Kindly wait over there. I'll let you know soon if we have a match."

The woman curtsied gratefully and hurried away to a chair.

"Next," called Certainty.

But the next patron in line was Aurelia. The mage looked radiant in her silver robes, and she wore her hair loose and flowing that morning. Hope was curled around her neck like a fluffy, scaly scarf.

"Hello," said Aurelia. She leaned over the counter and gave Certainty a quick kiss, dislodging Hope in the process. The cat-dragon gave a disgruntled yowl and stalked off among the shelves; Certainty knew she was on the hunt for shiny things to add to her growing hoard beneath the counter. "Aren't you going to ask me what I'd like help with, Master Librarian?"

"I'm working, dear," said Certainty severely, though she could feel herself smiling, too, which might have undermined the sincerity of her chastisement.

"So am I," said Aurelia brightly. "I've just heard from one of the other Guild farspeakers. The one posted in the Long Sea aboard Admiral Vagan's ship. They have a small problem that they wondered if the Library might have a solution for."

"Oh?"

"It turns out that Admiral Vagan gets terribly seasick."

"But... *Admiral*..."

"Yes," sighed Aurelia. "I know. Evidently he's been hiding it for his entire career by developing an unhealthy addiction to anti-nausea potions and gingerroot, and now they've finally all grown ineffective."

"You know, you could have just farspoken the request to me," said Certainty, teasing. Then she felt that faint, familiar ringing in her mind, and let it open to Aurelia's voice.

"I could have, but then I wouldn't have been able to kiss you, now would I?"

Certainty couldn't help it. She blushed.

Aurelia smirked at her, her eyes promising that they'd continue that particular conversation later. She nodded toward the artifact record books behind Certainty. "So do you think we've got anything in there that might help?"

Certainty grinned. She always liked this next part.

"Novice Geranium—your assistance, please?"

Her assistant popped back out eagerly. "How many searches?"

"Two," said Certainty. "A poet in search of inspiration, and an admiral in search of a cure for seasickness."

Novice Geranium considered this for a moment, then pulled several inventory books off the shelves and spread them out on the counter. "Then I'd try these first."

Certainty smiled at her. "Well chosen, Novice." Geranium would make a fine Deputy Librarian someday (even if "Librarian Geranium" was rather a mouthful). She had good instincts, good organization, and a good way with people, which was probably more important than anything else, if Certainty were being honest. People were trickier than artifacts, any day.

With Aurelia watching, Certainty rolled up her sleeves and placed her hands on the books in front of her. She took a breath and let her magic leap to her fingertips, as warm and familiar as the sun.

"Hello, old friends," she thought at the books beneath her hands. *"We need your help again . . ."*

ACKNOWLEDGMENTS

Book Two is always the hardest, or so everyone has cheerfully reminded me. I certainly hope they're right, and that the days of me desperately scanning my kitchen drawers for inspiration while muttering made-up magical spells are well and truly behind me. We'll see!

I owe a great big thank-you to everyone involved in making this book a reality.

First, to my unflappable agent, Paul Lucas, whose sartorial flair is matched only by his literary taste—thank you for all the guidance and wisdom every step of the way, and for not flinching at all when I told you that I'd written an entirely different book than the one we'd initially sold as Book Two, and could we possibly ask about swapping this one in, pretty please? I'm so grateful to have you always by my side and in my inbox. (Thank you, also, to the rest of the Janklow & Nesbit team, including Nathaniel Alcaraz-Stapleton and Lansing Clark, for your hard work and support!)

To Jess Wade, editor extraordinaire—thank you for always getting the vibes of my stories, even when the aluminum scaffolding of plot is barely standing and very wobbly. Without you, this book would be . . . well, perhaps not totally nonsensical but definitely *less* sensical. (Especially the skyfire. Who'd have thought that magical things going *boom* might be such a headache?) I'm so grateful that I get to work with you in shaping my stories, and to have found such a champion for them.

The whole team at Ace has also been absolute heroes; a massive thank-you to Gabbie Pachon, for fielding my anxious emails and doing so much of the invisible and important work of Getting Books Published; to Stephanie Felty, Yazmine Hassan, Jessica Mangicaro, Elisha Katz, and Tyler Simon, for making sure people know I (and, more importantly, my books) exist; to Caitlyn Kenny and Kristin del Rosario, for shepherding this book from ugly Google Doc to beautiful and typo-free pages; and to Christine Legon and Sammy Rice, for their expert management of very complicated publishing things I don't fully understand. Thank you, also, to Katie Anderson for the gorgeous US cover design, executed with absolute magic by the wonderfully talented Devin Elle Kurtz (whom we are so extraordinarily lucky to have snagged!). Devin, your art so perfectly captures the feeling of this story. I'm in awe.

Not all authors get to be as lucky as I am in having not one but two stellar publishing teams bringing their book into the world. I owe a metric ton(ne) of thanks to the fantastic folks at Hodderscape. To Molly Powell, my UK editor: I was truly thrilled for you when you went on a wonderful and well-deserved sabbatical . . . and I was also extremely selfishly glad when you came back. Thank you for your unwavering enthusiasm, for always seeing the heart of my characters, and for helping me find the best way to tell their stories!

My gratitude also goes to Sophie Judge for doing seemingly everything at once with impeccable grace, and to Kate Keehan for knowing everyone in the UK and shepherding my awkward

ACKNOWLEDGMENTS

duckling self from interview to interview. Thank you, also, to the rest of the Hodderscape team, especially Jo Dickinson, Laura Bartholomew, Rachel Southey, Catherine Worsley, Sarah Clay, and Daisy Woods for the stunning UK cover design (so wonderfully illustrated by Lydia Blagden—thank you!).

To my beta readers and writing friends (especially Bonaparte Dynamite, Dragons & Tea, Inklings, and ESFF peeps): thanks for making writing much less lonely. I'd never manage to finish writing a book without having people to ramble and vent to, people to gently tell me when a plot point makes absolutely no sense, and people to reassure me that I had not, in fact, "used up" all my writing ability on Book One.

To my family—thank you for not pointing out that I utterly neglected to include you in the acknowledgments of my first book. It's possible, of course, that you didn't notice because you didn't read it, in which case it seems like fair should be fair? (Alex, if you're reading this, have your mom text me the code word "catdragon" and I'll buy you Pop Rocks and a Minecraft thing.) I must admit that pretending you all won't read this makes it easier for me to say that I love you all and I'm grateful to have you in my life.

And to Sarah, Rebecca, Olivia, Andrea, Julia, Alice, Elaine, Gen, Eliza, Frances, Kate, Quenby, Lucy, Maiga, John, Sangu, El, India, Emmy, Jules, Bori, Samantha, Catriona, Georgia, Stephanie, Amy, Nadia, Grace, Genevieve, and all of the other wonderful authors who make a point of lifting fellow writers up, whether through blurbs or reposts or just a kind word—thank you. I hope to follow your example for as long as I get to be here.

To Petrik, Kel, LeeAnna, Lucile, Teresa, Nils, Beth, Eli, Sunni, Jenny, Claire, Milo, Megan, Agatha, Liz, and all the other booksellers, librarians, reviewers, bloggers, bakers, and readers who read *The Teller of Small Fortunes* and took a chance on this next book: You have my deepest thanks. Your support means everything to me. I hope you love this book as much as the first one, or at least pretend convincingly enough that I can't tell the difference.

Finally, to Drew, my husband (goodness, that sounds like I'm writing to you during wartime, doesn't it?)—you're my favorite and I love you. I would have dedicated this one to you if not for, you know, the sapphic-ness of it all. Just didn't feel right, somehow. Sorry!

Whew.

In short: It takes a village to raise a child. It takes two and a half villages to publish a book. Thank you to my many villages. Any remaining mistakes are mine alone (though I'm very happy to blame the dog).

THE KEEPER OF MAGICAL THINGS

JULIE LEONG

READERS GUIDE

DISCUSSION QUESTIONS

1. What was your favorite minorly magical artifact?

2. How do Certainty's and Aurelia's relationships with their families influence their actions and beliefs?

3. How did Certainty and Aurelia's relationship evolve from their first meeting in the High Mage's office to their last? How did the relationship weave into the story's overall themes?

4. The village of Shpelling undergoes a significant transformation. How does the village's rejuvenation parallel Certainty's and Aurelia's personal journeys? (And was it really the magic of the artifacts that transformed it?)

5. Why do you think Certainty was so driven to help the residents of Shpelling?

6. Did you find Tobias's background and motivations sympathetic? In what ways is he both similar to *and* different from Certainty and Aurelia?

7. How did the story's setting influence its tone? How different would the story have felt if it had been set entirely in Margrave?

8. What do you think the novel suggests about happiness, self-worth, and fulfillment? Which moments best capture these ideas?

9. Would you want to read another book set in this world? If so, who or what would you want it to focus on?

Photo by Drew Regitsky, 2023

A daughter of Malaysian Chinese immigrants, Julie Leong grew up across suburban New Jersey and Beijing, China, and managed to feel equally out of place in both. She studied economics and political science at Yale University and was briefly an investment banker before coming to her senses and jumping to a tech job instead. She is now also a well-rested bestselling author of fantasy novels and lives in San Francisco with her needy dog, her less-needy husband, and one thoroughly self-sufficient Meyer lemon tree. When she's not writing, she enjoys making unnecessary spreadsheets and flambéing things.

You can find her online, where you're also very welcome to send her photos of your cat(dragon)s.

VISIT JULIE LEONG ONLINE

JulieLeong.com
JulieLeongBooks
𝕏 JulieLeongBooks

Ready to find
your next great read?

Let us help.

Visit prh.com/nextread

Penguin
Random
House